A Medical Correspondent for ABC News and Professor of Medicine at Michigan State University, Marshall Goldberg is the author of THE KARAMONOV EQUATIONS; the popular Dr. Lassiter novels—fast becoming "cult" books among medical students; and CRITICAL LIST, on which the NBC mini-series was based.

In NERVE, his newest medical thriller, the worlds of science and sports collide with chilling results.

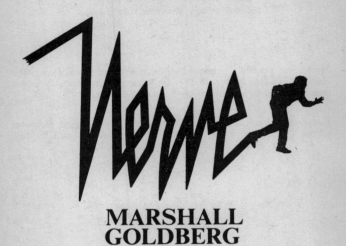

Nerve

MARSHALL GOLDBERG

BERKLEY BOOKS, NEW YORK

To
Lieut. Colonel (ret.) Ken Kay—
mentor, editor, indispensable friend.

The author gratefully acknowledges permission to quote from "The Gambler" by Don Schlitz, © 1977 by Writer's Night Music. All rights reserved. Used by permission of Writer's Night Music.

This Berkley Book contains the complete text of the original hardcover edition. It has been completely reset in a typeface designed for easy reading, and was printed from new film.

NERVE

A Berkley Book / published by arrangement with
Coward, McCann & Geoghegan, Inc.

PRINTING HISTORY
Coward, McCann & Geoghegan edition / September 1981
Berkley edition / August 1983

ISBN: 0-425-05593-0

A BERKLEY BOOK® TM 757,375
Berkley Books are published by The Berkley Publishing Group,
200 Madison Avenue, New York, New York 10016.
The name "BERKLEY" and the stylized "B"
with design are trademarks belonging to
Berkley Publishing Corporation.
PRINTED IN THE UNITED STATES OF AMERICA

1

Unable to sleep, Adam McKinnon rose from bed in the hazy light of dawn and switched on his desk lamp. Opening the notebook entitled "Experiments in Choline Metabolism," he turned to a blank page and wrote: "Perhaps Einstein was right: God does not play dice with the universe. But He *does* gamble with mankind, and His game is stud poker! His face-up cards are Irony, Impermanence, False Hope, and Tribulation: His hole card is either Immortality or Oblivion, but you have to bet your life to call Him on it."

One week before, feeling he had nothing to lose, Adam McKinnon had called the bet and seemingly won. Now he was ready to cash in his winnings. His prize, he knew, would not be eternal life but immortality in the Freudian sense: the mass love of anonymous people. Though science had provided his stake, the sports world would provide his payoff, and he picked boxing for the first installment.

Twelve hours later, Adam McKinnon, gym bag in hand, climbed the creaking stairs to Boston's Front Street Gym and entered unnoticed. It was a spacious room with two regulation-sized boxing rings in the center, wooden bleachers on the left,

1

and an exercise area with wall pulleys, sawdust-filled heavy bags, and platform-mounted light bags in the rear. Pungent odors of arnica and liniment wafted to his nostrils. In the background, Adam could see a young Negro doing sit-ups on a padded bench. Nearer the entrance, a tall, stooped, silver-haired man stood by the ice-glazed window over the street. The older man was Al Lakeman, Boston's leading fight trainer—as preeminent in his field as the presidents of Harvard and M.I.T. were in theirs, though the recipient of far fewer applicants for his college of hard knocks. For ten years after World War II, the Front Street Gym had rivaled Stillman's in New York as a breeding ground for professional pugilists and gathering place for fight promoters, high rollers, odds-makers, and sports scribes. But the postwar boxing boom had long ago peaked, and, despite the periodic boosts given it by Muhammed Ali, declined steadily. From a high of fifteen in the mid-Fifties, Al's stable of fighters had shrunk to three, leaving him more and more time to spend at his window-side retreat.

As Adam would soon learn, Lakeman was a shrewd, cynical, intensely private man who seldom used his office in the front of the gym except to telephone or catch the late-afternoon racing results on the radio. Too many hustlers, con men, moochers, or kibitzers tried to trap him there. He preferred his window, where he could give them a fish eye, a glad hand, or a polite brush before turning to supervise the action in the ring.

Now, emerging from his reverie, Al was momentarily startled to see an intruder standing in his shadow. Blinking, he rasped, "Yeah? What can I do for you?"

"You're Al Lakeman?" asked Adam, overcoming the tightness in his throat brought on by the realization that he was about to perform what his scientist friends would call "the crucial experiment."

Al nodded impatiently.

A loud thudding began to resound throughout the gym. "And that's Todd Tanner pounding the heavy bag?"

"Right again."

"I'm Adam McKinnon." He extended his hand.

Al took it briefly. He could have added, "Glad to meet you," but he wasn't and he didn't. Al was sixty-eight years old, fighting a cold, and bushed. Moreover, it was past five, the gym's closing time, and he was anxious to lock up and go home. Pulling up his sweater collar against the chill on his neck from the leaky weather-stripping of the window, he asked, "What do you want, mister?"

"I want to spar with Tanner. Three rounds."

Al hooted derisively. "Come again?"

Adam repeated the request, prompting Al to shake his head and crack, "Jesus! Must be a full moon out tonight."

When his ridicule drew no response, Al shrugged and sized Adam up. He stood a few inches taller than Al's six feet, and although it was hard to tell under his winter clothes, probably weighed one-hundred-eighty to one-hundred-ninety pounds. He was certainly well and expensively dressed, even color-coordinated: brown leather coat, tan cashmere sports jacket, sharply creased gabardine slacks. From the old-fashioned leather gym bag by his feet, Al lifted his head to peer into Adam's eyes. If a guy was a nut, he could usually tell by the shifty, unfocused look in them. But Adam's gaze was steady, the slight upthrust of his jaws conveying impatience. Finally, Al asked, "You a boxer?"

"Used to be. Amateur, mostly. A little semipro. I want to start up again."

Al suppressed a smirk. "Anything's possible, I guess. How old are you?"

"Forty-five," Adam answered without hesitation.

"And you want to be a pro boxer? Little late, don't you think?"

Adam shrugged. "Archie Moore was going strong at forty-five."

"Nobody in the fight game ever knew how old Archie really was," Al pointed out. "Besides, you're not *that* good, are you?"

"I'm better," said Adam flatly.

Al snickered but wasn't amused. A cocky claim like that, at one of his favorite fighter's expense, rankled. "Are you, now?" he mocked. "Well, seein' is believin'."

"That's why I'm here, why I want to spar with Tanner."

Al took out the stub of a cigar from his pocket and lit it. "So you want to spar with Tanner," he said, exhaling smoke. "What makes you think Tanner would spar with you? It's not amateur night, you know."

Half-grinning, Adam fanned away the cloud of smoke from his face and dug out his wallet. He opened it and gave Lakeman a hundred-dollar bill.

Al looked at Benjamin Franklin's picture and asked, "What's this for?"

"For Tanner—if he can hit me once in three rounds. One solid punch."

"W—what?" Al's laughter made him choke on his cigar spittle. He plucked the stogie from his mouth and waved it almost threateningly. "Now wait a second, pal. Let me get this straight. You're willing to pay Todd Tanner a hundred bucks to go three rounds with you—right? It goes without saying he'll hit you. No-hitters belong to baseball, not boxing. Oh, he'll hit you, all right! I'll bet another C-note on that."

"How about betting something else?"

"Like what?"

"Like, if I go the three rounds unscathed—eh, untouched— you'll take me on. Be my manager."

Al shook his head in disbelief. "Manage you for what? A bout with one of your keepers at Boston Psychopathic . . . ?"

Before Al could continue, Harry Patashnick, co-owner of the gym, shouted from the office doorway, "Hey, Al, you about ready to lock up?"

"In a minute!" Al shouted back. "Say, Harry, c'mon over here. I want you to meet a guy with real *chutzpah.*"

A portly man with an arthritic gait weaved his way to them between the ring and the bleachers. "Harry," Al said, "meet Adam McKinnon."

Harry shook hands and said to Al, "So, what's the deal?"

Al explained.

With a skeptical look at Adam, Harry said, "That's crazy, Al!"

"I know, I know. But the money's real. What do you think?"

"You in good health, mister?" Harry asked Adam. "No heart or head condition?"

"I feel fine."

"Well, you look all right," Harry granted. "At least, on the outside. . . . You seen a nerve doctor lately?"

"A psychiatrist?"

"Yeah, a psy-chiatrist. Somebody who treats delusions of grandeur."

Adam laughed and shook his head.

"Maybe you should. You're talking crazy, you know?"

"Maybe. But what the hell—it's my money and my neck. I say Tanner can't lay a glove on me. If he does—" Adam shrugged—"I lose and won't ever bother you gentlemen again."

Harry and Al exchanged doubtful looks.

"Look," Adam pleaded, "if I can't do what I claim, how long's the bout going to last? Ten, twenty seconds? Why not leave it up to Tanner?"

Al snapped the hundred-dollar bill in his hands and reluctantly nodded.

"What do you make of this guy?" Al asked Harry after Todd Tanner had recovered from his surprise, agreed to the match, and taken Adam to the locker room to change into boxing togs.

"*Meshugge*," Harry said in Yiddish. "A real *meshuggener!*"

"Yeah, but remember Dempsey, the first time Doc Kearns laid eyes on him?"

"Al—*Gottenyu!* What's gotten into you? The man's forty-five, twice Tanner's age. Might as well be ninety for a boxer. What if he gets hurt?"

"He won't. I told Tanner to land one good punch and then coast with him."

"Still, why risk it? The guy's obviously mental."

"Why not? What else interesting's happened up here lately? This way Todd gets his hundred bucks and you get a good story to tell your drinking buddies at Dumphey's."

2

Forty seconds into round one of the three-round bout, Todd Tanner's confident expression began to sour. At the opening bell, he had shuffled in, feinted with both hands to freeze his opponent in place, and snapped a long left jab to the head. The punch missed Adam's jaw by a fraction of an inch. Two more jabs also missed, but the right cross couldn't miss, thought Tanner; he was too close, practically toe-to-toe. With a shoulder-jarring jolt, he felt it land—on leather, not on bone. Infuriated, Tanner unleashed a roundhouse right, which, to his amazement, breezed through the space where Adam should have been and, with his momentum twisting him completely around, grazed his own left shoulder.

"What the hell—" Tanner muttered in self-disgust. Even as a novice, he had never looked this awkward. Retreating a step, he glanced worriedly at Al Lakeman standing on the ring apron.

"Nail him, for Chrissake," Al shouted, "and let's go home!" Turning to Harry Patashnick, he grumbled, "What's with Todd, anyway?"

Tanner nodded and advanced on his opponent, eyes gleaming with the intent to not only hit Adam but to hurt him as well.

Adam stared back impassively, while mocking Tanner with his stance. Though only a few feet separated them, his arms hung loose by his sides.

"Jesus!" Lakeman grunted. "This guy's not only cocky but crazy."

Seething, Tanner bit down on his rubber mouthpiece, balanced himself on the balls of his feet and bore in. He feinted with a left hook and when Adam failed to react, threw it—a short vicious blow with all of Tanner's two hundred pounds behind it. It was his most effective punch, the one that had decked numerous opponents, and, halfway through the swing, he knew it was dead-on target. It had to connect—if not on Adam's jaw, then on his head or shoulder. There was simply no way he could avoid it at this range. Yet, once again, Tanner smacked leather, not flesh or bone. With incredible luck or skill, the dude had picked the punch out of the air as cleanly as a Jack Johnson or Jersey Joe Walcott in their prime. Confused and off-balance, Tanner lurched forward to clinch and punish his opponent with body blows. But again Adam was too quick. Nimbly leaping back and sideways, he evaded the glove meant to hook him around the neck and pull him in. Taking a stumbling step forward, Tanner let him get away. He shook his head, not to clear it of pain but of fury, while struggling to regain composure. Though the round was turning into a humiliating debacle for him, he was enough of a professional to know it would be futile to brawl instead of box. Even with two rounds left in which to redeem himself, Tanner sensed his hundred-dollar prize slipping away. Yet what flustered him far more was knowing that his opponent—twenty pounds lighter, twenty years older, a boxing nobody—was making him look like a stumblebum in front of Al Lakeman.

As he circled Adam, hoping to tire him or force him into a misstep, Tanner began to sweat, despite the chill air of the gym. With each sudden stop or reverse, water poured off him.

"Thirty seconds," Lakeman announced and Tanner immediately moved in. Wide-based, arms pumping, willing to take three punches to land one, he leaped forward, bulling Adam toward a corner before a pair of stinging jabs closed his eyes. Opening them to aim a flurry of blows at Adam's midsection, he saw only the ring post in front of him. His opponent was gone. Suddenly, Tanner flinched, fearing a blow to the head from his blind side, but when he spun around, Adam was back in the center of the ring.

This can't be happening, Tanner thought wildly. It's unreal! No man alive, not even a scared alley cat, could move that fast. He was tempted to hurl himself across the ring and tackle the guy just to lay hands on him, prove he was solid flesh, not thin air.

At the bell ending the round, Todd Tanner strode dispiritedly to his corner and sank down on the stool.

"What the hell's the matter with you?" Lakeman growled. "That guy got you hypnotized?"

"No, he ain't got me hypnotized," Tanner said irritably. "He's just quick. I never seen nobody that quick before."

"He don't look so quick to me," Al lied. "You're just telegraphing your punches."

"Like hell!" Tanner sputtered. "I've been snappin' them off like always, like you taught me. But never mind what I'm doing. What I want to know is, what *he's* doing?"

"He's boxing your ass off—that's what! Making you look like a clown."

"Oh, yeah?" Tanner glowered. Then he shrugged, "Okay, I admit it. But how?"

"I don't know how. The guy's forty-five fuckin' years old, for Chrissake, and looks it. So settle down and box him sensibly. Jab him at long range until you can figure out his moves."

"Okay!" Tanner said and stood up, breathing deeply, storing wind, determined to cast off his feelings of humiliation and doubt. After all, he told himself, he was no preliminary palooka but a main-eventer, a silver medalist in the 1976 Olympics, New England's top heavyweight, and ranked tenth in the world. He also had Al Lakeman for his trainer and manager. He had worked too hard to persuade Al to take him on, instead of retiring as Al had planned, to throw it all away now.

The bell rang and Tanner sprang from his corner to mid-ring, making Adam step back hastily and circle left. Tanner circled with him, trying to inch closer with each step, to move within punching range. He flicked a left jab, which fell short, and continued to circle, bouncing lightly on the balls of his feet. Lakeman had said to jab the guy, keep him moving, tire his legs out, and Tanner was doing it. Though he had given up hope of outboxing his elusive foe, he longed to nail him with one good punch and not just for the bet. He could use the money, but mostly he dreaded having to face his friends when word got out that a middle-aged white man had boxed his jock off.

Suddenly, he thought of Muhammad Ali's "rope-a-dope" fight with George Foreman in Manila. Foreman was younger and stronger, but Ali was smarter; psychology, not strength nor endurance, had won the fight for him—that plus Ali's greater reach. Well, his reach was as long as Ali's; why not use his tactics?

"Hey, man, you boxing or boogying?" Tanner taunted, as they circled.

Adam smiled, but said nothing.

Abruptly, Tanner stopped in mid-ring, dropped his guard, and beckoned Adam forward. "C'mon," he said, pointing to his chin. "Hit me! One free punch."

Adam glanced at Lakeman who, surmising what the usually workmanlike Tanner was up to, shouted, "Hey, Todd, quit grandstanding, and start boxing!"

Tanner sighed and shuffled forward sluggishly. Suddenly, he switched to southpaw, leading with his right instead of his left, momentarily confusing and immobilizing Adam as he tried to adjust. Leaping forward, Tanner snapped a long right jab to the face. As he expected, Adam stepped inside it, letting the jab whiz by his cheek. Tanner immediately brought up his left hand from groin level in an uppercut, rising up on his toes for maximum leverage and follow-through. Failing to see the bolo punch until it was only inches from his chin, Adam flung himself back against the ring ropes. Jubilant at finally having his tormentor off-balance, Tanner took quick advantage. He spread his stance and, with both hands pumping furiously, charged forward to crowd Adam into the nearby corner and pound him insensible.

Ten feet away, Al Lakeman gripped the ring ropes and leaned forward to observe the action closely, intending to stop it before McKinnon could be badly hurt. What he saw, however, made him gape so wide that he nearly lost his cigar.

Crouching and weaving to the right, Adam ducked Tanner's lead left hook, blocked his right cross, and deftly slipped by, letting Tanner's forward momentum slam him into the ring post. Lakeman was awed: the evasive maneuver had been executed with the grace of a bullfighter's classic pass with a *muleta*.

Spinning around with the startled look of a man stabbed in the back, Tanner's feet twisted and he stumbled sideways, barely managing to seize the ring ropes to keep from falling. Pushing off, he blinked sweat from his eyes and searched bewilderedly for his opponent. Adam stood at the center of the ring, staring back. When Tanner made no move, Adam beckoned with his glove, mocking him with his own gesture. Quivering with rage, Tanner lunged a step forward, paused, shook his head, and dropped despairingly on the nearest stool.

The bell ending the round did not sound until a second later, but Tanner's capitulation was clear. Al Lakeman moved to his side and stared worriedly at him. He wasn't hurt or even winded, he was simply demoralized, Al realized with a mixture of pity and pique. Then he turned to Adam McKinnon, his mind racing. In fifty-two years in the fight game, Al thought he had seen it all—the upsets, the dives, the ring deaths—but never anything like this. In the glare of the ring lights overhead, he was momentarily overcome by a dizzying sense of unreality. But this was no cinematic fantasy, no *Rocky III*, he told himself; it was as real as the beaten boxer slumped on the stool below him and must be dealt with.

Patting Tanner's sweaty shoulder, he said, "Take a shower, Todd. Then we'll talk." He was about to tell McKinnon the same thing when he saw that he had climbed out of the ring and was headed for the locker room.

Cocky bastard, thought Al, and wondered if he ought to charge him the usual ten-dollar fee for using the gym facilities. But he knew he was avoiding the real issue. McKinnon had won his bet, making Al his manager, and where that arrangement would lead was anybody's guess. Though it wasn't his nature to overdramatize, one fact seemed clear: if McKinnon outclassed other heavyweights the way he had Tanner, he was going to explode on the world of boxing like an atomic bomb!

When Harry wheezingly sidled up to him, Al rolled his eyes heavenward and sighed, "Looks like I got me a forty-five-year-old heavyweight."

"I don't know, Al," said Harry fretfully. "I saw what you saw, but I still don't believe it. It's . . . it's too—" He groped for the word.

"Unnatural? That what you mean?"

"Yeah. Unnatural! Like a guy running a two-minute mile. I just don't know what to make of it."

"What time you meeting Mel?"

Harry looked at his watch. "Around now. At Dumphey's."

Mel Waldman was a sports columnist for the *Boston Globe* and Harry's son-in-law.

"Go ahead then. After I have a little talk with this forty-five-year-old wonder, I'll join you."

"Sure you don't want me to stick around?" Harry had promised to meet his son-in-law to discuss family problems with him, but he was also filled with intense curiosity.

"No. I'll fill you in later." At the look of indecision on his partner's face, Al snapped, "For Chrissake, Harry, put it in perspective! What we just saw was a helluva fine boxing exhibition, not the Second Coming! Maybe the guy's not really forty-five, or maybe he's hit on some special training gimmick. Believe me, there's an explanation—a logical one—for what we just saw. Soon as I find out what it is, I'll let you know."

Harry nodded and moved to the coatrack by the door. He struggled into his heavy overcoat, bent stiffly to slip on his galoshes, and wrapped his wool scarf around his neck. Outside, he plodded down Front Street, slipping and sliding on the ice, gasping in the stiff wind, but sunk deep in thought.

A widower with two married daughters, emphysematous, arthritic, and almost seventy years old, Harry Patashnick was a lonely and largely spent man. Without the gym—a money-loser—and boxing, he would have no place to go each day and nothing to interest him.

Yet, as he lumbered along Front Street, Harry began to feel less discouraged over the decline of the sport he so loved. Despite his labored breathing and aching joints, he actually found himself smiling. The remarkable performance he had just witnessed in the gym had somehow lifted his spirits. He felt invigorated, less decrepit, not so useless. The reason, he realized, was magic.

People craved magic. Believing it had once belonged to them, they yearned for its return. Proof of magic would crumble the foundations of science, refute the Darwinian theory that man had evolved from apes, foster hope of heaven and fear of hell. How could a Godless universe, governed by random chance, exist in the light of magic? It was no wonder people hungered so for it, even if their only taste came from a movie projector or television tube: Superman, Wonder Woman, Mandrake the Magician. Better to read about the miracles in the Bible, thought Harry, than watch such schlock.

But as much as he yearned for proof of magic, too, Harry did not delude himself that McKinnon's gym exhibition was supernatural. Like Bob Cousy winning a game at the last second with a sixty-foot jump shot, or Dan Larsen pitching a World Series no-hitter, it had merely defied the odds. Nothing more. Yet, even if what he saw in the ring was not magic, Harry was transformed by it. In what was doubtless their final round together, life had suddenly showed him something new! That, at least, was magical, even if Adam McKinnon was not.

3

After Harry left, Al Lakeman went to his tiny, memento-strewn office to make some phone calls before Tanner and McKinnon returned. Prominently displayed on its walls were autographed photographs of the two heavyweights and one middleweight Al had developed into world champions. The last had been retired from the ring ten years and Al's one hope for a fourth before retiring himself lay in Todd Tanner. It was more than wishful thinking on his part. Todd not only had a near-perfect build for a heavyweight—long arms and legs for reach and stride, and a heavily muscled torso—he also had the right temperament.

Despite his mulatto skin, Tanner insisted he was pure black, and Al did not doubt it. He ran a boxing gym, not a country club, and couldn't care less about his boxer's ancestry. Tanner was a clean-living bachelor out of the Pennsylvania coal country who yearned to become world heavyweight champion after narrowly missing being Olympic champion. That was all Al had known, or needed to know, about him—until now. It was one thing to be defeated in the ring, another to be demoralized, and he could only hope that a cold shower would ease the wound to Tanner's pride.

When Al ended his last phone call, he saw Tanner standing

outside the door and beckoned him in. Ordinarily, Tanner looked him in the eyes when he spoke. Now, he stared at the floor as he announced, "I quit!"

Al said nothing.

"I said, 'I quit!'"

Al nodded. "My eyesight's dimming, but there's nothing wrong with my hearing."

Tanner glared at him, expecting more of a response. Then the sullen set to his face softened and he said, "Should I quit?"

"What for?"

"What you mean—what for? You were there. You saw it! That guy made me look like a lead-assed pug. A palooka. It was—you know—humiliatin'."

"So?" Al gestured dismissingly. "The guy gave you a boxing lesson. . . . You've been outboxed before."

"Never that bad! Not by an old man!"

"What if it had been Muhammed Ali—Ali in his prime? Would you want to quit then?"

Tanner shifted his feet uneasily. "This guy ain't no Ali. . . ."

"That's right. He's better."

"Better!" Tanner bristled. "What do you mean?"

"What I said. You're no prelim-fighter, Todd. You wouldn't be tenth ranked if you were. But that guy put on the single best boxing exhibition I ever saw. In all my years, I never seen anybody slip and block punches better."

Lakeman's extravagant praise of McKinnon surprised and flustered Tanner, deepening his discouragement. "Well, shit, if he's *that* good, take him on. No sense wastin' your time on me."

"Hold on!" Al barked. "Just hold on. If you want to quit—which would be just about the dumbest thing you ever did—that's your business. Just don't go telling me my business, understand? Before I take a fighter on, I want to know certain basic things about him: like what kind of a guy he is, where he's from, who taught him to box. And right now, I know nothing about this Adam McKinnon—if that's even his name. Let me tell you, Todd, when a forty-five-year-old guy shows up out of nowhere who can box that good, you know where I figure he learned? In prison, that's where."

"Hey, yeah!" Tanner's eyes gleamed with enlightenment. "I get your point."

"Good. So let's just leave it like that for now," said Al,

figuring he had mollified Tanner enough. "I got a bunch of questions to ask this McKinnon when he gets out of the shower and he better come up with convincing answers. Otherwise, you're not likely to see him up here again. So just bag any thoughts of quitting until I can fill you in tomorrow—okay?"

"Yeah, Al. Sure. . . . Just one more thing. You don't think I was drugged, do you?"

"Drugged? How?"

"I dunno. Maybe he rubbed something on his gloves."

"They're our gloves, not his, and he put them on in the ring. You don't feel drugged, do you?"

"Naw, not really. Just sick to my stomach. . . . I suppose this'll be all over town tomorrow!"

Al frowned. "It better not! Harry'll keep his mouth shut. I'll see to that. And I expect you to do the same."

"Don't worry about me," said Tanner morosely and then brightened. "Thanks, Al. Thanks a lot. See you tomorrow."

"Yeah, fine," Al muttered. He'd better warn Harry fast, he thought, though not for the reason he gave Tanner; not to save the young boxer from embarrassment. He had a more compelling reason for not wanting word of his new heavyweight's prowess spread around town.

"Well," Al began, when Adam McKinnon entered his office, hair still wet from the shower, "that was quite a show you put on."

"Glad you liked it," Adam replied.

Al reached in his sweater pocket and handed over a crumpled bill. "Here's your hundred back."

"Thanks. This also makes you my manager, I presume?"

Al shook his head. "Not just yet."

"Oh? I thought that was my payoff. I didn't know there were conditions."

"Nobody said there were."

"Then why the hedge?"

Al stared hard at him. "Who the hell are you? I mean, *really*."

"I gave you my right name. Want to see my driver's license?"

"Matter of fact, I do."

Adam smiled sardonically. "Smart move." He took out his wallet and passed the plastic-covered license to him.

Al compared the photograph with Adam's face and handed the license back.

"Well—?" Adam prompted. "Notice any discrepancies? Name and age, exactly as stated?"

"Age is right. Little more to the name, though. Like the M.D. at the end."

"So I'm a doctor. I would've told you, had you asked. What's so special about that?"

"Might explain a few things."

"Like what?"

"Like why Tanner never laid a glove on you. . . . What kind of doctor are you?"

"Professor of medicine. At Tufts."

"Professor, huh? I'm impressed. Any specialty?"

"Uh huh. Neurology."

"Not pharmacology?"

Adam's eyes widened in surprise. Lakeman's power of deduction was impressive and would have to be taken into account in future dealings between them. "I do some of that, too. My research is in neuropharmacology."

"Hmm," murmured Al, smiling with satisfaction. "Have a cigar?" He opened the box on his desk.

"No thanks. I prefer a pipe."

"Figures. . . . Funny, I've known a few pro boxers over the years who wanted to be doctors, but never the other way around. What sort of research you doing in neuropharmacology?"

"Nothing earthshaking. Mainly in patients with senile dementia. You familiar with the condition?"

"Not exactly, but I get the general idea. What do you do with them?"

"Well, like many neurologists worldwide, I've been trying to find a substance that will penetrate the brain and arrest or reverse the degenerative process. Restore mental function."

"Any luck?"

"Not so far. Nothing original, anyway."

"But I'll bet you've had *some* luck of *some* kind. Otherwise, you wouldn't be here."

Adam smiled fleetingly. He had already decided how much he dared tell Lakeman and was close to that limit. "What do you mean?"

"Well," Al continued, "what makes a good boxer? Punch and agility—right? And agility comes from quick reflexes. I

know how quick your reflexes are; I saw them. What I don't
know is how they got that way. Suppose you enlighten me?"

"Would you believe no sex and daily meditation?"

"Not even if you were a priest," said Al flatly.

Adam hesitated. "Exactly how important is it that you know,
Mr. Lakeman?"

"Very! In fact, essential. The one answer I need before I'll
agree to manage you."

"Why?" Adam demanded. "Why's it so essential?"

Lakeman drew on his cigar and exhaled slowly, watching
McKinnon intently, expecting him to squirm, disapointed when
he didn't. "Well," he said, "let's say you discovered a new
drug, a nerve-stimulant of some kind that really speeds up your
reflexes. Makes you twice as quick as the next guy. And
suppose, after you win a few fights all hopped up on this stuff,
the Boxing Commission finds out about it. They're no
dummies, you know. They're bound to investigate a forty-five-
year-old boxer who moves quicker than a cat. So, you get
barred from the ring, and me along with you. Only I don't have
doctoring to fall back on. I'm out of work for good."

"I heard you were close to retiring anyway."

"You heard right. But I've been clean all these years, and I
want to go out that way. So how 'bout leveling with me, Doc?
Just what kind of drug are you taking?"

"What if it wasn't a drug but a new training method: a
combination of diet, special exercises, and certain nutrients—
naturally occurring ones—taken in large amounts? Would that
take you off the hook with the Boxing Commission?"

"It might. If *that's* really what it is."

"It's close."

"Close?" Al repeated dubiously. "Close is a loaded word in
sports. Usually applies to losers. Even if what you just said *is*
close, I get the feeling the truth is a lot more complicated. Even
illegal."

"No, not illegal, since the nutrient is not strictly a drug.
Certainly nothing that could be classified as a 'controlled
substance.' More like a vitamin."

"But it does speed up your reflexes—right?"

Adam nodded. "Rather remarkably. You saw what I can do
in the ring. I can do even better in handball or Ping-Pong."

"I don't doubt it. But I'm only interested in boxing. Tell me
more about this nutrient you're taking."

"Sorry," Adam said, shaking his head, "but I can't just yet.

Not until I publish a report on it. You see, it also happens to be a major medical discovery. Quite possibly, a Nobel Prize-winning discovery.''

Al's eyebrows lifted. "So you're not only after the heavy-weight crown, but a Nobel Prize, too! That's quite a parlay, Doc.''

Adam returned his smile. "I'm not quite that greedy. I don't want to be world champion—in fact, with Ali retired, I'd rather not be. I just want to make a million bucks at it.''

"A million, no less. On one bout?''

"One or two. Three at the most. After that, I retire. From boxing, that is. Try my hand at some other sport, like stakes handball or hockey.''

Al shook his head in wonder. "You know, you're beginning to spook me with all this wild talk. Still, if what you did to Tanner is a fair example, you might just pull it off!''

"I might. If it's finessed just right. That's why I came to you. Except for a few handball players at the Y, and one amateur boxer, nobody else has seen me in action. And nobody else will until the price is right.''

Al squinted. "I'm not sure I follow you.''

"Don't worry, you will. You'll catch up in a minute, and then step out ahead. I'm depending on it. . . . Take Todd Tanner, for example. A very popular boxer around these parts. Gate-wise, he'd be a hell of a good opponent for my first bout. But do you think he'd agree to fight me after today?''

"I know damn well he wouldn't.''

"That's right. Neither would any other 'name' boxer who'd sparred with me. Who wants to lose to a middle-aged freak?''

"Yeah," said Al, "I see what you mean. So what's the answer? How do we line up a big-money bout?''

"I'm leaving that up to you. There must be a way. Give it some thought, and I'll be by tomorrow to hear what you've come up with.''

Adam stood up and Lakeman followed. Coming around his desk, he asked, almost pleadingly, "Why don't you just settle for the Nobel Prize?''

"It's iffy. And it doesn't pay as well. I'm giving myself a year to make a fortune at sports. Maybe rewrite a few records. Then back to medicine.''

"Well, if your discovery's as important as you claim, I suppose you've earned a crack at the big bucks.''

"Oh, I've earned it, all right," Adam said ruefully. "In

ways you'll never know, or want to. . . . Well," he added, slipping into his leather overcoat. "See you tomorrow."

"Bring your gear," Al told him.

"Oh? Got another sparring partner lined up for me?"

"Either that, or I'll get the zoo to loan me a kangaroo."

4

Dumphey's Bar, in the shadows of the elevated train tracks running to and from Boston's South Station, was a dingy oasis for neighborhood sports buffs. Open to the general public all day and most nights, it was as exclusive as the Harvard Club after major sports events at the Garden. Started by Alderman Shane Dumphey shortly after repeal of Prohibition, the bar had been sold in 1940 to a group fronted by former heavyweight Jack Sharkey, and the name changed to Sharkey's Bar. But Sharkey was no Jack Dempsey, either as a boxer or a tourist draw, and was eased out a few years later. Then, with the decline of boxing and the rise of the Boston Celtics' basketball dynasty, the name was changed to The Celtics' Corner. Finally, an Italian businessman and boyhood friend of Dumphey had bought it and, as a sentimental gesture, restored his name to the establishment—though little else. The furnishings remained essentially the same as from the beginning: a wooden bar long enough for fifteen elbow-rubbing patrons, a row of six pay phones along one wall, and a dozen or so sets of sturdy oak tables and chairs.

When Harry entered, breathless and shivering, the place was

empty. Moving to the bar, he pressed his ample belly against it and bellowed, "Hey, Moe! It's me, Harry. Anybody home?"

He heard the gurgling flush of a toilet and, in a moment, the bartender emerged from the men's room. Moe Malone was a short, broad-shouldered, barrel-chested man whose arms and wrists were impressively thick and muscular as befitting a former A.A.U. weight-lifting champion and Boston's foremost Indian arm wrestler. A dent in his domed forehead was a perpetual memento of the time he had been hit with a lead pipe by a would-be robber. Concussed and temporarily blinded by blood gushing from the wound, Moe had still kept his feet. And the sight of the stumpy man, his face twisted into gargoylelike ferocity, had so terrified the robber he fled without emptying the till. That had been five years earlier and nobody had tried to rob Dumphey's Bar or its hardheaded bartender since.

Moe raised the panel in the bar and walked through to wash his hands at the sink. "Wouldn't you know," he groused, "no customers for a solid hour but the moment I step into the crapper, you show up."

Harry shrugged apologetically. "Mel been in?"

"He called. Said to tell you he'd be a few minutes late."

"Considerate boy. . . . So, Moe, how's business?"

"Like the Celtics. Runs in streaks." He reached for a beer mug. "The usual?"

"Schnapps first. Beer later."

"That's a switch. What's the occasion?"

Harry pointed to his throat, indicating dryness, and whispered, "The schnapps."

Moe poured the whiskey into a shot glass and passed it to him. *"L'chayim!"*

Harry nodded, gulped the drink down and sighed contentedly. "I just came from the gym, Moe, and I'm going to tell you a story you won't believe."

"You're probably right about that," rasped the bartender, his face distorted by a colonic cramp. "So—tell me. I got to work a disco at eight o'clock."

"Okay, okay," Harry said. "Around five o'clock, while Al is working with Todd Tanner and I'm balancing the books, this stranger comes in carrying a gym bag. A tall, well-built guy, but no spring chicken. Looks forty, says he's forty-five. Walks up to Al, takes out his wallet, and hands him a hundred-dollar bill." Harry paused to clear phlegm from his throat.

"What for?"

"He wants to go three rounds with Todd Tanner, which, ordinarily, Al would never allow. So the C-note is a come-on." Again Harry paused, his breath wheezy. Gesturing patience, he took out a medicated inhaler from his pocket and inhaled a few whiffs. "Now, this is the crazy part," he continued. "Tanner gets the hundred if he can hit this guy once in three rounds of sparring. One solid punch. Crazy, huh?"

"Sure is!" Moe agreed. "Todd moves fast for a heavy-weight. Punches fast, too. . . . So what's the scam? What's the guy's stake in this?"

"If Tanner can't hit him, Al agrees to be his manager."

"This guy a pro?"

"Wants to be."

"At forty-five? You've got to be kidding! A black man?"

"No, white."

"Got any marks on him?"

"Naw, nothing except a slightly dented nose. A clean-cut guy, square-jawed, cropped gray hair. A Burt Lancaster-type. Had a funny way of walking, slow and tight, like he's wearing leg braces. In the ring, though—*Ach, Gott!*" Harry raised his hands to his cheeks in wonder.

The next moment, the front door opened with a howl of wind and slammed shut. Moe glanced up, recognized Harry's son-in-law, and said. "Here's Mel. . . . So go on. What happened next?"

"Wait!" Harry urged. "Let me tell Mel, too."

"Now!" Moe insisted, feeling the start of another gut spasm. "Did Tanner lay a glove on him or not?"

Harry wagged his head. "As God is my witness, not once. Todd must've thrown thirty, forty punches. This guy slipped or blocked every one. I tell you, Moe, I've never seen anything like it."

"Huh!" Moe grunted. He waved at Mel Waldman as the lanky, bespectacled, bushy-haired columnist walked up, scowled, and said, "I don't get it."

"Get what?" Mel asked, taking off his eyeglasses and wiping them with a napkin.

"How a middle-aged guy—how old did you say, Harry, forty-five?—how a forty-five-year-old guy could go three rounds with Todd Tanner and not get hit once."

"W—what?" Mel scoffed. "Did Todd have one hand tied behind his back? His feet in lead boots?"

"Nope," said Harry. "It was straight sparring."

"Impossible!"

"That's what I'd think, too," Moe said. "But Harry, who last I knew still had all his marbles, swears he saw it."

"Now, wait a minute!" Harry protested. "Let me tell Mel the whole story."

"Go ahead. And if any more customers come in, tell 'em to wait. I'm going back to the can."

By the time Harry repeated the tale to his son-in-law, Moe had returned from the toilet and Al Lakeman was walking in the door.

"Al!" Harry cried. "Am I glad to see you. These two skeptics here—one my own son-in-law—don't believe me. Straighten them out."

Al did not need to ask what Harry was referring to. The original excitement, the special status conferred on him by being an eyewitness to the extraordinary event, still shone in his eyes. "What Harry saw, I saw," Al said. "It's true. The guy's name is Adam McKinnon, he's forty-five, according to his driver's license, and—get this—he's a doctor. A Tufts professor."

The gloating expression on Harry's face turned to bafflement at this new information. "Why, Al?" he blurted. "What would a doctor want to be a fighter for? It doesn't make sense."

"Oh, yeah?" Al countered. "Since when doesn't making big money make sense? He figures he can earn a fast million bucks, and after what he did to Tanner, I'm not saying he can't."

Draining his bourbon highball, Mel Waldman knitted his thick brows and said exasperatedly, "Listen, I've heard you both out, but I still don't believe it. Something's fishy somewhere."

"My cynical son-in-law," Harry chided. "Better you should be covering politics than sports."

"Aw, c'mon, Harry," Mel snapped. "I like a tall tale as much as anybody, but I'm not *that* gullible. I couldn't write a word about this until I saw the guy in action for myself."

"Good!" Al Lakeman said. "That's exactly what I want. Don't write a word. Not yet, anyway."

"Oh? How come?"

"The doctor made an interesting point. The more boxers who find out what he did to Tanner, the fewer who'd be willing to fight him. So, instead of arguing about what happened or didn't happen let's put our heads together and figure out how to get the Doc a big-money bout."

"A million-dollar one?" Mel taunted.

"It's possible," Al said. "With teamwork and careful planning, it could be done. How about it, Harry? Who knows better than you how to build up a gate?"

Harry pondered. "In the old days, maybe. But now gate receipts are small potatoes compared to the TV take. An old-timer like me couldn't negotiate that kind of deal. You need a sports agent or lawyer—even both. That's how Bob Arum and Don King operate."

"Hey, hold on!" Mel protested. "If this is just bullshitting—okay. But you can't really be serious. Jesus Christ, Al, you're one of the most level-headed men I know. How can you even think about promoting anything of this magnitude after seeing a forty-five-year-old amateur spar three rounds?"

"Just thinking out loud, Mel. Just thinking out loud. I've no intention of approaching anybody until I'm sure what I saw today was real. If the Doc shows up tomorrow, he goes three rounds with Tommy Harms, the fastest middleweight around. I want you there, 'cause if he passes that test, we move!"

"Move?" Mel puzzled. "Which way?"

"We go see Aaron Robards. After being elbowed out of big-time fight promotions by the black entrepreneurs, Aaron's itching to get back in. And, providing he's willing to come up with a modest stake, we'll show him how."

"How modest?"

"Fifty grand or so. Nothing he can't manage out of petty cash."

"Moe, pour me another drink," Mel said. "A double! Al, much as I respect you, I find it hard to believe a cagey operator like Robards is going to gamble fifty thou on a middle-aged doctor with fast reflexes, even on your say-so."

"I don't get it either," Harry said. "What's the fifty G's for?"

Al gestured tolerantly. "To get a big-name heavyweight, active or retired—a Ken Norton or Joey Jakes—to box a few rounds with the Doc in secret."

"In secret!" Mel cried. "What do you mean by that?"

"In a television studio. So we can get the Doc's performance on tape."

"Then what?"

"Then Robards shows the tape to a few select fight promoters and TV sports executives. To prove our man's for real. Book him into one of the big arenas like Madison Square Garden or the Pontiac Silverdome."

"Against who?" Mel asked.

"Somebody good but not great. A George Chuvalo or Jerry Quarry-type. A crowd-pleaser, but nobody in the top ten. Not yet."

"Okay," Mel admitted. "I follow you so far. The Doc does his act on national TV and is an overnight sensation. What next? A bout with the heavyweight champ?"

"No, not him. The Doc doesn't especially want the crown. He wants the million bucks. And there's one heavyweight who could pretty well guarantee it for him. Especially since the champ ain't too eager to fight him. Can't say I blame him, either. That guy's cracked more skulls than a brain surgeon."

"Coleman Jackson?" Mel speculated.

"The same."

"Jesus, Al," Harry questioned, "you think the Doc would go for it? A million dollars won't do him no good in the morgue."

"He'll see that it's a natural," Al said.

"Sure—for an undertaker," cracked Mel.

"I know Coleman and he's no animal," Al said. "He's a serious student of boxing. I also know Bucky Miller, his manager, and think I can make the match."

A thoughtful pause ensued as the four envisioned the possibilities. Finally, Mel Waldman spoke: "Look, Al, I hate to be a spoilsport, but I don't believe in flying saucers or Uri Geller or this forty-five-year-old doctor who's faster than a fly. I especially don't believe he got that way through secret Yogi training or supervitamins or drinking jet fuel for breakfast. I don't doubt that you and Harry saw what you saw, and you can bet your life I'll be there tomorrow to see for myself. But I'd sure feel better about it if the guy was a plumber, not a doctor. To me, him being a doctor means one thing—drugs. And drugs that can alter human behavior or performance scare the piss out of me. Besides, they're illegal."

"The Doc claims he's not taking any drugs."

"Any *known* drugs, maybe. What if he's concocted a new one? It's his field, for Chrissake. All you've got is his word on it."

"So what do you suggest?" Harry asked worriedly.

"Get some advice from another doctor. One who knows about the latest research on nerve-stimulating drugs. Better yet, one who knows this McKinnon personally, what kind of guy he is, and what he's been working on in the lab. What I'm trying to say, Al, is before you let this doctor dazzle you with his footwork, find out how he learned to dance so good."

Gravely, Al nodded, "I tried, believe me; but all the Doc would admit to was following a training program of special exercises, diet, and nutrient supplements."

"What sort of nutrient supplements?"

"Naturally occurring ones, *he claimed.*"

"Yeah," Mel said skeptically. "Well, where can I get my hands on some? Might do wonders for my tennis game."

Al shrugged. "He won't talk about it. Says the nutrient represents a major medical discovery and he doesn't want anybody filching it from him until he publishes a paper in some medical journal. Makes sense, you know."

"All right," Mel conceded, "so he won't tell us about it. But maybe he'll tell a fellow doctor, one he trusts to keep his mouth shut, so this other doctor can then assure us it's legit. Fact is, Al, I'd insist on it if I were you. Make it a condition of handling him."

"Hmm," Al mused. "It's worth a try. But who gets to pick this doctor go-between, him or us? Got to be us—right?"

"How about Harvey Larkin?" suggested Harry.

Al's mouth twisted derisively. "'Lumbago' Larkin, the liniment man! Shit, he couldn't tell a concussion from a cold!"

"Well, he does work for the Boxing Commission," Harry pointed out.

"Sure, since his brother-in-law, the political hack, got him appointed. . . . Come to think of it, I *do* know a doctor. A damned outstanding one. Better yet, he's an ex-boxer himself. Used to work out at the gym once or twice a week until about ten years ago. Dan Lassiter."

"Lassiter!" Mel exclaimed. "The general director of Commonwealth General? I didn't know you knew him, Al."

"For almost twenty-five years. Since his medical school days. Yeah, Dan Lassiter's our man, all right. I'll check with McKinnon tomorrow and if he doesn't object, I'll give Danny a call."

"What if he does object?"

"I'll call anyway!" Al rose and reached for his mackinaw. "Well, see you guys tomorrow." He scanned their faces.

"Jesus, if this works out—if this guy's for real—what a ride we got ahead of us!" He looked mischievously at Harry. "Worth sticking around for, huh, old friend?"

"Halevai!" Harry said.

"What's that mean?" asked Moe.

"It means, 'Saints preserve us' in Yiddish," Mel explained.

5

The dense snowfall did not faze Adam as he left the Front Street Gym. Not even a hailstorm could have pounded the smile from his face or dampened his exhiliration. Step one of an elaborate plan to bring him fame and riches, advance science, wreak havoc on professional sports, and maybe even get Lakeman to switch to a better brand of cigars had gone smoothly; his vision, born of dead-end desperation, was that much closer to reality.

Al Lakeman was exactly the right man for his purposes, although he doubted Lakeman shared the same high opinion of him. Most likely, he thought Adam arrogant and evasive, even egomaniacal. But his brash behavior had been calculated to irritate the crusty fight manager into letting him spar with Tanner. No doubt, Lakeman would be amazed to know how morose and ineffectual Adam had been recently—how close to suicidal depression the loss of a woman and her unborn child had brought him. That knowledge might well make Lakeman feel more sympathetic toward him, but Adam wasn't ready to reveal himself in that way yet. Not until the mystique he was in the process of creating had outlived its usefulness.

Turning up his coat collar against the driving snow, Adam

hurried to where his Corvette was parked on the street. Risky as it was—sports cars were stolen even in heavy snowstorms—he had left it unlocked. With his extra-quick muscular movements, trying to insert keys into keyholes gave him fumbling fits—perhaps mostly psychological now, but still maddening.

He slid under the wheel of the four-year-old Corvette Diana had unloaded on him, started the engine, and waited the five minutes it usually took this marvel of General Motors' design and engineering to get its gears together and go more than a foot without stalling. The car would have defeated even a master automotive mechanic. The headlights wouldn't retract; the automatic choke stuck, flooding the carburetor; and the Positraction, installed to prevent rear-wheel slippage, actually made the car spin out on ice and snow. But maybe he was being too hard on General Motors, Adam considered. They'd merely built the car. Diana had driven it, and she could be as rough on a car as on a relationship.

The Corvette was almost an extension of Diana herself: sleek, attention-getting, temperamental, capable of exceptional performance if pampered with frequent tune-ups; both of them complicated mechanisms demanding constant attention and expensive maintenance.

More than anyone, Diana was responsible for his present plight and his triumph. Even in the ring with Tanner, thoughts of her had fleeted through Adam's mind. *Diana, the Huntress*. How the name fit! They might still be together had he not refused to be her prey.

He released the clutch and the Corvette, as if to spite him, promptly stalled. Maybe he ought to slip it a little of the so-called nutrient he was taking to soup up its fuel-metering system? He started the engine again, along with the windshield wipers and defroster, and slumped back to wait for the carburetor to clear. As he did, his thoughts returned to Al Lakeman and the one potential trouble spot in their developing relationship. What he had revealed about his remarkable reflexes could conveniently be called a half-truth, if there were such a category. But it was as meaningless as semicancerous or semipregnant, making his story either an exaggerated truth or a minimal lie. It *was* a nutrient, an essential one, and it did occur naturally, only not in humans. Oh, well, he thought philosophically, it would all come out eventually—in the newspapers, the medical journals, his diaries. And, after all, it was *in the interests of science*.

Ah, Doctor Faustus and the interests of science. What a euphemism! Even the medical atrocities of Auschwitz were allegedly "in the interests of science." The grisly comparison held a special meaning for Adam: he had such a fierce aversion to being a victim that it ruled his life. Having felt that way even since they institutionalized his father, locked him away in a tiny room looking out on a crumbling concrete wall, Adam had only lately come to despise himself for it. Losing self-control, risking all to regain it, he had succeeded beyond belief. His gamble with God—technically, a suicide attempt which could still end up as one, though the process would be prolonged—had won him greater control of his body than any man before him had ever possessed.

Control, Adam mused. In an existential world, how important that seemed as a palliative against foreknowledge of death. Mind control, within the limits of sanity, meant little, but body control in sex and sports—what a premium death-fearing man placed on that! Otherwise, sports would remain as much a child's amusement as tiddledywinks.

He let out the clutch again and the Corvette, as if bored with idling, moved forward into the flow of traffic.

Cautiously, Adam drove up the slippery, cobblestoned incline to his Beacon Hill apartment. Snowflakes danced like sprites beyond his windshield. Sprites! He remembered reading Pope's *Rape of the Lock* in college: Belinda guarded over by a force field of thousands of tiny sprites. Feeling similarly protected by his new powers, he repressed elation, knowing that his slipping, sliding car was distinctly devoid of magic. Suddenly, he spotted headlights sweeping the top of the hill and heading towards him. He braked and the motor stalled. Cursing, he started it again and went shuddering forward until his headlights illuminated the front of a taxicab and he feared there wasn't enough room for them to pass between the high snowbanks. Since he was almost at the top of the hill and the cab had just turned onto it, he had the right of way. He slowed to a crawl. The taxi didn't. He saw the gleam of eyes and teeth on the cabbie's face as the two vehicles, front bumpers almost brushing, squeezed past.

Confidence, thought Adam. Despite the thin line dividing it from recklessness, how zestful it made life!

Without further incident, he eased the Corvette into his

driveway, cut the ignition, and waited while the engine dieseled before wheezing to a halt.

"Is that all?" he asked aloud. The engine responded with one more turn. The last word. Yup, Diana's car, all right, he thought wryly. As he started to take the key from the ignition, he suddenly changed his mind. He had been cooped up alone in this small, outrageously expensive Beacon Hill apartment almost a week now and was sick of it. Even though he was tight-muscled and sore from his sparring with Tanner, he craved more action. And he knew where to find it.

For years, Adam had swum and played handball regularly at a private sports club in New Haven. On moving to Boston, however, he had discovered that racquetball had largely superseded handball at such clubs and the only place for a decent game was the YMCA. But tonight, Adam did not hear a single thwack of a handball hitting a wall as he climbed the circular iron staircase leading to the observation gallery. A quick inspection of the four courts confirmed they were empty. He was both surprised and disappointed. Handballers were a hardy lot, as fanatically devoted to their sport as golfers, and it usually took more than a heavy snowstorm to keep them away. He had particularly wanted a tournament-class player to test his newfound agility on, or maybe even hustle one of the hustlers.

Ah, well, there would be other nights, he thought, and went to the snack bar for a bowl of soup and a sandwich. At the counter, munching on potato chips and a minuscule hamburger, sat a lanky blond man in his early thirties Adam had never met but recognized instantly. Had Charlie Nash been Chinese, or a citizen of virtually any foreign country, he would have been a national hero. He was Boston's top Ping-Pong player, one of the best anywhere. Adam had watched him compete against formidable opponents at the Y twice and marveled at his mastery of the sport. Although Adam had played tournament Ping-Pong in his youth, and once or twice a year since, he was hardly an accomplished player. Yet that, too, was changing. Two nights before, after a few games to adjust his stroke, he had given a Ping-Pong opponent a good thrashing. But did he dare challenge a player of Nash's ability? Taking the next stool, Adam looked at him, feigned surprise, and said, "Aren't you Charlie Nash? I'm Adam McKinnon."

"Evening." Nash shook hands. "You live here?"

"No."

"Just like the food, huh?"

"Not particularly. In fact," Adam said, glancing from the remnants of Charlie's overfried hamburger to the waitress listlessly sweeping the floor, "I just lost my appetite. . . . Interested in a game?"

"I was," Nash said ruefully. "Drove ten miles in this slush, but my partner never showed up. He's a fireman, so maybe got called to a fire, though it beats me how anything could catch fire in this snow."

"I'll play you," said Adam matter-of-factly.

Nash scrutinized him. "I've seen you around. Handballer—right? Never saw you at the tables, though."

"Gave it up a few years ago."

"How come?"

"No competition," Adam lied. In a reprise of his brash performance at the Front Street Gym, he was giving Nash the same come-on.

"That's my line." Nash glanced at his watch, hesitated, then shrugged. "Oh, what the hell. I'll give you a go. What do you want to play for, stakes or sport?"

"Sport," Adam said. "Wouldn't want to hustle you."

Nash made a wry face. "That's my line, too. . . . Okay, Mac," he said and saw Adam wince at the nickname, "you got yourself a game—short as it will be."

"Good."

"No competition," Nash repeated mockingly. "What Y you been playing at, the YWCA?"

"It was a couple of years ago. You weren't around then."

"Could have been when I was in Korea, keeping an eye on the DMZ. But enough talk. Let's play."

The gameroom contained two Ping-Pong tables, two pool tables, a scattering of foosball and air-hockey platforms, and a hawk-eyed custodian perched behind a small counter. Nash removed a can of balls and a leather-protected paddle from his gym bag. Shedding its cover and holding the paddle in an Asian-style "penhold grip," he took several wrist-loosening practice swings. Adam picked up a paddle from the other table.

"You going to use that?" Nash sneered. "There's hardly any rubber on it! I've got an extra you can borrow. Just don't let it bang the table or drop it. I don't want it bruised."

Adam took the paddle from him with thanks.

"How many points you want?"

"As many as you're giving."

"Ever play in any 'Fed' tournaments?" Nash asked, referring to the International Table Tennis Federation.

When Adam looked blank, he sighed, "I gather not. I'll spot you twenty. Want the serve, too?"

"No, you can serve."

"Okay. Here goes."

Nash tossed the ball about a foot in the air and drove it across the net at medium speed to Adam's right side. Adam returned it with a backhand chop. Stepping back, Nash let the ball drop to table height and, with a sudden, whiplike stroke, smashed it back. The shot was perfectly placed, just grazing the table edge on Adam's side. Adam leaped back and reached down. Knowing it was an unreturnable shot, Nash glanced at the gameroom custodian for his reaction. But to his utter astonishment, the ball sailed back over the net and bounced in his face. Mouth agape, he exclaimed, "How the hell did you return that?"

Adam shrugged modestly. "Just luck, I guess."

"Sure," Nash spluttered. Picking up the ball from the floor, he tossed it to Adam. "Let's hope so."

It had been a lucky shot, Adam conceded, driving his first serve into the net. The fault made him acutely aware that Nash would be a much tougher opponent than Tanner. Beating an expert Ping-Pong player required a masterly offense as well as defense, and he wasn't sure he was capable of mounting one.

Staring intently across the table at the far left-hand corner, Adam's serve skipped over the net, hugging the right border, a deceptive stroke, usually good for one point a game against an average player. But Nash was not average. Though caught off-balance by the direction of the ball, he managed to reach it and backhand it back. But his momentum carried him too far left and Adam returned the ball diagonally to his right.

Futilely, Nash lunged for it, but it was just out of reach. "Not bad," he said grudgingly. "Not bad at all. . . . Well, now that you can brag to your friends you beat Charlie Nash, sort of, let's play some real Ping-Pong. How many points you want this time?"

Adam smiled. "How many do *you* want?"

Nash's eyes widened. "Oh, I get it. The reverse hustle."

Adam looked baffled. "What do you mean?"

"You're putting me on."

"No, honest—"

Nash sighed. "Okay, you know what a hustle is, when you

play less than your best to keep the mark coming back for more. Well, in a reverse hustle you go all out from the start, make a few fast points and a lot of smart-ass remarks to get the guy you're playing so mad he'll be off his game. Get it now?''

Adam nodded.

"Then let's play. No spots, no cupping on serve, strict tournament rules—okay? Much as the word chokes me, the loser—meaning me—serves first.''

Switching to the more conventional "shake-hands" grip, Nash's right arm arched back and whipped forward, sending the ball spinning over the net twice as fast as before. Adam's return sailed over the end of the table. His next two also overshot the table, as he struggled to adjust his swing. He let the fourth serve bounce beyond him before reaching back and slamming it down the middle. Nash returned it weakly, trying but failing to put enough backspin on the ball, and Adam put it away. Expecting a repeat, Nash stepped back quickly following his next serve, but before he landed on his heels, the ball skipped past him. Instead of retreating, Adam had leaped forward and, with timing only his super-quick reflexes were capable of, backhanded the ball before it reached the end of the table.

"Jesus," Nash muttered. "You sure you're not a Jap in disguise? I haven't seen a shot like that since Ogimura in his prime!''

Adam bowed humbly. He was playing better than expected, but he was running out of surprise shots. His first serve overshot the table; his second bounced too high and Nash smashed it back so hard that it rebounded several feet over Adam's head. He kept his next three serves lower and within bounds, but ideally placed for Nash's forte, his forehand topspin slam. Adam managed to return the last of these successfully, making the score 7–3.

Thereafter, the lead see-sawed back and forth in paradoxical fashion. Though the advantage was usually with the server, Adam won most of his points during Nash's service by shrewdly mixing volleys of short and long strokes. And Nash took equal advantage of his weak serve. Finally, the score deadlocked at 20–20. Again, Adam looked to his left while propelling his serve down the right-hand edge. He didn't expect Nash to fall for the maneuver a second time, and he didn't. Sliding sideways, he returned the serve with a vicious backhand chop. The ball rocketed forward, tipped the top of the net, and tumbled downward. Leaping forward, Adam managed to scoop it up with his paddle before it bounced twice, and lob it back. Nash waited for the ball to drop to shoulder level and then, with a looping overhead swing, smashed it back. The ball hit the middle of Adam's court and rebounded ten feet in the air. Backpedaling furiously, Adam leaped high, and slammed it back with even greater force to bound a good two feet above Nash's reach. The Y attendant, the sole spectator to their match, gaped in astonishment. It was the sort of volley he was more accustomed to seeing in badminton than in Ping-Pong.

Clearly unnerved, Nash sent his first serve into the net and his second off the side of the table. Without a word, he turned sharply and strode to the drinking fountain. He gulped thirstily, wiped his mouth with his hand, and said, "Well, that's two games you won off me."

Adam looked up at the wall clock. "Still half an hour till closing time. Let's keep playing."

"Sure," Nash said tersely. "Why not? What have I got to lose—except my mind? Look, Mac—or whatever your first name is—I've been beaten plenty of times before, but never by anyone who plays like you. I coach teen-agers who can serve with more zip. But not even Stellan Bengtsson, one of the greatest defensive players in the history of the game, could match some of your circus returns. Nobody, and I mean *nobody*, can backhand my serve immediately after it bounces. Nobody has that kind of split-second timing. So how come you do?"

Adam shrugged. "I don't know. I've got good hand-to-eye coordination."

"You do, huh? How did you get it?"

"Practice," Adam said not very convincingly.

"Practice! Against who? Superman? A robot?"

"Look," Adam hedged, "it's a long story. Suppose we play a few more games and I'll tell it to you over a couple of drinks."

"Okay," said Nash reluctantly. "I guess I need the practice—a hell of a lot more than I thought. I don't know if you heard about it, but the North Korean government has invited a team of Americans over there to play their boys this fall. And I intend to be on that team. I missed last year's championships in

Pyongyang because of hepatitis. But I'm not going to miss this trip; I've got a few scores to settle with those gooks. . . . You know," he added with a grin, "we'd make a hell of a doubles team!"

6

The gameroom custodian got so engrossed in the marathon final game between Adam and Charlie Nash that he let them play past eleven P.M. By then it was too late for the drinks and explanation Adam had promised, so he and Nash parted outside the Y after agreeing to a return match two evenings later.

When Adam got home, he should have been exhausted from so much exercise. Instead, he was charged with energy. He unlocked the front door with comparative ease and almost bounced into his apartment. "Jesus," he exulted, "I feel good!"

And so you should, he told himself, beating Boston's top boxer and Ping-Pong player in one day!

Adam and his inner self talked to each other more and more these days to prove that they were compatible and, with the possible exception of acute schizophrenics, trial separations didn't work. He also had a less glib reason. Since his plunge into the unknown the week before, there seemed to be two Adam McKinnons: the feckless, bet-hedging "old" one—long on responsibility, short on self-esteem—and the bold "new" one—awesomely self-assured and inspirational, despite the discouraging probability that his stay would be brief.

Late as it was, there remained the letter he had to write. He sat at his desk and composed rapidly:

To: Dr. Kurt Eliasson,
Chief of Neurology,
Karolinska Institute and Hospital,
Stockholm, Sweden

Dear Kurt,

With deep regret, I am writing to inform you that I won't be able to attend the Second International Symposium on Neurotransmitter Metabolism at your institution in July. The last meeting was a stunning success, and I was greatly pleased to be invited to chair a subsection at the forthcoming one. However, since my last letter to you, tentatively accepting the assignment, I have decided to take a year's sabbatical and am uncertain where I will be this summer.

Although my team has continued its clinical trials with choline therapy in the treatment of various dementias, our results remain inconclusive and we have very little new to report. As I'm sure you'll understand, my dual responsibilities as chief of neurology and project director have grown so overwhelming that I need some time away from the hospital to regain my perspective and develop some personal life. Adding to the pressures I'm under, the National Institute for Nervous and Mental Diseases has recently notified me that it is terminating my research grant as of this July. I had hoped their review committee would decide otherwise, but I simply cannot furnish them with the sort of clear-cut results they evidently expect. As a sop or consolation prize, they have asked me to make some project site visits for them, but I hate sitting in judgment of other researchers as much as I hate their doing it to me. So I have postponed any decision in this regard and for the next few months plan to do little more than read, have a few brain-picking sessions with my neurochemist friends at M.I.T., and loaf. I may do some traveling as well, having an itch to visit Paris again and satisfy my craving for croissants and French coffee. My itinerary might include a side trip to Sweden, too, and if so I will inform you well in advance. I do want to keep my options wide open, though, and so feel it best to withdraw from participation in your conference now. I'm confident you can find a suitable replacement.

Wishing you and your conference every success, I remain,
                              Your friend and colleague,
                              Adam McKinnon, M.D.

There! he thought with satisfaction. That was done. He liked
Kurt, a big bear of a man with lusty appetites for food and
women, and regretted passing up the pleasure of seeing him
again. But the conference would be a waste of time; he was
light-years ahead of any of its participants, and he had no idea
where he would be in July, even if he would still be alive. One
thing seemed certain, however: if he survived long enough for
his plan to work, Kurt, along with the rest of the world, would
definitely know where *he* was and what he was doing. A
sudden thought made him laugh out loud. Since he had no
intention of adopting a pseudonym, or hiding the fact that he
was a medical doctor, he was certain to hear from the twelve-
man grant-giving jury of the N.I.N.M.D. They were bound to
ask for an urgent meeting, which he would refuse, and for
tickets to his next fight, which he would not refuse, providing
he could seat them in the very last row of the arena, the proper
place for such a far-sighted group.

Bitter, Adam? whispered his inner self.

Damned right!

But you didn't have the data, did you?

No, but it was their timing. They hit me when I was down.

Meaning?

Meaning that, after Diana left, I still had my research to
keep me going. I still had hopes of finding a cure for senile
dementia.

Because of your father?

You know damned well because of my father!

Don't be so touchy. Want a drink?

Sure, and a little music.

Anything in particular—Brahms? Beethoven? Segovia?

Later. Right now, I think I'd like to hear my favorite country-
western sage.

Diana had introduced him to the modern pop-rock singers,
the Carly Simons and Rod Stewarts, but Kenny Rogers was his
own find. And the lyrics of his gigantic hit record. "The
Gambler" had become as personal a philosophy to him as
Thoreau's or Osler's. He put the record on the turntable, poured
himself a drink, and looked for a place to sit. The living room
offered few choices: leather-covered couch, wicker chair by the
window, cushions piled on the floor in the corner. When, at

Diana's insistence, he moved into this expensive apartment, he
had sold most of his own furniture because it clashed with hers.
Now, with her pieces gone, the place was virtually bare. He
flopped down on the couch, sipped his drink, and listened
intently to "The Gambler," as the gravelly deep voice of
Kenny Rogers filled the room:

> You got to know when to hold 'em, know when to fold 'em,
> Know when to walk away, know when to run!
> You never count your money when you're sittin' at the table,
> There'll be time enough for countin' when the dealing's done.
>
> Every gambler knows that the secret to survivin'
> Is knowin' what to throw away and knowin' what to keep.
> 'Cause every hand's a winner, and every hand's a loser,
> And the best that you can hope for is to die in your
>   sleep. . . .

Rogers was certainly right about one thing, Adam mused:
after he'd had his year of high adventure, his revenge of sorts,
the most he could probably hope for was to die in his sleep.

Thoughts of the physical damage he might be doing to
himself unnerved him. But not for long. By nature, he was a
pragmatist—the year-long interlude with Diana his only lapse.
He was also a competent neurologist and did not delude
himself about the potentially lethal complications. From the
moment he had plunged into self-experimentation, and survived it, he had figured on a year. And a year could be a very
long time when each of its 365 days were as full as this one had
been.

He looked at his wristwatch: a little after midnight. In a few
hours, he had an anniversary of sorts. Exactly one week ago,
around three A.M., he had done it. He had dissolved three
teaspoons of L-butyrylcholine in a tall glass of ginger ale,
stared at the amber liquid a moment, and—without any toast,
prayer, incantation, or last words—gulped it down. It was a
dramatic moment and, with a little help from the weather,
could have been melodramatic. But the night was clear and
calm; no thunderclaps or bolts of lightning. The powder had
not bubbled or foamed, simply dissolved in the drink. It tasted
bitter, but more ginger ale washed the bitterness down. For the
next few minutes, Adam felt light-headed, but attributing it to
hyperventilation slowed his rate of breathing. Though he did
not really expect anything drastic to happen immediately, he

had his tape recorder running to capture his last words if that proved to be the case.

The spool of tape whirred softly, recording nothing but the tick of the kitchen clock and his heavy breathing. More minutes passed. Aside from mild nausea, Adam felt nothing except a little foolish. His dramatic gesture was turning out to be a dud. No hair sprouted on the backs of his hands, no spasms contorted his face; Doctor McKinnon was obviously not going to turn into Mr. Hyde tonight.

But then what should he expect? He had already fed the LBC to six of his rhesus monkeys. One had promptly vomited it back, but he hadn't observed any deleterious effects in the others. Not immediately, anyway. By rights, he should have conducted the standard toxicity tests on rats before moving on to monkeys, but Adam had impetuously omitted that step. Diana had left him the previous day, returning to her ex-husband in San Diego, and he was deeply depressed. Without her, he had only his research to occupy him. And although a meticulous investigator in the past, he just didn't want to bother with the preliminary step of poisoning the rats. It would take him at least two weeks to find the LD-50—that daily dosage of the chemical that would kill half the rat colony—and he wanted results sooner than that to dull the pain of Diana's departure.

Saying nothing to his three co-workers, he had let himself into the lab late one evening and fed the LBC to his monkeys in their favorite cocktail of emulsified bananas and honey. He observed them intently for the next two hours and, when nothing adverse happened, went home. Six hours later, however, he was awakened from sleep by a distraught animal-keeper; the monkeys were going crazy.

"Crazy?" Adam asked sleepily. "In what way?"

But all he could get from the elderly diener was that the monkeys were yelping incessantly and staggering around their cages. Hastily, Adam dressed and drove to the hospital to check them. What he saw made his heart sink. Removing them, one by one, from their cages and examining them thoroughly, he could find no abnormalities in their vital functions, no evidence of acute toxicity, nothing except frequent muscular twitches and gross incoordination. They couldn't even dip their drinking cups into the water trough to slake their thirst or grip their trapezes for a swing.

That same morning he called his three co-workers together

and confessed his act. They were stunned, but not totally condemning, knowing something of the turmoil in Adam's personal life. A discussion ensued as to whether one monkey should be sacrificed to find out if the choline analog had done any structural damage to its central nervous system. But the group decided to wait and see if the monkeys' incoordinated state was permanent.

Desperately hoping it would pass, Adam visited the animals immediately upon arrival at the hospital each morning and before departing each night for the next several days. But they remained so incoordinated that they couldn't scratch their noses without slapping themselves in the face.

Adam spent hours pondering what could have gone wrong: Was the dosage of LBC he had fed them excessive? Had it mixed poorly with something in their diet, or interacted with some residual effect from the last drug they'd received? Each possibility would have to be investigated in his next series of experiments. Then had come the letter from the N.I.N.M.D., terminating his research grant and the funds to purchase more monkeys. Adam had had grant proposals rejected before, and taken it in stride, but this time he was crushed. Not only was he still despondent over his break-up with Diana, and guilt-ridden for neglecting the rat-toxicity studies, but totally stymied. None of the dozens of researchers into pre-senile and senile dementia had yet discovered a form of choline, or any similar compound, that could penetrate the blood-brain barrier and restore normal memory function. Nor had a variety of other treatments, from megavitamins to neuropeptides, worked. And here he was, an established expert in the field, who had recently hit upon a promising new approach to the dementia that had devastated his own father, only to be told by a group of pontificating, jealousy-ridden men meeting in Washington, D.C., "Sorry, you may need the money to make a major neurologic discovery, but you're only a small-time investigator, and we *do* have our priorities." Even worse, they were turning thumbs down on the most original idea Adam had ever had in all his years in the largely depressing subspecialty of neurology.

It was he, and he alone, after an almost irrelevant discussion with an amateur ornithologist, who had the inspiration to study choline metabolism in birds; to spend months isolating the peculiar choline analog, initially only a faint spot on a chromotographic analysis paper, that they manufactured in flight; finally, to isolate and purify enough of it for testing in laboratory animals. He'd done all of this amid personal bliss that suffused him with energy, and personal chaos that drained him of it. To what end? To turn six normal rhesus monkeys into uncoordinated, face-slapping creatures who could no longer feed or wash themselves? To be told by the N.I.N.M.D., "You're simply not top-drawer, so no more monkeys." So be it then, Adam had decided. But not even the hierarchy of the N.I.N.M.D., appalled as it would doubtless be, could stop him from experimenting on himself.

All these thoughts had traversed Adam's mind as he sat at his kitchen table waiting for the foreign chemical that now flooded his nervous system to affect him.

Fifteen minutes had wrought little change; he experienced no twitches, no tremors, nothing. Maybe he hadn't even absorbed the stuff, he speculated, feeling increasingly foolish. The tape recorder beside him beeped, indicating it had reached the end of the spool, and he hadn't said a single word into it. "Oh, shit!" he groaned; all that wasted worry and tension. Obviously, the monkeys metabolized the LBC differently from him.

Or so he thought, until he reached for the half-empty quart of ginger ale to pour himself a glass. His right hand shot out, sweeping the bottle off the table and smashing it against the floor. Clumsy clod, Adam thought, and started to rise to clean up the mess. The chair flew back and so did he, toppling him to the floor.

"Jesus Christ!" he cried as he banged his head on the linoleum. He tried to rub the sore spot, but didn't even come close. As his arm flopped around looking for his head, sudden fear clutched him, along with bewilderment. Impatiently, he had waited for something to happen, and something was— acute cerebellar degeneration, spinal cord disruption, choreoathetoid spasms? He might be dying, and the tape recorder was off! Somehow, he had to rewind or reverse the spool. Even though he had no clear notion of what was happening to him, or what he could do about it, his scientific duty took priority.

Painfully, he sat up, tried to stand, and found himself flat on his back again. His left arm had buckled, not because it was weak but because he hadn't positioned it properly. And when he'd tried to push off on his right leg, it just slipped forward. So he was back on the linoleum, maybe for the count of ten.

But even worse than fear of dying was fear that his death would
go unrecorded. Adam didn't belabor what his political science
friends would call "the worst scenario." Instead, he lay still,
relaxed as best he could, and tried to analyze the situation.

He wasn't dying and he wasn't paralyzed; he was simply
uncoordinated. Somehow the LBC had rapidly penetrated his
spinal cord without passing the blood-brain barrier. At least it
wasn't disrupting his thought processes as yet. He could get up
from the floor if he wanted to; it would just take time, effort,
and extreme concentration.

It did. Finally getting his supporting arm in position and
pushing off slowly with his right foot, he rose, or more
accurately, sprung up—immediately losing his balance and
falling forward against the table. Now what? he thought,
before reminding himself of the tape recorder. He reached for
the eject button and hit the back of the machine. He was
uncoordinated, all right. He had seen patients with Saint
Vitus's Dance do better! When he willed his hand to move, it
certainly responded. In fact, it literally leaped. Dry-mouthed,
he ignored the tape recorder momentarily and reached for the
drinking glass, promptly knocking it to the floor. The people
downstairs must be wondering if Diana had returned and they
were in the midst of another of their noisy parties.

Suddenly, a deductive flash illuminated his mind. Maybe he
wasn't uncoordinated, after all. Maybe, like its function in a
bird in flight, the LBC had increased his nerve conduction
velocity, doubling or even tripling his reflex speed. If so, he
could control his muscular movements, provided he compen-
sated by doing it very slowly and deliberately. Again, he turned
to the tape recorder, fixed his gaze on the eject button, and
willed his right hand to reach out and his index finger to
depress it. With cogwheel rigidity, Adam's hand moved
towards its target and, after a few near misses, found the right
key. He repeated the same maneuver several times with steady
improvement. He even managed to eject the tape, turn it over,
and replace it so it was ready to record—a laborious task,
taking several minutes and beading his forehead with sweat.
When it was finally accomplished, Adam faced an unexpected
dilemma: with conjecture overloading his brain, he couldn't
think of anything to say.

If his hypothesis was correct, if the LBC had not disrupted
his coordination centers but merely speeded up his voluntary
reflexes, he wanted to be able to prove it. And despite the

numerous obstacles he would have to overcome to obtain such proof, he wanted it *now*—which meant he had to find some way to get it to the hospital. The electromyogram machine in his research lab could provide an objective measurement of his nerve conduction velocity and the necessary confirmation of his theory. All he had to do was figure out how to get there from here. Driving was out. It even took several tries to dial the number of a taxi company, but finally he did.

"Emergency, Doc?" the cabbie asked as Adam climbed into the back seat.

He nodded, trying to appear as calm as possible and somehow remain on the seat each time the cab swerved. He'd had the foresight to pluck a ten-dollar bill from his wallet before leaving the apartment, and kept it clutched in his hand to pay the cabbie on arrival. At the hospital, he went immediately to his basement laboratory. It was 6:45 A.M. Should he wait for a co-worker to appear and run the EMG on him? No, he decided, wanting to keep his discovery secret for reasons not altogether clear to him. The next obstacle Adam faced nearly defeated him: he could not fit the key to his laboratory door into its keyhole. Trying every conceivable maneuver, from placing his finger on the keyhole first and then quickly replacing it with the key, to repeated straight jabs at it, he simply couldn't coordinate the exchange. Even a blind man could have done it more easily.

Hearing footsteps along the corridor, he turned and saw a night orderly approaching.

"Having trouble, Doc?"

"Yeah," Adam admitted. "For some damn reason, I can't get my key in the lock."

"Sure it's the right key?"

"I'm sure," Adam said with a slight edge to his voice. "You want to give it a try?"

Taking the key case, the orderly fitted the protruding key into the keyhole and opened the door without difficulty. With a questioning look, he passed the case back to Adam.

"You feeling all right, Dr. McKinnon?"

"Fine," Adam replied, "just a little shaky from too much coffee."

"You do look sort of peaked."

"Do I? Must be the fast life I lead."

"You?" The orderly regarded him skeptically. "Don't tell me you're one of those secret swingers?"

"Outswing any monkey in there," Adam said, glancing at the open lab door. "Well, thanks for your help. See you around."

"Sure, Doc," said the orderly, moving on with a perplexed look.

Inside the laboratory, Adam went immediately to the electromyogram and turned it on. Omitting the usual disinfectant swabbing, he inserted a needle electrode into the skin immediately above his left ulna nerve where it wound around the elbow, and another into the bony knob at his wrist. With mounting excitement, he pressed the firing button and watched the oscilloscope screen come alive with the graphic depiction of a nerve impulse. The computer attached to the machine clicked rapidly and gave him a reading: 136.6 meters per second. Adam was thrilled. Normal nerve conduction velocity ranged between fifty and sixty-five meters per second, and though many drugs and diseases could slow it, none had ever increased it significantly.

At one A.M., Adam still wasn't sleepy. Whimsically, he decided to stay up until three to celebrate a full week since his discovery. And what a week! Like a recovering stroke victim, he'd had to re-learn the simplest tasks. His handwriting had become an illegible scrawl; his typing worse. Much as he disliked the feel of an electric razor against his skin, he didn't dare use a blade unless he shaved next to the hospital's blood bank. Eventually, he learned to harness his quickened reflexes, and only wished he could teach his hapless monkeys to do the same. Each morning he got to the hospital at six-thirty, a half-hour before his co-workers, to run an EMG on himself. The measurements showed that the LBC was long-acting, his nerve conduction velocity decreasing only ten meters per second in the forty-eight hours since he'd taken it. But that merely represented his response to a loading dose; still to be determined was how much of a maintenance dose he would need and how often?

On the fourth day, he received what turned out to be a fortuitous phone call from Dr. Keith Harrison, his regular handball opponent, challenging him to a match. With mild misgivings, Adam accepted and got to the court an hour early to test his new reflexes.

It proved a wise precaution. Like a handball player trying to hit a much deader squash ball, he kept swinging too soon.

Even when Keith showed up, he was still missing half his shots. Lamely, he invented an afternoon eye appointment and persistent blurred vision from the drops used to dilate his pupils.

"Why didn't you tell me?" Keith admonished. "We could've canceled."

"Naw," said Adam. "It's getting better."

How much better soon became apparent. After winning the first ten points, one less than a shutout, Keith suddenly saw his lead vanish as his opponent made first one, then a series of near-impossible return shots.

Losing the game 21—12, Keith glared at Adam and demanded, "What the hell's going on? I don't mind getting beat, not even blowing a ten-point lead, but I've never seen you—or anyone—get such a jump on the ball."

"Sonar," said Adam.

"Sonar?" Keith exclaimed. "What's that supposed to mean?"

"It means, I can tell where the ball's headed by the sound it makes when it hits the wall."

"Is that so? And you learned all that since we played last month?"

Adam smiled sheepishly. "I might as well confess. I took off a week to attend a handball clinic in Chicago run by Paul Haber. Learned a lot of tricks from him. Judging the direction of the ball from its sound was one."

Keith sighed exasperatedly. "Well, why didn't you say so?"

"I wanted to be sure I'd improved first."

"Improved! Jesus, you're a world-beater, blurred vision and all. At least, you were this game. Let's see if you can keep it up."

For the final two games, Adam flubbed enough shots to keep the score respectably close, but had he chosen to, he could have beaten Keith 11–0 both times.

The match was a revelation to Adam two ways: first, his eye muscles seemed to have accommodated to his faster reflexes. Not only did he react quicker to a shot but the ball appeared to be moving slower. As a neurologist, Adam was familiar with this phenomenon and its cerebellar-spinal tract rewiring mechanisms. It was another bit of information to file away for inclusion in the papers he planned to write on LBC. The second revelation was far more complex and preoccupied him in the shower and on the drive home.

Since most popular sports demanded quick reflexes, and their champions were those athletes whose neuromuscular responses were conditioned to react with the least delay to the relevant stimuli, a whole new world had opened for him. If his newly acquired agility on a handball court could be transferred to a boxing ring or hockey rink, say, he could rapidly dominate professional sports, become the nation's most versatile, highest-paid athlete. All it would require was giving up his medical practice for a while and jeopardizing his life again—not at some future sporting event, but this very night and for many nights to come.

Back at his apartment, Adam went into the bathroom, opened the medicine cabinet, and reached for the pint-sized jar of LBC on its shelf. Holding it in front of him, he smiled, remembering the television commercial in which a whirlwind rose out of a bottle of household cleanser, and debated whether to take another dose now.

His nerve conduction velocity had decreased another twenty meters per second in the last twenty-four hours, obviously too small a decrement to prevent his spectacular handball play, but quite possibly enough to hinder what he planned to do next. What made him waver, however, was knowing that the second dose of LBC might be almost as risky as the first. Even if he escaped an acute allergic reaction and its extremity, anaphylactic shock, he still had the hazard of cumulative toxicity to worry about. The fact that his monkeys showed no signs of blood, liver, or kidney damage gave him small comfort, since each had received only a single dose.

He remembered how discouraged his late friend, Nobel-laureate George Cotzias, had been when his original L-Dopa preparation produced severe bone marrow depression in several of his Parkinsonian patients. George had given it to them in what was then considered to be unusually large, eight-to ten-gram amounts; Adam had taken, and was planning to take again, even more massive doses of L-butyrylcholine.

But for the moment, bone marrow toxicity remained only a theoretical possibility. Much more worrisome was the *probability* that, if he kept taking it, the LBC would gradually replace all the acetylcholine, the natural chemical transmitter at his nerve junctions, making his nervous system totally dependent on a continuous supply. To stop it at that point might well result in a drug-withdrawal state more life-threatening than that of a heroin addict going "cold turkey" or an alcoholic in

D.T.'s. He would, in all likelihood, develop acute myasthenia gravis: a debilitating neuromuscular disease whose victims could barely open their eyes, chew food, or breathe on their own. That chilling prospect gave Adam pause and he took the jar of LBC with him to the kitchen to ponder his decision further.

Unlike his mental state of a few days ago when his life seemed bereft of pleasure or purpose, he was much less depressed now, less disposed to act rashly or recklessly. Moreover, he faced a gamble of mean consequences: should he continue on LBC, the chances of developing physical addiction and myasthenia gravis on withdrawal were high, and the chances of recovering from it unknowable. The sensible course would be to stop his self-experimentation until he could learn more about LBC's long-term effects from his monkeys. But to retreat now, to rejoin the ranks of the safe and sensible, was too reminiscent of the old Adam and he was loath to resurrect him. Something extraordinary had happened to him during the handball match: he felt as if he had broken through barriers of human perception into some mystical realm. It was such a surreal, surpassingly liberating sensation that Adam longed to recapture it. For perhaps the first time in his life, he could understand and share in Einstein's belief that a sense of the mystical was "the source of all true art and science."

Whatever the reason, whether to advance science or his own selfish ends, Adam simply could not stop now. For the second time that week, he dissolved three teaspoons of LBC in ginger ale and gulped the mixture down. He was prepared for as violent a reaction to the chemical as the last had been and was pleasantly surprised when it did not occur. Aside from feeling mildly nauseous and uncoordinated for the next hour or so, nothing else happened.

Subsequently, Adam tried to sleep, but his busy brain refused to cooperate. Just before dawn, he drove to an all-night drug store that stocked a large selection of paperback books and bought a copy of *The Guinness Book of World Records*. It sat now on his nightstand beside two library books: *Dr. Jekyll and Mr. Hyde* and *The Invisible Man*.

7

Adam went to bed shortly after three and fell into a deep sleep. He was wakened twice—once briefly by the clatter of snowplows clearing the street under his window and then permanently by a nightmare out of his military past.

Captain Adam McKinnon had served in the U.S. Army Medical Corps from 1959 to 1961—the last eighteen months at the 196th. Station Hospital, Paris, France. Europe was at peace, the U.S. was not yet embroiled in Vietnam, and Adam had been under fire only once as medical officer of an air-evac team bringing Americans out of the Belgian Congo in the early days of the Lumumba-inspired civil war. Casualties were minor: an Air Force mechanic and a civilian slightly wounded by sniper fire at the moment of takeoff. But for a few memorable moments, with bullets whistling overhead and pinging into the metal skin of the helicopter, Adam had known the heart-pounding, cotton-mouthed sensations of mortal fear. The mission earned him a Letter of Commendation and a new respect from combat veterans at the officers' club bar, nothing more.

Now, sleeping fitfully at dawn, his brain charged with the extraordinary events of the day before, and possibly because

Buglerian theory was correct—conscious pleasure was, indeed, unconscious pain—Adam returned to that remote grasslands in a vivid, violent dream.

Stanleyville was in flames. Smoke billowed from burning buildings and grass huts. Interspersed with bird squawks and hysterical monkey shrieks, the air crackled with automatic weapons' fire. The staccato bursts came from mutinous Congolese soldiers hiding in huts and doorways along the route Adam's medical team had to travel to reach the airstrip where their evacuation helicopters were waiting. They rode in a jouncing jeep with a machine gun on a swivel-head tripod mounted in the rear. Bracing himself as best he could, Adam crouched up front beside the driver, cradling a Thompson submachine gun in his arms. Time after time, as their jeep sped through the heart of the city, enemy soldiers sprang up from ambush with pointed rifles. But Adam always fired first, and the soldiers fell back with riddled chests and agonized faces. His gun barrel grew almost too hot to touch and his shoulder ached from the recoil, but instead of repugnance or remorse, wild exhilaration filled him as he slew men by the score.

Finally, they were out of the city, beyond the paved highway, bouncing along a rutted dirt road cutting through the grasslands. Nearing a Y-shaped intersection, they spotted a jeep full of black soldiers bearing down on them from the right fork. It carried no flag or military markings, nothing to indicate if its occupants were Lumumba loyalists or insurgents.

But as the distance between them closed, Adam saw a woman standing up in back—a tall, strikingly attractive woman, white blouse gaping wide, blonde hair tied back by a scarf, blue eyes shining excitedly as she held a stubby Uzi submachine gun in her hands.

Were they friends or foes? Adam wondered frantically as both jeeps entered the intersection together and drew parallel. Suddenly, Adam's driver, ducking as his windshield was shattered by a hail of bullets, shouted, "Shoot the fuckers!" Instantly, Adam swung his gun around, his finger tightening on the trigger. But before he could fire off a burst, he saw a bullet strike the girl—now clearly Diana—in the throat. In slow motion, he saw her flesh part, her torn carotid artery gush blood, and the bullet exit from the side of her neck below her ear. Appalled, but fascinated, he watched her drop her machine gun and clutch her throat, her eyes glazing with

*terror. In disbelieving horror, he saw her reach down into what
must have been a medical kit on the seat, seize a scalpel, and
without hesitating plunge it into her neck, moving the blade in
a circular motion like someone coring an apple. My God! he
thought, aghast. She was performing a tracheotomy on herself!*

Shuddering, Adam woke from the dream, blinking his eyes
repeatedly to rid his retina of its ghastly afterimages.

The woman *was* Diana, he was convinced of that; but what
the hell did it all mean? Was she the enemy? Who fired the
bullet that struck her in the throat? He? Most puzzling of all,
why did she attempt the tracheotomy on herself?

It was not until he had started shaving that the symbolism of
the dream dawned on him. In plunging the scalpel into her
neck wound, Diana was not trying to save her life at all. *She
was cutting her own throat!*

Had the abortion inflicted that mortal a wound on her
psyche? All he could ever get her to admit was, "I simply
wasn't ready for motherhood. My mother wasn't ready either,
which cost me eighteen thousand dollars' worth of analysis!"
Adam never really bought that explanation. It sounded too
glib, too rehearsed, more psychodogma than gut-spilling truth.
If it were true, why had she longed to get pregnant in the first
place; made it a precondition of their living together? But he
had never pressed her for a more convincing answer. The
abortion was over, their relationship irreparably damaged and
soon to end, so what was the point? How could a man hope to
understand something so intimate, even mystical, as the
feelings of an expectant mother for her unborn child? Yet, for a
time, while the abortion was still a raw wound in both of them,
and his pride kept him from asking her directly, he speculated
endlessly over her motive.

It could have been mere vanity. Diana had loved her
enlarging breasts, but not her thickening waistline. She
bemoaned that her best dresses no longer fit; that she could not
wear her bikini on the Bermuda vacation they had planned. But
Adam could not believe that was enough of a reason. He gave
her credit for more character than that.

Fickleness, then? In the most memorable of "Dianaisms"—
those aphoristic remarks derived from years of psychoanalysis
or her own keen powers of observation—she had said: "If you
order them, you can't cancel them!" She had made the
statement after a close friend from San Diego had rid herself of

an accidental pregnancy. And Adam, unaware and unsuspecting that Diana, influenced by her friend to consider abortion, too, had said it mainly to convince herself, had nodded in agreement. Her pregnancy was hardly accidental. It had been discussed for weeks, regarded as a more lasting bond between them than marriage, and once "ordered" taken root with extraordinary dispatch—only three days after Adam himself had pulled her interuterine coil. A happy time, the happiest they had known together followed, lasted two and a half months and ended abruptly with Diana's announcement that she no longer wanted the baby. Beyond that she refused to elaborate, even to discuss it, leaving him but a single choice: she could have her abortion in San Diego the next day or, if he wished to accompany her, locally within a week. Adam had chosen the latter, needing the extra time to try to dissuade her. It proved an exercise in futility. He got a catalog of complaints about living in Boston, living with him, but no real insight into why she had changed her mind, actually grown to fear motherhood. Fear what? he had demanded. The added responsibility? The increased chance of an abnormal child because of the cigarettes, alcohol, and sleeping pills she consumed less of but refused to quit? Eventual widowhood because he was twelve years older? But he never got an acceptable answer and the mini-execution proceeded on schedule.

In vivid, imperishable detail, he remembered sitting in the surgical lounge of the small, outlying hospital where Diana was being aborted, actually hearing the sucking sounds of the vacuum extractor and empathically feeling himself being swallowed up, his own flesh sundered. The brutal procedure, so awesomely Godlike in its finality, shook him severely. Moments earlier he had wanted desperately to do something to stop it, but knew not what. He *could* go beserk: barge into the operating room, yank the plug of the vacuum bottle from the wall, assault the gynecologist, get arrested, make newspaper headlines, become the latest *cause célèbre* of the right-to-lifers. The temptation was overwhelming. But he did nothing; it was not then in his nature.

Moreover, having never opposed the concept of legalized abortion before, he had to wonder how paternal and pure his objections really were. He had wanted to father a child, but he also wanted to insure Diana's fidelity. He loved her; she brought gaity and excitement into his dreary, work-oriented life. And although he had never openly admitted it, the thought, the mental imagery, of her in bed with another man was almost unbearable. Intellectually, he knew that sex stripped of procreative potential was merely a physical act. Yet, for two people to reap its full reward, they had to feel a sense of exclusivity, of almost hermaphroditic oneness, impossible to achieve if either took other lovers. What he wanted was an old-fashioned, till-death-do-us-part commitment from Diana and had thought having a child with her might insure it.

Wrong thinking! he had bitterly come to realize; wrong regarding Diana and quite possibly wrong regarding most of her contemporaries. "Women have sex, men have power, and each wants the other," Diana was fond of quoting. But was it true? Had the main affinity between men and women degenerated into deal-making?

One thing Adam did know: the abortion had destroyed more than a fetus. By plunging him to such depths of self-disgust, it destroyed forever his tolerance for his old, ineffectual self. The evidence was incontrovertible. He had swallowed the LBC.

He had heard nothing from Diana since she left Boston almost three weeks ago, and had no great desire to hear from her now. But the implications of the dream, whether real or imagined, left him inexpressibly sad—for both of them.

With sunlight streaming through the French doors into his living room, Adam spent a relaxing afternoon reading and listening to music before going to the Front Street Gym. Al Lakeman and Harry Patashnick were there with two other men. One, Adam recognized as Tommy Harms, a Filipino-American and Boston's top middleweight until a detached retina ended his boxing career. Adam later learned that even though the eye had received laser treatment, which usually prevented a recurrence, Al Lakeman refused to let Harms fight anymore. Instead, he had found him a good job as boxing instructor for a string of boys' clubs, and called on him often to help train his fighters.

"Hey, man," Tommy said with a broad grin while shaking hands, "Al tells me you're real quick slipping and blocking punches. Well, I'm quick, too, at throwing them—so let's see who's the quickest. Just don't hit me in the left eye, if you can help it."

Adam looked at the thick scar tissue around Harm's eye and promised to be careful. Then, Harry Patashnick tugged his arm to introduce the other man.

"Doctor, this is my son-in-law, Mel Waldman, sports writer for the *Globe*."

"Nice to meet you," Adam said, "I read your column almost every day."

"Glad to hear it," Mel replied, scrutinizing him intently.

"Mel'll want to ask you a few questions after the sparring," Harry mentioned.

Adam's smile faded, and he glanced suspiciously at Lakeman. "Okay, but all you'll get will be what I told Al yesterday. So what's the point?"

"I'll fill you in on the point later," Al growled. "You want a big-money bout—right? A million-dollar one? To get it, we're gonna need Mel's help."

At Adam's dubious look, Al added, "If I didn't trust him, he wouldn't be here. . . . Go change!"

Adam shrugged and headed for the locker room. Having seen Harms fight twice at Boston Garden, he understood why Al wanted them to spar. Harms threw combinations of punches almost too fast for the eye to follow.

"No head gear?" Harms questioned, once they were in the ring. "That's not smart, man."

"I'll take my chances."

Harms shrugged. "I got to wear mine, understand?"

"That's okay."

Harms shook his head. "You're somethin', you know that. Got me a little psyched already."

The difference between Todd Tanner and Tommy Harms was that Tommy had a sense of humor. Here he was, a veteran boxer, not so long ago the *numero uno* middleweight contender, up against a forty-five-year-old doctor and he couldn't land a punch. Not that he didn't try! He tried every move and maneuver he knew. At the opening bell, he had bounced into punching range, glided left and flicked out a jab that fell short, glided right and threw another one that Adam blocked, came straight on with a lightning-fast combination of punches, left jab and right cross, as if his two arms were connected by a pulley. It was possible to slip the jab or block the cross, but few fighters had ever done both—not the way Adam did. Instead of backing away, as expected, he stepped forward and inside, taking the jab on his left shoulder and blocking the cross with the palm of his glove.

"*Aie Krai!*" Harms muttered in Spanish, and moving out of range, gave Al Lakeman a shrug and a smile, Darting in and out, he threw an assortment of punches that either hit Adam's gloves or thin air—mostly air.

Gradually, Tommy's smile faded as his pride began to nag him. This guy *was* quick—quick as the darting tongue of a lizard up close, but not quite so quick moving forward or sideways. Maybe he could use that to his advantage? Again he shuffled forward, gloves held close to his face. Then, instead of gliding from one side to the other before unleashing a punch, he jumped, turning Adam constantly in a half-circle. Finally, he bounced to the right a split-second before Adam could swing his shoulder around, threw a left jab to stop the shoulder in mid-swing, and then a vicious left hook. Adam managed to deflect the hook inward, away from his face, and took it on the clavicle. It stung. He stung Harms back with a cross to the jaw and clinched.

"You okay?" he asked.

"Me?" Harms sounded surprised. "I'm fine. You move good, but you don't hit too hard."

Pushing Adam away, he was about to try his side-to-side jumps again when the bell rang. He looked around for Al Lakeman and was surprised to see him talking to Mel Waldman. Harms was irked. Al hadn't even watched that last flurry of punches.

"Throw combinations," Al told him while sponging his face. Tommy swallowed hard. He *had* been throwing combinations, dozens of them, but was too polite to contradict his old trainer. "Hey, Al," he ventured, "maybe I should try tricks."

"What do you mean, tricks?"

"You know. Butting, tripping, thumb-in-the-eye. Tricks!"

Al hesitated, glancing over his shoulder at Harry Patashnick and Mel Waldman with a mischievous gleam in his eyes. "No. No tricks. But you can kiss him, if you get close enough."

Everybody laughed, except Todd Tanner, sitting in the bleachers behind Harms's corner. He couldn't decide whether Tommy's poor showing against McKinnon made him feel better or worse. Though it took some of the shame from his own shoulders, it was bound to raise McKinnon's standing with Al Lakeman. Tanner could hardly wait for the sparring to end, so he and Al could talk.

Harms began the second round with the same tactics that had almost worked at the end of the first: jumping from side-to-side with both hands held in close, ready to strike at the first opening. But recognizing the danger of being drawn off-balance by either an effective feint or a misstep, Adam went on the offensive. Aiming low to miss Harms's eyes, he watched for him to square his shoulders after each side-leap—the signal that a punch was coming—and then beat him to it.

"Good jab, man," Harms grunted in the next clinch. But, seeing the sullen glint in his eyes, Adam grew wary—with good reason. Harms pushed him off and, against the rules, simultaneously launched a vicious uppercut. Caught flat-footed, Adam arched back to his limit, feeling his opponent's glove brush his chin. The blow left Harms off-balance, too, and Adam landed a right cross to the jaw that floored him just as the bell rang. Helping Harms up, Adam saw that he was shaken but not hurt.

"I deserved that," said Harms manfully, and draped his arm around Adam's shoulders. "Hey, Al!" he shouted, nodding at Adam, *"Mucho talencio!"*

Adam looked at Lakeman. "You satisfied?"

"Yeah," Al said grudgingly. "Get dressed. I'll be in the office." He waited for Adam to climb down from the ring before saying to Mel Waldman, "Ever see anybody like him before?"

"No, never," Mel replied. "I'm excited."

"You're not the only one. Come on in the office. We'll have a drink to celebrate."

Al Lakeman seldom made mistakes in handling fighters. But he made two that afternoon: He forgot about the talk that he had promised to have with Todd Tanner. And he forgot that Todd was in the bleachers when he closed the door to his office without a word. A few moments later, Tanner stalked out of the gym, smoldering.

"All right," Al said after Adam joined them. "You asked me to come up with a plan to make you a million bucks and I have. So listen carefully."

Adam did, nodding approval when Al had finished describing it. "When do we meet this Aaron Robards?"

"Three tomorrow afternoon. At his office in the Prudential Building."

"That soon, huh?"

"I just got off the phone to him, setting it up."

Adam turned to Mel Waldman. "You going to write about this?"

"You bet. . . . When the time is right. Until then, not a word."

"Sounds good," Adam said.

"There's a catch," Al added.

Adam sighed, "Isn't there always."

"You're good, McKinnon," said Al. "You've proved that twice now. You can beat any boxer around, in my opinion. That's not the issue. The issue is how you got that way. Neither Mel nor I believe that cock-and-bull story about a special diet and nutrients. We think you could be on stimulant drugs. And if you are, we want no part of you."

"I see," said Adam. "Well, how do I convince you I'm not?"

"You don't. I know a fair amount about caustics and hemostatic solutions to stop bleeding from cuts. Otherwise, I don't know a damn thing about drugs. So it's not me you have to convince, but a doctor we know."

Adam frowned. "Gentlemen, that's not a catch, it's an impasse. I'm simply not ready to do that."

"Why not?" asked Mel Waldman.

"I already explained that to Al."

"And Al passed your explanation along," Mel said. "But what if it's a doctor you can trust to keep his mouth shut?"

"You know someone like that?"

"Al thinks he does."

Adam's eyes locked with Lakeman's. "And who might that be?"

"Lassiter," Al replied. "Dr. Dan Lassiter. Know him?"

Adam hesitated. "Not personally. But I know of him."

"Enough to trust him to act as a go-between?"

"Hmmm." The question put Adam in a bind. To refuse to confide in a doctor of Lassiter's repute on the pretext that he might steal his discovery would be paranoid and absurd. But to tell Lassiter the truth about L-butyrylcholine was running an enormous risk. If he failed to convince him that LBC should be classified as a nutrient, not a drug, he could forget about Lakeman's cooperation. On the other hand, Adam knew that he would likely need a doctor himself before too long, and even though Lassiter was an internist, he was also head of a major hospital with numerous neurologists on its staff.

"Well?" Lakeman challenged. "What's your answer?"

"My tentative answer is that I *do* trust Lassiter. If I have to confide in any doctor, it might as well be him. Have you mentioned anything about this to him yet?"

"No," Lakeman said. "But I'll call him as soon as you give me the word."

"You know him that well?"

"For twenty-five years," Al said proudly. "He's an ex-boxer himself, you know."

"He's also a pretty fair handball player, I hear."

"That, too."

"Okay," Adam said reluctantly, "go ahead then. Have him call me and we'll set up a meeting."

Looking relieved, Al said, "I'll do that."

"I suppose you'll want Lassiter's verdict before we meet Robards?"

Al grinned. "I sure as hell would've if you'd hedged. But this way, I'm willing to go ahead."

"Generous of you," Adam said wryly.

"Oh, I'm a generous guy. Let's hope Robards proves as generous."

"Think he will?"

"Are you kidding! A white heavyweight who isn't connected—meaning, owned by the mob? He'd hock his office chandelier for a piece of you!"

8

Blinking in the bright sunshine outside the Front Street Gym, Todd Tanner pulled down his cap and rapidly walked away, wanting to get out of this part of town where all the shopkeepers, cops, and drifters knew him. He hadn't wanted to talk to anyone but Al Lakeman that day, and since Lakeman had cold-shouldered him, he was in no mood to rap or hassle with some street dude.

Better not to talk at all, he thought. Boston had been good to him; he was the most popular fighter in town. Born in the anthracite coal country near Scranton, Pennsylvania, Todd Tanner owed everything to boxing. It had been his ticket to see the world. In five years, he had fought in twelve countries on four continents, picking up a fair knowledge of other cultures in his travels. He had come a long way from the smoky skies of Scranton and never meant to go back. But without Lakeman to guide him, he might easily get turned around.

Invariably, life's choices had been presented to Todd Tanner in simple, take 'em or leave 'em terms. This seemed no different now.

Since his first Golden Gloves bout at age twelve, Todd had climbed into hundreds of rings because of what his father taught him long ago. Franklin Tanner was past forty when Todd was born, a coal miner bowed by the burden of supporting a wife, four children, and three older relatives, and beginning to suffer from "black lung" disease. A proud man who prized self-reliance above all other virtues, he instilled it in his children.

At six, Todd had run home crying from Sunday school, his good suit ripped and soiled, beaten up by a boy two years older. His father heard his tearful account and thrashed him, warning that if Todd ever got hit again without hitting back he better not come home, because the strapping he'd get would hurt worse than any bully's fists. His devout mother might tell him to turn the other cheek, but his father lived in this world, not the next, and those were the rules. Like the leftover neckbones and grits for dinner or his brothers' hand-me-down clothes, he had but a single choice: take it or leave it.

Ever since that day, nobody ever punched Todd without being punched back. He might, and often did, come home disheveled and bruised, but never crying.

At puberty, Todd began to shoot up and fill out. Although his classmates continued to hound him, they grew more careful with their taunts. The older, stronger ones bragged they could whip him, but kept postponing the proof. It wasn't that Todd had grown tired of fighting; it was simply that he was beginning to punch too hard.

Actually, Todd missed the schoolyard fights. Many of the white boys he fought later became friends, proud of their tough, touchy black classmate. They encourged him to take up boxing, enter the Golden Gloves tournament, and cheered wildly when he won the state championship in his weight class. After that had come the Olympic tryouts and Al Lakeman.

Getting Al Lakeman to handle him was the best thing that had ever happened to Todd. By the time he had won his Olympic silver medal, he was not only ring-wise but career-wise, knowing that, without the right representation, he'd be pushed too fast, over-matched, exploited, and tossed aside. Then where would he be? What, besides boxing, did he really know? It would be back to leftovers.

Al Lakeman had saved him; under Al's tutelage, he had gone undefeated in twenty-two professional bouts. Until yesterday, everything had been going just fine. Then this McKinnon had showed up, suckered him into a few rounds of sparring, humiliated him in front of Al Lakeman. Worst of all, he had hit him without Todd hitting back. Nobody had done that since he was six years old! And the final insult was the way Lakeman ignored him today

Dusk found Todd Tanner on a bench in the all-but-deserted Boston Common. He had no idea how far he had walked or where—only that his mind had been more in Scranton than in Boston, his thoughts mostly of his taciturn father, now near death, in a nursing home there. In all their seventeen years together, Todd could remember only three times that they'd really talked. The first was after that bully had bloodied him at age six and his father, with his razor strap, impressed on him the importance of self-reliance. The second, after they'd moved to a racially mixed neighborhood and he was called mulatto the first time.

Franklin Tanner had not seemed particularly upset. He advised, "Pay it no mind, Son."

"But how come my skin is lighter than Josh's, and Luke's and Jesse's?" Todd said, referring to his three brothers.

Franklin Tanner hesitated. Todd was barely eleven, but he realized kids learn about life early in mining towns. "Well, your Ma's light-skinned. Guess you just favor her."

"Guess so, Pa," Todd said, embarrassed to say what was really on his mind.

Sensing it, Franklin Tanner laughed. "Look, Son, knowin' your ma like I do, the only man but me she'd ever let in her bed is the Good Lord Himself. And that would make you the black Jesus. Any more questions?"

Todd gulped. "How soon's supper?"

That memory gave Todd his first smile of the day.

Their third conversation came after Todd made the U.S. Olympic boxing team and told his father he was thinking of turning professional.

"You're good, Todd," Franklin Tanner had replied. "Mighty good. And I'm not gonna try to stop you. But I can't honestly say I like the notion of a son of mine ending up another nigger gladiator."

"What you mean, nigger gladiator?"

"Well, I know some history. I know most of them Roman gladiators were slaves, which meant most were blacks. How come you don't see many white kids boxing any more? 'Cause their folks want them to do more with their lives than entertain a bunch of Romans."

"But I'm better'n any white kid, Pa. I can really make a name for myself."

"I know you can, Todd. But just remember one thing: Until you get to the top, the very top, you're gonna have to do as you're told. And some of those who'll be doing the tellin' ain't gonna have your best interests at heart. Look how bad they cheated Jack Johnson and Joe Louis. So don't hurt nobody more'n you have to, don't do nothin' dishonest, and, above all, don't let nobody abuse you."

Todd remembered. And suddenly, the feeling that had tormented him, made him as restless and driven as a man possessed for the last twenty-four hours, had a name: abuse. McKinnon had not merely outboxed him, he had set him up, psyched him out with that hundred-dollar bet, embarrassed, and abused him.

Well, then, Todd thought with cold hard anger, can't sit here all night. Got to go have a talk with that man. He rose and crossed the street to a drug store, where he looked up Dr. Adam McKinnon's address in a telephone book. Then, he went there and waited for him to return in the shelter of an adjacent doorway.

Todd Tanner wanted to talk to Adam, but he meant to do other things, too. The only question was the sequence he would follow. Watching Adam park his Corvette in front of the toney Beacon Hill apartment building decided him.

Adam still had trouble putting a key in a keyhole, especially an iced-over one. He had to drop his gym bag on the curb and use both hands to lock the car. Suddenly, he sensed danger; warning signals, triggered by Tanner's shadow or his barely audible footsteps in the snow, sounded an alarm in his brain. He tensed, straightened, and swiveled his neck to the right. Tanner swung at the same time, so that his fist entered Adam's field of vision an inch from his jaw. Only his extraordinary reflexes allowed even a token attempt to evade the blow. He jerked his chin down and away—not enough to escape the punch, but enough to keep it from landing squarely. The next instant, a pressure-pain seemed to shear his head from his neck, scintillating lights showered on his retina, and he collapsed on the icy pavement.

"There," said Tanner in satisfaction as Adam fell. He had accomplished his goal, hit the unhittable man. A sense of sweet revenge should have surged through him. Instead, his spent anger gave way to frightful anxiety. Below him, Adam lay motionless, neck half-twisted, face buried in snow.

"Oh, Lord," Tanner groaned, his chest heaving and his stomach sickening with incipient panic. What do I do now? I can't just leave him? What if I broke his neck? What if he's dead? Naw, he told himself, his jaw might be broken but not his neck. Even so, I can't leave him to freeze. Cursing his own incredible stupidity, Todd took the key case from the car door and stuck it in his pocket. Then he lifted Adam by the armpits and hoisted him over his shoulder in a fireman's carry.

Moan! Make a noise! Anything! Todd silently pleaded as he carried Adam up the walk. But he remained unnervingly silent. Twice, Todd had to put him down while he hunted the right keys to open the outside door and the one to his apartment.

He read the two names over the doorbell and wondered who Diana Acheson was, figuring she was McKinnon's live-in girlfriend and praying she wasn't inside. To his relief, she wasn't. In fact, there was so little furniture in the living room the place hardly looked occupied. He lowered Adam to the couch, put a cushion under his head, and was immensely relieved to hear him groan.

Todd knew little medicine, but he had a professional boxer's familiarity with broken jaws. Lightly, he squeezed every inch of bone from the angle of Adam's jaw to his chin between thumb and fingers. Each time he did so, Adam groaned louder. Finally, his eyes opened, rolled aimlessly in their sockets, and focused on Tanner.

"What—?" Immediately, Adam winced at the twinge of pain triggered by the movement of his jaw. "What the hell are you doing here?"

Dumbstruck, Tanner managed to mumble, "I'm, uh, I'm here to help." As he let Adam mull that over, he saw a half-dollar-size spot beginning to turn purplish-blue on the underside of Adam's jaw. "Hey," he suggested, "let me make you an ice pack for that bruise."

The look Adam gave him indicated complete comprehension. "Thanks, Tanner. The icebag's in the top drawer left of the sink."

"I'll have it for you right quick." Todd headed for the kitchen.

"There's a phone in the kitchen, too. Use it to call the police."

Tanner stopped in mid-step. Pivoting, he blurted, "Police? What you want to call them for?"

"I've been attacked with a deadly weapon. It's a reportable crime. A felony."

"What deadly weapon? I didn't hit you with no weapon."

"But you did hit me, right? I'm still dazed, but I can figure that out. And being a professional boxer makes your fists a deadly weapon. You're in trouble, pal."

Tanner's face sagged. "Look, Doc, can't we—uh—talk this over?"

"Hard to talk." Adam pointed to his jaw.

"Maybe the ice pack'll make it easier?"

"What the hell got into you, anyway?"

Tanner gestured helplessly. "I'll get the ice pack."

"Use some of the ice to fix me a good stiff bourbon, too. The bar's in the corner."

"Sure, Doc. Then we'll talk, huh?"

The icebag eased the throbbing in Adam's jaw, but not his anxiety. If the jaw was broken, his boxing career was ended. But before facing up to that possibility, he wanted to hear Tanner out.

Once past his shame and embarrassment, Tanner was surprisingly articulate. Adam admired his honesty, could even sympathize with the inner turmoil that had provoked Tanner's attack. But he didn't say so; he wanted Tanner to sweat, just as he was sweating, over a possible broken jaw.

"Anyway, why I did it ain't so important as what I did," Tanner concluded. "And that was wrong. It deserves punishment. . . . Here—" he thrust his chin—"go on take a poke at me."

Adam smiled sardonically. "Good Old Testament justice, huh? Not a bad idea. . . . Tell you what, Tanner: let's you and me take a ride to the hospital, where I can get X-rayed. If my jaw's broken, I'm going to break yours. You know why?"

Tanner shook his head.

"Just so I can see the look on Al Lakeman's face when we tell him his two top heavyweights have broken jaws."

Tanner's eyes widened and then he broke into a laugh. "You know, Doc, you're okay. Maybe you and me can be friends."

"More than friends."

"What do you mean?"

"If the jaw's okay, sparring partners."

Tanner's smile faded. "I guess I owe you that much. But I got ambition, too, Doc."

"Not like mine. My ambition starts where yours ends." Tanner looked puzzled.

"You want to be heavyweight champ, right?"

"Right!"

"Well, I don't, and Al Lakeman knows it. All I want out of boxing is a million-dollar payoff, and Al thinks he can get it for me."

"Against who?"

"Coleman Jackson."

Tanner stared. "Coleman, huh? Wow! He's one mean mother."

"You afraid of him?"

Tanner scowled. "Not afraid. Just not ready yet."

"Well, you will be. You spar with me a month and Jackson's going to seem so slow you'll beat him to the punch every time. Like shot-putters practicing with twenty-pound balls so that the sixteen-pounders they use in competition seem light."

Tanner was intrigued. "Yeah. I see what you mean. Up against you every day, I'm bound to get quicker. Only, how come you don't want to be champ?"

"No time. I'm giving myself a year's break from medicine, and there are other sports I want to try. Now, get your coat. Can you drive a Corvette?"

"I can park one. I can park anything. Used to do it for pocket money."

At the New England Medical Center Hospital, Adam advised Tanner to stay in the car. "Don't think I'm ashamed to be seen with you, for God's sake. But they know me in there, and everybody in town knows you. If my jaw's broken, someone just might put two and two together. . . ."

"Gotcha," said Tanner and slid down in the seat.

A half-hour later, Adam climbed back into the car.

"Well?" Todd asked anxiously.

"We lucked out. No fracture."

9

Aaron Robards—lawyer, agent, sports promoter—could best be described as a relatively honest con man. With W. C. Fields he believed that, "You can't cheat an honest man," but there were enough dishonest ones around for him to make a very prosperous living. His suite of offices on the forty-fourth floor of the Prudential Building reflected it. Entering with Al Lakeman, Harry Patashnick, and Mel Waldman, Adam first noticed the glamorous but decorously attired receptionist at the antique desk and then the obviously expensive sculptures, mobiles, and paintings. On one wall alone, he saw a Spritzer, a Miro, and a Chagall lithograph.

"The sports promotion business must be booming," he remarked to Mel.

"In most places, it is," Mel answered, "but not in Boston. That's why Aaron's eager to see us. Probably drumming his fingers on his desk right now, waiting the obligatory five minutes before calling us in. He doesn't want to appear *too* eager."

"Cynic."

"Naw. Aaron's all right—in fact, a lot better than most. Ever hear of Sam Silverman?"

Adam shook his head.

"Well, Sam was a big man in this town for years. Booked the fights at the Garden. Somehow, he took a liking to Aaron, hired him as an office boy when Aaron was just a kid. Showed him the ropes. Once, Aaron got beat up by a hood because he wouldn't tell him Sam was hiding in the john. After that, they were like father and son. But those were the old days when matchmakers like Sam made matches, not deals. You know, this guy fights that guy on Friday night. Never mind the network subsidies, the replay rights, the closed-circuit TV cut, the satellite charges—they didn't exist. So Sam got pushed out of the fight game unceremoniously a dozen years ago, and Aaron wants back in."

Intrigued by a Utrillo on the back wall, Adam was about to inspect it when a buzzer sounded and the receptionist said, "Gentlemen, Mr. Robards will see you now."

Harry Patashnick and Al Lakeman preceded Adam through the door and were greeted effusively with handshakes and hugs. Then, Adam was introduced to Robards: a medium-tall, silver-haired man with wily eyes and a disarming smile.

"Nice to meet you, Doctor," he said. "I've been hearing amazing things about you, the most amazing being that you're the same age I am."

"Thanks," said Adam laconically.

Robards reached around Adam to shake Mel's hand. "Hi, scribe," he said. "Liked what you wrote about me last month."

"You did?" Mel looked askance. "Sure you read it all? I was expecting a libel suit."

Robards grinned. "Why? If you'd written what an honest, high-minded operator I was, I'd be out of business. . . . Take the average, talented, but not super-talented, hockey or baseball player I represent. They know they're not worth half a million bucks a year when the president of the United States only makes two hundred thousand and a Harvard professor thirty. They don't want anybody high-minded representing them; they want somebody ruthless—at least as ruthless as the guy representing the owner. So when a popular sports columnist calls me a *gonif*, I thank him."

"You're welcome," Mel said.

"But I'm not going to pull any of my usual schtick with Harry and Al. They're almost family."

"I'll drink to that," Harry said.

"Good." Robards pressed a button behind his desk and a panel of the bookcase slid open to reveal a well-stocked bar.

"Impressive office," Adam said.

"You think so?" Robards looked pleased.

"I was particularly impressed by the art collection."

"Don't be." Robards poured and passed Harry a tumbler of Ambassador Scotch. "They're fakes. All except the Utrillo. I bought that before I discovered my clientele couldn't tell a Rubens from a *Playboy* centerfold. Anybody else want a drink?"

When no one did, Robards said to Adam: "Doctor, since there's a chance we'll be working together, let me show you how outrageous a con man I can be."

Robards leaned back in his chair and pushed a concealed button. The telephone buzzed instantly and his secretary said through the amplified speaker, "Mr. Roone Arledge on the line. Should I put him through?"

"Please do, Miss Rich," Robards replied.

"Aaron!" boomed a hearty voice that Mel Waldman recognized as that of Roone Arledge, president of ABC News and Sports.

"How are you, Roone?"

"Fine, fine. Listen, I just got out of our board meeting and I wanted to give you the good news. The deal you proposed for 'Wide World of Sports' is all set. . . ."

The conversation between the two went on for the next five minutes before ending with the usual pleasantries. Hanging up the phone, Robards turned to Mel Waldman and said, "Mel, you're the expert. Recap what Roone promised."

"A lot of up-front money and below-the-line cost splits, and twelve weeks of guaranteed air time. But I'll be damned if I know what for."

"For nothing. It's a tape I spliced together to impress the rubes."

"Does Arledge know about it?"

Robard's grin widened. "I played it for him last time he was here and he laughed himself sick. He'd deny it, of course, but it wouldn't do him any good." He winked conspiratorially. "I got another tape of his reaction while listening to it. You going to write about it?"

Mel hesitated, causing Harry to look sternly at him. "Sure," he finally said. "In my next novel."

Robards turned to Adam and sighed, "Okay. Let's get to the business at hand. Al's filled me in on what you want and what you can do. I even checked with Tommy Harms, who thinks you're some kind of will-o'-the-wisp who can dematerialize at will. But that's beside the point. Mind giving me a little demonstration?"

Adam looked surprised. "Boxing, in here?"

"No, no, I just want to see how quick you are. Stand up, please, and extend your hands, palms out."

Robards stood, too, and dug some change out of his pocket. "Now, I'm going to put a quarter in each palm and hold my hands about a foot above yours. The trick is to see if I can grab those coins before you can close your fingers around them."

"Doesn't sound too hard to me," said Mel, the perpetual skeptic.

"Then let me try it on you first," Robards replied.

Mel took the quarters and extended his palms. Robards stared at him with almost hypnotic intensity for several moments and pounced. The next instant, the quarters were in his hands. He did it three times before Mel gave up.

"Now, your turn, Doctor," said Robards, a gleam of anticipation in his eyes. Adam extended his hands, quarters in place, and waited. Robards smiled, pounced, and came up empty-handed.

"Very good," he complimented. "First time I've failed in years."

"Anything else?" Adam asked.

"No. . . . Well, would you mind the handkerchief trick, Al? Open-handed, of course, so nobody gets hurt."

"No," answered Lakeman, "provided you don't injure the hand that's going to sign our fifty-thousand-dollar check. . . . Aaron's going to place two handkerchiefs on the rug," Al explained to Adam. "You stand on one, he on the other."

"Then what?"

"He'll try to hit you."

Reluctantly, Adam agreed. "How about a little side-bet?" he proposed.

"Like what?" asked Robards.

"Like the Utrillo."

"Against what?"

"The purse for my first fight."

"I'll do better—you win the first fight and I'll give you the Utrillo."

Both men removed their jackets and Al measured the distance between the handkerchiefs with Robard's desk ruler. Then the two took their positions and Robards began swinging. To his chagrin, Adam did not even use his hands to block him, simply ducked and twisted away. Growing arm-weary after a dozen futile swipes, Robards conceded defeat. "Amazing!" he said breathlessly and sat down at his desk. From the middle drawer, he took a cashier's check and handed it to Al.

"See?" Robards said, "I trusted you."

"Good thing you didn't play that Roone Arledge tape for me earlier," Al remarked. "If I'd have known you two were so chummy, I might've asked double."

"Don't worry, Al, we'll all make money. Better yet, we'll own the Garden again and Arum and King can go choke on their chitlins."

"Halevai," Harry intoned.

"Who've you decided to use for the videotape?" Robards asked Al.

"Jakes is in the best shape."

"That the only reason?"

Al smiled. "Well, Joe Justin's in Philly, Norton's in Dallas, and Jakes is in Las Vegas, shooting a movie. That answer your question?"

Before Robards could reply, his desk panel buzzed.

"Mr. Larry O'Brien calling, Mr. Robards," said his secretary.

"Oh, balls!" Mel Waldman gibed, "O'Brien is too square. Tell her to play the Pete Rozelle tape."

"What happened to your jaw?" Al asked as he and Adam rode down in the elevator.

"I banged it."

"On what?"

"A bedpost," Adam lied.

"A bedpost, no less! Must've been an interesting evening."

"It was," said Adam, wondering if Al had a puritanical streak.

"Well, try to be a little less frisky in your leisure pursuits from now on, will you?"

"Sure, Al. You contact Dan Lassiter yet?"

"Tried. He's out of town for a week. You're still willing to talk to him, aren't you?"

Despite Adam's nod, Al looked concerned.

"It has to be that way, you understand. I don't deposit Robards's check until Lassiter clears you."

10

Three days before Adam and his entourage were to leave for Vegas, he finally heard from Dan Lassiter.

Lassiter's call reached him at the Front Street Gym, where he lay flat on his back while Todd Tanner pounded him in the stomach with a medicine ball.

"Hey, Doc!" Al Lakeman shouted from his office. "Phone call."

Adam gestured for Todd to help him up. Rubbing his aching belly muscles, he went to the office, crossing paths with Al in the doorway. "Who is it?" he asked.

"Dan Lassiter."

At his anxious look Adam smiled. Lakeman didn't want anything to burst his fantasy bubble either.

Adam picked up the phone. "McKinnon here."

"Dan Lassiter. Al Lakeman wants us to get together for some strange reason. At least, he's being mysterious as hell about it. But Al and I have been friends for a long time, and if you don't object, neither do I."

"I don't object at all. . . . You're a handball player, I hear."

"An aging one, but I can still go a game or two. What've you got in mind?"

"A match, and dinner afterwards."

"Sounds good. When and where?"

"The Huntington Avenue Y at seven P.M. I'll reserve the court."

"Hold on, while I check my calendar. . . . Okay, you're on."

"Are you still a class-A player?"

"Yeah—barely. How about you?"

"I'm in a class by myself." Adam smiled as the boast rendered Lassiter speechless. "See you at seven," he added and hung up.

"Hey, Lakeman!" he shouted in the raucous way Al usually called people to the phone.

"Yeah?" Al said, returning to the office.

"Expect a call from your friend Lassiter any minute now."

"Oh, yeah? Why?"

" 'Cause I challenged him to a handball match tonight."

"So? Why should he call me about that?"

"It's the way I challenged him. He's going to want to know a lot more about me than you've told him."

"I haven't told him hardly anything."

"Good. Keep it that way."

"You gonna hustle him or something?"

"Al!" Adam feigned hurt innocence. "I'm surprised at you. Now that I have you and Robards for front men, my hustling days are over."

"Got something funny in mind, though, don't you?"

Adam shrugged. "A little surprise, then after the little surprise, a bigger one. Just do as I ask—okay? You'll hear about it."

Al opened his mouth as if to protest, threw up his hands in surrender, and walked away.

The medical directory Adam consulted couldn't tell him what his potential nemesis looked like, but he learned that promptly at seven on the handball court. Lassiter was a tall, very trim man, with the slightly flattened nose of an ex-pugilist and gray-flecked hair. He looked younger than his forty-eight years except for the crows' feet and open-pored crescents of skin around his eyes. They were, Adam speculated, the eyes of a man who had accumulated experience, good and bad, far beyond his years.

"Al Lakeman is afraid I'm going to hustle you," Adam said, after shaking hands.

"Are you?"

"The ungentlemanly thought never entered my mind."

"Then let's play for the dinner tab."

"No," Adam said firmly, "dinner's on me."

"Drinks, then?"

"You're going to need more than a few."

"Just exactly what do you intend to do to me?"

"Three things: give you the worst drubbing you've ever had on a handball court; ask you to be my personal physician; and tell you one of the wildest stories you've every heard."

Lassiter's eyebrows lifted. "Sounds like a lot for one evening."

"Perhaps. But the handball part won't take long."

It didn't. Adam showed Dan nothing during their warm-up play, and lost the wall toss to see who served first. Dan sent a Z-shaped serve bouncing off the front wall, the right forewall, and diagonally across the court, expecting Adam to let it rebound off the left rear wall and return it after it had bounced in mid-court. It was the customary way to play such serves. But Adam surprised him. He let the ball hit the left wall, rebound sideways about a foot, and slammed it into the left forecorner on the fly: a perfectly executed kill shot. Dan did not see this. It was too dangerous to watch an opponent return a serve; the ball might accidentally hit him in the eye. He merely heard McKinnon's glove smack the ball sooner than he had expected, and a split-second later, saw it roll dead in the corner.

"What happened?" he said in wide-eyed wonder.

"You lost the serve."

"I know, but how?"

Adam explained.

"If you say so," Dan frowned, thinking nobody had that kind of coordination.

Adam served Dan a similar Z-shot, which he played in the standard way, waiting for the ball to bounce in front of him and then lofting a ceiling shot. To his satisfaction, the shot hit the ceiling close to where it joined the front wall and came down at a steep angle—giving his opponent three options, none easy. He could hit it immediately after its first bounce at mid-court, stretch high and reach it before the ball hit the back wall, or try to play it off the wall before it plunged to its second bounce on the floor. Disregarding the danger, Dan watched McKinnon struggle with the difficult return. What he saw made him blink in astonishment and virtually concede defeat. McKinnon chose none of the options. He let the ball drop to waist-level and, before its first bounce, drove it diagonally into the right forecorner.

Picking up the ball, Dan tossed it to Adam with the comment, "You're right. You *are* in a class by yourself. Do you have any weaknesses at all?"

"A mediocre serve. A strictly defensive left hand."

"That's it?" Dan said dispiritedly. "In that case, let's make the game eleven."

Adam eased up a bit, winning the shortened game 11–6.

Afterwards Dan sighed, "Okay. You've achieved your first goal: you beat my ass in handball. Let's go shower, only give me a head start. You're probably quicker than I am at that, too."

Adam smiled and put his hand lightly on Dan's shoulder. "The third goal's the toughest. Please try not to get too pissed off at me until we get to that."

They drove in separate cars to a waterfront seafood restaurant and asked for a quiet table.

"This way, Doctors," the headwaiter said, and led them to an alcove, taking their drink orders enroute.

"You any good at small talk?" asked Dan, thirstily waiting for his rye and ginger ale.

"Terrible," Adam said, "as my ex-lady friend kept reminding me."

"Me, too, as my wife keeps reminding me."

Their drinks came. Dan took his gratefully, swallowed, and said, "How long have you been at the New England Medical Center Hospital?"

"Around three years now."

"And before that, Yale—right?"

"Right," said Adam, surprised.

"Look, I admit I got damned curious about you after our phone conversation and called Al Lakeman back. But he'd left. So I looked you up in the *Directory of Medical Specialists*."

Adam laughed.

"What's so funny?"

"I did the same with you."

"Well, nothing like researching a subject. . . . Why'd you leave Yale?"

"After seventeen years, I was beginning to get smothered in ivy. Tufts needed a clinical neurologist to replace Sullivan when he retired, and I wanted to be closer to M.I.T."

"Why M.I.T.?"

"My research is in the field of senile dementia, and some of their neurochemists are doing interesting work there."

"So I understand. I heard Whitten lecture on his choline therapy recently. Sounds promising."

When Adam didn't answer, Dan asked, "Well? Isn't it?"

"I suppose. It's certainly helped the health food stores sell a lot of lecithin."

"Meaning—"

"Meaning that, after three years of clinical trials with the stuff, I've just about given up on it. It's worthless for advanced dementia. It may help presenile Alzheimer patients if given *early* enough, but how do you decide that? You can't do brain biopsies on every patient who complains of forgetfulness. And you can't diagnose Alzheimer's without the biopsy."

Dan sipped his drink. "So what's to be done for the millions of Americans with memory impairment?"

"I've been working along two lines. First, to try to develop a blood test that will pick up Alzheimer's in its earliest, potentially reversible, stage. That presupposes a lot, however: that its cause is either autoimmune, or due to some intracellular chemical deficiency—and there's not a bit of hard evidence it's either. The other approach is a little further out. Maybe the fundamental problem is not diffuse damage to the millions of memory cells, but to a memory-control center, a sort of central clearing house. And if that's so it might well be correctable."

"By what?"

"By a more powerful derivative or analog of acetylcholine. Look how long it took George Cotzias before he perfected L-Dopa therapy for Parkinsonism. Small doses did nothing, the R-form didn't work, and the racemic mixture proved toxic to the bone marrow."

"Good point," said Dan. "Are you on to anything like that?"

"Maybe more. I might just have found it."

The waiter brought menus. Dan set his aside and, with a nod from Adam, ordered another round of drinks. "That would be one hell of an accomplishment," he said. "Are you willing to talk about it?"

"I'd rather not. But Al Lakeman, who swears I can trust you, insists on it."

"Al Lakeman!" Dan exclaimed. "Jesus, I forgot about him. What's Lakeman got to do with this? He's not your patient, is he?"

"No, he's my trainer and manager. You see, I'm giving up medicine temporarily to take a crack at professional boxing."

Dan started. "You're doing *what!* Are you out of your mind? You'll get killed, or at least crippled, at your age."

"That's possible," Adam admitted, "but unlikely, since I don't plan on getting hit. Sounds preposterous, I know; that's why I wanted to play handball with you before we had this talk. Would you laugh in my face if I told you I'm probably the best handball player in the world right now?"

Their drinks arrived. Dan took his time with his before answering Adam. "No," he said slowly, "I certainly wouldn't laugh, not after the drubbing you gave me. But that doesn't make you the best in the world. After all, I'm forty-eight and, even in my prime, I was never any Paul Haber or Jim Jacobs. What's your point?"

Gesturing patience, Adam said, "In a minute. Al tells me you're an ex-boxer. You still follow the fights?"

"Locally, I do."

"Then you've probably seen Todd Tanner and Tommy Harms in action."

"You bet. Too bad about Harms, but Tanner's a real comer."

"Dan, this'll be hard to believe, but I sparred with both of them in the last week. Neither one could land a single solid punch. Ask Lakeman. He'll confirm it."

Dan looked incredulous. "How's that possible?"

"You saw how quick I am on a handball court? I'm even quicker in the ring. I slipped or ducked or blocked every punch they threw."

"Jesus!" Dan rasped. "That's almost—" he hesitated— "super-human!"

The waiter approached to take their dinner order, but Dan sent him for more drinks. Adam's remarks had him so baffled he barely felt the alcohol he had imbibed. "Now, look!" he said when the waiter was gone, "I'm tired of marveling at your stunts like some kid at his first circus. So let's review what you've said: first, you're a neurologist doing research on senile dementia. Second, you've isolated a choline derivative that can penetrate some theoretical CNS memory-control center. Third, at the ripe age of forty-five, you're the world's best handball player and possibly the world's best boxer. And since you say you don't like to make small talk, I assume there must be some connection between all this and me. Right?"

"Right."

"Then suppose you tell me what it is."

Adam started to speak, faltered, and fidgeted.

Watching him, Dan couldn't help feeling a measure of satisfaction. McKinnon had kept him off-balance, physically and mentally, all evening. Now, it was his turn. "I'm waiting," he said.

"Dan, I don't really want to tell you this—not because I'm afraid you'll steal it, put your neurology staff to work on it, and publish first. You couldn't, even if you were a cutthroat grant-grabber—which you're certainly not. I'm doing it only because Al Lakeman insists. He's no fool. Much as he'd like to end his career in a blaze of glory, he knows no man my age can become a superathlete without some gimmick; some drastic chemical alteration in his neuromuscular system. And he's right. I told him I was taking a special nutrient supplement that speeds up my reflexes, but he wants you to confirm it, to assure him I'm not on some kind of stimulant drug that will get him in trouble with the Boxing Commission. Follow me so far?"

Dan nodded. "Well, are you?"

"Am I what?"

"Taking a drug?"

"I'm afraid it's too complicated to answer straight out like that. In fact, before I elaborate, I'd like to make a rather unusual request. I want you to tell me something personal about yourself, so personal you wouldn't want anyone else in the medical community knowing it."

"You want *what?*" demanded Dan. "You can't be serious?"

"Dead serious."

"Good God!" The corners of Dan's mouth twitched as he wavered between scowling and laughing. "I hate to sound coy, but I hardly know you."

"True. But you are about to learn something of immense importance about me—my deepest secret. If I want Lakeman for my manager, I've got to tell you. He's given me no choice."

"But I *do* have a choice," Dan countered. "And what you're asking is so presumptuous as to be absurd. It doesn't even make sense."

Adam gestured placatingly. "Then let me try to justify it. . . . Ever do any death counseling?"

"No," said Dan. "Too hung-up on death myself, I guess."

"Well, I have. Bob Lifton talked me into it at Yale. It was damned tough. Just getting the patient to talk to me—a total stranger—was hard enough. Then you had to get him to reveal his most intimate thoughts and fears. I finally managed to break through this resistance by confiding personal things about my own life, even my sex life, that I wouldn't want anyone else to know. You could call it mutual blackmail; we had the goods on each other. The approach worked; it worked so well I had to give it up. The shared confessions made the patient my most intimate friend of the moment and, when he died, I lost that friend. After several such experiences, I couldn't take it any longer."

"I couldn't either," said Dan sympathetically. "So that's what you're after—mutual blackmail?"

"If you're willing."

"I don't see what I stand to gain, but—oh, hell, let me think about it while we order dinner."

"All right," Dan began after the waiter had taken their orders and left, "I'll play along, if only to find out how you play handball so well. When I was a med school freshman, I did a very bizarre thing. I was assigned a young cadaver to dissect and, for some strange reason, probably because I personalize and hate death so much for robbing me of my whole family—mother, father, older brother—by the time I was sixteen, I became obsessed as to who the guy had been in life. I found out, too: a boxer named Rick Ferrar, and Al Lakeman was his manager—which is how Al and I met. I also found out that Ferrar had been murdered."

"Murdered! How?"

"A blow on the head. We discovered an egg-sized hematoma on top of his brain when we sawed off his skull. Anyway, with the help of a black friend of Ferrar's named Lem Harper, I found out that two local hoods had been hired to make the hit. Never mind why. One hood was killed in an automobile accident that I caused, since he was trying to kill me at the time. The other, Lem Harper took care of. Two people in the world know that story—Al Lakeman is one of them."

Adam stared for a moment. "Thanks . . . for trusting me."

Dan shrugged. "Your turn."

"Okay. I moved from Yale to Tufts with two of my three original co-workers, hired a biochemist, set up my lab, and spent the next eighteen months feeding choline to dozens of patients and getting nowhere. Then, by sheer luck, I attended Jean Mayer's annual faculty party and got cornered by a professor emeritus of biochemistry who happened to be an amateur ornithologist. He was a charming old coot, afraid of getting senile and interested in whatever I had to say about it. Then, out of the blue, he mentioned something absolutely mind-boggling. 'You know,' he said, 'if I were studying choline metabolism, I'd study it in birds.' 'Why birds?' I asked. 'They fly, you know?' he said—a gratuitous remark if ever I heard one. But then he made his point. Not only did he know bird morphology, but damned near everything about their metabolism. Like the fact that they lack thyroxine-binding proteins; the thyroid hormone they secrete goes directly to their tissues without any carrier-protein hanging it up in the bloodstream. 'No time,' he explained, 'not when they're in flight.' He speculated that they must've evolved some bio-chemical mechanism to speed up their nerve transmission, too, and suggested I might look into it."

"Which you did?"

"We nearly got pecked to death collecting specimens, but my team did analysis after analysis of micro-nerve punctures until a pattern of sorts began to emerge. At rest, ninety percent of the neurotransmitter substances at their synapses is acetyl-choline and ten percent is something else. Immediately after flight, however, the amount of that something else doubles, and during flight, I suspect, supplants acetylcholine completely."

"And that something else is?"

"A chameleonlike choline derivative that can add and shed a few carbon atoms like mad: L-butyrylcholine. Took us eight months to synthesize enough of it to try on animals."

"What happened?" asked Dan between mouthfuls of food.

Adam described his discouraging result with monkeys and how he went on to fateful self-experimentation.

Dan nearly dropped his fork. "You must've been crazy!"

"No," Adam replied calmly. "Merely suicidal. Scientif-ically suicidal, actually. It's not unheard of. Werner Forssmann won the Nobel Prize for having the guts to thread a catheter into his heart. He was lucky to survive. I lucked out, too. I am now the only man in existence with bird-in-flight neurotransmission."

Dan shook his head in wonder. "Has it affected you mentally?"

"I seem to require less sleep, which may just be due to my general state of euphoria. Either it doesn't penetrate the brain, or else a brain enzyme rapidly converts it back to acetylcholine."

"Even so, I think what you did was insane, and damned dangerous."

"I agree—especially since I have no idea what the long-term effects will be. That's why I need you to be my doctor. The monkeys have partially recovered, but I don't plan to re-treat them."

"Why not?"

"I'm saving the stuff for myself. According to my nerve conduction velocity, I need a supplement dose every three to four days."

"Oh, great!" Dan groaned. "What happens if you can't get off the stuff?"

"I can always make more. It's not that hard to synthesize. Look, Dan, you may think I'm ready for the funny farm, but actually I'm a damned good neurologist. I've thought a lot about all the complications I might develop and am willing to risk them. Anyway, it's all in a good cause—considering the potential benefit of LBC to others. For example, I've got a young patient in the hospital with the worst case of myasthenia gravis I've ever seen. Everything—anticholinesterases, steroids, thymectomy, even plasmapheresis—has failed. All that keeps him alive is an iron lung—one of the last of those relics in the city. He also happens to be the half-brother of a friend of mine."

"And you believe L-butyrylcholine might help him?"

"It might, but I don't dare try it until I learn what it does to me over a period of time. There's a whole host of neurological diseases, from depression to Huntington's Chorea, that involve neurotransmission, and might benefit from it, too."

Picking at his salad, Dan mulled over Adam's rationalizations. "It's possible, I suppose, that you've hit on the greatest neurological discovery since L-Dopa. But that remains to be proven. In the meanwhile, you expect *me* to keep tabs on you? Do you want to sign your post-mortem permit now?"

"Sure," said Adam agreeably. "Anything for science."

"What made you suicidal, anyway?"

"A woman."

"You *are* crazy!" Dan said in disgust.

At the end of dinner, Adam asked, "What are you going to tell Al Lakeman?"

"To padlock his gym and keep the hell away from you!"

"Seriously."

"Seriously, I'm not sure. If what you told me is true, LBC is not a simulant, since it doesn't affect the brain. And being a neurotransmitter, at least in birds, it's not exactly a drug, either. Frankly, I don't know what the hell it is."

"Would you call lecithin a nutrient?"

"Yeah, a worthless one."

"Tryptophan?"

Dan hesitated. "I don't know. The F.D.A. is having a hell of a time with that one."

"Choline?"

"I suppose."

"Then why not L-butyrylcholine?"

Dan sighed. "I honestly don't know."

"Look, if you're worried about Al Lakeman getting in trouble with the Boxing Commission, don't be; I've covered my tracks pretty well. Two of my three co-workers are going to spend six months in Edinburgh studying with Christie. The third is a grad student working on an immunoassay for Alzheimer-damaged brain cells and doesn't know LBC's composition. No toxicology lab in the country could detect the stuff in my body fluids. It took me weeks to notice its faint spot on the chromatograph paper, and I was on the alert. You and I are the only people who really know what I'm taking."

"It's bound to come out sooner or later, though. The press will see to that."

"I'll beat them to it. I'm giving myself a year and then publishing a medical paper on the stuff. You can be co-author."

"Suppose you don't last a year?"

"You can still be co-author, only your name can go first."

Sighing deeply, Dan stood up. "Be at my office at nine sharp in the morning for your first check-up. . . . Oh, and thank you—for dinner, and for my first trip to 'The Twilight Zone.'"

11

Among the dwindling population of professional boxers, Al Lakeman was owed as many favors as a philanthropic politician. Joey Jakes never forgot that, shortly after he'd turned professional, Al picked him to substitute for an injured boxer in a main event at Boston Garden. Fourteen bouts later, Jakes was matched against Larry Holmes for the W.B.A. version of the heavyweight championship of the world. He was even ahead of Holmes on points when an accidental head butt cut a deep gash over his left eye and the fight had to be stopped. So Joey never became the heavyweight champ and his boyishly handsome face was permanently disfigured by a jagged scar that ran from his left eyebrow to the corner of his eye. To his amazement, the scar made his fortune.

With his Adonislike body and a modicum of acting talent, Jakes became a movie actor, specializing in bad-assed villains. When the phone call came from Al Lakeman, he was making a Western with James Garner in the Nevada desert outside of Las Vegas. Jakes was pleasantly surprised to hear from the famous fight manager. But even after a second run-through, Lakeman's proposal made no sense to him.

"Hey, Al, let me get this straight. You want me to spar three rounds in a television studio with a new heavyweight you're developing? A forty-five-year-old heavyweight! And for that you're willing to pay me twenty-five G's?"

"Not spar—fight. Go all out."

"I'm in great shape, Al. I could hurt him."

"You could, but he's quick as hell and hard to hit. Todd Tanner can't hit him."

"Todd can't? Jesus, if he's that good, what's to stop him from clobbering me? I'm in the middle of shooting a movie, you know? The producer wouldn't like it too much if I got my face punched in. What size gloves we gonna use?"

"Regulation."

"I don't know, Al."

"Look, Joey, my guy won't hit you hard enough to break a capillary. I promise you that. You don't have to tell your producer a damn thing."

"So what's the point of the bout?"

"Call it a preview of coming attractions. And the attraction we're after is Coleman Jackson. Bucky Miller isn't going to be interested in matching Coleman with some unknown. So, I got to show him what my man can do. Get the picture now?"

"Yeah, sort of. . . . You know, Al, if anyody but you was pitching this, I'd laugh in his face. Sounds more like a script for another dumb boxing movie than a real-life promotion angle. But since it's you, okay, set it up. Besides, I'd really like to see you again. I'm tired of having nobody to talk to but Indians and fag actors all day."

The chartered Lear jet left Logan Airport in midafternoon with Adam, Aaron Robards, Al Lakeman, Todd Tanner, Mel Waldman, and Ronald Warner, president of the Boston Garden Corporation, aboard. Harry Patashnick had been stricken by a flare-up of his chronic bronchitis and confined by his doctor to bed.

The jet had a well-stocked bar and liquor and conversation flowed freely among the passengers. After sipping a bourbon and soda with the others, Adam took the front-row seat beside Todd Tanner.

Watching them, Al Lakeman realized what close friends the two were becoming. It would have surprised him, if anything the eccentric McKinnon did could still surprise him. What preoccupied Al even more was the vast improvement Tanner had shown recently. He'd even begun to score on his agile sparring partner, maybe one punch in ten and mainly body blows—not because McKinnon was slowing down but because Todd was releasing his punches faster.

Turning in his seat to gaze out at billowy clouds, Al was suddenly struck by an intriguing thought. He was not a greedy man nor an opportunist, but as an expert in the psychology of boxers he saw a way he could manage not the world's best heavyweight, but the two best. The more he pondered the possibility, the more feasible it became. An occasional chess player, Al visualized a board with boxers and promoters for the pieces. If the bout with Joey Jakes went well tomorrow, he would be just two moves from checkmate; the king being Len Savitt, world heavyweight champion, and the key gambit being to rap Coleman Jackson, the leading contender.

Robards had engaged rooms at a plush motel a few miles from the Strip, and arranged for the taping at an NBC-affiliate TV station. Upon landing, he went there directly to supervise construction of a boxing ring and to instruct the production crew, Al Lakeman met with Joey Jakes at the motel to brief him, while Adam and Todd took a long run in the desert followed by a swim in the pool, a light supper, and bed.

At the opening round bell, the two fighters closed. Jakes, a thick-necked heavily muscled boxer, had been instructed by Lakeman to pull no punches, especially since the chairman of the Nevada Boxing Commission was a spectator, and did exactly as told. Moving forward and gliding sideways, he flicked a long left jab at Adam's face. Adam pulled back and picked off the follow-up right cross with his glove as easily as if Jake's best punch were a baseball. Tanner, standing at ringside, grinned. Al Lakeman, behind Adam's corner, did not; he had seen Jakes fight too many times before and knew what he could do. Known in the trade as a "swarmer," willing to take punches in order to land them, he maneuvered Adam out of the center of the ring and charged him, swinging. Adam slipped his lead punch, stepped nimbly aside, and let Jakes stumble into the ropes.

So it went for two rounds—Jakes swarmed, Adam evaded. Al Lakeman was pleased, but vaguely bothered. Finally, he figured out why. Before the third and final round, as Adam sat mildly breathless on his stool while Todd Tanner sponged his face, Lakeman leaned close to his ear and said, "Let him hit you."

"What!" protested Todd Tanner, as surprised as Adam. "Why you want him to do that?"

Al gave Tanner a sharp, silencing glance. "You got that, Adam? I'll signal when there's ten seconds left in the round, then let him hit you."

"What for?" Tanner persisted.

Al turned to him with scorn. "Will you butt out?"

"I don't get it. Why get hit when you don't have to? Adam could get hurt."

"He's going to get hit because he *does* have to. Otherwise, I'll never be able to line up a 'name' fighter for him. Jakes is so arm-weary now, he won't hurt him." Again, Al leaned toward Adam. "You get the picture?"

"I'm beginning to," Adam admitted.

"As for you," Al told Tanner, "I'll explain later."

Tanner recoiled slightly at the anger in his manager's eyes, then took a last swipe at Adam's face with the sponge. "Watch out for the jaw," he cautioned.

Adam nodded.

"Last round," Al shouted at Jakes. "Give it your best shot."

Jakes smiled around his mouthpiece and gave Al the thumbs-up sign with a gloved hand.

Bemused by Lakeman's instruction, Adam backpedaled and circled Jakes at arm's length for the first forty seconds of the round. Although being hit by a man as strong as Jakes was a dismaying prospect, he could understand Al's reasoning. The videotape was primarily a lure for big-time fight promoters, but it would also be viewed by potential opponents, and if a talented boxer like Joey Jakes couldn't lay a glove on him, what chance had they? So Al was right, Adam conceded, and only wished there was some way his manager could take twenty percent of the punch.

When he estimated that two minutes had passed in the round, Adam began to move in; to punch instead of merely counterpunch and get Jakes riled. He feinted with his left, then right, and with his opponent's guard spread, snapped two stinging jabs off his nose. Jakes winced, and moved back, expecting Adam to disengage. Instead, he bore in, landing a hard left to the kidney and an uppercut to the midsection. Jakes grunted and clinched. Adam pushed him away and waited for the defensive jab that Jakes was sure to throw to fend him off. He stepped inside it, seeing his opponent's right hook descending almost as if in slow motion. It hit his cheekbone with concussive impact. He reeled back, and Jakes was immediately upon him, pummeling with short hooks and crosses; then, as Adam doubled over, turtlelike, to protect his head, shifting his attack to the body.

Al Lakeman leaned over the ropes in alarm; Adam hadn't waited for his signal and there were still fifteen seconds left in the round. Still doubled over, Adam swung sharply to the left, hoping Jakes would aim his punches in that direction, and then to the right before straightening. Redirecting the left hook he had launched downwards, Jakes turned it into an uppercut which Adam, head still spinning, barely evaded. The momentum carried Jakes forward, and Adam immediately clinched. He took two stiff punches to the ribs, but held on until, to his relief, the bell rang.

With an accusing glare, Tanner snapped at Lakeman, "You satisfied?"

"Very," said Al and climbed through the ropes to help Adam to his corner. "You okay?" he asked.

"Fine," Adam said through clenched teeth. "But no retakes."

The next instant, Jakes threw his arms around Adam in a sweaty embrace. "You're all right, man! Best damn boxer I ever faced." He turned to Al. "You get what you wanted?"

"You did fine, Joey."

"Yeah!" Jakes said, his pride restored. "Another thirty seconds in the round, I would've had him."

Todd Tanner was about to retort when Al shushed him. "Uh, Joey," he said. "I wonder if you'd mind doing me another little favor?"

"What's that, Al?" asked Jakes, feeling expansive.

"Go a round with Todd."

Jakes looked as surprised as Tanner.

"I don't know. . . . I might be fighting him for real someday."

"An easy round—head gear, sixteen-ounce gloves, you know. Nothing that'll even work up a sweat."

"Well, okay," Jakes agreed reluctantly, "only how come?"

"Todd's got a flaw he's been working on and I want to see if he's corrected it."

Jakes nodded and turned to Tanner. "Hey, brother, see this pretty face? Don't you bruise it, hear? Not for free."

"Don't worry," Todd said. "As a *movie actor*, I'm one of your biggest fans."

"What flaw?" he asked Lakeman after Jakes had gone back to his corner.

"Your motor mouth."

"Aw, come on, Al, be serious. I'm entitled to a little respect, too."

"And you're getting it. More than you realize," Al said enigmatically. "Now, go change."

Watching Todd spar with Jakes confirmed Al's hunch. He was indeed two moves from checkmate—from a virtual monopoly on the boxing world's heavyweight division.

12

Ribs stinging, cheekbone throbbing like a gigantic toothache, Adam lay in the sun by the pool while Al Lakeman, Aaron Robards, and Ronald Warner were holed up in Robards's suite plotting his future.

"You hurtin'?" asked Todd Tanner on joining him.

"You could say that," Adam said dryly. "Jakes hits hard, but not as hard as you. I still can't chew on that side of my mouth."

"You took his punch pretty good, though."

Adam grimaced. "Maybe I should've gone down, made Lakeman's little scenario more convincing. Hey! You looked damned sharp against Jakes, too—beating him to the punch like that."

Tanner grinned. "Thanks to you. Pleasure fighting someone I could hit for a change. Tell the truth, Doc, I wouldn't mind fighting him for real."

"Don't tell me, tell Lakeman."

"I already did."

"What'd he say?"

"Somethin' didn't make a whole lot of sense: that he had to get you in position on the board before he could make his move with me. I asked him—what board? And he says, a chess board. You play chess, Doc?"

"Used to. As a kid, I played a lot with my father."

"Know what he meant?"

Adam reflected. "Sounds like a combination move to me." At Tanner's frown, he added, "Cheer up. It means Lakeman's got big plans for you. Bigger than you think."

Todd sighed hopefully and looked up to watch a shapely female dive off the high board. "Nice," he said.

"What—the dive or the diver?"

Tanner shrugged. "Been meanin' to ask you," he began hesitantly, "who's Diana Acheson?"

Adam sat up and stared at him. "How'd you know about her?"

"Her name's on your doorbell."

"Ah, yes, so it is. God knows why I leave it there. I sure don't want her back."

Not wanting to pry further, Todd said nothing.

Adam appreciated his tact. Yet, surprisingly, he wanted to talk about Diana. "She's a doctor," he said. "I met her around a year ago and, after a few dates, she moved in with me."

"You're a fast worker, Doc."

It had been fast work, Adam mused. Dinner the first night to discuss Diana's half-brother, Jon, the severe and intractable case of myasthenia gravis that he had mentioned to Dan Lassiter. Dinner the second night to discuss Diana's deteriorating marriage and Adam's reasons for staying single all these years. No plans for dinner the third night until a snowstorm canceled her return flight to San Diego. Without confessing it until they were in bed together, each had cheered on the snow, caring not a bit when it closed Logan Airport for three days. By the time the planes were flying again, it was agreed that Diana would divorce her husband, a step she had been contemplating anyway, give up her HMO-based general practice in San Diego, and move to Boston. Adam, in turn, would give up his bachelor apartment on Canterbury Street, find them a place on Beacon Hill, and father the child Diana longed for but her husband, a dermatologist and avid outdoorsman, had opposed.

"Sometimes, slow is better," Adam finally said. "You get less loving in the short run, but it stands a better chance of lasting."

"Glad to hear that, Doc. Sex is supposed to be bad for a boxer—though I never knew why."

"Al Lakeman tell you that?"

"Al!" Tanner almost gasped. "Lord, no! But I heard it from other fighters who heard it from their managers."

"Well, Todd, I don't want to promote any loose habits, but as a doctor I can tell you that's a crock. Sex burns about eighty calories of body energy and a few M&M candies replenish them. The only reason I can think of why managers ban sex before a fight is 'cause they can't collect their twenty percent cut."

Todd chuckled. "Ain't that the truth! Remind me to buy some M&Ms."

Adam topped off his sunbathing with a swim, dressed, swallowed a few more painkillers, and went to Robards's suite. Lakeman was still there, but Waldman and Warner had gone.

"You gamble, Doc?" Robards asked him.

"Every day."

"Really? Where?"

"At the hospital. With patients' lives."

Nodding, Robards said, "Then I suppose roulette wheels and crap tables would seem pretty tame stuff. . . . Joey Jakes called. They finished shooting their film today, and are having a cast party at The Aladdin. Jim Garner will be there, and if meeting him doesn't interest you, there'll be the usual bevy of starlets. Joey practically begged me to bring you. So what do you say?"

Adam turned to Lakeman, slouched on the couch puffing a cigar. "You going, Al?"

"What for? I already met Garner. And ogling a bunch of busty starlets will just remind me of the miseries of old age." Al eyed him slyly. "Now, if you were to slip me some of your so-called nutrient . . . ? Naw, you go ahead. Just make sure nobody hugs you too tight. Or kisses that left cheek.

"Tut, tut, tut," Al added hastily, as Adam started to swear, "I only did what had to be done. Otherwise, you couldn't get a fight with King Kong."

The mezzanine ballroom of The Aladdin seemed a spectacularly gaudy scene to Adam, although probably commonplace for Las Vegas: disco lighting, a long, delicacy-laden hors d'oeuvre table down the middle of the room between dance floor and mixing area, a bar in each corner, an eight-piece orchestra on the strobe-lighted rear stage.

"Hey, Doc," shouted Jakes. "Glad you could make it. Aaron here didn't think this was your scene. But what the hell, you earned some relaxation, and this is the place. C'mon, let's join the sybarites. . . . How about that word, Aaron?" Jakes grinned at him. "Shows you what a year at U.C.L.A. can do for a pug like me."

Robards winked, spotted a friend and drifted off, leaving Adam and Joey alone.

"Your face hurt much?"

"Not as bad as my ribs."

"Yeah, I always was a better body puncher than headhunter. You gave me a few lumps, too. My nose is still bleeding on and off, so no coke for me tonight. Hardly use it, anyway. A boxer needs his nose. How about you?"

"Same. Doesn't do that much for me," said Adam, based on the one time Diana had coaxed him into trying it.

"Always wondered what docs do for kicks. Want to level with me?"

"Wrong guy to ask. I'm pretty square."

"Well, you name it," Jakes said with a sweep of his hand, "we got it. . . . I asked Tanner about you—how you learned to move so quick. Says you got some secret training method. That true?"

"Something like that."

"Hmmmm," Jakes mused. "If I decide to try for a comeback, I want an appointment with you. You help me improve like you did Tanner, I got a real shot at the title—providin', of course, you're not the titleholder."

Before Jakes could continue, an exquisite girl in her twenties caught his arm. "Hey, Joey, how about introducing me to your friend?"

"Sure," Jakes said amiably. "Amelia Martens, meet Dr. Adam McKinnon."

"Doctor!" she exclaimed, wide-eyed. "I thought he was a boxer."

"He's both."

"Really! Well, good. I can't talk boxing, but I can medicine. My daddy was a doctor, killed in the Korean War. My ex-fiancé is a doctor, too. More witch doctor, actually; he went into psychiatry."

"Well," Jakes said tactfully, "why don't I leave you two to talk medicine while I see Syd Pollack about my next movie. But let me warn you about Amelia, Doc. We were freshmen together at U.C.L.A. and she's as smart as she is pretty. Worse than that: she doesn't *play* hard to get, she *is*." Jakes gave Amelia a challenging look. "Didn't you ever hear about 'time's winged chariot,' child?"

"I heard, Joey, but the only flapping around here is your mouth."

"I leave the lady to you, Doc," said Jakes with a slight bow and sauntered off.

Watching his elegantly tuxedoed figure depart, Amelia said to Adam, "I hear you gave him a boxing lesson today."

"Word gets around fast."

"I heard it from Joey himself. He really admires you."

"Thanks. Only he got his licks in, too. One pretty painful one."

"Oh? Where?"

Adam pointed to the bruise on his cheek. "He also banged up a slab of ribs."

"Still hurt?"

He nodded.

Amelia looked sympathetic.

"Mind if I ask you a rather dumb question?" he began awkwardly.

"No." Amelia smiled. "Not if I can ask you one, too. You go first."

"Okay. I hardly ever go to movies or watch anything except news on TV, but your face seems familiar. Why's that?"

"Not just my face, I bet. My body, too. You see, I model between pictures. My latest pose was for Maidenform Bras and has been in a lot of newspapers and magazines. That's probably what you remember."

"Probably," Adam said, looking a bit bemused.

"Now, my turn: do you have prematurely gray hair?"

Adam laughed. "No, it's aged right along with me. I'm forty-five."

"And a professional boxer?"

"Aspiring to be."

"For God's sake, why?"

"It's a long story. I'd tell it to you, but I shouldn't monopolize that much of your time."

"Well," she said boldly, "I want to monopolize you. How much do your ribs hurt?"

Adam rubbed his hand along his right side and winced.

"Enough. And I'm afraid to drink with all the painkillers I've taken. I'm still nauseous from them."

Amelia hesitated, as if debating the wisdom of what she was about to say. "I don't shoot up or sniff," she began, "but I *do* know what's good for bruised ribs."

"What?"

"Heat. And maybe a little pot."

"I'm not sure I follow you."

"You'll have to, if you want my sure-cure remedy." The baffled look on Adam's face made her smile. "I've got a sauna in my room, and a bag of 'Maui Wowee.' You're welcome to both, providing you don't mind leaving the party. And you promise to explain about yourself."

In her room, Amelia turned on the sauna and took the telephone off the hook. Then, she said, "Excuse me, while I put on a swimsuit."

"What do I put on?"

Amelia smiled. "I can loan you a sarong."

"I'll settle for a large towel."

"All right," she said and headed for the bedroom. In the doorway, she paused. "There's a *New West* magazine on the desk. The bra ad I mentioned is on the next to the last page."

Adam picked up the magazine and flipped to the back. She was right; that was where he had seen her face. But it was her full-breasted, sensual figure that now held his eyes. A gold necklace dangled into her cleavage and the pink sheen of her body blended with the fleshy-pink satin lingerie she wore.

Moments later, they were sitting side-by-side in the sauna sharing an expertly rolled joint.

"What happened with your fiancé?" asked Adam. "If that's not too inquisitive . . ."

"Oh, him," she said. "Everything was fine while he was interning. But then he got weird after starting psychiatric training."

"Been known to happen."

Ruefully, Amelia nodded. "'Sometimes a cigar is just a cigar,' Freud said. But I couldn't convince Fred of that. Especially during sex. He insisted on knowing everything I felt and why. Asked so many questions I became anorgasmic."

"Temporarily, I hope."

"I don't really know." Taking a final drag on the joint, she smiled enticingly at Adam and said, "I lured you here to find out."

An hour later, at the end of a tense silence, he reached for his undershorts.

"I'm really sorry, Adam," she said contritely.

He smiled resignedly. "So am I. More surprised than sorry."

"This really never happened to you before?"

"Scout's honor. I've been impotent from time to time—what man hasn't? But I never ejaculated prematurely. Not three times in an hour!" Damned LBC! he thought. Did it have to quicken *every* muscular response in his body?

"Maybe you ought to see a sex therapist?"

"I used to live with one. She was a family practitioner who did sexual dysfunction therapy, too."

"And it never happened with her?"

Adam shook his head.

"Oh, dear," uttered Amelia, crestfallen. "Then it must be me."

"If that's true, which I doubt, it must be because you're the most beautiful woman I ever made love to. Maybe I was too overawed to—"

She cut him off. "Don't analyze it! Please!"

Adam sighed. She was much more upset than he was, and he understood why. Knowing nothing about the LBC, she could not possibly grasp the hilarious irony in what had happened. Nor did he dare explain.

"But I really like you!" she wailed. "I mean, you really appeal to me. Now, I suppose you'll never want to see me again."

"Wrong!" Adam said emphatically. Going to her desk, he wrote on a piece of paper. "Here," he said a moment later. "My Boston phone number and address. I'd love to see you again. Soon!"

Smiling, Amelia took the paper. Then, she looked glum again. "I don't suppose you'd spend the night?"

Adam got back in bed and took her in his arms. "I'd be delighted," he said, "providing you're willing to do two things."

"What?" asked Amelia anxiously.

"Autograph that bra ad and then stay in my arms."

13

At seven A.M., Adam gave Amelia a long, last hug and left. Outside the hotel, he got into a cab, directed the driver, and slumped back in the seat. Suddenly, he was overcome by a seizure of barely muted laughter. The Greek dramatists had a term for it: the fatal flaw. Oedipus, Agamemnon, Achilles, all had one, but none like his! LBC made him the planet's quickest human, *in* and *out* of bed. He wondered if *The Guinness Book of World Records* had a category for ejaculations per hour? The absurdity started him laughing again, prompting the cabbie to remark, "Good time, huh?"

"Right."

"Guess you came off a winner."

"Something like that."

"You a vacationer or a player?"

"A player," Adam said. "Definitely, a player."

Baggy-eyed and bone-weary, Adam boarded the plane back to Boston an hour later. Confessing his torpid state, though not its cause, to Todd Tanner, he took the seat in front of him. Behind them, in the semicircle of seats at the rear, Lakeman,

Robards, Waldman, and Warner were in an animated discussion.

Although aware that they were deciding his boxing future, Adam was too exhausted to join in. He drank a Bloody Mary, put his head on a pillow, and fell asleep. When he woke, hours later, Aaron Robards was in the seat beside him. "Time to talk," he said. "You awake enough to listen?"

"Barely," Adam muttered.

"Coffee?"

"Strong coffee."

Robards summoned the steward and waited for Adam to sip his first cup. "All right," he said briskly, "let's talk business. Chances are, your first fight will be at Boston Garden. We're seeking bids from six major arenas, but Ron Warner was damned impressed by what he saw and is offering a floor bid of two hundred grand in exchange for first refusal—that is, the right to top any higher offers. Frankly, Adam, I think that's the most we can get."

"Okay, so I fight at the Garden. Who do I fight?"

"Ever hear of 'Mean Joe' Metcalf?"

"The defensive tackle for the Pittsburgh Steelers?"

"No, that's 'Mean Joe' Greene. Metcalf played defensive end for the Buffalo Bills. A real bruiser. Six-foot-five and two hundred and sixty or seventy pounds. But he figured he was worth more than the Bill's owner would shell out, so he quit at the start of the season and turned boxer. He's had six pro bouts so far, none against 'name' fighters but no pushovers either, and won them all by kayos. Four in the first round. It was Ron Warner who suggested him, since Metcalf's played a lot of football in Boston and is well-known—in fact, hated with a passion—by Patriot fans. But Al had reservations."

"What kind of reservations?"

"Well, he's not only a good seventy pounds heavier than you, but wide as a door. Takes up a lot of space in the ring, leaving you less room to move around."

"What sold Al on him?"

"Mel saw his last fight. Metcalf's so muscle-bound he telegraphs every punch. You can box circles around him."

"Small circles, considering his size."

"We also discussed Mike Rossman, the ex-light heavyweight champ turned heavyweight. He's much quicker and more ringwise than Metcalf. Could give you a lot more trouble."

Adam drank a second cup of coffee. Then he turned back to Todd Tanner: "Who would you rather go up against, Todd, Metcalf or Rossman?"

"Metcalf, I guess. Tackling's against the rules."

"Good point. Okay, Aaron, 'Mean Joe' it'll be. Anything else?"

"Warner wants the fight in three or four weeks, since he's got some open dates then."

"Three or four weeks, huh? Doesn't leave much time for a buildup."

"We discussed that. But Mel thinks he can handle it. He's going to screen the Jakes videotape for some of his sports buddies next week. . . . *'Magic' McKinnon versus 'Mean Joe' Metcalf*. Got a catchy ring, don't you think?"

" *'Magic'*—who?" Adam protested. "That's pretty corny, wouldn't you say? Mel think that up, too?"

"No. Actually, it was Harry Patashnick's idea. He thinks there's something magic about you. And what the hell—the nickname didn't hurt Earvin 'Magic' Johnson's basketball career any."

Adam nodded resignedly. "Anything more?"

"One last thing. Mel's first column about you will be in Wednesday's newspaper—so be prepared. Your life'll never be the same again. Change to an unlisted telephone number. Use my answering service if you want. And get any unfinished business at the hospital out of the way. You might even consider dropping by a costume shop and picking up a disguise, *à la* Floyd Patterson."

Adam stared at him. "Surely, you jest."

"I'm giving you fair warning," Aaron said flatly. "It might not happen next week, or the following one, but once you demolish Joe Metcalf, you're going to be pestered by every reporter, talk-show host, cereal manufacturer, and sports groupie in the state. Harry Patashnick won't be the only one who thinks you're magical, and the rest'll want to get close enough for some to rub off."

"Jesus," said Adam, massaging his brow. "I'm not sure I care for that much notoriety. In fact, I don't care for it at all."

"What'd you expect?" Robards chided. "To fight incognito? Nothing like it would happen to Todd here. Nor should it. He's twenty-five years old and been a boxer most of his life. But you're forty-five and a doctor to boot. Don't you think the public will wonder about you? Wonder, hell! You'll be every middle-aged weekend athlete's dream. They're going to eat up every word written about you. Face it, Adam, you're going to turn the sports world upside-down. Which is maybe what you've intended all along. So don't say you haven't been warned. . . . Want more coffee?"

"Would you, after hearing what I just did?"

"No, I'd want a good stiff drink."

"That's exactly what I want, too."

Brooding over Robards's words, Adam remained silent the rest of the fight. He had three days before Mel Waldman's column appeared in print and the hospital personnel began buzzing about him. If Walt Carson started early Monday morning, he could synthesize enough LBC to last Adam a year. That would solve one problem. If he sent Carson and Jill Jamieson, his other biochemist co-worker, to Edinburgh ahead of schedule, the reporters couldn't get at them. Will Rankin, his graduate student, had to stay on to care for the monkeys, but he was a neuroanatomist, not a biochemist, and knew nothing about the composition of the choline analog. The only laboratory equipment Adam needed was the electromyogram to measure changes in his nerve conduction velocity, and since it was portable, he could take the machine home with him. That should keep the reporters at bay for a while. But he was not so naive as to think that he could keep his discovery a secret indefinitely. Sooner or later, they were bound to ferret it out. He could only hope it would be later.

Dan Lassiter's office, palatial in comparison to the smaller, quainter offices of other local hospital directors, was on the twentieth floor of the new Commonwealth General Hospital in Weston. His private secretary, Hedley, announced Adam's presence and was told to send him right in.

"Well," Dan said, eyeing the discolored cheek, "I see you're still in one piece."

"Bruised but unbowed—in fact, doubly bruised."

"I only see one. Come into the examining room and strip down so I can take a look at the other."

"It's not visible," said Adam dolefully. "But it's dealt a crippling blow to my male ego."

"Meaning?"

With a straight face, Dan listened to his sexual misadventure with Amelia. But when Adam himself grinned, he broke into a loud laugh. "Well!" he said, "I'm not totally unsympathetic, but it's something of a relief to know you're not a complete superman. How do you feel otherwise?"

"Physically, fine. Psychologically, a little shaky." He related the gist of Aaron Robards's warning.

"That *does* present a problem," Dan agreed. "Al Lakeman would kill me for suggesting this, but is it too late to back out?"

"No, but I don't want to. My life's been too routine, too static, for too damned long. I'm learning a lot about myself and it's not all bad. I need a favor, though. A big one."

"Name it."

"Being on a year's sabbatical, I've arranged coverage for all my private patients, except one, the severe myasthenic I told you about. His name's Jon Acheson, and we've gotten pretty close. In fact, he's the half-brother of the woman I was living with. Anyway, he needs special care and I wonder if you'd accept him as a transfer. Jack Morris, your chief of neurology, is an expert in myasthenia and could consult on him. But I'd want you to be his personal physician."

"Any particular reason?"

"Yes. I have a theory of sorts as to why he's so refractory to therapy. I think he's suffered some structural damage to his synaptic cleft, so that acetylcholine simply doesn't fit into its receptors on the membrane any more. There's a chance—admittedly, slim—the LBC might, and if he deteriorates any further, I'd like you to try it on him."

Dan looked doubtful. "That's asking a lot, Adam. Legally, I'd have to get permission from our research committee, and the F.D.A. first."

"I realize that."

"You also realize it would give away the secret of your super-reflexes?"

Soberly Adam nodded. "Even so, I can't justify withholding it if it's his only chance to live."

"He wouldn't by any chance be Diana Acheson's brother?"

Adam could not conceal his surprise. "You know Diana?"

"I've met her. We served on an A.M.A. committee together. Knowing how you feel—or felt—about her, I won't say any more."

"Even if I ask you to?"

"Even then. At least, not here and not now. Maybe over drinks some night. . . . But I think it's damned decent of you to be this concerned about her half-brother and I'll help all I can. I'll reserve a bed on our neuro-vigil unit right away, so you can transfer him over here today. . . . Now, then, anything I can do for your, uh, sexual problem?''

"You can stop gloating!"

"Is that what I was doing?" Dan said innocently. "Must be my vengeful nature. You see, even though I'm happily married, I still prefer winning at handball to sex."

14

The morning of his last day of anonymity, Adam signed a six-month lease on a large North Shore duplex Harry Patashnick's real estate broker nephew had located for him, and arranged to have his furniture moved. He did not regret leaving Beacon Hill and its sepulchral setting—generations of famous Bostonians having died on this hilltop. It was convenient to the hospital and to downtown. But the rented three-room apartment with its high ceilings and antique plumbing was painfully haunted by Diana's lingering presence. Only yesterday, in a shadowy corner of the shower stall, he had found a disposable razor she had left behind and the discovery conjured up memories of showers together, of lovemaking in the shower stall or on the bathroom floor when the need was urgent and the bedroom too far away. Sex generated some strange current between them, achieving an intensity of union neither had ever experienced before. Sex and the profession they shared, the stimulation of discussing patients each evening, were the bonds that moored their relationship through countless emotional storms. That, and their desire to have a child.

It was Al Lakeman who advised him to rent a three-bedroom apartment.

"What for?" Adam asked.

"Well, with you and Todd doing roadwork together every morning, he might want to sleep over some nights."

"Okay. That's two bedrooms. Who's the third for?"

"A bodyguard."

"A *what?*"

"A bodyguard," Al repeated irritably, "—if one becomes necessary."

"Think it will?"

"Depends."

"On what?"

"If you beat Metcalf and how bad."

"And exactly who or what will this bodyguard be protecting me from—the mob?"

"Not the mob," Al sneered. "Your fans, dummy. Your fans among the press, who'd just love to trap you into blabbing something stupid and quotable; your fans among local he-men, wanting to take a poke at you; most of all, your female fans, dying to find out if you're as good in bed as you are in the ring. Muhammed Ali could lecture you on that occupational hazard. He had four bodyguards, by the way, but you'll have to make do with one."

"Got anybody in mind?"

"Matter of fact, I do. Meet me at a bar called Dumphey's after training some evening and I'll introduce you to him. . . . Speaking of training," Al continued, "I want you to step up the pace. I know you can box, but not how hard you can hit. So better figure on the Metcalf fight going the full ten rounds. Which means you've got to be in top shape. Can't ease up or slack off for a second, 'cause 'Mean Joe' can put you away with one punch. I guarantee it, understand?"

Adam nodded.

"One good thing about that bruise Jakes gave you and the one you supposedly got from a battling bedpost," Al said sardonically. "You're beginning to look like a fighter!"

At the end of that afternoon's workout, Adam felt unusually fatigued and stayed under the shower a long time, soaking the soreness out of his muscles. He had taken his last dose of LBC three days before and was due for another, so that might be the cause. Or it could be the extra rounds he had sparred with Tanner. Or even his apprehension about the effect of Mel Waldman's column in the *Globe* tomorrow on his life. Though he was moving on a fast track these days, he had yet to settle into it with any degree of ease.

From the Front Street Gym, Adam drove to Commonwealth General Hospital to visit Jon Acheson at his new quarters. Picking up the consulting doctor's pass Lassiter had left for him at the reception desk, he went directly to Jon's room on the neuro-vigil unit.

As always, the sight of the young man's head protruding through the tight rubber collar at the end of the iron lung gave him a pang of pity. With the TV set playing loud enough to overcome the swishing of the bellowslike machine, Jon did not hear him enter the room. But his handsome face brightened when Adam came into view. "Hi, Doc!" he shouted and pushed the button by his hand that shut off the TV. "Great to see you."

"Same," Adam said. "How do you like your new home?"

"The Taj Mahal of hospitals! I like Lassiter a lot, too. He's got his biomedical engineers working on a souped-up pneumatic vest that he hopes will spring me from this capsule. I told him the one you tried didn't work and why, but he thinks they can surmount that with some new, space-age technology."

"That'd be great! What else is happening?"

"Oh, the usual. I hold court at least twice a day for every medical student, intern, and resident who's never seen a case of myasthenia gravis or an iron lung before. I lecture the neuro-residents on the latest theories and treatments for the disease. And I do my best to shock the gray ladies by telling them that too much sex overtaxed my parasympathetics and got me into this fix. Aside from that, it's business as usual. How about you?"

"Oh, it's taken a little time to get used to, but I'm beginning to enjoy my sabbatical."

"Lassiter tells me you wiped him out in handball. But he said it with a grin, so I guess he's not too sore. You play tennis, too?"

"Some. I plan to play a lot more this summer. Get ready for Wimbledon, you know."

Jon shared his smile, never suspecting that Adam might mean it.

"That's my game. We'll have to play sometime. . . . You know, when you guys finally figure out a cure. You'd better do it soon, too."

"Oh? What's the rush?"

"My minister, high Episcopalian but a closet Catholic, I suspect, is talking about raising the money to send me to Lourdes." Jon grinned. "I sure hope this iron lung can float! Incidentally, been reading some Ernest Becker on your recommendation. I'm about halfway through *The Denial of Death*. Heavy stuff. Wait 'till I finish, then we can talk about it."

"Fine," Adam said, glancing furtively at his watch. He had a Ping-Pong match with Charlie Nash at eight o'clock. In the ensuing silence, he steeled himself for Jon's inevitable question.

"Hear from Diana lately?"

"No," Adam said, "have you?"

"Got a call from her when she reached San Diego. She practically drove straight through, naturally. Blew a tire in Nevada, but other than that, made it back without being robbed, raped, or otherwise molested. I called her after being transferred here. She was surprised to learn you'd taken a year's sabbatical and asked a lot of questions. But I really didn't know what to tell her. Why are you?"

Adam hesitated. "Read Mel Waldman's column in the *Globe* tomorrow. That'll explain it as well as I can."

"Waldman?" Jon puzzled. "He's a sports writer. Why would he write about a neurologist? You into sports medicine or something?"

"Or something," Adam said evasively. "I'd say more, but I want it to come as a big surprise."

"You know, for a quiet guy, you're full of surprises. You and Diana getting together was one. Your splitting up another. I love that girl, but I don't pretend to understand her. Too bad you didn't ski," Jon said in a lighter tone. "Since there wasn't much else about you to criticize, she bitched a lot about that."

"Well, now she has her ex-husband to ski with."

"Yeah," Jon said sourly. "For that and not much else. Unless she develops some skin disease he can treat, I give their reunion a month."

"Then what?"

"Then I'm going to have to have a serious talk with her. Sometimes, I wonder who's worse off. I'm in pretty bad shape, but those are the breaks. I'm certainly not down on myself because of it. Just the opposite. I'm hanging on until the end. But Diana . . . I don't suppose there's any chance of you two getting together again?"

"Afraid not."

Jon tightened his lips. "Didn't think so. Well, come see me again soon."

"Count on it," said Adam and left, feeling the mixed relief and regret that talk of Diana always engendered.

15

Reverberations from Mel Waldman's column in the *Boston Globe* reached the coffeeshop where Adam usually ate breakfast before he got there. As the waitress wrote down his order, he overheard the middle-aged man at the next table say, "Hey, Pete, did you read Waldman this morning?"

The man with him put his fork down. "Yeah! I did. Think this McKinnon's really as good as Waldman says?"

"Beats me. But imagine a guy our age fighting 'Mean Joe' Metcalf! Hell, I wouldn't fight Metcalf even if he tried to rape my wife."

"Why should you? She outweighs him."

"It's glandular, she says. Maybe this McKinnon is some kind of gland case, too?"

Not quite, thought Adam, turning to watch the waitress pour his coffee. He had a copy of the *Globe* folded beside him. But he hadn't read Mel's column yet; he wasn't ready. Before his eggs and bacon arrived, he heard his name mentioned twice more by other patrons of the coffeeshop and felt the first uncomfortable twinges of notoriety. Though he was still a private person, his name was becoming public property—to be discussed as freely as politics or the weather.

Sipping his second cup of coffee after breakfast, Adam finally opened the newspaper to Mel's column. Entitled, "The Front Street Gym Phenomenon," it ran longer than usual, a full page and a half. Its hype surprised him, until Adam remembered that Mel was not unbiased. Without being deliberately misleading, his purpose was to publicize the hitherto unknown Adam McKinnon, arouse public interest in him as a marvel of the age, and build up the gate for the Metcalf fight. If the comments he heard in the coffeeshop were indicative, Mel was succeeding grandly.

Impulsively, Adam telephoned Al Lakeman to tell him he would not be working out today. He gave no reason and Al didn't ask. After Mel's column, the gym would probably be crawling with fight fans, especially gamblers trying to get a line on the Metcalf-McKinnon bout, so Al was not averse to Adam staying out of sight.

The end-of-March day was clear and cold. Adam got into his car and drove off with no particular destination in mind. He considered going to New Haven to visit old friends, but was not feeling that sociable. What he really wanted was solitude and space in which to come to grips with whatever was troubling him and try to put it to rest.

Remembering a long stretch of beach outside of Gloucester with a good restaurant at the end, Adam headed towards Cape Ann. He got there in two hours and started hiking along its frozen sand, the choppy Atlantic on his right, high dunes on his left, and a biting wind in his face. Soon, he felt isolated, insignificant, lonely.

His isolation, he knew, was largely of his own making. Broodingly, he accepted that his life-endangering act of swallowing the LBC had been precipitated by more than his break-up with Diana and the loss of his research grant. Deep beneath these disappointments lurked the real reason for his discontent: the one face-up card God had dealt him—had dealt all mankind—that he could not abide: impermanence. The impermanence of all living things. The knowledge had festered in him ever since the death of his mother when he was twelve. Had he been subtly suicidal since then? Was that the reason he avoided marriage and children so long? Diana's persistent probing had helped him verbalize some of it, but, despite her urging, he refused to be psychoanalyzed. Yet Freud was right: you spend the first half of your adult life trying to rewrite the script of your childhood, erase infantile frustrations and adolescent hurts. And Ernest Becker was right: you spent the last half brooding about the imminence of death. Was there no respite, no breathing spell?

But he was falling into his usual trap, Adam realized; worrying about the problems of mankind when he should be concentrating on his own lonely plight. Although it was within his grasp, having been won fair and square, Adam no longer wanted the adulation of the crowd but the love of the kind of women he had known long ago.

Thinking of his mother, Adam suddenly understood the impulse that had brought him to this remote Cape Ann beach. It was where she used to bring young Adam to meet his father when he returned from his weekly lectures at Brown.

His thoughts drifted back to those happy times. . . .

Adam McKinnon was born in Newton, Massachusetts, a city traditionally divided between the "Hill" and the "Lake." The division carried more social than geographical significance, since the hill was not the highest in Newton and the lake was merely a pond. But the hill contained the elegantly landscaped Victorian houses from which the professional class commuted to their Boston offices. The lake was where the bakers, gardeners, shopkeepers and repairmen who served the hill-dwellers lived in their cheap houses and crowded flats.

Adam grew up in a border area between hill and lake occupied primarily by middle-aged, middle-class couples. An only child, he would have been a lonely one in the largely childless neighborhood except for his close, satisfying relationship with his parents. Adam's mother, Eva McKinnon, was a frail, lovely woman with a damaged heart from rheumatic fever in her youth. She had borne Adam at grave risk, and knowing that her life expectancy was limited, cherished him the more dearly.

His father, Harold McKinnon, a professor of physics at M.I.T., was a sedate, scholarly man who lavished all his spare time on his family. He had a dry, deadpan sense of humor and delighted in responding to Adam's endless questions with either valid answers or nonsensical ones and making him divine which was which.

"Why did the dinosaurs go extinct, Dad?" Adam would ask.

"Bad table manners. After a while, nobody would serve them. So they starved."

"How come I can never kick a kickball past the pitcher's mound?"

"Quite simple. Kickball is a game of impulse and momentum. The greater the impulse you impart to the ball, the farther it goes. The greater angular momentum your leg gains as it swings, the more impulse you impart. The longer your legs, the greater the momentum. Your legs just aren't long enough yet."

When Adam was twelve, Eva McKinnon's rheumatically scarred heart finally failed, ending the happy portion of his youth. There were times after his mother's death when he felt as if he had lost not one parent, but both. Grief-stricken, Harold McKinnon withdrew into his study and a near impenetrable shell, leaving Adam alone in a suddenly incomprehensible world.

"Why did Mom die, Dad?" he would ask.

"Of a weak heart."

"But why did she have to have a weak heart? I mean, who gave it to her?"

"I don't know. It was God's will."

"Where is she now?"

"With God."

"Is God cruel?"

"God is God. Now leave me alone, son. I have work to do."

His father could have spared Adam a great deal of anguish and misdirection had he only sat him down and explained death. He was not insensitive to his son's need, but he was too distraught to satisfy it. He hired a cook-housekeeper and secluded himself in a morbid world of psychic pain and bereavement, leaving Adam to find his own answers.

Eventually he did. He decided to find out what made people sick, what had made his mother die. He started with the *Britannica Junior Encyclopaedia,* reading every medical article in it, before moving on to medical texts from the public library. He lacked the chemistry and biology background to understand most of what he read, but at least he was doing something. His sense of bewildered frustration began to fade.

Gradually, Adam's father emerged from isolation and again talked to him, took him places, answered his questions. But he refused to explain the scientific concepts that Adam couldn't grasp. Harold McKinnon wanted nothing to do with science. Despite his years of dedicated service to it, science was a false god who gave false answers. Instead, Harold McKinnon reinvested his faith in the Christian Lord, telling Adam at dinner one evening that he was resigning his M.I.T. professorship and going to divinity school. But by the time he graduated and could offer his son other answers to the puzzle of life and death than those of misguided science, Adam was beyond his reach. His search for the cause of his mother's death had led him to the obsessive ambition to become a doctor.

To Adam's methodical mind, that meant doing well enough in his studies to get into a top college, medical school, and hospital residency program. He became Newton North High School's most conscientious student. He also went out for track, boxing, and hockey, and although not naturally athletic drove himself so hard that he made the varsity in all three sports by his senior year. Boxing, in particular, gave his anger and frustration release and his coach was amazed at how such a quiet, studious youth could turn into such a raging competitor.

Whenever Adam took time from training and studying to think about his life, he would be racked by an almost intolerable loneliness. He had a few casual friends on the track and hockey squads, but none understood his moody drive, nor did they try. Girls intrigued him, and some made overtures, but he could never think of anything to say to them and was far too busy to go out on dates. For his father's metaphysical, rhetoric-filled world of conjecture and sermonizing, Adam could only feel contempt, although he loved his father unconditionally.

In his senior year, Adam was accepted at both Harvard and Yale, and chose Yale as being the farther away. He left Newton the next fall with excitement and relief to be free of unhappy memories, the intrusions of his father's congregation into their home, and, most disturbing, his father's puzzling personality change.

Adam did well at Yale and his letters home reflected his satisfaction with the progress he was making. His father's replies, however, baffled him more and more. They would begin by describing the latest happenings in Newton or at his church and veer off suddenly on some irrelevant, almost nonsensical tangent. There would be allusions to obscure Biblical or Talmudic passages Adam couldn't possibly know; pages of disjointed and incomprehensible anti-science arguments or ecclesiastical advice. He would ask questions about Adam's courses and living arrangements that had been answered several times before.

Home for Christmas, Adam found his father's behavior as

erratic as his letters. He would put a book in its proper place on the bookshelf and then search the house for it. He would promise to pick Adam up at the library or YMCA and forget all about it. He could never remember what day it was or when Adam was supposed to return to school and, even in repose, he wore a permanently perplexed, almost pained, expression on his face.

He explained his absent-mindedness by claiming his thoughts were on a higher plane now, but Adam was unconvinced, finally persuading his father to see a doctor. The diagnosis was dooming: pre-senile dementia. There was no treatment, no way to arrest the progression of the disease, nothing except to provide for institutional care. In the next few years, Adam watched the one person in the world he loved degenerate from a highly intelligent scientist and clergyman into a babbling, drooling old man who could no longer feed, dress, or wash himself. Adam visited him faithfully at the Newton Convalescent Center every other weekend, even after his father had ceased to recognize him. And long before Harold McKinnon died, he had made up his mind: instead of becoming a cardiologist, as he had originally planned, in order to cure cases like his mother's, he must find a cure for the horrible "locked in" living death that had destroyed his father. He would specialize in neurology.

16

At nine A.M., the weekend janitor at the downtown San Diego Medical Arts Building unlocked the outer door to Dr. Diana Acheson's fourth-floor office and reversed the sign on it to read, THE DOCTOR IS IN.

The doctor wasn't in, he knew, and might not be in, but those were her instructions and she was a generous tipper.

Diana was, in fact, en route—a minor miracle under the circumstances. She sped down the coast highway in her Porsche convertible, top down, hair flapping in the breeze, tape deck blaring, head pounding, hands so shaky from the Dexedrine taken earlier that she had to grip the steering wheel tightly to keep the car from straying into another lane. Out of necessity, not caution, she kept one eye on the speedometer and the other on the road; one more speeding ticket and she would lose her driver's license.

God, she was dehydrated! She could barely produce enough saliva to chew the sugarless gum in her mouth. Usually, she started her day with a potful of coffee and two or three bottles of Pepsi to replace the fluids that the previous night's alcohol consumption had made her piss away. But she'd overslept this morning and had to slake her thirst by guzzling water from the shower nozzle.

Saturday morning office hours were the pits, anyway, she groused. She would be glad when her practice built to the point she could eliminate them. But she had wanted to be in private practice and not answerable to some penny-pinching HMO administrator, wanted a downtown location, and the income she generated on Saturdays helped pay the exorbitant rent. Office hours or not, she never should have drunk so much last night. There were probably other things she shouldn't have done either, but mercifully she couldn't remember them. Oh well, Ted, her ex-husband and self-appointed house-mother, would doubtless give her a full accounting when she got home.

Why did she tolerate him? Security, that's why. Not the security provided by his lucrative dermatology practice, but the security of having somebody at home with her. As her last analyst kept insisting, she had trouble individuating. Individuating, indeed! She was afraid that, without Ted around to talk her out of it, she might blow her brains out. Actually, they lived together more from habit than choice; that and mutual perversity: they simply weren't through punishing each other for past wrongs. She hoped he won his tennis match at the club this morning; it would put him in a better mood the rest of the day.

Diana took the downtown exit off the expressway and almost immediately braked for a light. Exhaust fumes from a rickety vegetable truck ahead of her started her coughing and gagging. "Damned Mexicans!" she muttered.

The instant the light changed, she twisted the wheel hard to the left and, with a blast of her horn, cut in front of the truck.

The young blond driver thrust his arm out the window and gave her the finger.

Diana chuckled. "Damned *blond* Mexicans," she amended.

Two blocks further down, she shot up the parking ramp to her office building, waved to the gatekeeper, and screeched to a halt in her assigned space. Grabbing her oversized purse, she dashed for the elevator in her spiked heels, slipped on an oil patch, and barely avoided falling by steadying herself on a car fender.

Oh God! she thought, that was close. With her hair already a frizzy mess, all she needed was to walk into her office smeared with oily dirt to send her patients scampering for the door.

In the elevator, she fumbled in her purse for comb and

lipstick, trying to restore a semblance of neatness to her appearance. At the fourth floor, she pressed the hold button and checked her face in her pocket mirror. Not bad, she thought, except for the eyes. Her puffylidded, bloodshot eyes betrayed how rotten she really felt. She glanced at her wristwatch, the one Adam had given her for her thirty-second birthday. But she couldn't dwell on him now. She was already running a half-hour late.

She paused before the office door to straighten her dress. THE DOCTOR IS IN, all right, she reflected ruefully: In pain, in debt, in analysis again, in a purgatory of her own making. Actually, she wasn't doing all that badly; she hadn't dreamt about the abortion in almost a week, or thought about it for the past two hours.

Opening the door, she piped a cheery, "Good morning!" to the five patients waiting for her and walked briskly past the empty receptionist's desk to her inner office, dying for the bottle of Pepsi in her refrigerator. Still fuzzy-headed and yawning incessantly, she debated whether to take another Dex to revive her, but decided on coffee instead. Too much Dex made her talk so fast her patients had difficulty understanding her.

She donned a long white coat and sighed at her last-minute inspection in the mirror. Two years, she reckoned, three at the outside, and the face would be beyond the magic of make-up. No discerning male would give her a second glance. She almost looked forward to it. She had never much enjoyed sex, except with Adam, and in her own inimitable style had screwed that up. Enough! she pleaded with her inner tormentor and turned toward the door to immerse herself in her patients' problems instead of her own.

At noon, Diana ushered in her last patient, a wealthy, distinguished-looking businessman suffering from long-standing impotency, and spent forty minutes counseling him. He saw her, in preference to Masters and Johnson, because beautiful women were at the root of his problem, and she *was* beautiful. Diana did not need to point this out to him; he had been in analysis almost as long as she and was well indoctrinated in the theory of "reaction-formation." She had seen him three times now and hoped she could go on seeing him much longer—not only because he was her richest patient but because he represented an escape hatch. An encouraging word from her and he would take her anywhere she wanted, for as long as she wanted. Technically, it would be a violation of the Hippocratic oath, but Diana had violated other oaths with impunity, not the least that of holy matrimony. Nonetheless, she felt she was helping him, and he claimed she was, although listening to him talk about his seductive mother was as tedious for her as it was painful for him. Mothers! Hers was a lulu. If humans could reproduce asexually like flatworms, Freud might have become a strudel chef and psychiatry never invented. Yet, despite all her negative feelings about "momism" she had wanted to be a mother herself. Too bad she'd lacked the staying power.

"Uh huh, that's fine, Max," she said, when he paused, even though she had not heard a word for the last minute.

"You sure?" he asked dubiously.

"There are no right feelings or wrong feelings, only feelings," she said glibly to cover her lapse. "But store the thought. We'll get to it next session."

"Okay." He stood up and stretched. "Can I escort you to your car?"

Diana smiled warmly. "Please do. Rape's bad enough any time. But Saturday morning rape. Ugh!"

Although still hung over, Diana brightened as she drove up the hill to their oceanfront home—Ted's home, actually; he had bought her out when they were divorced, but it was she who had found and furnished the place originally. "Hello!" she shouted on entering and, getting no reply, headed for her bedroom. She slipped on her bikini and, gin and tonic in hand, went looking for her ex-husband, finding him sitting by the pool, putting together a jigsaw puzzle. Ted was the only grown man she knew who pursued that juvenile pastime, claiming it helped him think. Think about what? she wondered, observing his intense concentration. About her, no doubt, and almost certainly nothing good.

"Hi!" she said airily, testing the water, so to speak.

"Hi," he replied in a neutral tone.

"How'd you make out in tennis?"

"Split. Too hot to play the deciding game."

"Oh." Diana pulled up a deck chair and spread a towel over its foamrubber cushions. Unfastening her bikini top, she lay on her stomach, facing him. Intuitively, she knew something was troubling Ted and waited worriedly but impatiently for him to bring it up.

Finally, he did.

"You never told me that guy you lived with in Boston was such a—" Ted paused to flex his biceps—"he-man."

Diana raised up on her elbows, exposing her breasts. "Adam?" she said, puzzled. "What do you mean?"

"There's a story about him in the paper today; how he's turned professional boxer."

"Adam?" she repeated, looking utterly bewildered. "You can't be serious!"

"Oh, no?" he said irritatedly. "Read for yourself." He took the paper from the chair beside him, folded it, and tossed it to her.

Diana had to duck to keep from being hit in the face.

"But it *can't* be Adam," she protested. "He's . . . he's . . ."

"Too old?" suggested Ted snidely.

"That, and, well—just not the type. I mean, he's lean and muscular, but not at all aggressive."

"Then what the hell's he doing fighting Joe Metcalf? Metcalf, for your information, used to play defensive end for the Buffalo Bills. He's six and a half feet tall, almost three hundred pounds, and isn't called 'Mean Joe' for nothing! Either your ex-boyfriend is Superman in disguise, or there's a hell of a lot you haven't told me about him."

"I haven't told you much of anything," Diana countered. "You never wanted to know. But it can't be Adam. Must be somebody else with the same name."

"Oh, sure," Ted said scornfully. "There must be dozens of forty-five-year-old Boston neurologists named McKinnon. . . . Look, instead of continuing this inane conversation, why don't you just read the story? It's on the front page of the sports section. Go on, read, damn it!"

Diana took off her sunglasses and stared. What in the world was going on with him? Or with Adam? For a moment, she felt dizzyingly disoriented. Finally, she opened the newspaper to the sports section and the headline: "MIDDLE-AGED DOCTOR HOPES TO ANESTHETIZE 'MEAN JOE' METCALF."

"Well?" demanded Ted when she put the paper down and reached for her drink.

"Well, what?" she snapped, her brain thrown into turmoil by the incredible career change in a man she thought she knew.

"What do you think now?"

She shook her head. "I don't know. . . . What do you care what I think anyway?"

"Well, if what they say about McKinnon is true, he sounds really tough. I'm surprised he never beat you up . . . or knocked you up."

Diana glared, trying to keep the sudden spasm in her stomach from her face. She had never told Ted about the abortion. Many times, roaring drunk or screaming mad, she had been on the verge of it, but her instinct—the same survival instinct that told her when to drive slower or steer clear of certain men in bars—stopped her. Still, she was curious why Ted seemed so upset about Adam; curious and, sensing his peculiar vulnerability, determined to find out. "Fix me another drink, will you?" she said casually.

"In a minute. Right now, I want to know what you're thinking."

"About what?"

"Adam McKinnon."

Diana smiled sweetly. "I'll hold the thought until you get me a drink."

Ignoring her request, he asked, "Are you thinking of going back to him? He can afford you now. If he beats Metcalf, he'll make millions."

"He made enough before. Not as much as you, but enough. Money was never an issue."

At the end of a deep breath, he said, "Was he good in bed?"

Now *that's* different, thought Diana. In a remarkable reversal of form, it was Ted who was spoiling for a fight. "That's none of your damned business! Adam never asked that about you."

"What would you have said?"

"I would've refused to answer—just as I'm refusing now. . . . Look," she fumed, "I'll get my own drink. And while I'm inside I think I'll give my brother a jingle to see how he's doing. But I'm warning you: when I get back, I want you to cut this bullshit and tell me what's really eating you."

Diana stood up, but before she could fasten her bikini top, he said, "I suppose you'll be making a trip to Boston soon."

"I might."

"Don't."

"Oh?" She stared challengingly at him. "Why not? Are you trying to tell me it would be taking a calculated risk?"

"Something like that."

Balefully, she nodded. "Well, right now, I'm only going as far as the kitchen. And tonight I'm going to the party at the

Cutlers', with or without you. After that, I'll let you know,''
she said and sauntered off.

Adam a boxer? Ted jealous? Heady stuff, she thought. It
wasn't turning out to be such a dull day after all.

17

Megan Donovan was the first woman to climb the stairs to the Front Street Gym in several years. There had once been a sign, NO WOMEN ALLOWED, by the door and a man at a turnstile to enforce it. But the sign was long gone and the man had quit after an irate wife, bent on retrieving her gambler-husband before he blew his paycheck, had spiked his shins with her high heels.

The man might have lasted longer had the gambler's wife possessed Megan's guile for penetrating male sanctuaries. At the top of the stairs, she squared her shoulders, lifted her chin, and strode through the door as if she were entering her own apartment. Aftre all, she reminded herself, by law she had as much right as any male reporter to enter a gym or locker room in search of a story. She glanced around haughtily; the place was almost empty. In the rear, a sweat-sheened black savagely pounded a heavy bag and a wiry Latin grunted through a series of sit-ups on a slanted board. Neither seemed to notice her.

Good, Megan thought. I'll just sneak behind the bleachers and wait for the show. She sidled along the wall, acutely conscious of her five-foot-nine height and the conspicuous chartreuse shirtdress she habitually wore for tough interviews.

Under the shadowy bleachers, she sat back on her heels and waited uncomfortably but expectantly for Adam McKinnon, the "Front Street Gym Phenomenon" to appear. For a variety of reasons, she had becomed intrigued by McKinnon after reading about him in Mel Waldman's column on the third day of her Boston vacation. Megan despised most professional sports, particularly the brutal ones like boxing and football, but she was a producer for "20/20," ABC's weekly news magazine, and whether home in New York or traveling, maintained a vigilant eye for possible show pieces. Moreover, she had known Mel since working as a journalism intern at the *Globe* between her junior and senior years at Yale, and considered his writing the least objectionable in the sports section. Mel's idol was Red Smith, and although he never expected to top Smith's classic comparison of a fumble-fingered rookie shortstop to "The Ancient Mariner"—"He stoppeth one of three"—he strove to emulate his controlled syntax. But his column about this middle-aged doctor-turned-boxer was distinctly different. Instead of his usual cautious, wait-and-see attitude toward rising sports figures, Mel had been unrestrained in his praise of McKinnon. It made Megan wonder if Mel, now in his mid-thirties, and fifteen years past his varsity basketball days at Boston University, wasn't subconsciously betraying some of his fantasies and frustrations. Perhaps McKinnon was a symbol for him, as for other aging former athletes who must resent the huge sums paid to inarticulate twenty- or twenty-one-year-olds to play professional sports these days. But for God's sake, the man hadn't even had his first professional fight yet! What made Mel so confident in McKinnon's future success that he was willing to stick his neck out so far? Plant so many hooks in his column about him that it sounded to Megan like he was planning to write a series. A series! On an unknown, forty-five-year-old doctor who might have lost contact with reality! What the hell was Mel up to? Was he trying to create a mystique around McKinnon? If so, why?

And then she remembered: Mel's father-in-law was a fight promoter who happened to be co-owner of the Front Street Gym. Puzzle pieces connected into an unpretty picture. Had family loyalty or under-the-table bucks motivated Mel to write the piece? Or could McKinnon really be as talented as he proclaimed? Either way, Megan's curiosity was whetted. She tried repeatedly to reach Mel that day. But nobody answered his office phone, so she let it go, knowing they would be at the same sports banquet the following evening.

Luckily, Megan and her escort, a sports programmer for the local ABC affiliate, were seated across from Mel at one of the long banquet tables. He seemed delighted to see her again and praised her hair-do and gown extravagantly, but that was all she got out of him. To the steady stream of skeptical colleagues who stopped at his chair he talked with incessant enthusiasm about McKinnon.

Megan's escort confided to her that Al Lakeman was supposed to have a video tape of McKinnon sparring with Joey Jakes he was showing around to sports promoters and network TV representatives, although he had not seen it himself as yet.

Hearing this, and hearing Mel's colleagues baiting him with taunts about the mysterious McKinnon, Megan became convinced there was a "20/20" story here. Though Mel's advice to his doubters remained the same: "Don't take my word for it. Come see McKinnon in action for yourself, April seventeenth at the Garden," she resolved to get an interview with him well before that time.

After the banquet, she cornered Mel and made him admit there was a McKinnon-Jakes videotape. He promised to invite her to its press premiere in a week or so, but flatly refused to give out McKinnon's phone number or address. Al Lakeman had him "under wraps" until the Metcalf fight and there was simply no way he could help her. But later Megan overheard him tell a *Sports Illustrated* photographer that McKinnon worked out evenings at the Front Street Gym after its five o'clock closing time.

So here she was, ruining a perfectly good pair of nylons, kneeling under the bleachers and impatient for something to happen.

At last, it did. A muscular black boxer crossed in front of her and climbed into the nearest ring. When he turned to shed the towel draped over his shoulders she recognized him, despite the protective headgear covering most of his face, as Todd Tanner. Holding on to the corner ropes with his gloved hands, he did several deep knee-bends and then began jogging around the ring. He was followed up the ring stairs by an elderly, white-haired man in a heavy coat sweater whose face was unfamiliar to Megan but whose manner conveyed authority. "Attaway, Todd!" he shouted. "Get those shoulder muscles loosened up, too. And, remember, counter-punch! Let him come to you, commit himself, and then *bamm!*'' He slapped his fist into his palm. ''You're scoring on him more and more each session.''

Tanner stopped jogging and began shadowboxing. Then he glanced at the ring stairs and his punches seemed to lose a little snap. Climbing up was a tall, white man with chiseled features and short-cropped gray hair. His body, though sinewy and fit-looking, seemed spindling beside the massive Tanner. Megan stared: *This* was Adam McKinnon? He looked more like a middleaged jogger or squash player than a professional fighter. Who was Mel trying to fool?

But when the sparring began, Megan quickly changed her mind. The man moved like quicksilver, darting from one spot to another so smoothly that she could hardly follow his movements. Todd Tanner stalked him determinedly. But, like his warm-up punches, he hit only air.

''Damn it, counter-punch!'' the old man shouted at Tanner. ''You know he's going to throw triple combinations, so straight jab him in between. And get your chin down. Take his jabs on your head gear, hear?''

Todd nodded, and stopped dead in the center of the ring. Adam immediately closed the distance and unleashed a series of combinations consisting of two left jabs and a right cross.

''Good, Adam. Good!' the old man said. ''Now start mixing up your pay-off punch. Instead of the cross, try a hook or uppercut. That's it. . . . That's it!''

The sparring lasted exactly twenty minutes. In the fourth round, Tanner finally landed a stiff jab that reddened Adam's nose and made the old man crow with delight. Adam retaliated with a hard hook to the side of Tanner's face that might have floored him had not his head gear absorbed most of its impact.

The sudden flurry of blows made Megan realize she had not been following the sparring for some time. Instead, she had been watching Adam. There was something immensely attractive about him—perhaps the balletic grace of his moves or the calm expression on his face through the most punishing exchanges.

Megan had never liked athletes much. Even at Yale, where most of the best-looking men were jocks, she'd steered clear of them. For many athletes, stars and subs alike, she believed the compulsive drive to excel often hardened into an obsessive need to be right, leaving no room for compromise and no retreat into life's comfortable middle ground. Sometimes, when Megan scored a telling point in an argument with a jock, she would see deep, personal resentment in his eyes. And when one of them pressed her to go farther in sex play than she permitted, he seemed less driven by honest desire than by the victory he would achieve by subjugating her resistance and her will.

The only jock she dated more than once in college had confirmed her prejudices. Glen was a tall, dark-eyed embodiment of her high school dreams. He was also a closed-minded male chauvinist. They lasted a month while she tried to convince herself he couldn't possibly be so insensitive, and he realistically recognized that brainy, good-looking girls like Megan were hard to find at Yale. Finally, the day came when she started to refute one of his more inane remarks and he stopped her with: "Be careful, you've already got two strikes against you. You're middle-class Irish, and only so-so in bed."

Swept up in a venomous rage, she screamed, "No, it's three! I was stupid enough to let your princely body blind me to your frog-sized mind. So just get lost before I puncture your overblown ego with a few sexual comparisons of my own."

And that was the last of Glen. To Megan, he so typified the jock species that she wanted nothing more to do with them.

Until now. This Adam McKinnon was certainly no run-of-the-mill jock; not with his M.D. degree and all the mystery enshrouding him.

Megan emerged from reverie to realize that McKinnon and Tanner had finished sparring and were climbing out of the ring. She jumped up, banged her head on the bleacher seat above, and sat back down again. Then, clutching her notebook, she scrambled out from under the boards and ran towards the ring.

"Ah, Dr. McKinnon," she called, "could I speak with you for a moment please?"

"What the hell?" Al Lakeman rasped.

Adam turned, panting from his workout, and said, "Yes?"

Megan came to a halt in front of him. Their eyes met, hers greenish-blue and wide with excitement, his gray and weary.

"Dr. McKinnon, I'm Megan Donovan. I work for '20/20' and I wonder if I could have a few words—"

"Reporter?" Al Lakeman barked. "Out!"

"Wait a second, Al," Adam said. "If we're going to give her the heave-ho, let's do it like gentlemen." Turning back to Megan, he said, "I'm sorry, but I'm not ready to give interviews. When I am, I promise you'll be one of the first, Miss, ah—"

"Donovan. Megan Donovan. I hope you mean that."

"Okay, that's gentlemanly enough. Now, out!" Lakeman bellowed. "No women allowed in here. No reporters, and especially no women reporters!"

Megan smiled at Adam. "I warn you, I don't give up easily."

Again, his gaze was drawn to her remarkably expressive eyes; they literally glittered with determination. He smiled back and trudged off to the locker room.

As soon as she got to her sister's house, where she was spending the week, Megan telephoned Av Westin, executive producer of "20/20."

"Av, listen," she began before he had finished saying hello, "I've got a gem of a piece for you. Did you get the Waldman column I mailed you? Oh, good! Well, I just got a sneak look at this Adam McKinnon working out and he's for real. He could easily be the next heavyweight champ. That, plus his age and profession, makes for a terrific human interest angle and I think I can get the lowdown on him, if you give me a few days to dig on it."

Westin was skeptical, but after ten minutes of Megan's persuasion gave in and okayed the assignment.

Must get an interview somehow, she thought, hanging up—which meant starting with background research and asking doctor friends in town if they knew him and could introduce her.

Dr. Adam McKinnon's biographical sketch in the *Who's Who in Medicine* she read at the library was impressively long, but only two facts in it were of practical interest. He was a Yale graduate, too, and he was single—which fed Megan's fantasies. But neither would help her get an interview. His home phone number was unlisted, and no matter what subterfuge she tried, the hospital operator refused to give it out. Neither her family doctor, her gynecologist, not the few other doctors she knew were acquainted with him, though some were familiar with his reputation and work. The next day, she went to his laboratory at the Tufts-New England Medical Center Hospital, where a graduate student told her Dr. McKinnon was on sabbatical. What now? she wondered. The time Av Westin had given her was running out.

As a last resort, she decided to go see Mel Waldman. Even though Mel wasn't a womanizer as far as she knew, Megan wore her "seductive" outfit: a fairly low-cut, hip-hugging, black dress and stiletto heels. She surveyed herself in the mirror: breasts too small for enough cleavage to fill out the plunging neckline, hips a bit wide, but the high heels made her legs look long and sleek and the black fabric set off her pale skin nicely.

Pausing nervously to gather breath and courage outside Mel Waldman's office, she could hear the murmur of voices within and wondered if Adam McKinnon was there. What a break that would be! Finally, she knocked.

"Come in," said Mel's voice.

Megan entered. Instead of McKinnon, a bald, paunchy, elderly man sat in the straight-backed chair beside Mel's cluttered desk.

"Megan!" Mel exclaimed. "How nice to see you again. Not holding any grudges, I hope? From what Al Lakeman says, you came as close to getting an interview with Adam McKinnon as anybody, and that's saying a lot. Megan, meet my father-in-law, Harry Patashnick. . . . Harry, this is Megan Donovan, an ambitious but good-hearted TV producer. Her father was Tim Donovan, the legendary police reporter for the *Boston Post*."

Megan extended her hand. "I'm happy to meet you, Mr. Patashnick."

Harry took it and smiled. He liked to look at pretty girls and this one was stunning.

Anticipating her next words, Mel said, "Don't tell me why you're here, Megan. I'll tell you—mainly because I have a deadline in fifteen minutes. You want to interview Adam McKinnon for a possible spot on '20/20.' For this, you're willing to: A) presume upon my good nature; B) buy me a two-pound lobster at Pier Four; C) offer me a night of illicit bliss, even though my father-in-law's here. So unless you're holding a real kicker in your hand, my answer is: sorry, but leave your phone number."

Megan bent to thrust her face almost against his. "Mel," she pleaded, "I *need* this interview."

Mel pulled back, shaking his head in mock sympathy. "I know, kid, your job depends on it. Westin produces shows, and either you produce for Westin or it's back to 'WKRP in Cincinnati.'"

"Little wonder the Irish went into politics, not the professions," Megan complained. "They had to outdistance the Jews."

Mel looked astonished. "You dare make an anti-Semitic crack in front of my father-in-law?"

"It was a compliment, dummy. My way of admitting defeat. . . ." She grimaced. "Look, Mel, I'll give it to you straight. I want to meet McKinnon for more than professional reasons."

Mel smote his breastbone with his fist. "Be still, my jealous heart!"

"Well, Mother always wanted me to marry a doctor."

"Not exclusively a Jewish mother's ambition, eh?"

"This conversation is beginning to confuse me," Harry protested. "Would somebody mind filling me in?"

"Sure, Harry," Mel said. "Megan would be glad to. You're the sympathetic type." He looked thoughtful. "Or should I have said avuncular?"

"The word you want, Mel, is *brush-off*," she said coolly. He shrugged apologetically. "Still friends?"

"I suppose so. I'm still going to need you."

"Well, that's playing it as it lays." He turned to Harry. "How would you like to buy this pretty lady coffee and give her some background on the fight game in this town. Not too deep, however. Nothing that'll get any of us indicted."

"With pleasure," Harry replied. "But don't forget, Mel, I'm a promoter. It's in my blood. And I've promoted a lot more than prizefights in my day."

"Before we order," said Megan as she and Harry sat at a coffeeshop table, "let's get something straight. I'm extremely frustrated, which means I'm going to eat a lot, and I'd feel guilty sticking you with the tab. So Dutch-treat, okay?"

"Sure," Harry agreed. "But before you go ruining your figure, maybe I can relieve some of your frustration."

"How?"

"First, tell me what you meant when you said you wanted to meet Adam McKinnon for more than professional reasons."

Megan started to make a glib retort, but something in his look of gentle wisdom inspired confidence. "Harry, I . . . I don't exactly know. I only saw him box a few minutes and exchanged a couple of words, but he's been on my mind ever since. And that bothers me . . . a lot."

"Why should it bother you?"

"Because I don't know him from the original Adam—which means his attraction is purely physical. And that's pretty shallow, don't you think? Highly unprofessional, to say the least." She laughed mirthlessly. "I'm supposed to be tough, resourceful, tempered in the blast furnace of network television production. So why the hell am I daydreaming so much about Adam McKinnon? Just because he seems different from any man I've known before? Because he excites me physically? That's so indiscriminating it makes me cringe. You'd think a woman of twenty-eight would know better, wouldn't you?"

"Megan—" Harry began, but was interrupted by the waitress. He ordered coffee, and Megan, true to her word, ordered two Danish, a double cheeseburger, and a bowl of chili.

"Megan," he began when the waitress left, "why bother with all this analysis? In my business, you get a hunch. Maybe it's good, maybe not so good, but what's life if not hunch-playing? So you play it."

"Play what? I'm not even in the game," she said, looking down at the table. "Besides, you make it sound so simple."

"In some ways, it is simple. . . . Look, let me ask you what might sound like a dumb question, but hear me out." He paused to add emphasis to his next words. "Do you believe in magic?"

"What kind do you mean? The magic of television? That's just illusion. The magic of beauty lotions? The magic of oven cleaners?"

"Maybe the magic of coincidence."

She gave him a questioning look.

"I mean, here you are, a woman I met ten minutes ago, who could have spent the time coaxing or conning me into telling you all I know about Adam McKinnon. Instead, what do you do? You tell me you're lonely. Well, I'm going to tell you something I don't know for a fact but know in my bones. I've watched Adam McKinnon when he didn't know it, and the look in his eyes is the same as yours. So, I'll tell you what I'm going to do. If you promise to meet me for coffee sometime soon, I'll give you his address."

Megan's eyes shone with gratitude.

"Wait a second, let me remember it first." Harry tapped his forehead. "It's, ah, it's 211 Northshore Boulevard. Should I write it down?"

"I'll do it," Megan said, scribbling the address in her notebook. "Harry, I don't know how to thank you."

"Well, one way," he said, "is to cancel that junk-food order you gave the waitress. Settle for coffee and *one* Danish, and spend the next ten minutes just chatting with me."

"You got a deal," she said happily.

18

Megan's courage faltered when Adam opened the door. To see his face in reality again after so much fantasizing unnerved her. He looked older and more drawn than she remembered. Or perhaps she had merely idealized him. He stared at her curiously, as if trying to place her.

"Yes?"

"Megan Donovan, Dr. McKinnon. Remember? The female booted out of the Front Street Gym?"

"Ah, yes." Adam smiled as he recalled Al Lakeman's tantrum. "I *do* remember. I also remember your telling me you don't give up easily. How did you find me?"

"Must we talk on your doorstep, Dr. McKinnon?" Megan gave him her most ingratiating smile and sighed with relief when he invited her in.

My God! What a mess! she thought after Adam took her coat and led her into the living room. If his housekeeping reflected his mentality, it was a wonder that he could speak coherently. Except for the stereo, the couch, and the floor pillows, the room was a jumble of wooden boxes, piled newspapers, and partially unpacked cartons of dishes, books, magazines, and clothing.

She stepped through the clutter and sat down on the sofa, propping her feet on the edge of a wooden box of framed pictures.

"Now, Miss Donovan—uh, it is *Miss,* isn't it?" he asked, hovering above her.

"Yes," Megan said.

"How exactly did you find me? I'm supposed to be incommunicado. Who's the squealer?"

"A man with your best interests at heart."

"Meaning what?"

"Meaning, he thought you ought to meet me."

Adam squinted, about to demand more of an explanation but deciding to postpone it. The truth was, he was glad to see her. "You know, Miss Donovan, even if you are a reporter-type, which I'm supposed to avoid like the plague, would you like a drink?"

She beamed. "I'd love one."

Looking for the glassware box amid the clutter around him, Adam asked, "I don't suppose you do housework, do you?"

"Only windows. I'm exclusive."

"Ah, well. We're all specialists of some kind."

In the ensuing silence, she looked up. Adam hadn't moved. Instead, he stood staring down at her in a bemused way. She smiled and said, "The drink, Doctor."

Adam dug two glasses out of a box and started for the kitchen. He paused. "I hope you don't mind bourbon. I know it's a man's drink, but it's all I've got."

"Man's drink, my foot! When I was fifteen, I could match my father shot for shot and still walk a straight line when he could barely stagger to the bathroom."

Adam eyed her dubiously. "You are kidding, aren't you?"

"Well, sort of . . . though my father did drink a lot. Bourbon, Scotch, rye, whatever. . . ." Lowering her eyes, Megan noticed the photograph of a tall, fur-draped blonde in the box her feet rested on. She picked it up. "Well, this is a chic lady! She not only has the *Town and Country* look I've always wanted, but the fox coat. Who is she, may I ask?"

Adam glanced at the photograph, then away. "That's Diana—correction, that *was* Diana. Dr. Diana Acheson. She left a couple of months ago to go back to San Diego and her ex-husband."

Megan studied the photo. "I might be mistaken, but I seem to detect the gleam of a bitch in her eyes?"

Adam blinked in amazement. "You can tell that about her from her picture? It took me a year to realize it, to make myself accept it."

Megan looked sympathetic. "The power of self-deception. It has no correlation at all with I.Q.—or maybe an inverse one. I went through a similar experience myself recently."

"Want to talk about it?"

"Not cold sober. Seems to me you offered me a drink. Make it a double."

"Straight or mixed?"

"The glasses you're holding don't look big enough for more than a shot and an ice cube."

"I've got bigger ones," Adam said hastily. "Be right back."

He returned with two tall, ice-filled glasses and sloshed bourbon into one until Megan said, "Whoa! That's plenty."

Adam poured himself the same size drink, then held it out. "A toast?"

"To what?"

"To love—'a triumph of hope over experience.'"

"That's George Bernard Shaw's line. And he was referring to marriage, not love."

"Well, whatever he was referring to, he never would've written it if he had known Diana."

"Was it that bad?"

"Bad? Yes—no—well . . ." Adam took a long swallow. "Diana's usually the last person I like to talk about. But since you asked, drink up, and I'll tell you a long story—providing you don't mind stories that don't end happily ever after."

"I'm glad this one didn't," Megan said boldly.

"Oh? Why?"

"Because then I wouldn't be here alone with you."

"Hmm. You not only know your own mind, you speak it."

Megan returned his stare with equanimity. "Well, this is good bourbon. And you're good company. So the statement stands. Now tell me about Diana, and I'll tell you about some damnfool lawyer who didn't know a good woman when he had one. And at the end of this mutual therapy session we'll know each other a whole lot better than if we'd started off by asking, 'What school did you go to?'"

He grinned. "You really don't waste words, do you?"

"Well, as my father used to say, 'Never waste words or whiskey. You never know when a short fall's coming'. . . .

As you might gather, I loved my father very much. About as energetic as a hippopotamus, but the best reporter this town ever saw. I always had the hunch he was so easygoing because he had life figured out—or, at least, sorted out into what was important, and what wasn't. But if he did, he died before he could tell me. . . . Now, go on with your story."

"Okay," Adam said after a pause. "But you realize, of course, that you won't be able to use any of this."

"That all depends on what I want to use it for, doesn't it?"

"I thought you worked for '20/20'?"

"Oh, did I forget to tell you? I also moonlight for *The National Enquirer.*"

"Are you always this witty?"

Megan drained her drink and shook her head. "No, its just a cover-up. The truth is, I'm nervous as hell. . . . Dr. McKinnon," she ordered, "refill my drink, clear away this couch so you can sit beside me and then prepare yourself for what's known in the trade as an unsolicited editorial statement."

Adam laughed and complied. "Okay," he said, gazing into her eyes—green? blue? aquamarine?—he couldn't quite tell in the artificial light. "And now for that editorial. . . ."

"I don't know this Diana," she began, "or what she's really like. But somehow I get the feeling she's the sort of woman who hurts people too much. I get that feeling from you, the look on your face whenever you mention her, and I don't like people who hurt other people too much. It's an indulgence that I, for one, can't afford."

Her stern expression intrigued Adam. How could she be so intuitive? For the first time he found himself speaking freely about Diana. He launched into a long, unsparing account of their relationship, admitting his share of the blame, blaming himself too much.

"Will you stop!" Megan suddenly protested. "You're being absolutely ridiculous, and I hope you realize it. How could you possibly hope to win with someone like that? She wasn't a woman you loved; she was a patient you foolishly tried to cure. So what if she was good in bed—no, you didn't come right out and say it, but I got that implication. A lot of neurotic women are. It isn't sex with them, it's combat. She wanted you to try to dominate her so that she'd ultimately defeat you and prove her own strength. I could go on and on, but what it boils down to is that you were in a no-win situation and lucky to get out of it."

Adam refilled their glasses. "You know, Miss Donovan, that's quite a skillful analysis. How did you come by such insights?"

"I've been in a few no-win situations myself."

"With that 'damnfool' lawyer?"

"He was the last one. Sad to say, he had predecessors." Suddenly shy, she took a pack of cigarettes from her purse. "Mind if I smoke? I allow myself ten a day, and so far I've only smoked five. I have a feeling, though, the next five are going to go quickly."

"Not at all," Adam said, and dug a glass ashtray out of an open box.

Megan studied the scrolled emblem engraved in its center. "Ah, yes, the old *'Lux et Veritas.'* Brings back memories."

"You're a fellow Yalie? What year?"

"Class of '74."

"My God, I was there then, too! Think of all I missed, holed up in my laboratory. Now I *do* want to know something about you. Skip the 'damnfool' lawyer. Tell me some of the bare essentials."

"All right," Megan reluctantly agreed. "But after practicing this on so many job interviews, I'm going to give you the *Reader's Digest* version. Born right here in Beantown to a newspaper reporter father and a schoolteacher mother who wrote Gothic romances on the side. One brother, now working for the U.S. government in Nairobi, and one sister, married and still living in Boston. Attended public high school thirty pounds overweight, which gave me plenty of time to study and get top grades while others went on dates. Got into Yale as a member of the first class to ever accept women, shed the thirty pounds the summer before I started, and had a wonderful time. Wrote for the *Daily,* got noticed by the dean when I wrote a particularly inflammatory article about the Black Panthers, but otherwise was your average, grade- and diet-conscious student. Graduated with a respectable G.P.A., accepted at Columbia Journalism School, wrote for a bunch of New York papers—wrote well, paid a pittance. So quit that and landed a job as researcher for '20/20.' Worked my way up to producer and a salary that would hurt if I lost it, which means compromising my journalistic standards from time to time, but not my integrity, and here I am—sitting next to you on the couch of your extremely messy apartment, three sheets to the wind and steady as she goes. See? I told you it would be boring."

"That's the *Reader's Digest* version," Adam reminded her. "You wouldn't have a *Playboy* version, would you?"

As he bent to freshen her drink, Megan regarded him with mock suspicion. "You're *obviously* plying me with liquor."

"Plying myself, too."

"True, but after all, I'm the one who's supposed to be pumping you. How could this Diana-what's-her-name be dumb enough to leave a man so intelligent, attractive, and incredibly athletic?"

"I wasn't, then."

"You weren't what?"

"Athletic."

"What do you mean? According to Mel's column, you were too busy doing other things, but there must be more to the story than that."

Adam described his father's death and his twenty-year search for a cure for senile dementia. "Sports didn't seem too important," he concluded, "compared to that."

"So, what made you change your mind?"

"An abortion," he said, and related the scarifying experience of journeying to Weyland with Diana for what was euphemistically termed an "elective termination of pregnancy." The *election* ended in a tie, one for, one against, generating an abundance of anguish and tearful recriminations, but no stay of execution. The abortion not only destroyed their child and the few illusions he still harbored about Diana, but inflicted Adam with a sense of failure his work at the hospital couldn't overcome.

"Didn't it ever occur to you that she *had* to have the abortion?" Megan pointed out. "Maybe she wasn't spiteful or punitive at all; maybe she just realized she didn't have it in her to be a mother and wanted to spare you, the child, herself, the inevitable torment."

"Is that a woman's point of view?"

"Not necessarily. Just an outsider's trying to be objective. Much as it still hurts, Adam, you're lucky she made that decision."

"Am I?" he said testily. "I could have raised the child myself."

"Well, it wasn't your last chance. Wouldn't it be better to raise a child *with* a mother?"

"I don't know. From what I've been reading, not many women want children any more. Do you?"

Megan hesitated. "Frankly, yes. I know many career women who want children, with or without marriage. And you'd be good father material."

"What exactly is that supposed to mean?"

"I guess it means I'm pretty tipsy and my feelings are beginning to show, so let's change the subject. Tell me why you decided to take up professional boxing this late in life."

"That's the one thing I can't tell you."

"Why not?"

"I can't even tell you that."

"Oh, come on," Megan protested. "Let's not start putting up barriers now."

Adam was tempted to tell her about the LBC, but held back. Though she seemed to accept, even warm to, his fallible human side, he was less certain how she would react to his near-infallible physical transformation, especially since it was chemically induced. Moreover, he knew it would be foolish to trust any reporter with his secret at this stage. Too much was at stake. "Oh, just call it insurance," he said evasively. "Insurance that you'll come back to see me again."

"That's really not necessary," she replied. "Not necessary at all."

"I believe you, Megan. I really do," he said, taking her hand. "But it's getting late and—"

She looked at him warily as he faltered and his hand tightened around hers, expecting a pass. "And what?" she asked.

"How did you get here, car or taxi?"

"Car," she answered, feeling relieved and disappointed.

"I'm not kicking you out," he said gently, "I'm just calling the end of round one. Round two starts tomorrow night at eight o'clock, if you're willing? No, wait—I've a better idea. Meet me at Maître Jacques and I'll buy you dinner to keep up your strength. Is it a deal?"

"Ðeal!" Megan said delightedly. "Now help me up, and lead me through this minefield you call a living room."

"Are you sure you're in shape to drive?" Adam asked at the door.

"As good shape as you are to drive me."

"You could always spend the night?"

"No, that would be spending more than I'm ready to. I'm frugal in some ways."

Adam smiled, realizing how much he enjoyed her company; how long it would seem until tomorrow night.

"Good night, Megan," he said softly and watched from his doorstep until she was safely in her car.

19

It was Friday night.

During Adam's childhood, Friday nights meant boxing—at the local arena, on radio, later on television. He thought back to the Gillette-sponsored broadcasts with Bill Stern providing the commentary and Dan Dunphy the blow-by-blow description from ringside. He also recalled the duPont Company's dramas and their catchy sign-off slogan, "Better things for better living through chemistry."

Boxing and chemistry; he had finally combined the two, thought Adam as he sat on the padded training table in his dressing room while Al Lakeman expertly wrapped heavy cloth bandages around his hands to protect his knuckles.

"Hey, Al," he said suddenly, "listen to this. Time: around ten P.M. on a cool April night. Place: Boston Garden. Person: Adam 'Magic' McKinnon. Right?"

Lakeman gave him a peculiar look. "So?"

"So, it means I'm oriented times three: time, place, and person. I'm not hallucinating, confabulating, or otherwise spaced out. I'm actually going to have my first professional fight in a few minutes."

"You a little nervous, Doc?"

Adam winked at Todd Tanner across the room. "A little."

"Well, what do you know—"

"Surprised?"

"Uh huh. Relieved, too. Nice to know you're human, after all. There's a packed house out there. And with all the angles Aaron's worked with TV, the take's growing like Topsy. So all you have to be nervous about is a six-foot-six, two-hundred-and-sixty-pound bruiser named 'Mean Joe' whose snarls to the press have made clear what he plans to do to you."

"I can understand smashing me to a pulp, but there's a rule against tearing me limb from limb, isn't there?"

"Yeah. Only a crowd who hasn't got its money's worth can do that."

"Joey Jakes is pretty pissed at Metcalf for what he said," Mel Waldman remarked. "He called again last night to make sure I print his answer—most of which is unprintable. I kept telling him that Metcalf's crack that he was acting, not boxing, in the three rounds he went with Adam, was just wishful thinking on 'Mean Joe's' part, but Jakes is still pretty steamed up. Says it sounds like he took a dive, and Metcalf better apologize or else."

Adam welcomed the banter between the four men in the room (Moe Malone, guardian of the door, comprising the fourth) since it helped take his mind off the imminent bout and his other problems.

Except for meeting Megan and the pleasure he took in their deepening relationship, the last two weeks had been difficult for him. With the press and television buildup for the Metcalf fight exceeding all expectations—Aaron Robards had even arranged for clips of his videotaped sparring with Jakes to appear on network evening news reports—Adam had been forced into almost monastic confinement. Todd Tanner and Moe Malone were his roommates, and even though Moe was a surprisingly good cook and Todd arranged brief but blissfully relaxing rendezvous with Megan, he was acutely aware of the penalty for his burgeoning fame. But that was merely annoying. A much more alarming problem was regulating his daily dose of LBC. It was now clear that his body was developing a tolerance to the neurotransmitter, necessitating increasing dosages at more frequent intervals to maintain its effectiveness. At first, Adam had taken ten grams every three to four days. Now, to keep his nerve conduction velocity above one hundred twenty meters per second, he needed fifteen grams every other day. Moreover, its effects did not wear off gradually but abruptly, leaving him weak and tired; in short—myasthenic. He was also experiencing sharp pains in his wrists shooting up his forearms, usually at night and sometimes so severe they woke him up. They might be nothing more than wrist sprain from the hours spent pounding a heavy bag. Or they might represent a side effect of the LBC that made him shudder to contemplate—a complication so crippling that it could quickly end his athletic career.

By conscious effort, Adam pushed that unnerving thought from his mind. While Al Lakeman tied on his boxing gloves and Moe Malone massaged his shoulders, he concentrated on Megan. Although he wouldn't let her shoot the TV piece she wanted, he had kept her in Boston by getting her an exclusive interview with Aaron Robards. Initially, Aaron was leery, not wanting to reveal his more devious operations. But Adam and Megan had persuaded him that national publicity was bound to win him more clients as well as make him the envy of his rivals. Against program policy, Megan had even promised Aaron script approval of the correspondent's commentary. She was as eager to stay in Boston as Adam was to have her there.

"Your muscles are awfully tense, Doc," Moe Malone said as he continued to knead him. "They're actually jumping."

"Didn't you hear what he said earlier?" Al gibed. "The nerveless neurologist is nervous."

Even without Moe's reproving look, Al regretted the remark instantly and patted Adam's shoulder. "Don't worry, Doc. You'll do fine against that klutz. I'm pretty relaxed about it myself."

"I bet you are," Adam replied, "I was always relaxed, too, when one of my patients had his skull cracked by a neurosurgeon. Never hurt me a bit."

"Well, nobody's going to crack *your* skull," Al said defensively. "Not Metcalf, anyway. Football players, for Chrissake! What the hell they know about boxing? You ever fight one, Todd?"

Tanner grinned. "Lots. In Golden Gloves. Like chopping down tall trees. Just be sure when they fall, they don't fall on you."

"See?" Al said. "Metcalf's no boxer. He's a boa constrictor who'll try to crush you in the clinches. So just stay clear of them."

Adam nodded, half-listening. He *was* nervous, too nervous, and began to wonder if the supplemental dose of LBC he'd taken at noon was causing it. His muscles were twitching, his wrists aching, and he felt slightly nauseous. "How much time?" he asked Al.

Before Lakeman could send Moe Malone to find out, Mel Waldman returned to the dressing room. The semifinal bout had just ended. The time was now.

"You want to pray or something?" Al asked awkwardly.

Adam stared at him, barely suppressing a laugh. "Are *you* a religious man, Al?"

"I'm no churchgoer, but I believe. How 'bout you?"

"My father was a minister."

"That so?" Lakeman muttered, surprised by the disclosure. Again, he realized how little he knew about this man. "Still alive?"

Adam shook his head. "Died three years ago. Actually, stopped living twenty years earlier when he turned senile."

"Sorry to hear that," said Al softly.

Is God cruel? Adam remembered asking his father that when he was twelve years old and getting no reply. He was tempted to ask Lakeman the same question, but this was hardly the time or place. Besides, he knew the answer. God was neither kinder nor crueler than any other poker-dealer, and Adam had already played his make-or-break hand. "Come on," he said, springing off the table. "Let's go meet 'Mean Joe' Metcalf!"

Flanked by Todd Tanner and Moe Malone to protect him from crazies in the crowd, Adam strode down the corridor to the arena floor. Metcalf had already made his entrance amid a spatter of applause and a loud chorus of boos and catcalls. When Al saw him lumber up the stairs and into the ring, he told Adam to wait. "Stay here a minute or so. The crowd paid to see you, not him. So give them a chance to turn around. Build up a little suspense."

It worked as Al anticipated. The crowd began to shout and clap impatiently, but not until the timekeeper clanged his bell to speed them up did he give Adam the signal to go.

From the back of the arena the ring blazed like a nebula of blinding light, reflecting off the canvas and obscuring the ringside seats in a whitish haze. Momentarily fascinated and a little awed, Adam needed a slight shove from Lakeman to start him moving. The shout: "There he is!" rose and spread from the rear rows to the front. Suddenly, sixteen thousand pairs of eyes were staring at him and the roar was deafening. It subsided slightly as he climbed the steps to the ring apron, scuffed his shoes in the resin box, and ducked through the ropes with an agile bounce. Comments from the more vocal members of the crowd cut through the din:

"Is there a doctor in the house?"

"Hey, Doc, you got guts, but I don't wanna see them!"

"Hey, 'Magic,' take your Geritol tonight?"

"Limber up," said Al Lakeman curtly. He tugged Adam's robe off, revealing his pale torso and black satin trunks. A murmur arose from the spectators. Although he was flat-bellied and well-muscled from weeks of hard training, Adam knew he must look puny when compared with Metcalf's gargantuan physique.

"Don't worry none that he's bigger'n you, honey!" a woman shrilled. "He's just a nigger and they ain't no good!"

Adam glanced at Todd Tanner. "Nice, huh?"

Todd shrugged. "Been so long since I fought anyone but a Negro, I almost forgot about that stuff."

"Ignore the bitch, and start loosening up!" rasped Lakeman and, betraying his own tension, pushed Adam forward. Yet, even as he began his arm-stretching, knee-bending exercises, part of Adam's mind remained enthralled by the fantastical qualities of the scene.

The bell clanged for the fighters to meet in the center of the ring to receive the referee's instructions.

"Metcalf's going to say something to rattle you," Al warned. "Don't answer back."

Al was right. Looking down at Adam contemptuously, "Mean Joe" sneered, "Hey, 'Magic Man,' better pull a disappearing act, if you know what's good for you."

Adam said nothing, turning Metcalf's sneer into a snarl: "Gonna break your bones good you mutha!"

"What'd he say?" asked Al when Adam returned to his corner to wait the opening bell.

"He threatened me!" Adam reported with an air of huffy indignation. "For no reason!"

Todd Tanner guffawed.

"What are you laughing at?" Al demanded.

"Doc, here. He's his old self again."

"Yeah," said Al dubiously. "Just remember to stay out of clinches."

"I will!" Then, with a look of distaste, Adam added, "I don't even like the man."

Shaking his head, Al Lakeman inserted Adam's mouthpiece. "Don't get too cocky, Doc."

Adam nodded. For some unaccountable reason, he had shed his nervousness and felt ebullient, even euphoric. At the risk of constricting Lakeman's coronaries, he suddenly decided to change the fight plan they had worked out, especially the opening. Confident that Metcalf would come out swaggering and snorting at the bell, Adam was supposed to circle defensively, let his opponent miss enough punches to grow arm-weary before trying to score himself. That was the agreed-upon strategy until something—the rising roar of the crowd, the dazzling lights, the knowledge that the fight was on national closed-circuit television and would be re-run the next day on network channels—inflamed Adam and made him reconsider. The bell rang and like a sprinter off the starting blocks, he almost flew across the ring. As predicted, Metcalf flexes his muscles and snorted—once. Before he could exhale again, Adam had bounced three quick jabs off his nose and followed through with a right hook to his eye. That brought the crowd to its feet, screeching in pandemonium. Adam back-pedaled, turned to wink at Lakeman, and waited for Metcalf's reaction. With his vision blurry and blood trickling from his nostrils, Metcalf was about to charge at Adam like a wounded bull when his manager shouted, "No! Box him!"

Metcalf paused, torn between frenzy and caution. He shuffled forward, counting on his bulk and reach to force Adam into a corner where he could close or clinch with him, break his ribs with body punches. When he reached mid-ring, Adam began circling, picking three of his left jabs out of the air before Metcalf exploded in predictable rage and charged. Suddenly, his body seemed to be going one way and his head another as Adam peppered his nose with lightning jabs. Blinded, Metcalf swung wildly with his left, then his right. The right caught Adam on the shoulder and sent him stumbling against the ropes. But Metcalf was in no shape to take advantage. By the time his vision had cleared, Adam was back in the center of the ring, bouncing agilely on his toes.

"What the *hell* you think you're doing?" Lakeman growled at Adam after the round had ended and he was back in his corner.

"Scoring points."

"That so?" Al said sardonically. "How's your shoulder feel?"

"Sore."

"Well, your jaw'll feel even sorer if he lands a lucky punch there. So listen to me, and listen good. Right now, Metcalf's manager is telling him to hit you any place he can, especially on the arms. Hit 'em so hard you can barely lift 'em. That's what he's going to try to do and that's what you've got to avoid. Even with gloves on, that fuckin' brute can probably break your armbone if he hits it square. You want to win this fight, go back to slipping and ducking. Got it?"

Across the ring, Adam could see Metcalf's manager talking furiously in his fighter's ear, probably telling him exactly what Al had predicted. With his left shoulder throbbing, he glanced up at the astute Lakeman and nodded.

Six rounds later, having evaded innumerable punches, ducked dozens of wild swings, and escaped all but one clinch—a stumbling misstep that had left his right kidney and rib case aching—Adam realized he needed to change strategy.

In the earlier rounds, the crowd had loved his moves and maneuvers, chanting "Magic! Magic! Magic!" each time he sidestepped the charging Metcalf and set him stumbling into the ropes. But by now, the action had grown too repetitive and the fickle were switching allegiances, shouting to Metcalf to land one good punch. Conscious of the changing mood, Al Lakeman made a difficult decision. "Listen, Adam," he said between the seventh and eighth rounds, "that ox is pretty arm-weary. He can still put you to sleep with one good punch to the jaw, but I doubt he can hurt you much to the body. The question is, do you think you can put him away?"

"A knockout?" Adam panted.

Al shook his head. "I'm thinking TKO. You already cut him over his right eye—work on it. Open it wider, make it bleed good, and maybe the referee'll stop the fight. It's risky, but the fight with Coleman Jackson won't be worth a million, it'll be worth two or three times that, if you can do it."

"I'll try," Adam said. He rinsed his mouth, spat into a bucket, and stood up.

"You got to do more than just hit him in the eye," Todd Tanner advised as he reinserted Adam's mouthpiece. "You got to hit and rub—rub your glove over the cut before pullin' back." Todd illustrated with his fists. "But be careful, Doc. It leaves you wide open for a left hook."

At the bell, Adam again moved out of his corner like a sprinter. Metcalf was barely off his stool when Adam's jab caught him above the right eye. Metcalf countered with a left hook, but Adam blocked it with his elbow and bounced three more jabs off his target. By the time he backpedaled, it had begun to bleed. Adam circled out of range until he got Metcalf to circle with him, then darted in and out through his defenses to jab and rub. But his opponent grew wise to the tactic. The next time Adam landed the jab, he didn't counter with a left hook to the head but to the body. It hit Adam just below the breastbone, knocking the wind out of him. He clinched, hugging Metcalf as hard as he could to pin his arms down, but unable to match his strength. Breaking Adam's grip, Metcalf drove a stinging punch under his heart before the referee stepped in to separate them.

Every inch of Adam's rib cage hurt now and he circled rapidly trying to get his wind back. But Metcalf was in trouble, too. His cut eye bled profusely; the thumb of his right glove was soaked red from trying to wipe blood away from his field of vision.

Knowing the round was nearly over, and hoping one more assault might open the cut beyond repair, Adam burrowed in, taking a jarring punch on his shoulder and barely ducking one to the head, but jabbing the eye repeatedly. Howling in pain, Metcalf tried to ward him off with a backhanded swing—a flagrant foul. The referee stepped in to warn him of it and the round ended.

"Nice job," Al said to Adam before taking a closer look at him. He was ashen-pale, drenched with sweat, and panting.

"You all right?" Al asked worriedly.

"Hurt like hell," whispered Adam, his breath so shallow he could hardly speak.

Al looked across the ring at the referee and house doctor leaning over Metcalf. "Well, let's hope that was the last round."

Another tense minute passed as the referee told the time-keeper to delay striking the bell. The doctor dabbed at Metcalf's eye with cotton gauze and peered at it with his penlight. Finally, he beckoned the referee and said something.

The sudden scowl on Metcalf's manager's face told Al all he needed to know. "It's over!" he cried, and impulsively hugged

Adam. Todd Tanner and Moe Malone slipped through the ropes to hug him too.

"Easy!" Adam pleaded. "I hurt!"

As the referee signaled for the ring microphone to be lowered, the crowd quieted down, waited for the ref's voice to boom, "Winner by a technical knockout in the eighth round— Adam McKinnon!" and then went wild.

Adam looked around for Megan, who was supposed to be sitting beside Harry Patashnick at ringside, but the wall of spectators surging toward the ring blocked his view.

"Police escort!" Al shouted at the referee. "A whole squad! We don't step out of the ring until we get 'em!"

The referee nodded and bent to the timekeeper, who signaled the police with several clangs of his bell. Meanwhile, Todd Tanner, arms spread and hands balled into fists, protected Adam's rear, Moe Malone and the referee his flanks, and Al Lakeman his front. Sportscasters holding microphones tried to shove their way toward him, but were thwarted by Lakeman who kept shouting, "Later! Let's get him out of here before there's a riot!"

Metcalf, his eye bandaged, waved congratulations at Adam across the crowded ring, and Adam, pinned in tightly, managed to wave back.

Finally, a squad of police entered the ring and lined the stairs leading down from it. Unable to restrain his joy any longer, Todd Tanner began jumping up and down, pounding Al Lakeman's back and shouting, "He did it, Al! He did it!"

"He sure did!" Lakeman shouted back, beaming at Adam now resting on a stool and thinking of Tanner: you'll do it, too.

20

The sensation began to build while Adam was still in the ring, making him reluctant to leave it. It grew as he struggled through the horde of screaming, worshipful fans so that when he reached the dressing room he barely felt earthbound. Maybe it was the massive outpouring of adrenalin, or maybe the LBC was finally affecting his brain, but by the time Adam stepped into the shower he felt as if he had ascended beyond this solar system into another where he, not the sun, stood at the center.

But the omnipotent feeling abated when he stared at the reflection of his battered, all-too-mortal body in the bathroom mirror. Slowly, painfully, he dried himself off and got dressed. Then he sat on the commode for several minutes trying to collect his thoughts before signaling to Moe Malone to unlock the door. His elation had given way to a strange, detached mood. The fight with Metcalf seemed days, not minutes, ago. In the shower, he had struggled with an amorphous thought that would not quite come clear. Whatever it meant, it left him vaguely fearful. Whether the LBC was slowly killing him or letting him live life to the utmost, no longer seemed to matter. Night was coming; he needed help. He needed a guide to help him traverse its timeless passage. He had a premonitory sense that the Metcalf fight had been the last eerie flare of light before nightfall—the night he was suddenly afraid to face alone. Or was it merely his habitual loneliness breaking through? But that was easily remedied. Beyond the plywood door, a throng of people waited to congratulate him, interview him, adore him.

From the questions he could hear shouted at Al Lakeman, it was apparent the newsmen were in a quandary. What does a reporter think, or say, or write, when magic comes true? Against enormous odds, David had slain Goliath, Cassius Clay had defeated Sonny Liston for the heavyweight championship of the world. A slingshot explained the first; natural talent, the other. But how could they explain him?

That was the question they harassed Al Lakeman with in the dressing room. Even though Harry Patashnick and Mel Waldman were screening the mob in the outside corridor and telling the police who to let in, the room was still packed. The privileged visitors looked first for Adam McKinnon and, failing to see him, headed for either Al Lakeman or Aaron Robards. Al was no ingrate; these were old friends or influential members of the press and he was obliged to talk to them. But with his voice growing hoarse and his nerves frayed, he reached his limit. He grabbed Moe Malone by the arm and told him to bring, drag, or bodily carry Aaron Robards to him. When he did, Al huddled with Aaron in a protected corner. "We gotta put a stop to this!" he rasped.

"How?" Robards asked.

"Set up a press conference where they can interview Adam to their heart's content, and then get them the hell out of here."

"When?"

"Monday or Tuesday."

"That's three or four days away. They won't like it. Why not sooner?"

"I'll tell you later."

Robards wanted to argue, but the haggard look on Lakeman's face stopped him. He climbed on top of the training table and made the announcement. As expected, there were howls of protests and pleas for special consideration. But he finally prevailed and the dressing room slowly emptied. With breathing space restored, Al Lakeman lit a cigar, took a single puff, and erupted in a fit of coughing as the smoke irritated his raw throat. Recovering, he scanned the faces in the dressing room and asked, "Where's Lassiter?"

"Had to go back to the hospital," Mel Waldman told him. "Said to bring Adam over there if he needed medical attention."

"Well, let's find out," Lakeman said, and when Adam appeared, asked. "How do you feel?"

"Like I was mauled by a gorilla."

"That's not far from the truth. Metcalf break anything—like a few ribs?"

Adam grimaced. "I feel like I'm breathing fire, but I don't think so."

"Want Lassiter to check you? Take X-rays?"

"Tonight?"

"Up to you . . ."

"Then I'll pass. See how I feel in the morning."

"Great fight, Doc!" Mel Waldman said. "I shudder to think what I'd have done if you lost. Now my reputation as a sports seer is skyhigh."

Adam smiled and turned to Lakeman. "What next?"

"A press conference Monday or Tuesday at one of the hotels. You're going to be asked a lot of tough questions, so think up some good answers."

"A press conference," Adam looked dismayed. "Is that really necessary?"

"It's necessary," Al said flatly. "Now that they know you're for real, not merely a figment of Mel's imagination, there are a lot of questions they'll want answered. Especially—well, I don't have to tell you what they'll pump you hardest on."

Wearily, Adam nodded.

"So," Al continued, "you either explain it convincingly to them or the Boxing Commission. But don't worry—I won't let it drag on too long. I hope to make an announcement that'll send them to the telephones and cut it short."

"What kind of announcement?"

"I'll let you know as soon as it's set. Aaron and I'll be doing a helluva lot of traveling this weekend. A lot of fast-talking, too. But let us worry about that. You worry about what you're going to tell the press. Use plenty of fancy medical terms. The more the better, to confuse them. Shouldn't be too hard—you confuse me enough already."

"I still don't like it," Adam said.

"Neither do I," Al admitted, "which is why I want to get a few signatures on contracts beforehand."

"Feel like celebrating?" Robards asked. "There's a party at Dumphey's."

Adam exchanged looks with Todd Tanner. "No, afraid not."

"Just as well," Al interjected. "They're a rowdy bunch. . . . Get your gear and we'll have the cops take you out of here. I'll call you at your place Sunday night to let you know how we made out."

"Fine," said Adam. Turning, he whispered something to Todd Tanner.

"In one of the most remarkable displays of boxing skill ever seen in these parts," the sports broadcaster began excitedly, *"Adam 'Magic' McKinnon defeated 'Mean Joe' Metcalf tonight by a TKO in the eighth round . . ."*

"Switch to some music, will you?" Adam asked Megan as they drove along the highway toward Gloucester.

"Must I?" she said plaintively. "I want to hear what he says about you. I'm really interested."

"In 'Magic' McKinnon or the man you're with?"

"Aren't they one and the same?"

"Not really."

"Oh?" she mused. "In that case, I'd have to say I'm more impressed by 'Magic.' I just love to watch him box. But—" she added, reaching for his free hand, "I'm much fonder of the man I'm with." She shivered excitedly. "I can hardly believe we're finally going to spend the night together. Frankly, Adam, I was beginning to wonder if you'd ever ask."

"Worry you?"

"Yes, it worried me. Your kisses were passionate enough— quite marvelous, in fact—but when you never went any farther—well, I was afraid I just didn't appeal to you in that way."

"In what way?" he taunted.

"Oh, come on. I know if I take enough time with my hair and face and stick to my diet, I'm attractive. But as for sensual—"

"You're sensual."

"Then, what?"

"Don't you know about boxers in training?"

"Oh, no!" she protested. "You're not going to pull that fairy tale on me. Todd Tanner already told me the facts about that—facts he claimed he got from you. Want an M&M?"

"Hmm," he murmured, "I didn't know Todd was such a talker. How'd you get him to open up?"

"I think he feels sorry for me, knowing how stuck I am on you."

"He knows I feel the same about you."

"Do you?" she asked softly.

Adam squeezed her hand. "I do."

"Then, what?" she repeated. "I *want* to make love to you."

"Look, Megan," he began slowly, "I care about you. Deeply. But that creates more problems than it solves. Please don't forget—I am two people, and it's getting more and more confusing. It's also beginning to scare me."

"What are you trying to say, Adam? What scares you?"

"I was brooding about that in the shower after the fight. What's scary? The dark, mostly—meaning the unknown. You see, Megan, like it or not, that's where I'm headed—into some vast unknown."

"I'm sorry, Adam, but I simply don't know what you're talking about."

"I realize that," he said. "And I'm finally ready to explain it all to you."

"When?"

"As soon as we're in bed together and you're in my arms."

"All right, fade out and segue to the bedroom scene," she said flippantly, trying to conceal the anxiety she felt for him.

Naked, at last, in a motel bed, feeling the electricity of her supple body against his bruised one, Adam kept his promise to explain. Since she already knew about his disastrous liaison with Diana, he glossed over that. Otherwise, he spared her nothing, not even his sexual debacle with Amelia. When he finished, Megan gave him a look of tender concern and said, "Marry me."

"You're crazy!"

"No, merely Irish and fey. I mean it—marry me."

Adam said nothing.

"Oh, come on," she pleaded, "don't keep me in suspense. I've never proposed before."

Adam hugged her tightly, but she broke free and impatiently raised an eyebrow. "Ask me again in a year," he said.

Megan pouted. "I may not want to in a year."

"In that case, you've no business asking me now. Marriage should be forever, remember?"

"Tell you what," she proposed, "I'll ask you again in a year, providing we spend the time practicing."

"Practicing what?"

"Living as man and wife. Oh, I know it didn't work with Diana, but I'm not her. I'm smarter and tougher in ways that count. So how about it, Dr. McKinnon? Want to try me out for a year?"

"Hussy!"

"Worse. A horny hussy—or is that redundant?"

"Have a heart."

"I do. A big one. And it's full of love for you. Give 'Magic' McKinnon the night off. He's earned it. It's you I want. Quiet, considerate you. You know when I first realized I was in love with you? Not just infatuated or curious about how you'd be in bed, but really in love? When I heard how Todd Tanner feels about you; how he adores you."

"Adores?"

"Oh, I know that's not the way a grown man usually feels about another. More father-son stuff. But it applies."

"Sure what you're feeling isn't father-daughter stuff? After all, I'm much older."

"Oh, ancient! But what would you have me do? Go back to dating younger New York men? Spend another seven years nursing their fragile egos? Patch things up with my lawyer friend, who kept dragging me to porno flicks and tried to talk me into group sex? Damn it, Adam, there's a war on! Men and women are skirmishing everywhere and long-term planning is out. So what if you are seventeen years older and if I marry you I'll probably end up a widow. Think of all the great times we'll have ahead. After all, wouldn't you rather be gifted with a bottle of aged Benchmark bourbon than a case of beer?"

"Depends. If I were marooned on a liferaft or in the middle of Death Valley, I might opt for the beer."

Megan sighed exasperatedly. "Thank you, Albert Einstein, for this latest example of Relativity Theory. . . . Look, wise ass, I made you an offer—a rather generous offer, in my opinion. Either accept it, reject it, or . . . or . . ."

"Or what?"

"I've had my first one-night stand. And you've got a woman scorned on your hands."

"Are you threatening me?"

"Of course. Why waste words trying to convince you of my

desirability when I've got the goods on you? Either we live together or I go public with what I know."

"You wouldn't!"

"No, I suppose not. I'm too decent a sort. But are you sure that stuff you're on isn't dangerous?"

"I'm not sure at all. That's the main reason I'm reluctant for us to get too involved."

"Well, I'm willing to risk it if you are."

"Megan, kidding aside, wouldn't you be better off with a younger man?"

"Oh, Jesus!" she groaned. "Even though Metcalf didn't hit you in the head, I just might, if you bring that up again. Now quit your stalling. Are you going to make a semihonest woman of me or not?"

Gently, Adam caressed her shoulder and breast. "All right, move in—if you're sure that's what you want?"

Ignoring his wince, Megan rolled on top of him, smiled lustfully, and said, "*Very, very* sure."

21

Memphis, Tennessee, Coleman Jackson's hometown, was sweltering in the noonday sun when Al Lakeman and Aaron Robards left the airport terminal to find a taxicab.

"Jesus!" Lakeman groaned. "It's like a furnace. Sure hope Bucky Miller's house is air-conditioned."

A cab pulled up and they climbed in. Al gave the driver Miller's home address in the "Beale Street" black section of Memphis and then lit a cigar.

"How long have you known Bucky?" Robards asked.

"Oh, years and years. Got his start as a sparring partner, then assistant trainer, for Jersey Joe Walcott. Been in the fight game ever since. He's a soft-spoken but shrewd-minded guy. Very religious, too. Wouldn't talk business on a Sunday."

"Think you can persuade him to sign?"

"A million-buck guarantee can be very persuasive."

"What if he wants more?"

"It's negotiable."

"What about Coleman?"

"He'll do what Bucky tells him to," Al predicted. "With Savitt playing hide-and-seek fighting those South Africans, nobody's exactly breaking down his door with offers."

"Still, I hear he's a funny guy. Never says two words to the press, and that look in his eyes spooks out a lot of opponents. Might be more of a problem than you think."

Al shrugged. "Maybe, but I doubt it. I thought it through pretty carefully. If it's not money he wants, it's recognition."

"Think Adam can beat him?"

"I wouldn't be here if I didn't."

"What if Jackson thinks so, too? That's not the sort of recognition he wants."

"No, but I still got a pot-sweetener. He'd have to be punchy to turn that down."

"I've got to admit," Robards said, having heard a detailed description of Al Lakeman's psychological double play on the plane ride down, "you're holding some pretty potent cards. And I don't know who can play them better than you can."

Miller and Jackson lived in a large, white-columned house bordering on a meadow at the very edge of the "Beale Street" section. Meeting them at the door, Miller shook hands warmly. He was a tall, big-boned man in his mid-sixties with kinky white hair, large expressive eyes, and a dignified, almost patriarchal demeanor. He wore a white shirt open at the neck and baggy black pants held up by blue suspenders.

"Welcome to Memphis, Mister Al! And you too, Mr. Robards," he said. "Sure nice of you to fly all the way down here to see us, especially the very next day after your boxer's big fight. Must be something mighty important you want to discuss."

"It is, Bucky," Al said, beginning to perspire heavily. "It is."

"Well, come on out to the back porch. Got some big ceiling fans to keep it cooler there. Coleman's running, but he'll be back soon. How about fixing you gentlemen something to drink?"

"What have you got in stock?" Al asked.

"Coleman and I don't drink, but there's gin and bourbon for guests who do. Specialty of the house, though, is iced tea with mint. Very refreshing."

"Sounds good," Al said, and Robards nodded in agreement.

"Well, all right. Follow me on out back, and I'll tell Rosa, our housekeeper, to fix some."

The screened-in back porch ran the width of the house. It was furnished with couches, card tables, easy chairs, and a hammock at one end. Four overhead fans whirred softly, keeping it comfortably cool.

"My hearin' ain't too good," Miller said, "so let's all sit around the table, if that's all right with you gentlemen?"

Al and Robards drew up chairs flanking Miller and made small talk until a Mexican girl brought them the iced tea and a plate of cookies.

"Well," began Al, after slaking his thirst, "I've got a proposition for you."

"I know you have," Miller chuckled. "I know you have. You want my boy to fight your boy. Trouble is, your boy's forty-five years old. It ain't natural, a man turning pro at that age."

"That's true," Al admitted. "I thought the same at first. But he's for real, believe me."

"Oh, I believe you," Miller affirmed. "Tell the truth, I called Metcalf's manager, Lindy Shaw, this mornin' to get his e-valuation."

"What'd he tell you?" Al asked.

"That your McKinnon ain't no hitter, but just about the best boxer he ever saw. Moves faster than any man ought to be able to move."

"Against Metcalf, maybe," Al pointed out. "But Coleman's a lot quicker."

"Even so, they went eight rounds and Shaw says Metcalf only landed four punches. You can't call that natural, can you, Al?"

"No, but this McKinnon's a neurologist, a nerve doctor, and he's developed a training method to speed up his reflexes."

Miller cocked his head at Al. "Mind telling me a little more about this here training method? I don't want you giving away no secrets, but I'd sure like to set my mind at ease on a few points."

"Well, most of it *is* secret—even to me. Involves a lot of electronic gadgetry to measure what's called 'nerve velocity,'" said Al glibly. "I don't even pretend to understand it myself. But you know how those Yogis in India can slow their heartbeat and breathing to practically nothing—well, McKinnon can do the opposite. Speed things up instead of slow 'em down. That's about all I can tell you, Bucky."

Miller stared penetratingly at him. "Now you and me, we known each other a good many years. And you always been straight, Al. But you're not telling me the one thing I got to know: is your man on drugs?"

"No!" Al answered. "I had a doctor friend, name of Lassiter, head of one of Boston's biggest hospitals, check him out. And he's not on stimulants of any kind."

"You swear?"

"I swear what I just told you is the truth. He does take a nutrient supplement of some kind—stuff he says is necessary to keep his nerves from running out of juice."

Miller frowned. "What you mean, a nutrient? I ain't sure I know what that is."

Al looked at Robards as if cuing him in. "It's like a vitamin, or the protein pills weight-lifters pop," Robards explained. "I don't know exactly what it is either, but Dr. Lassiter does, and he says it's a naturally occurring substance and in no way a stimulant."

Miller shook his head dubiously. "I don't know. Gentlemen, I just don't know. Something mighty strange about a forty-five-year-old heavyweight."

"I've given you my word," Al reminded him. "And Aaron here, who'll be promoting the match, is willing to give you something else."

"A million-dollar guarantee," Robards said. "That's *minimum*. If we can pack one of those domed football stadiums, and the TV money comes through, your end of the take may be closer to two."

"Two million dollars!" Miller mused. "My, my, that's certainly a tidy sum. Never had no pay-off like that before. Sounds almost too good to be true."

"First million's guaranteed," Robards reiterated.

"So it is, so it is," Miller muttered, looking preoccupied.

"And let's face facts," Robards continued. "Your fighter's good, maybe too good. Which is why he hasn't had a bout in six months. Savitt certainly wants no part of him, and neither do the other top contenders. You know as well as I a layoff that long isn't good for a boxer."

"Oh, I know," Miller admitted. "Indeed, I do. But Coleman's an obstinate man who suffers the sin of pride. Says if he can't fight Savitt, he don't want nobody else."

"Not even for a million dollars, maybe two?"

"Maybe not even then. I just don't know. Let me tell you a little about Coleman, so you'll understand what I mean. Nature's been good to him; for at least seven generations, his family's been pure-bred black and free. His grandfather was the country's best black wrestler in his day, and his father was on his way to becoming a champion fighter 'fore he got himself killed in a construction accident. Coleman himself was an all-round athlete in high school. Could've had his pick of college scholarships. But he turned 'em all down and instead took training to be a prison guard. Know why?"

Lakeman and Robards shook their heads.

"Well, this part is confidential, but I think it's important you know. He had a goal in mind—a mighty sinful goal; what you'd call an obsession. He wanted to get assigned to the penitentiary where they keep James Earl Ray and beat him to death with his bare hands. Lucky for both of them, he never got the chance. When Ray made his jailbreak a while back, Coleman left his prison post at the other end of the state and almost drove himself wild looking for him. That got him fired from his job and concentrating full-time on boxing."

"Does he hate *all* white men that much?" Robards asked.

"No, he don't. Only James Earl Ray. One of his regular sparring partners is white and he gets along fine with him. Then, of course, Jake Knowles is his trainer and he's white. But he's a mighty prideful man, Coleman is, and he's got his mind set on being world heavyweight champ. Believe me, that means more to him than a million, even two million, in the bank. . . . More tea, gentlemen?"

As he poured, Al Lakeman pondered. Jackson's fanatical streak perturbed him and he wished there were some other opponent for Adam who would be as big a drawing card. But that wouldn't mesh with the rest of his plan, so it had to be Jackson. After a meaningful glance at Robards, Al played his trump card. "Bucky," he began, "what if we could offer Coleman more than a million-dollar guarantee. What if we could more or less promise him a shot at the heavyweight title?"

Hastily putting the tea pitcher down on the table, Miller stared at Al. "How? How you gonna do that? Savitt's people won't even talk to me on the telephone."

"I'm not surprised. Until the public starts clamoring loud enough for a match between Savitt and Coleman, why should they? But what if Savitt was no longer champ? What if somebody else was?"

"Like who?"

"Like Todd Tanner. Take my word for it, Bucky, Tanner has improved enormously. He can whip Savitt right now."

Miller's brow furrowed. "Maybe so, maybe so," he conceded. "But how you gonna match them up?"

"That depends on you."

"Me!" Miller exclaimed. "How?"

"Look, Bucky, if Coleman signs to fight my man, that takes the pressure off Savitt to fight him for a while. And if McKinnon beats Coleman, it takes Savitt off the hook indefinitely."

Miller blinked in confusion. "But if your man *beats* Coleman, how in heaven is that going to get him a shot at the title?"

"Because—and this is strictly between us—McKinnon isn't interested in the title. He only wants to fight Coleman for the money. Win or lose, he quits boxing the next day. You have my solemn word on that."

Miller sighed. "Al, you got my head spinning like a top. How 'bout explaining all that to me *slowly?* Like I was slow-witted?"

"Sure, Bucky," Al said. "Number one, Coleman signs to fight Mckinnon in two to three months. Aaron has the contract drawn up and in his pocket now. Number two, we fly to Houston, tell Savitt's front man about it, and confidently predict McKinnon will win. By that time, they'll have seen the replay of the Metcalf fight on TV and be inclined to believe us. Number three, I make a deal with them: If Savitt signs to fight Todd Tanner now, I promise he won't have to meet McKinnon. Otherwise, he will—the public will demand it—and, if McKinnon can beat Coleman, they know damned well he can beat their man. But that won't happen if they go along with the Tanner match, 'cause for some reason, probably medical, that I'll have to think up between today and tomorrow, I'm going to insist McKinnon retire from the ring. Number four, Tanner beats Savitt, and within six months, no longer, I promise he'll give Coleman a shot at the title."

"My, my," murmured Miller. "With a head for strategy like that, you ought'a be an army general, Al, not a fight manager. That is some campaign plan."

"I admit it's complicated, Mr. Miller," Robards interjected, "but I make complicated deals all the time and I think this one will work."

"You know, Mr. Robards, I do believe you're right."

"Then, the next step is up to you," Al reminded him.

"You mean, convincin' Coleman?"

"That's right."

"How much time I got?"

Al looked at his watch. "Our flight for Houston leaves in four hours."

"Rosa!" Miller called out and, a few moments later, the housekeeper appeared. "Mr. Jackson back from his run yet?"

"*Sí*, Señor Miller." She pointed to the ceiling. "Upstairs, under the water."

"I better go up and have a preliminary sort of talk with him. Might take a while, so get Rosa to fix you some drinks. She knows how. She used to work as a barmaid in Juárez."

Al and Aaron asked for gin and tonics and, once alone, settled back to talk.

"Well," Robards said, "what do you think?"

"I think we've got him. The part about him wanting to kill James Earl Ray bothers me, though."

"A lot of blacks feel that way."

"Yes, but they don't get prison jobs to get at him. Ever see Jackson fight?"

"Yes, he's ferocious."

"You're not kidding! As fearsome as Sonny Liston was and a lot better boxer. I don't like some of the things I've heard about Jake Knowles, either. He was a college football trainer for a while until he got fired for slipping amphetamines to the players. I wouldn't like to be in Adam's shoes if he has to fight some hopped-up fanatic."

"Nor would I," Robards agreed. "Any suggestions?"

"Yeah. Wait until we get their signatures on the contract and I'll have a little talk with Bucky about Knowles."

Robards nodded. "Think things will go as smooth with Savitt's people?"

"Smoother," Al predicted. "Why the hell do you think I insisted on taking the early-morning flight down here? Miller talking to Metcalf's manager on the phone is one thing, him seeing Adam in action on TV another. Savitt's group will not only have seen him, but spent a sleepless night worrying about him. Which leaves us just one major hurdle—how Adam handles himself during that press conference on Tuesday."

22

The McKinnon press conference was a major media pseudo-event: a "hot ticket" in the parlance of the newsgathering profession. Aaron Robards, who was in charge, had made sure of it. Experienced, efficient, glib as an evangelist, though careful to promise no more than he could deliver, Aaron was in his element. Had the telephone been a musical instrument, he would be an acclaimed virtuoso; if the Second Coming of Christ needed an advance person, he would be the logical choice. He had computer printouts of the key people to call, the staff—three of his own and five borrowed from Ron Warner—the extra telephone lines, the hotel accommodations, everything, except enough time. With only twelve hours to do the job, time had to be rationed out by the minute.

After returning from Houston with Al Lakeman late Sunday night, Aaron slept briefly, collected his team, and by eight Monday morning, had begun to contact the sports editors of over two hundred daily newspapers, the sports directors of radio and television networks, and a select group of magazine writers. He spoke to the more influential himself, leaving the rest to his staff, but keeping himself available for any persuasive personal touches. They were seldom necessary.

Virtually every Sunday newspaper in the country had featured
a detailed account of the McKinnon-Metcalf fight in its sports
section, and millions of viewers had watched the replay on
Saturday afternoon television. All Aaron and his staff usually
had to do was give the time and place of the press conference
and make hotel reservations for those requesting them. What
took the most time was dealing with those reporters trying to
get an exclusive slant on the miraculous McKinnon and a jump
on their colleagues. But Aaron had long ago solved that
problem with an ingenious, push-button device on his telephone that generated bursts of static so he could conveniently
curse the telephone company and curtail the conversation.

By four P.M., Aaron and his co-workers had contacted most
of the sports-reporting world east of the Mississippi and were
moving sunward. Finally, at eight P.M., the last West Coast
newspaper had been reached, television crews from the three
major networks were in Boston and at the Sheraton, where the
press conference would be held, and all Aaron had left to do
was answer the scores of messages that had flooded his office
switchboard. At least a dozen, to his surprise, were from
foreign correspondents asking to attend the conference; their
interest piqued his curiosity, but he had no time to speak to any
of them nor ponder its implications.

At two A.M., Aaron returned his last phone call and with his
heart skipping every third or fourth beat from the countless
cups of coffee he had drunk, he took a Valium and lay down to
nap on his office couch. Before leaving, Cindy, his most nubile
secretary, volunteered to stay behind and give him a back rub.
After a moment's temptation, he politely declined her offer in
favor of the Valium. He needed sleep, for which a clear
conscience was conducive, more than sex, especially with an
impressionable twenty-two-year-old who also happened to be
an excellent secretary.

With that potential pitfall behind him, Aaron spent his last
waking moments worrying about whether the four-hundred-
seat banquet room he had chosen would be big enough for the
crowd he expected, and whether Adam McKinnon could cope
with all the questions that would be fired at him without losing
his composure or divulging more about his secret nutrient than
he intended. That was Al Lakeman's biggest concern; Lassiter's, too, who promised to be there but not to rescue Adam if
he got into trouble over the definition of what was a nutrient
and what was a drug.

He was confident that most of the media sports reporters he had called would show up. Their vast, Nielsen-rated, circulation-sustaining public demanded an explanation for the "Magic Man's" magic and they had to come up with one. It didn't matter that most of them knew that what looked to be magic was merely advanced scientific knowledge and technology. It was the illusion that enthralled the magic-craving public. Aaron himself might have enjoyed believing that a modern Merlin had cast an enchantment on Adam McKinnon. But knowing the truth had not diminished his fascination with McKinnon's performance against "Mean Joe" Metcalf, nor did it dim his expectations against Coleman Jackson. On that comforting reflection, Aaron drifted off to sleep.

He was up by seven, having breakfast with the hotel manager by eight, inspecting the fourth-floor conference room and the camera setups by nine, and meeting with Lakeman, Waldman, Warner, and Patashnick in a nearby vacant suite by nine-thirty. "Where's Adam?" he asked.

"He'll be along," Al Lakeman said confidently. "Tanner and Malone will get him here a bit before ten."

"That's cutting it a bit close," Aaron fretted. "Channel Five is carrying the press conference live."

"Relax," Lakeman said. "If they're late, you can entertain the crowd with some sleight-of-hand."

"Are you kidding?" Aaron exclaimed. "I'm so wired I couldn't even hold a quarter in my palm, let alone grab one out of somebody else's."

Al Lakeman smiled. "What's got you so jumpy?"

"I haven't switched to Sanka like you have," Aaron cracked. "Aw, what the hell—long as you're not worried over what McKinnon tells the press, why should I be? Have you talked to him about it?"

"Tried. But what with Tanner jumping up and down over his title fight and Adam cooing over his new girlfriend, their place was a madhouse Sunday night. I wasted more breath trying to warn him about a few things yesterday at the gym. Gave me that old doctor line: 'Don't worry!' So I'm not worrying. I'm not digesting my breakfast, either. Got gas bottled up at both ends, so don't seat me near a live mike. How's the house?"

"Packed. The security guards have let in almost three hundred so far, including—get this—two Russian correspondents from Tass."

"Russians, huh?" remarked Mel Waldman. "Well, it figures . . ."

Lakeman gave him a quizzical look. "How so?"

"The Olympics, Al. They're out for blood after the 'no-show' we pulled the last time. A team of American athletes with Adam's super-quick reflexes could turn the games into a rout. Which would serve the Russkies right, after all the drugs they use. Practically their whole team takes something called pangymic acid. Supposed to be a vitamin and worthless, but who knows?"

"Humph," Al snorted. "You got to be a druggist to coach sports these days. Well, I'm glad the bastards are here. Let 'em sweat!"

Robards looked at his watch. "Speaking of sweating, it's five minutes to ten."

"Mel," Al Lakeman said, "take a look down the corridor towards the service elevator to see if they're coming, will you please?"

Mel rose, stretched, and started out of the room. But before he reached the door, it opened and filled with Todd Tanner's bulk.

"Everything's cool," said Tanner and stepped aside to let Adam and Moe Malone enter. Adam was wearing the same color-coordinated turtleneck sweater, cashmere sports coat, and gabardine slacks he wore his first night at the Front Street Gym. Lakeman marveled at the recollection. Could only two months have passed since then? It seemed more like two years.

"Nervous?" Robards asked Adam.

He gestured equivocally. "Little trouble sleeping."

"Try sleeping alone," gibed Lakeman, again registering his disapproval of Megan moving in with him.

Adam rolled his eyes upward. "Al, it's not a mortal sin anymore."

"Yeah, says who?"

"The good book . . . *The Ann Landers Encyclopedia.* Besides, we're engaged."

"Mazeltov!" Al said grudgingly.

"Will you two stop!" pleaded Robards, and eyed Adam earnestly. "Some final advice: be sure you understand the question before you try to answer it. If not, make them repeat it, and if you don't like it, tell them—politely—to shove it."

Adam nodded. "Don't worry, Aaron. I've handled press conferences before."

"There's that good, old 'Don't worry' again," Al jeered. "So you've handled press conferences, have you? To medical reporters—right?"

"Right. So?"

"So they were pussycats compared to these guys. They're all would-be Howard Cosells who've learned *chutzpah* pays from him. Don't think they haven't done their homework, either. They've talked to your old Newton high school teachers and Yale boxing coach and anybody else who might be able to give them the tiniest bit of dirt on you. So don't try to snow them."

"Thanks for the tip, Al," Adam said dryly. "Now if you'll excuse me, I'd like to use the john."

"Moe's in there," Tanner said.

"Well, get him out!" Robards shouted. "It's ten o'clock, for Chrissake!"

Tanner hesitated. "Moe don't like to be rushed."

"Never mind," said Adam hastily before a flushed-faced Robards erupted. "I didn't get too much sleep last night and a little bladder pain might help keep me awake." He took a moment to straighten his turtleneck collar, and to Aaron Robards's relief, said, "Let's go."

Robards led them through a side door onto the banquet hall stage. There was a lectern at its far left and a table with four platform microphones on it in the center. The table was for Adam, Lakeman, Tanner, and Robards, but a flatulent Al Lakeman preferred to lean against the side wall and took Tanner with him.

Robards put Adam in the end chair and moved to the lectern. The noisy crowd grew silent when he tapped the microphone. "Ladies and gentlemen, welcome!" he began. "I'm Aaron Robards and my job's to introduce Dr. Adam McKinnon." He paused for the ripple of applause. "Dr. McKinnon's here this morning to answer your questions—provided they're brief, not too outrageous, and of general interest. Please refrain from asking him what's good for a bad back, tennis elbow, hangover, or any other of your professional infirmities. Dr. McKinnon has temporarily traded his stethoscope for a pair of boxing gloves. Also, since this press conference is being televised live, please preface your question by giving your name and media affiliation—okay?"

Aaron paused a beat for the perfunctory nods and then concluded by saying, "Now, since you've all come to hear Dr.

McKinnon, not me, I'll turn the mike over to him. . . .
Ladies and gentlemen, I give you the 'Magic Man' of boxing,
undefeated in—let's see—oh, yes, exactly one professional
fight, Dr. Adam McKinnon!"

Adam rose, amid applause, and replaced Robards at the
lectern. He scanned the crowd until he spotted Megan at the far
right of the front row and, diagonally across the room, in the
end seat nearest the rear exit, Dan Lassiter, obviously positioned for a fast getaway. Adam smiled at Megan and, on
perverse impulse, waved to Lassiter to draw attention to him.
Then he turned to face his audience, building suspense by
remaining silent for several seconds. Finally, he said, "All
right, to get right to the pay-off question, you want to know
how I did it—right?"

"Right!" a chorus of voices shouted.

"Damn!" whispered Lakeman to Todd Tanner. "He
shouldn't stir them up like that."

"Aw, Doc can handle them," Tanner ventured. "Least, he's
relaxed."

"Yeah," Lakeman said sourly. "Relaxed, short on sleep,
and in love. I been meaning to talk to you about that."

"Me!" Tanner protested. "Why me? I had nothing to do
with it."

"I ain't so sure. Especially after the dainty way you two
been sparring lately. Those powder-puff punches you been
throwin' at each other. . . . Now, hush up. I want to hear
him, not you!"

Tanner sighed patiently. He was too grateful to Lakeman for
his upcoming title bout to take offense at anything he said.

Adam pointed at a middle-aged man with his arm up in the
front row. The man rose and approached the nearest microphone. "Carr, *New York Times*," he said. "Okay, Doctor,
since you brought it up, how did you do it? Specifically, how
did a man your age and with your background develop the skill
to TKO a giant like 'Mean Joe' Metcalf? And I do mean
specifically."

"I'm sure you do, Mr. Carr," Adam replied. "And I'd like
to answer you with specifics. But—" he gestured apologetically—"if I did, then you could do it, too."

"Is it *that* easy?" Carr asked in amazement.

"No." Adam corrected himself. "I spoke too glibly. It's not
easy at all. It takes a great deal of rigorous training. And the
willingness to absorb a lot of stiff physical punishment, as one

look at my badly bruised ribcage will attest to. But it's not impossible for most reasonably fit men to learn. It takes a mastery of certain carefully monitored exercises, a strict diet, and special nutritional supplements. That's all I'm prepared to say about it right now."

The audience murmured its discontent and Carr put it into words for them. "That's not saying very much, Doctor. If you aren't willing to give us more to go on than that, you're just wasting our time."

Adam met his challenging stare without blinking. "I understand your feelings, Mr. Carr, and I'd like you to try to understand mine. That way, maybe we can compromise. After all, if I were a nuclear physicist, you might ask me to describe the basic principles behind the neutron bomb, but you wouldn't ask, or expect me to tell you, how to build one."

"Is there a parallel?"

Adam looked confused. "What do you mean?"

"I mean, you've obviously made a major medical discovery: something that makes you twice or three times as quick as the average man. If you can endow others with the same agility— as you claim—it'll hit the sports world like an atomic bomb! Instead of amateur and professional athletes, we'll be dividing them into McKinnon-method and natural ones. That'd cause quite a shake-up, wouldn't you agree?"

Adam shrugged. "To some extent. But I think professional sports can survive it, just as the game of football survived the legalization of the forward pass and basketball the slam-dunk. It might take a period of adjustment, but it'll get done."

"But is that fair to the athletes who make their living at sports now?" the reporter standing next to Carr blurted into the microphone without first identifying himself. "The 'Mean Joe' Metcalfs, or whomever your next ring opponent will be?"

"Whether it's fair or not, I can't say. Are advances in any profession fair to those whose skills they make obsolete? It depends on your particular point of view. Look at it another way—why shouldn't a forty-five-year-old athlete get a crack at the million-dollar salaries now given a lot of twenty-one-year-olds?"

The implications of Adam's statement sent a stir through the audience. Ignoring the hand-wavings to either side of him, the unidentified reporter asked, "Is that a distinct possibility?"

"A possibility—yes. But hardly a probability at this time. My method won't be generally applicable until I've managed to iron out a few important wrinkles in it. So all those millionaire athletes who might be watching can breathe easy for a while.''

Reluctantly, the reporter sat down and Adam recognized a bushy-browed man in thick, horned-rimmed glasses in a middle row.

"Joe Haliday, *Detroit Free Press,*" he said. "How long did it take you to develop your training method, Dr. McKinnon?"

"I've been working on it intermittently for the last twenty years. As I indicated earlier, it's not quite perfected yet, but enough so that I decided to give it a try.''

"A very impressive try," Haliday added, "as I'm sure 'Mean Joe' Metcalf would agree. But why now? Any particular reason?"

Adam nodded. "A very basic one. I needed the money."

Some of the audience laughed aloud; others snickered. "Funny," Haliday said, looking dubious. "I thought doctors made plenty of money.''

"Uh huh. Some do. But the majority, including myself, make about half as much as major league baseball players— averaging between seventy and eighty thousand a year. It wasn't enough for my purpose."

"And what might that be?"

"Medical research. I don't want to make myself out another Albert Schweitzer, but I was working on a promising new treatment for senile dementia—senility itself—when my government grant ran out. Since they wouldn't renew it, I decided to try to earn the funds I needed to continue, myself."

Haliday's face furrowed. "Do you mean to say that, because some government agency refused to renew your research grant, you turned to professional boxing?"

"That's exactly what I *am* saying, Mr. Haliday."

"But weren't there other sources of funds available to you? Private foundations and so forth?"

"Yes. But they're iffy, and I was in a hurry. I still am. I'm giving myself a year to make all the money I can at professional sports. After that, it's back to medicine and research."

Haliday shook his head in wonderment. "Another Albert Schweitzer or not, you're sure putting your brains and guts on the line. For the record, what government agency turned you down and why?"

Adam hesitated. Then he shrugged. "The National Institute

for Nervous and Mental Diseases. As to why, that's for them, not me, to say."

"Why'd you pick boxing?"

"The biggest and fastest payoff. After all, Muhammad Ali must've made seventy, eighty million dollars from his bouts. A mere million would suit me fine."

"Come on, Joe. Sit down!" The thin-featured, thirtyish-looking woman next to Haliday said it loud enough to be picked up by the microphone. "Give somebody else a turn."

Adam grinned. "How about it, Joe? Feel like taking the hint?"

Haliday flushed. "Okay, but you might not like what's coming, Doctor."

The woman glared at him before she spoke. "Faith Falconer, the *Springfield Republican*," she said crisply. "You did something extraordinary last Friday night, Dr. McKinnon, and provocative as your remarks about medical research might be, they're quite beside the point. I got out of bed this morning and paid the toll on the Mass. Pike for one thing and one thing only: I want to know how you did it."

The bluntless of her question drew a round of applause. But before Adam could answer, she preempted him. "Okay, okay, you've already said that you're not going to tell us the nuts and bolts of your training method and I accept that. You also said, or at least hinted, you'd be willing to describe the general principles behind it. So, instead of beating around the bush, how about letting us have them?"

"The bitch!" Al Lakeman growled to Todd Tanner. "I'd like to let her have something else."

Straight-faced, Adam asked, "Would you get to the point of your question, Miss Falconer."

The audience tittered as Faith Falconer's jaw went slack. "Would I what?" she almost shrieked.

Adam gestured placatingly. "Just kidding. Or, to put it another way, I thought you'd never ask. I only wish I had a blackboard and piece of chalk available. But Aaron Robards has nixed that request. Afraid I might get too pedantic. So you'll just have to bear with me while I try to make the connection between my being a neurologist and a boxer."

"That would be most appreciated, Dr. McKinnon." Unable to resist, Falconer turned to stare down her detractors.

"All right," Adam said. "First of all, let's play with a few facts. The human brain contains approximately one hundred billion neurons, or nerve fibers. Each neuron connects with ten to twenty thousand others through electrochemical switches called synapses, making a thousand trillion interactions. In other words, it's *one hell of a computer*. But there are at least two major differences between electronic computers and the human brain. Firstly, no computer yet built is capable of self-programming or changing its programming by rewiring itself as the human brain can do. Secondly, in a computer information can be processed serially at a very rapid rate; in the brain the rate is much slower, but the information can be handled on millions of separate channels in parallel. This represents both an advantage and a disadvantage. On the plus side, it allows us to recognize patterns in ways no contemporary computer can match. On the minus side, with so many neurons interacting to a given stimulus, the signals can get scrambled, activating both excitatory and inhibitory neurons simultaneously and making our muscular response slower and clumsier than we might wish."

Adam paused to clear his throat. "How can we overcome this handicap? Channel our nerve impulses more tightly to improve the speed and precision of our response? Practice is one way. The more we practice a given movement, the more we reinforce the memory circuits controlling that movement and the more automatic it becomes. But practice has its limitations, since it cannot, of itself, turn on the switches to the muscles we want to use and shut off the switches to the ones we don't. To accomplish that takes more of a conscious effort—one whose progress can be measured electronically and so improved on. What I'm talking about can be loosely—very loosely—compared to biofeedback training in which the subject wills his brain to put out more alpha waves by watching their production on an oscilloscope screen. Only, in my training method, it's not alpha waves that are monitored but nerve conduction velocity: the speed in meters per second in which a spinal cord impulse can traverse a peripheral nerve to move a muscle. Do you follow me so far, Miss Falconer?"

"Pretty well. But please remember we're sports, not science, reporters, Dr. McKinnon, so keep it simple."

Adam nodded. "Do my best. Now a few more facts to tie things together. Different type nerves in our brain and body fire at different rates. The larger A-type fibers, which are insulated by what's called a myelin sheath to keep its electrical charge from dissipating, can carry approximately two thousand impulses per second. In contrast, the slower, uninsulated C-type fibers can carry only a few impulses per second. So the speed in which a brain signal triggers a given response is governed largely by two factors: the type of nerve fiber that transmits it and the electrochemical efficiency with which it can cross the synaptic junction that connects one neuron to another and the terminal branch to the muscle bundle, which then contracts or relaxes. Now this synaptic delay usually takes around half a millisecond, or one two-thousandths of a second. But it's variable and can be altered to some degree. In other words, if you can decrease this delay, you can react faster to a given stimulus, such as getting out of the way of a punch. Now perhaps you'll perk up your ears when I tell you this is where the nutrient supplements I take fit in. The synaptic junction consists of essentially three parts: the presynaptic membrane, which contains numerous vesicles, or packets, of a nerve transmitter substance called acetylcholine; the synaptic cleft, which is the spacial gap between two neurons; and the postsynaptic membrane, which contains specific receptor sites for the acetylcholine molecules that bridge the gap and fire the next nerve in line. These acetylcholine molecules shoot across the synaptic space at an incredible rate of speed—something on the order of one hundred microseconds per packet. Thus, the actual delay is infinitesimally short. However, what's important to keep in mind is that these synaptic junctions fatigue more easily than the nerve fibers themselves and so represent a bottleneck of sorts. And since the speed of muscle contraction depends on the ability of acetylcholine to excite this connecting chain of neurons, it can slow our reaction time. Furthermore, this chemical transmission involves five or more separate and distinct stages, beginning with the synthesis of the acetylcholine molecules at the nerve endings."

Again, Adam paused, wishing he had a blackboard handy to illustrate what he was saying. He would have insisted on one if his purpose had been to enlighten, not confuse, his audience. "Now, some of these rate-limiting steps can be manipulated and some cannot. For example, the calcium ion is essential for the acetylcholine molecules to get through the presynaptic membrane, so a shortage of calcium can delay their passage and an abundance can perhaps speed it up. Certain other protein-building substances called amino acids, such as glutamate and aspartate, can, in themselves, trigger the postsynaptic membrane to fire and thus potentiate the action of acetylcholine. Other amino acids, such as glycine, and the muscle-paralyzing poison, curare, can inhibit its action and so slow or stop the propagation of the nerve impulse. . . ."

Faith Falconer pursed her lips in frustration as she desperately tried to follow Adam's reasoning. She scribbled furiously in her notebook, but each chemical name that rolled off his tongue became another stumbling block slowing her down. In contrast, Al Lakeman who had not understood a single word of Adam's for the last five minutes, smiled contentedly.

"So part—a small part—of the nutrient supplements I take," Adam continued, "consists of calcium, glutamic acid, and aspartic acid. Its major ingredient, however, shall remain nameless for the present—though I assure you it is a naturally occurring, not a manufactured, substance. . . . Are you still with me, Miss Falconer?"

"Barely, Dr. McKinnon. I'm counting on your promise to tie things up."

"All right. Nerve conduction velocity measurements normally range between forty and seventy meters per second. I've managed to raise mine from sixty to one hundred thirty meters per second—making me twice as quick as I was before. How? By three aids. First, by learning to better channel and increase the speed of my neuromuscular responses by monitoring them on a machine called an electromyogram which measures nerve conduction velocity. Second, by minimizing the delay, or lag time, of my nerve impulses at synaptic junctions through special nutrient supplements. Third, by maintaining the tone of my resting muscles through techniques developed by Dr. James Mather at Stanford and familiar to most kinesthesiologists. Those are my methods—and their basic principles have been known for a long time. In fact, many years ago, a colleague of mine ran electromyograms on the old Brooklyn Dodgers baseball team and found one of its players, Duke Snider, had a nerve conduction velocity measurement twenty percent faster than any of his teammates. Snider also happened to be their best hitter at the time—which is understandable since he could wait twenty percent longer than anybody else before deciding whether or not to swing at a pitch. So you see, Miss Falconer, the correlation between what I'm measuring and what I can do is pretty close."

"Thank you, Dr. McKinnon," Faith Falconer sighed. "All I can say in reply is that sports ain't never going to be the same."

"Dr. McKinnon! Dr. McKinnon!" The insistent voice rising

above the ensuing din came from a slight, bow-tied man in the middle of a rear row. Adam called on him next and waited while he struggled through a tangle of legs to reach the aisle microphone. "Dr. McKinnon," he repeated in breathless relief. "My name is Estebrook, and I am a science reporter for the *Baltimore Sun*. Am I correct in assuming that most of your research and experimental treatment of senile dementia involved the use of choline supplements?"

Adam hesitated, regarding the well-informed questioner warily. "Initially, it did. But I abandoned that approach a few years ago when it became apparent it didn't work too well, especially in more advanced cases, and went on to try something new."

"But you have published several scientific papers on choline metabolism in recent years and remain a leading expert on that subject. In fact, I remember reading that you are to chair the section on choline metabolism at the Second International Symposium on Neurotransmitter Metabolism to be held in Sweden this summer."

"I *was* going to chair it. I've subsequently declined, since I've other plans for the summer. Exactly what those plans are will be announced shortly by my fight manager, Al Lakeman."

"But Dr. McKinnon," Estebrook persisted, "since, eh, since you *are* an acknowledged authority on acetylcholine and since that is the substance transmitting electrical impulses from one nerve to another, it strikes me that the two, your expert knowledge and your amazing transformation into a super-quick athlete, must be related somehow."

"A neat deduction, Mr. Estebrook," Adam acknowledged. "Would you like to carry that line of reasoning a step further?"

Estebrook's bow-tie rose and fell in unison with his glottis. "I'm not sure I can."

"Too bad," Adam said curtly and recognized a portly man in a black suit and brightly colored tartan plaid vest in the second row.

"McPherson, *Miami Herald*," he said. "You've put on a pretty good show today, Dr. McKinnon. You've got medical terms tap dancing on my brain like a chorus line of hoofers. But I've a cynical streak, and one or two things you said bother me."

"Then speak your mind, McPherson," Adam said, mimicking his brogue. "One Scot to another."

"Thank you, Dr. McKinnon. Think I will. You did mention,

didn't you, that you plan to try your hand at other sports besides boxing?''

Adam nodded. "Several. Tournament Ping-Pong, handball, racquetball, baseball, hockey—sports where a winning performance depends more on quickness of movement than speed or stamina.''

"That's what I figured. But to get to what's nagging at my mind. You said you needed a million bucks to continue your research—right? Well, you're bound to make two or three times that on your next fight alone. And many millions more on the other sports you mentioned. Is *all* this loot going into medical research?''

"The bulk of it certainly is. I don't preclude paying myself a handsome salary from it, though.''

"Figured that, too. Which makes it not quite so altruistic as you've made it sound. In fact, it strikes me as a bit of a hustle—a hustle at the expense of a lot of hard-working professional athletes.''

"If you're trying to portray me as more of a hustler than a do-gooder, McPherson, I'll tend to agree. But as one of the Black Panthers—Huey Newton, I believe—once said, 'Even doing good is a bit of a hustle.' ''

"Don't you give a damn what happens to professional sports?'' McPherson blurted. "It may not be the most important thing in your life, Dr. McKinnon, but as an ex-player and coach, it is in mine!''

"We all have our priorities, Mr. McPherson,'' Adam answered coolly. "I'm more worried about the millions of Americans who suffer severe memory impairment and are locked up and left to die in nursing homes each year than about the thousand or so otherwise healthy professional athletes who might lose their paychecks. Obviously, you feel differently.''

"Damned right I do!'' rasped McPherson. "And I'm still not ready to buy all that medical mumbo jumbo you've been spouting. If you're really on the up-and-up about your method and motives, then more power to you. But if you're not—if you're not—'' he said threateningly, "we'll find out and make sure the public does, too!''

Al Lakeman's mouth twisted into a tight scowl. "What the hell's that old coot griping about?'' he said to Tanner. "He's got gall accusing Adam of trying to ruin professional sports. He'd have to get in line behind the million-dollar bonus babies and

free agents to do that. Well, I've heard enough of this shit; I'm
going to put a stop to it right now!''

As Adam was about to recognize another questioner, he saw
Al Lakeman climb on to the stage, stride over to Aaron
Robards, and whisper in his ear. Aaron rose and came to the
lectern. "Ladies and gentlemen," he said, "it's now almost
eleven and for those of you who have noon deadlines to meet,
Al Lakeman has an important announcement—one I'm sure
neither you nor your newspapers would want to miss. Al—"
he beckoned—"come here."

"Good job, Doc," Al mumbled to Adam as he passed him.
Stepping to the lectern, he gripped its sides, cleared his throat,
and said sarcastically, "Friends, this is supposed to be a press
conference, not a wake for professional boxing. Truth is, the
old sport's healthier than it's been in years—and I've got the
proof to back me up. Over the weekend, Aaron and me flew to
Memphis and Houston and did a little negotiating. I think
you'll find the results newsworthy. First of all, we've signed
Coleman Jackson to fight 'Magic' McKinnon on the tenth of
July at either the Pontiac Silverdome or Caesars Palace in Las
Vegas—depending on who makes the best offer. Aaron's the
promoter, not me, and I don't go in much for hype. But
McKinnon versus Jackson—how's that for a match-up!''

The crowd murmured excitedly and a few reporters broke
for the exits.

"Hey, hold on!" Al shouted at them. "There's more. I told
you we also went to Houston, and we made out pretty well
there, too. On August twelfth, at a site yet to be determined,
Len Savitt will defend his heavyweight crown against Todd
Tanner. And that's going to be another hell of a fight. So let's
stop all this pissin' and moanin' about boxing, or any other
professional sports, being on the ropes. If you ask me, Adam
McKinnon's given boxing the biggest shot in the arm since a
loud-mouthed kid named Cassius Clay taught us a few things
about fight-promoting. Now, before you all stampede out of
here, I got one last thing to say. Aaron's a real pro who's got not
only McKinnon's and Tanner's best interests at heart, but
yours, too. He's also got an 'in' with the management of this
hotel and the telephone company. See those sliding panels in
the back of the room? Well, behind them, he's got three
portable switchboards and fifty telephones ready for you to
use. And, for those of you who might want to gab with Aaron
and me over a few belts, we'll be at Dumphey's Bar on Front

Street after one o'clock this afternoon. That's all I got to say, so go make your phone calls."

"Whew!" Al said to Aaron. "Glad that's over. Let's go back to the suite and rest up for a couple of hours."

"In a minute, Al. I want to talk to Pete Axthelm. He thinks he can get Adam's picture on the cover of *Newsweek*."

"Better than *Playboy*," Al remarked wryly and beckoned to Todd Tanner. "Grab Moe, and the two of you take Doc and his girl back to the suite. Tell Moe to stand outside the door and keep everybody out—and I do mean *everybody*—except the inner circle. Got it?"

"Got it!" Todd said smartly.

"I suppose you won't let me order you around like that once you're heavyweight champ."

Todd grinned and shrugged. "I will on the sly. Long as nobody else is around. . . . Anything else you want done?"

"Yeah. If that bastard, McPherson, shows up at Dumphey's, have Moe slip him a Mickey."

23

The press conference lasted fifty minutes. At its conclusion, Adam felt the same dizzying sense of relief that he had after the Metcalf fight. Though spared physical punishment, the mental tightrope he had walked so strained his nervous system that it now rebelled in screaming protest. His temples pounded, his eyes burned, and a gush of gastric juice seemed to be dissolving away his stomach lining.

Back in the hotel suite, he took a swig from the cream pitcher on the coffee table and mixed himself a weak Bloody Mary at the bar. "Cheers," he said to Moe Malone, standing by the door.

"Cheers! You did good, Doc."

"Think so?"

"You bet. James Michael Curley, rest his soul, couldn't have handled them newshounds any better. And he was the master! Hell, if Curley had ordered the Watergate break-in, he would've weaseled out of it by claiming it was the Dems, not him, that bugged the Oval Office and he was just getting even."

Adam chuckled. "Might've worked, you know," he said and wandered over to the couch. He sat down, sipping his drink and trying to quell his inner trembling, while waiting for the others, especially Megan, to appear.

Megan, he mused; she was the unforeseen element in his audacious scheme—not a fly in the ointment but a pearl in the oyster. How could he single-mindedly pursue his plan to conquer the professional sports world when his feelings for her kept sidetracking him? With her, he temporarily had it all; love, mission, money, fame. Without her, he was like a comet blazing across the media firmament on its way to fiery disintegration. He was a bust in bed and yet she seemed to love him all the more for it. Sex was supposed to be, "the most fun you can have without laughing," but their lovemaking refuted that supposition. With Megan's delightfully dry sense of humor, her assurance that she preferred nibbling to gorging to satisfy all her biological appetites, Adam had never laughed more during or after sex. Especially last night. Finally, at two A.M., he had given up trying to mount her, to maintain his erection long enough to satisfy her, not because she was complaining but because his bruised ribs hurt too much from laughing.

It was unfair, but he could not help comparing Megan and Diana in bed. Not once in the countless times he made love to Diana had he failed to satisfy her; he had not dared. Sex was a major weapon in her arsenal of ego-defenses. Going to bed with Diana was like climbing into the ring: a challenge, a contest of wills, a strange animalistic mix of attraction and aggression, true sexual combat. Their lovemaking was uninhibited, occasionally ecstatic, but the union that resulted was purely physical, cash on delivery from a checking account that accrued no interest. Diana never fell asleep pressed against him as Megan usually did; she did not like being touched in her sleep.

As he had hoped, Megan, escorted by Todd Tanner, was the first to reach the suite and Adam pulled her down beside him.

"Hey, Moe," he said, when Tanner left to look for Al Lakeman, "turn your back so we can neck."

Malone grinned. "Why stop there when there's a bedroom you can use?"

"Even better," Megan said, giving Adam a mock leer.

"I couldn't."

"Afraid for my reputation?"

"Afraid for Moe when he tells Lakeman where we are. It's not pleasant watching a man have a stroke."

Malone swung around at a knock on the door. "Relax," he said after looking through the peephole. "It's Dan Lassiter, not *Father* Al. . . . C'mon in, Doc."

"Well," said Lassiter, lifting an eyebrow as he saw Adam and Megan holding hands on the couch. "You two look cozy. . . . How're your ribs?"

"They hurt," Adam reported.

"As bad as your conscience?"

Adam looked momentarily baffled. "Oh, you mean the press conference?"

"Is *that* what it was? All I heard was a pitch by a snake oil salesman trying to con the local yokels into believing that the stuff he'd concocted was Nature's Own Remedy."

Adam frowned. "Was that your only reaction?"

"Noo," Lassiter drawled. "The other was to rush over to the D.A.'s office and see if he'd grant me immunity if I spill what I know about this scam now."

"I'll sue!"

"Over what?"

"Violating doctor-patient confidentiality. I'm still your patient, you know?"

Lassiter made a wry face. "Yeah, technically I suppose you are. At least, for the time being. After Coleman Jackson gets through unhinging your skeleton, you'll need a chiropractor to put you back together."

"How's Kris, Dan?" Megan said to change the subject. The four of them had gone out to dinner a week before and gotten along splendidly.

"Fine. She's in Chicago at a medical meeting. I'm flying out to join her this evening."

"How long will you be gone?" asked Adam, a note of concern in his voice.

Lassiter looked at him curiously. "Probably the rest of the week. Why?"

"I was planning to drop by to see you. . . ."

"Anything serious?"

"No . . . not yet," Adam answered enigmatically.

Lassiter glanced at his watch. "I can fit you in around two this afternoon."

After a moment's hesitation, Adam said, "It can wait."

Lassiter shrugged. "Suit yourself. I'll be at the Ritz-Carlton if you want to reach me. In the meanwhile, why don't you get a chest X-ray for rib detail just to be on the safe side? You still remember how to read a chest X-ray, don't you?"

Adam ignored the dig. "One more favor: write me a script for a hundred codeine tablets, will you? I'll pick it up from your secretary when I get the X-ray."

"A hundred!" Lassiter exclaimed. "You hurt *that* much? Look, maybe you ought to come by at two, so I can check you and the X-ray out?"

Adam glanced at Megan's intently watchful gaze and then at Lassiter, who suddenly seemed to comprehend his reluctance to reveal why he needed the painkillers in her presence. "Let's compromise," suggested Adam. "C'mon in the bedroom and I'll strip down so you can palpate my ribs. If you don't feel any jagged edges, we'll let it go until next week—okay?"

"Okay," said Lassiter, knowing such an examination was next to worthless but that it would give them privacy. "All right, let's hear it," he prompted when they were alone in the bedroom.

"It's not the ribs, Dan. Sure, they hurt—plenty—but not as much as my hands, especially the left one. It throbs so bad that I can hardly sleep at night."

"Your hands?" repeated Lassiter, puzzled. "Think you might've cracked some metacarpals?"

"I wish I had."

"Meaning what?"

"Meaning, that I'd much rather deal with that than what I'm pretty sure I *am* dealing with."

"Quit being so damned mysterious," Lassiter snapped. "Tell me what you're talking about."

"If it were a fracture, even one compressing my median nerve, the pain wouldn't be bilateral, it wouldn't spread up my arm like it does, and it wouldn't scare the hell out of me."

"I agree. So what do you think it is?"

"The carpal tunnel syndrome," said Adam, referring to the condition where the main nerve supplying sensation and muscle-flexing power to four of the five fingers is compressed by the tendons and ligaments surrounding it at the wrist.

"Makes sense," Lassiter mused. "So, what's scary about that?"

"Ever hear of a substance called 'nerve growth factor?'"

"Yes. There was an article in the *New England Journal of*

Medicine about it recently. But I only skimmed it, so enlighten me."

"It's a protein of some sort that's essential for the differentiation and survival of peripheral nerves. It hasn't been characterized as yet, and not much more's known about it."

"So?"

"So, I suspect the LBC I'm taking is either stimulating or acting similar to that substance. Making my peripheral nerves grow in order to better handle the increased number of impulses shooting down them. And if that's true, then I'm headed for *big* trouble. Not only the nerve trunks at my wrists and ankles will be trapped, but maybe a bunch of others."

"Yeah," Lassiter muttered, his face creasing. "Any atrophy of your thenar muscles yet?"

"Not noticeably." Adam extended his hands, palms up.

"Have you run an electromyogram on yourself?"

Adam looked chagrined. "No, not yet."

"Why the hell not?"

"Might be hard to interpret because of the LBC I'm taking."

"That the only reason?"

"I was afraid to," Adam admitted.

Lassiter smirked. "That's better. . . . All right, say you do have the carpal tunnel syndrome and it keeps progressing, thanks to that damned LBC you're on. What then?"

"You could try a cortisone injection?"

"I could—for starters. But you know better than I how seldom it works. And after that?"

"Tegretol?"

"Oh, good idea!" Lassiter mocked. "If it doesn't wipe out your bone marrow, you might buy another few weeks with it. Then what?"

"Hand surgery, I suppose. Right after the Coleman Jackson fight."

"Is that a promise?"

"More like a necessity."

Thoughtfully, Lassiter asked, "How long've you been on the LBC?"

"A little over two months."

"Which means at the rate your peripheral nerves are growing, you'll need surgery on both wrists, both ankles, and maybe a few vertebrae by July. Wouldn't it make more sense to push up the date of the Jackson fight, if you can, and get off the LBC as soon as possible?"

"It would, if I can get off it. . . ."

"What does *that* mean?"

Adam exhaled despairingly. "God only knows. Transient myasthenia gravis, most likely. Maybe worse. I don't even like to think about it."

"Nor I," Lassiter agreed. "Well, let's hope the codeine holds you for now. Be in my office nine thirty Monday morning and we'll discuss it further. Okay if I ask Jack Morris to sit in?"

"I'd rather you didn't. Not now, anyway. Let's see how I get along first. It could be something else, you know."

"Sure," Lassiter said disdainfully. "And Coleman Jackson *could* shower you with kisses, not kidney punches, in the clinches, but I wouldn't count on it." Adam's nervous laugh coaxed a smile from him. "What's that corny old movie line: 'Doctor, I *beg* you not to go on with these experiments?' "

"That's the one. But it's usually a deformed dwarf who delivers it."

"Yeah? Well, I might be a bit deformed when I get through kicking myself for ever getting involved with you."

"Say something reassuring to Megan on the way out, will you?"

"Like what? Like you can always plead insanity when your case comes to court? Megan's a pretty spectacular person, you know? I might be envious if I didn't have Kris. So it's not just you, your welfare, that you have to look out for. Lakeman won't suffer much. He's got that title bout for Tanner. And medical science won't suffer, either. You can always go back to animal experiments. So, unless you've got some hidden agenda, why not play it safe? At least think about it, will you?"

"I will, Dan," Adam said, wincing as he flexed his wrists before shaking hands. "I promise."

By the time Adam and Megan left the hotel, the overcast morning sky had cleared and the day was warm and sunny. Walking briskly beside him, she said, "Well, what's your pleasure? Lunch, a nap, a dirty movie—?"

Adam shook his head. "None of those. A drug store, a liquor store, and a bakery. Then a drive to the nearest beach and an afternoon of Omar Khayyám-like relaxation."

"I don't remember anything in the *Rubáiyát* about a drug store?"

"That's because old Omar didn't know about aspirin and antacids."

"Good thing, too. Otherwise, he might've written, 'A couple of aspirin, a swig of Maalox, and you beside me in the motel room.' It'd never play in Persia! Seriously, what do you want to do?"

Adam paused in mid-stride. "Get married. Make an honest woman of you . . ."

"I *am* honest. And you're either euphoric or punchy. I couldn't possibly take advantage of you in your addled state. Besides, you don't need a wife, you need a live-in physical therapist."

"I prefer your kind of massages. You proposed first, remember?"

"Don't remind me." As they reached the car, Megan dropped his hand and walked around to the passenger side, waiting for Adam to unlock the door.

"Let's go see your mother," he suggested after she had settled into the front seat beside him.

"My mother! What for?"

"Tell her the good news—you're marrying a doctor."

"Better than living in sin with one," she gibed before pausing and staring hard at him. "You're serious!"

"Matter of fact, I am."

"What in the world brought this about?"

"I like sleeping with you."

She flushed slightly. "And I thought I was a bit klutzy."

"I didn't mean sex. I meant 'sleeping' literally."

"I'm all over you in bed."

"I know. But you smell good and I like being touched."

"Not as much as *I* like touching you."

"Then we're compatible—right?"

"I suppose. . . . Oh, damn!" she lamented. "Why couldn't you just be an ordinary doctor, even a dentist, instead of 'Magic' McKinnon, the 'Front Street Gym Phenomenon'?"

"I wish I were that right now, too. But then we probably never would've met."

Megan pouted. "Oh, I know. I went after you because I wanted an exclusive, a boost up the slippery network ladder, and you . . . you wanted what? Not just sex. Probably a woman to help you lick the wounds left by the last one. Whatever the reasons, it's working. It's working better every day and I don't want it to end. So, instead of getting married,

I'd like a different kind of security. I'd like to stop feeling afraid."

"Of Coleman Jackson and what he might do to me?"

"No, what the LBC might do to you. That's what you and Dan Lassiter had your little chat about, wasn't it?"

Glumly, Adam nodded and started the car. "Well," he said a moment later, "aside from screwing up our sex life, it's not going to do anything more now. So let's head out to the beach."

"On one condition."

"What?"

"That we talk, really talk, like we're doing right now. That you don't clam up or doze off or retreat into your own little dream world. And that you promise to be properly admiring of me in my new swimsuit. I'm down to fighting weight, too, you know." Suddenly, she slid across the seat and hugged him, making him wince visibly. "Damn it!" she said exasperatedly. "If you keep on boxing, there won't be any place left for me to hold you at night. And just stifle any lewd remarks."

Adam did, as the fleeting erotic image he had conjured up gave way to a more urgent concern. A year, he reflected; he had given himself that long to reap the rewards of his chemically induced physical prowess. Now it seemed unlikely that he would have a full year, or even the better part of one.

As if to underline his uncertainty, the refrain from the song, "The Gambler," kept running through his mind while he drove through downtown traffic:

You gotta know when to hold 'em, Know when to fold 'em,
Know when to walk away, Know when to run!

24

A few years earlier, Adam had become briefly interested in
Catastrophe Theory, a new mathematical method, based on
tophology, for dealing with discontinuous and divergent phenomena. Its inventor, a Frenchman named Réné Thom,
claimed it could predict with reasonable accuracy the course of
human events, especially in those situations where gradually
changing forces or motivations led to abrupt changes in
behavior. Adam had attended a lecture at Yale by one of its
British proponents, and although the basis of the theory was
too abstruse for him to grasp, he found the concept fascinating.
Lately, he had been reading and thinking about it again. He
didn't need to consult one of its experts to recognize that his
grandiose plan carried a high potential for disaster. Even if he
had, it was unlikely that his personalized, three-dimensional
graph would have predicted the imminence of the catastrophe
awaiting him or identified its surprising cause.

The twenty-four hours spent with Megan at a Narragansett
beach motel were the happiest Adam had ever known; happier
even than the day he was accepted to medical school or the day
the army medical corps assigned him to France, instead of
Korea, as he expected. In the quiet interlude, he could, at

last, compartmentalize his thoughts, quell his anxiety over the
harm the LBC might be doing to his nervous system, be totally
receptive to what Megan said and felt. Despite the unresolved
issues burdening their minds, nothing of consequence was
discussed or decided; nothing allowed to disrupt the flow of
peace and contentment between them. It was a brief idyll of
wave-watching and stargazing and muted conversation that left
them feeling closer and more comfortable with each other than
ever before.

The next day also got off to a deceptively good start. From
the motel they drove directly to Commonwealth General
Hospital, where Adam had a chest X-ray and picked up his
codeine prescription. To his relief, the X-ray was negative for
rib fracture and, after dropping Megan off at the *Boston Globe*
for the job interview Mel Waldman had set up upon learning
she had taken a leave of absence from ABC, Adam went on to
the Front Street Gym. The door was locked and, when he rang
the bell, Tommy Harms let him in cautiously, having been
warned by Al Lakeman to keep reporters out.

"Well." Lakeman said with wry forebearance, "nice to see
you—even if you are three hours late!"

"Nice to see *you* any time, Al," answered Adam, suspecting from Lakeman's haggard look and reddened eyes that he
had drunk too much with his out-of-town cronies and was hung
over.

"Get changed!" Lakeman said brusquely and walked into
his office. He was still there, talking to Harry Patashnick, when
Adam returned in sweatshirt and trunks, so he did a half-hour
of calesthenics.

"Want to go a few rounds with Harms?" proposed Lakeman
after finally joining him on the floor.

"Would you," retorted Adam, pulling up his sweatshirt, "if
your ribs looked like this?"

Lakeman grimaced at the blue-black blotches and shook his
head.

"Where's Tanner?" Adam asked.

"Visiting his old man in Scranton. Be back in a few
days. . . ." Lakeman paused pensively. "You're a neurologist, so tell me something: is it possible for an otherwise
healthy guy not to feel pain?"

"Hmm," mused Adam, surprised and intrigued. "Theoret-
ically, a benign tumor or cyst in the region of the thalamus, the
pain-relaying center of the brain, could produce a hemi-

anesthesia; meaning, an absence of painful sensations over one entire half of the body. But I don't think it's possible to be *totally* insensitive and still walk around. Who're you talking about?"

"Coleman Jackson. Ever see him fight?"

Adam shook his head.

"Well, we've got films of him you can watch. You'll see what I mean."

Incredulously, Adam said, "Are you trying to tell me it doesn't hurt when he gets hit?"

"I'm not trying to *tell* you anything. But Harry and I ran three of his fight films while waiting for you today and not once, no matter how hard he was punched, did he even flinch. Naturally, he's never been knocked down or out. So, you being a nerve specialist and all, I thought I'd ask."

"That the only reason, Al? You wouldn't be trying to scare me into training harder, would you?"

"No need. A few minutes of seeing Jackson in action will do that. With your punch you haven't a prayer of putting him away, and he doesn't cut easy, either. So you'll have to figure on going the distance."

"Anything else?" asked Adam, his muscles stiffening as he cooled off.

"One more thing. He's a fast puncher. Almost as fast as Harms. So the key to keeping him off is the left jab. Work on that for a while."

With Tommy Harms bracing the heavy bag for him, Adam practiced his jab under Lakeman's watchful eye for three rounds. The mild twinges of pain spreading up his left arm each time his fist struck the sawdust made him welcome the bell ending the session. But before he could fully remove his gloves, Lakeman ordered, "One more. And this time really *hit* the big bag, don't just tap it."

Angrily, Adam drew his gloves back on and squared off. The moment the bell rang, he unleashed a punch at the bag whose transmitted force rocked Harms back on his heels.

"Harder!" Lakeman growled.

Adam faked with his left, then right, and launched a jab straight from the shoulder with all his one-hundred-ninety pounds behind it. Simultaneous with the smack of fist against bag, he grunted, feeling a lancinating pain shoot up his left arm. Shaken, he snapped off another jab which hurt almost as much.

Behind him, unable to see the pain in his face, Lakeman shouted, "Keep punching!"

Adam swung around. "That's it! That's enough!"

Lakeman blinked at his fury. "What'd you mean?" he stammered. "I'm the manager. I'll tell *you* what's enough."

"Not today," Adam warned. "I hurt!"

"So you hurt." Lakeman flung up his arms. "Hurting's part of the game. If you can't take a little pain, you don't belong in boxing."

"It's not a *little* pain, Al. It's a lot. So let's just call it a day, huh?"

Lakeman stared at him, shrugged, and dropped his eyes. "All right, all right," he said grudgingly. "Did Lassiter check out your ribs?"

"I got an X-ray this morning. Negative."

"Then why don't you go back to the hospital and get some hot packs and diathermy. Maybe that'll help?"

Adam nodded, purposely not telling his manager that it was his left wrist, not his rib cage, that hurt the most. It would take too much explaining. He took off his sweat-soaked gloves, dropped them on the canvas, and wandered toward the locker room, leaving Al Lakeman shaking his head in consternation.

Back in his North Shore duplex, Adam swallowed a grain of codeine, put a Segovia record on the phonograph, and sat down to wait for Megan to return. The codeine dulled his pain to a throb, and he drank a whiskey to deaden it further. Dreading what he had to do next, he climbed the stairs to his second-floor study, uncovered his electromyogram machine, and ran tracings on both median nerves at the wrist. The results confirmed his diagnosis and his fears. But when Megan bustled in, excited at being hired to write a thrice-weekly television commentary for the *Globe*, Adam was able to respond enthusiastically. Over drinks they discussed possible subjects for her first column—Adam again suggesting Aaron Robards as a motherlode of ideas and insights. When pressed for examples, he regaled her with tales of Aaron's more outrageous psychological ploys against network executives. But unable to maintain the mood, Adam grew progressively more subdued and preoccupied as the evening wore on, blaming it on his strenuous workout at the gym when Megan queried him about it.

They ate at a nearby Italian resturant, finishing off a bottle of wine over dinner and two more while watching TV at home.

Megan wanted to make love when they went to bed at eleven, but Adam was too drowsy from wine and still troubled by twinges of pain. To his relief, she fell asleep quickly; he took two more codeine and two sleeping pills, hoping to do the same. Gently disentangling himself from her arm, he slid to the edge of the bed, rolled on his side, and was just dozing off when Megan, tossing from a supine to a fetal position, jabbed her knees into the small of his back. With a surge of panic, he felt himself slipping off the bed. Thrusting out both hands to break his fall, he almost screamed at the searing pain that shot up his left arm.

"Oh, Adam! Oh, my God!" Megan cried, switching on the bedside lanp. "Are you all right?"

"Yeah," he said through gritted teeth. "Fine."

She leaned over to look at him, but he kept his back to her. "Are you sure?"

"I'm sure!" he snapped. "Shut off the light and go back to sleep."

Plaintively she asked, "Can't I have a good-night kiss?"

"In a minute, when I get back from the bathroom."

He waited for her to turn off the light and then rushed to the bathroom, barely making it in time. The moment the door closed behind him, he fell to his knees and vomited into the toilet bowl. He stayed in that position, taking deep breaths to suppress his gag reflex, until his nausea receded. With one hand on the top of the toilet and the other on the sink, he slowly pulled himself up to sit shakily on the toilet seat. From elbow to fingertips, his left arm stung as if scorched by flame. He tried to flex his wrist and barely stifled a scream. Finally, he risked standing, bracing himself on the washbasin and looking blearily in the medicine cabinet for his codeine bottle. Its safety cap almost defeated him, but at last he worked it open. He popped two tablets in his mouth and swallowed them dry. The codeine would take twenty to thirty minutes to reach peak effect, so he sat down on the commode to wait it out. With his bruised median nerve throbbing like an abscessed tooth, he wished he knew acupuncture, wished he had a local anesthetic in his doctor bag to inject directly in the nerve. But all he had on hand was an ampule of morphine that he was loath to use.

He hoped Megan had gone back to sleep and would not come looking for him, see him in this pitiful state. Either from the heavy dose of codeine or as a reflex response from his intense arm pain, spasms racked his stomach, doubling him up and making him frantic for relief. Though Tanner was out of town, he could wake Moe Malone and have Moe drive him to a hospital. But that was too risky: somebody might recognize him and leak the story to the newspapers. There was simply nothing to do except wait for the codeine to take hold.

Eyes aching from the harsh glare of fluorescent light off white tile, he rose and tiptoed out of the bedroom. In the living room, he turned on the TV for something to distract him. There was an old World War II movie on the screen, full of noise and action, but his arm hurt too much for him to follow the plot.

Twenty minutes went by, then thirty, but, instead of abating, the excruciating twinges climbed higher up his arm, as if the nerve were sputtering like a bomb fuse. He paced the floor, gulped whiskey until he retched, grew even sicker with the realization that the codeine simply was not working. He was on the verge of waking Moe Malone, but knew he could not endure another minute of this torture, certainly not the twenty or more minutes it would take Moe to dress and drive him to the nearest hospital. Almost crazed with pain, Adam lurched to the hall closet, pulled down his doctor bag from the shelf, and tore through its contents until he found the small leather case containing the syringeful of morphine.

Clumsily he twisted his trench coat belt around his left upper arm for a tourniquet and jabbed the hypodermic needle deep into an engorged vein in the crook of his elbow. Slowly, heedful that morphine injected too rapidly could cause severe vomiting, he emptied the last drop of the clear solution into his bloodstream. Then he released the tourniquet, withdrew the needle from the vein, and watched abstractedly as a trickle of blood ran down his forearm. Sluggishly realizing that it was *his* blood, he flexed his elbow to put pressure on the puncture and collapsed on the couch.

At last free of the maddening pain, a powerful detachment overcame him. He felt as if air, volumes and volumes of it, had replaced his brain substance, lightening his head like a balloon. His eyes seemed to leave their bony orbits and float up toward the light in the ceiling, dazzling him with its brilliance before sinking back into his skull. Blinded, he blinked repeatedly to rid his retina of the incandescent afterglow. But when his vision cleared, nothing looked the same as before. The furniture was fuzzy-edged, the walls were wavy, the room rocked, cradle-like, from side to side.

Strong stuff, marveled Adam, suddenly able to understand

why so few heroin addicts ever kicked the habit, why they were willing to risk so much, even their lives, to recapture this blissful state. Vaguely, his neurologist's mind tried to picture what was happening to him. With the pain-receptors in his mid-brain completely occupied by the morphine molecules, they could not relay warning signals to the command center in his cerebral cortex, thereby lulling it into a false sense of security. All seemed well with the world—if, indeed, there still was an outside world!

Whatever the mechanism, Adam's perceptions were radically altered. He felt buoyant, free-floating, liberated from the quicksand of his psyche's preoccupations with God, death, and meaning. Even as the room seemed to stabilize, the lightness in his head persisted, spilling over into his body and making him feel as if he could levitate off the couch at will. Levitate, hell! he thought expansively. Why not fly? With the avian-derived LBC firing his nerves, he was part bird, wasn't he?

He started to rise to his feet, but fell back feebly. He braced himself with his hands to try again, determined to go outdoors and flap his arms as fast as possible in hopes of emulating the aerodynamically ill-designed but high-flying bumble bee, when his brain's survival unit, its last in line of defense, swung into action, preempting the circuits feeding his delusional state and restoring some semblance of common sense.

All right, all right, Adam muttered to the chorus of nay-sayers in his head. To mollify them further, he remembered a line from Robert Louis Stevenson: "It's ill to loose the bands that God decreed to bind." Having ignored that dictum once before to his peril, the night he took his first dose of LBC, he decided not to push his luck.

Propping his head up on a cushion, he drew his left arm—his Achilles' heel—close and examined it as if it were a dismembered specimen. It looked mottled and swollen. He tried to visualize the Schwann cells lining his median nerve engaged in border warfare with the smaller, more numerous ligamentous cells squeezing it for space. Don't quit! he urged his embattled nerve fibers. Escalate! Use your cell-digesting lysosome sacs, your ultimate weapon. Launch an all-out lysosome attack, the microcosmic equivalent of nuclear war, against their front-line forces. Make them pay for their painful probes!

A loosely connected thought suddenly expanded into an insight of stunning force and clarity. Since nothing in life, not even life itself, came free, the price he would have to pay for continuing on his present course was pain. He could climb the ladder to success in sports as high as he wished, providing he could meet the ever-escalating price—and from here on it would be strictly pay as you go.

If necessary, as now, he could borrow to make some of the steeper payments, but morphine was the loan-shark of drugs whose debtors rarely got out of hock. Hereafter, he would try local cortisone injections, Tegretol, non-addicting analgesic or anti-neuritic balms, but no more morphine! That option was out—as was the year he had allotted himself in which to conquer professional sports.

Bleakly he wondered how long he did have? He would settle for three months—time enough to face Coleman Jackson and the North Korean Ping-Pong team and maybe a few other challenges—but he doubted he'd be given that much leeway. Even if the pain in his left hand was gone by morning, it would probably return each time he hit a punching bag, a handball, an opponent. So he did not have three months. A more realistic estimate might be a few weeks, even days.

The sensible thing, of course, was to quit now: let Lassiter put him in the hospital to wean him off the LBC and fervently hope his nervous system could survive the rigors of withdrawal. That would doubtless please Megan and infuriate Lakeman. Worse, it might jeopardize Todd Tanner's title fight. But even disregarding Tanner, Adam knew he wouldn't—couldn't— quit. He had always been a plugger, tortoise-slow at times, but tenacious. Still, it surprised him to realize how set he was on going the distance—the "distance" being the maximum amount of pain he could tolerate before it drove him mad or to a hand surgeon. Another and more perplexing reason was his determination to not only dumbfound but humble the sports and scientific worlds. Although his grudge against the government grant-givers was no mystery—in fact, was now public knowledge—what hidden motive had made him challenge the professional athletes? What drove him to not merely compete, but to conquer?

Was it simple greed? As that blustering reporter, McPherson, had pointed out, boxing would bring him far more than the million dollars necessary to continue his research. But accumulating more money than he needed had never ranked high on his list of priorities. He really wouldn't know what to do with great wealth; he lacked the imagination.

Revenge, then? Adam had played sports all through high

school and college. Had some long ago opponent so injured or humiliated him that he bore a deep-seated grudge against all athletes? He could remember no such incident. And although he disdained the militancy and commercialism of modern professional sports, he was out to beat the system, not reform it. But if revenge was not his motive, he sensed something closely akin to it was.

Suddenly, Adam had his answer. His obsession was fueled by anger—smoldering, implacable, gut-grinding anger. But not at any outsider. From start to finish, it was centered on his own ineffectual self.

What had he really built on the privileged foundation his parents, his education, his profession, had given him? He had never before fulfilled any of his deeper desires or brought any major projects to fruition. Nor had he risked much trying. He had gone into neurology, the most difficult and least rewarding of medical subspecialities, both because of his father and because it was safe. Most neurological diseases could be accurately diagnosed, many sufferers helped to heal themselves, few could be cured.

Even on those rare occasions when Adam broke out of his cautious rut to care deeply about someone or something, it usually turned out badly. Twenty years of intense research had not brought him even close to an effective treatment for his father's dementia. He had never made a close friend of a colleague or the women he periodically dated. The debacle with Diana was only the most flagrant of his sexual failures. He had even failed to meet the biological obligation to his species to father a child.

The one inspired idea he ever had, the isolation and testing of LBC, would also have ended in failure had he not dared fate and bet his life on it. So he had ample cause for dissatisfaction with the life he had led. But now that he knew what drove him, was it worth enduring another hellish night or all the pain-plagued days ahead? If not, he would have to delve into its subtler implications some other time. He would also have to try to figure out why he dreamed of drowning so much lately. Right now, barely able to keep his eyes open or his thoughts on track, he had more pressing matters to ponder and strategies to plan. If his magic show was soon to end, then he wanted it to have a spectacular, star-bursting, unforgettable finish.

First thing in the morning, he would list all the sports popular in the Boston area whose mastery depended more on quick reflexes than strength or endurance, and select the two or three at which he might excel. Then he would have Aaron Robards and Ron Warner arrange exhibitions for him in the next two weeks. With his showman's imagination and flair, Aaron should back him enthusiastically. Not so Al Lakeman; but he could get around Al by claiming his ribs hurt too much for sparring and this way he could stay trim. Finally, he would see Lassiter Monday morning, hoping a cortisone injection might buy him the extra time he needed.

No, not finally, Adam amended. Before setting his plan in motion, he would have to tell Megan what he was doing and why, trying to hide his underlying desperation. At least she should be glad to learn that, like a retired champion thoroughbred, "Magic" McKinnon would shortly be put out to pasture, if not to stud.

25

The postseason blues. George Sydney, general manager of the Boston Bruins, was mired in them. As he slumped in his leather-covered swivel chair, absently staring across his desk at the pictures and plaques on the side wall, his gaze fell on Bobby Orr's photograph. Orr in full flight was really something, he thought wistfully, fingering his 1972 Stanley Cup championship ring. But Orr was long gone and his "no stars" had been eliminated with ease by the Canadiens in this year's semifinals. So where did that leave him? Another season gone, another near-miss, another rebuilding program with a disgruntled coach who might or might not be around much longer. . . .

His melancholy musings were interrupted by the buzz of the intercom. "Mr. Warner and Mr. Robards to see you, Mr. Sydney," announced his secretary.

He pressed the call-box button. "Please send them in."

A moment later, Ron Warner bustled into his office, with Aaron Robards a few steps behind. Sydney gazed up at Warner, wondering where the seventy-year-old man got his boundless energy. It couldn't just be clean living, he speculated; a more likely explanation was that Warner's job, reputation, sense of self-worth did not depend on win-loss records. He rose to shake hands.

"George," Ron began, "I've got a terrific idea how to pack the Garden for the exhibition game against the Flyers on Saturday."

It was an unpromising beginning. Sydney was not too receptive to terrific ideas on this dreary Monday afternoon, even from the man who owned the arena his team rented. He sat back in his chair. "Okay, Ron. I'm listening."

"Use a substitute goalie. You don't have to sign him up, since it's just an exhibition."

"Why?" Sydney demanded. "Is something going on with Dale Clinton I don't know about?"

"No, nothing like that," Warner assured him. "It's just that the goalie I have in mind is bound to fill the house. He's the most-talked-about name in sports. Adam McKinnon."

Sydney stared. "I thought he was a boxer. What's the matter, isn't that sport rough enough for him?"

"George, we're trying to do you a favor," Aaron Robards interjected. "Turn an after-the-season exhibition game into a major sporting event. For all our sakes, we'd really like to see McKinnon in the nets against the Flyers."

Sydney rocked his chair to its full upright position. "Are you two out of your minds? The whole team works for the goalie, you know that. They protect him; he takes care of them. After what the Canadiens did to us, you really expect me to let the boys face the Flyers and their fans with a middle-aged amateur in the nets? Just to hype the gate? How much you paying McKinnon for this spectacle?"

"Nothing. It's a charity benefit, remember?"

"Then, what's he trying to prove?"

"Just that he's the world's best all-around athlete," Robards replied.

"That's all?" Sydney said with a mixture of skepticism and disdain. "And I suppose you think he is?"

"I'll know after Saturday night."

Sydney turned to Warner. "Look, with all due respect, Ron, I'm not running 'Celebrity Challenge' or a goddamn sideshow. I wish we'd never scheduled this exhibition game and I'm sure the Flyer organization feels the same way. But if we turn it into a circus, there'll be hell to pay."

Warner let him sulk a few moments before saying, "Now, hold on, George. Just hold on. We don't expect you to use anybody who isn't any good. Get Robin Redford up here and tell him to give McKinnon a tryout. If he can't hack it"— Warner shrugged—"don't use him. What could be fairer than that?"

Reluctantly, Sydney nodded. "Okay. Long as you realize that Redford's going to throw a fit over this. We're not exactly bosom buddies, these days. In fact, barely speaking."

"You're the general manager," Warner pointed out. "Redford takes orders from you. At least this way, you're giving him a choice: letting him decide for himself whether McKinnon's good enough to play part or all of the game. That's reasonable, isn't it?"

"I suppose so," Sydney conceded. "Let me call down and find out if Redford's had his slab of raw meat for the day. If so, I'll break it to him."

At two the next afternoon, Adam met Robin Redford in his rinkside office for instructions. Afterward, he wondered if the Bruins' coach had set a record for brevity. "So you're McKinnon," he had said and handed Adam a piece of paper. "Here's a release Sydney's lawyer drew up. Sign it! Then, get your gear on and go out on the ice."

"Anything else I ought to know?"

"Can't think of a thing," said Redford coldly and walked past him out the door.

Thirty minutes later, having donned his heavily padded goalie outfit and feeling as cramped as an astronaut in a spacesuit, Adam was sitting on the team bench, waiting for Redford to notice him. A huge player skated over. "Hey, Doc, I'm Ted McLennan. Mind if I ask you a question?"

"Go ahead," said Adam through his wire mask.

"Is your equipment brand-new or did you just skate through a car wash?"

Before Adam could answer, Redford appeared. "You ready, McKinnon?" he snapped and couldn't help grinning at the pristine state of Adam's gear. "Well, whatever else you are," he added, "you're certainly the neatest goalie I've ever seen."

Swinging around, Redford blew his whistle. The smack of sticks against frozen rubber ceased and the players gathered around the bench. "Gentlemen," he announced, "this is Dr. Adam McKinnon. He wants to play goalie Saturday night and Mr. Sydney has ordered me to give him a chance to show us what he can do. Mr. Sydney, I remind you, is the man who signs our paychecks. So we're going to humor him and if we get a few laughs ourselves, so much the better. . . ." Redford beckoned to a large man in a goaltender's uniform. "Dale, come over here a minute."

Dale Clinton, a veteran goalie, skated closer to the bench. His fiberglass mask was covered with dozens of dents and self-carved suture marks.

"Dale," Redford continued, "this gentleman would like your job on Saturday night and maybe next season. Would you be so kind as to show him where the crease is?"

A handful of players guffawed; the rest just stared at Adam, wondering what was going on.

Clinton motioned Adam to follow him to the near goal. Popping his mask up, he eyed Adam curiously. "So you want to play goalie, huh? Well, fine with me. I always welcome competition."

"Just for the one night," Adam explained. "Strictly a one-shot deal."

Clinton gestured tolerantly. "Whatever turns you on. Where'd you play before?"

"Yale," Adam replied. "A very long time ago."

"What position?"

"Defense. I've only played goalie a few times, mostly in pickup games."

Clinton nodded knowingly. "Figures. Most of the crazies I know are defensemen. Think they can always play goalie when they get older and slower. But it's not so easy, as you're about to learn. Anyway, you'd better stretch out unless you want to rip your hamstrings good."

Adam nodded and, grabbing the crossbar of the net, went through a series of bending and twisting exercises. At Adam's nod, Clinton banged his stick on the ice and called, "Hey, Ted, Neil, let's try some shots from the blue line." He backed into a corner of the rink, dug out some pucks, passed them to McLennan and Newton at the line, and raised his stick as a signal to get ready.

Facing the two players, Adam fought to quell a sudden attack of the jitters. McLennan was a mountain of a man, with massive shoulders and thick arms; Newton was even taller, with a shock of blond hair falling across his forehead. But before he could ever consider changing his mind, Newton strung out three pucks at two-foot intervals along the blue line, positioned himself at the left point, McLennan at the right, and waited for Clinton's stick to drop. The instant it did, McLennan skated toward the nearest puck and unleashed a powerful slapshot. Adam made a swipe at it, but it was high and sailed over the crossbar to bang against the Herculite behind the goal. The thunderous noise made Adam flinch and twist his neck around to see if the pane had broken. By the time he looked back, McLennan's second puck was in the air. Quickly, Adam lifted his right arm and deflected it off the glove holding his stick, feeling the sting but also feeling relief at having stopped it. A split-second later, the third puck was launched and sailing so fast that he perceived it as hardly more than a black blur until it was mere inches from his chest. In spite of his super-quick reflexes, he was unable to get his glove in front of it and it struck him square in the chest. Without his polyvinyl-and-felt chest protector, the blow might have shattered his breastbone. Even with it, the jar bounced him off the crossbar and shot pain from his spine to his toes. Shakily he straightened, balanced himself, and waited for Newton's series of shots. He blocked the first puck with his skate, the second one with his glove, and barely managed to deflect the third one from the upper left corner of the net.

Twenty minutes later, the entire team had circled around Adam and fired wrist shot after wrist shot at him from twenty feet out. Although numerous pucks stung him, none had successfully penetrated his often awkward blocks and deflections to the net. Neil Newton and Robin Redford stood at mid-ice, silently watching Adam's performance. Finally, Newton said, "Rob, this guy isn't bad. He plays some shots right back out front, but otherwise he's stopped everything we've thrown at him."

"Strange, damned strange," Redford muttered more to himself than Newton. Suddenly, he said, "Neil, tell the boys to quit snap shooting. I want them to slapshoot from right where they are."

Newton grinned. "You want us to kill the doctor, right?"

"No," Redford said contemptuously, "I want to see if one of you clowns can get one by him."

Newton passed the word and, within minutes, Adam was dodging a barrage of slapshots. The rifle-sharp noise of pucks caroming off posts, smashing into Herculite or fiberglass boards, reverberated in his head. He felt as if he were in the middle of a free-fire combat zone. But he was improving steadily, coordinating eye and limb movements in more fluid response to the essential rhythm. A couple of pucks got by him, one that he thought he had stopped on the ice with his skate, and another off his glove when he squeezed it shut too soon. But that was all; of the dozens of slapshots fired at him, those were the only ones that bulged the twine.

Skating over to Dale Clinton on the bench, Redford asked, "Well, what do you think?"

Clinton shook his head. "Christ, I don't know. All of a sudden, I'm worried. Where's this guy come from?"

Redford raised his eyes. "Heaven, maybe."

Dave Cartney joined them at the bench. "You see what that old boy's doing!" he said excitedly. "I don't believe it, but I can't get by him. I've had slapshots from fifteen feet out, and I can't score on him!"

Redford muttered, "I've seen enough." He blew his whistle and the shooting stopped. As the team gathered around their coach, Adam dropped exhaustedly to his knees. His flesh stung in a dozen places; his leg muscles ached and twitched and bunched up as if suffering a generalized charley horse. Neither his miles of roadwork nor hours or calisthenics had conditioned him to absorb punishment like this. He had stretched tendons and muscles farther than they had ever been stretched before. Even if he spent the night in a steamroom, he knew he would hardly be able to walk the next morning. He was also resentful that his "tryout" had been so severe and intended to make clear to Redford and his charges that he would tolerate no repeats.

That chance came when Ted McLennan skated up and hit his shoulder pads with his stick. "Good show, old man!"

In response, Adam's fist shot out, stopping a bare millimeter from McLennan's nose. The center blinked and drew back. "Hey, Doc," he blurted. "What gives?"

"Oh, nothing," Adam said, the edge to his voice belying the casual dismissal. "Just my way of saying thanks for the hockey lesson. Tell your teammates I'd be glad to return the favor if they'd care to drop by the gym some afternoon."

McLennan shook his head. "I don't think they will, Doc. I honestly don't think they will."

26

Although Adam's hockey magic remained to be demonstrated, his box office magic did not. All of the standing-room and scalpers' tickets had been snapped up well before Saturday's game time, filling Boston Garden to capacity for the second time in fifteen days. Banners hung from the balcony railing, proclaiming such sentiments as MAGIC, WHERE WERE YOU WHEN WE NEEDED YOU? and BULLIES, HAVE WE GOT A BIG MAC FOR YOU! Surveying the spectators from the press box, Mel Waldman saw a much higher proportion of women and children than usual. It did not surprise him; with Adam's goaltending as the main attraction, it was hardly an ordinary game.

Adam stood at attention in front of the home net while a local baritone sang the national anthem. Charged with excitement, the overflow crowd managed to restrain itself until the last line of the last stanza and then erupted in thunderous applause, drowning out, "home of the brave!"

Adam exchanged words of encouragement with the Bruins' starting five as they skated past him, whacking his leg pads with their sticks for luck. The Philadelphia players appeared less jaunty as they repeated the ritual at their end of the rink.

Since being eliminated in the Stanley Cup quarterfinals, they had not played in two weeks and were anxious to get this season-ender over, hang up their skates, and start summer vacations. Which is not to say they weren't "up" for the game. They all knew about McKinnon's one-sided ring victory over "Mean Joe" Metcalf and, like professional athletes everywhere, were intrigued by it. They had also read interviews in which McKinnon's teammates claimed that he possessed the "fastest glove hand in the league," but dismissed that as the usual media manure. Even if the Bruins had held their practice sessions under water, with a trained octopus in the nets, the Flyer veterans could not imagine it matching some of the miraculous goaltending feats attributed to Adam. Far from being intimidated by the pre-game boasts and sizable side-bets of the Boston players, the Philadelphia team was eager to expose "Magic" McKinnon for the rank amateur he doubtless was. It gave them an incentive to swamp Boston in this otherwise meaningless game.

The Flyers dominated the action from the opening face-off. Al Johnston controlled the puck, shoveling it to a defenseman before breaking for the blue line to pick up a perfectly executed cross-rink pass. Don Scholl, trailing him, veered to the left just over the line, beating the Boston defender, and Johnston slowed as he neared the net. Adam crouched, guarding the right-hand post with his glove arm. Misled by his boxer's instincts, he kept his eyes on Johnston's remarkably expressionless face.

The Flyer center bobbed his head and released a wrist shot that came at Adam waist-high. He raised his right arm to block it, but before leather and rubber collided, Scholl's stick appeared out of nowhere to deflect the puck down and to the left. Adam kicked his left leg out, catching the puck in midair and dropping it in front of the net. Scholl fielded the puck on his backhand and, with a quick flick of his wrist, drilled it into the left corner.

The crowd moaned. Adam retrieved the puck and glanced up at the scoreboard. A scant ten seconds had elapsed since the face-off.

McLennan skated over. "Settle down!" he urged. "That was our fault. Scholl shouldn't have gotten alone in front. We'll make sure it doesn't happen again."

"That'd be appreciated," said Adam, trying to hide his discouragement.

"One more thing," McLennan added. "To get an early line on a shot, don't watch a shooter's head or hands. Watch the puck!"

Thereafter, the Boston defense tightened, and Adam had to handle only five more shots, all long-range and easily blocked, until the final minute of the first period. With twenty seconds left, Swifty Baker, the Philadelphia winger, faked out a defenseman and skated through him. Tensely, Adam watched Baker streak toward him, his long, brown hair waving in the breeze of his incredible speed. Recalling McLennan's warning, he shifted his eyes from Baker's face to the puck. The Flyer forward shuffled it from backhand to forehand until he crossed the Boston blue line. Suddenly, his right shoulder dipped and he faked a slapshot. The deception worked—one of the few times Adam's super-quick reflexes proved a detriment. Before he could check himself, he had dropped to his knees, temporarily limiting his range and mobility. Baker took instant advantage, switching the puck to his backhand and lifting it high enough over Adam's left shoulder so that neither his glove nor stick could reach it.

As if launched by steel springs, Adam leapt to his feet and beyond, catching the puck in mid-flight on his shoulder pad and deflecting it over the net. It hit the Herculite and bounded back over the crossbar. With reflexes almost as fast as Adam's, Baker scooped up the bouncing puck two feet off the ice with the flat of his stick and batted it toward the open half of the net. Assuming he had scored, he turned and thrust his stick up in the air triumphantly, but there was no goal. Desperately jamming his own stick to the right, Adam had caught the puck on its butt end and batted it high and wide.

The roar of the crowd nearly drowned out the buzzer ending the first period. Wide-eyed with disbelief, Baker swung around to stare at Adam. "Didn't see that save. Must've been a hell of a good one!" He gave Adam a gap-toothed grin and skated to the visitor's bench.

Possibly because Adam's presence in the net made them lax, overconfident, shy of body-checking injuries, the second period was a defensive disaster for the Bruins. The Philadelphia players beat them to the puck repeatedly and Adam was shelled. In the first five minutes alone, he stopped twelve shots—the crowd chanting, "Magic! . . . Magic! . . . Magic!" after each spectacular save.

But before the period ended Ted McLennan intercepted a

clearing pass in front of the Philadelphia goal and shoved it in to even the score. Two plays later, Bobby Lucas beat the defense at the Boston blue line and streaked toward Adam. Dave Cartney, every muscle straining in all-out pursuit, could not catch up. In desperation, he dove forward on his stomach, flailed out with his stick, and snared Lucas's skate ten feet from the goal. Lucas tripped and slid headlong into Adam, piling them both into the net and knocking the goal from its pins.

Adam had received a sufficient assortment of blows in recent weeks to make him an expert in assessing, as well as treating, pain. What he felt now was top-of-the-scale; the worst ever. Lucas's shoulder had rammed into his stomach with such force that, despite his chest protector, it knocked the wind out of him. Beneath the great bulk of the Philadelphia player, Adam felt as if he were being crushed as well as suffocated.

After what seemed interminable delay, the Boston trainer, Danny Smith, managed to untangle them. Rolling on his side, knees drawn up, Adam continued to gasp and grunt. But before he could suck more than a mouthful of air into his burning lungs, a knife seemed to plunge under his heart, cutting the inspiratory effort short. He was certain he had cracked a rib or even torn it loose from his breastbone. But he had no time to consider the possible consequences now. Unable to breathe, barely able to moan, it took all his resources to keep from panicking. Seeing his distress, Smith reached inside his waistband and pulled up, simultaneously arching his back from behind. The maneuver worked. It was as if a constricting band around his thorax had been broken. At last, Adam could draw a shallow breath.

The next instant, the crowd came to its feet, booing, as the referee signaled a penalty shot for Lucas, who was sitting on the ice, rubbing his forehead where it had hit the crossbar, and looking dazed.

After a brief discussion with both coaches, the referee decided to clear the ice and play the extra fifty seconds in the third period. Adam was helped to the bench by Smith and Neil Newton.

Waiting for him to remove his mask, Robin Redford took one look at Adam's agony-twisted face and ordered him to the first-aid room.

"No!" Adam rasped.

"What do you mean—'No'?"

"I'm not moving."

Redford exchanged puzzled glances with the trainer. "Look, Doc," Smith said in a calmer voice, "I admire your guts, but you'd better let the team doctor check you over. The way Lucas barreled into you, you could have a fractured rib and punctured lung. So why not play it safe? Hell, it's just an exhibition game."

"I'm fine," insisted Adam, still unable to breathe without intense pain but loath to let the team physician, or Dan Lassiter, or Megan, talk him out of finishing the game.

Redford stared at him and shrugged. "Okay, McKinnon, have it your way. If you were an ordinary player, I'd bench you in a minute. But you're not an ordinary *anything*, and you played one hell of a period out there. So, if you want to go back in, I won't stop you."

At Adam's nod, Neil Newton grinned gleefully. "See, Rob. The Doc's a *real* hockey player; crazy like the rest of us!"

The third period began with Lucas's penalty shot. The referee placed the puck in the center face-off circle, checked to make sure that all players on both teams were behind the red line, and blew his whistle. Slowly, almost leisurely, Lucas approached the puck, picking it up on the forehand blade of his stick. Adam crouched in the center of the crease, still unable to draw a deep breath or move his left shoulder and arm without pain, but trying his best to ignore it.

Lucas swung to the left, circled back a little, and then spurted straight and hard toward the goal. Adam held his ground, knowing that if the Philadelphia forward faked him into making the first move, he might not recover in time to stop the shot. Fifteen feet away, Lucas broke sharply to the right and drew the puck behind the blade of his stick so that Adam temporarily lost sight of it. Suddenly, he fired a wrist shot toward the upper left-hand corner of the net. Adam lunged for it with his glove hand, but, with a stab of pain limiting his range, he could not quite reach it. The puck hit the junction between the crossbar and the post, fell into the crease, and flip-flopped on the goal line. Adam dove for it, covering the puck with his body. Pain flooding his nervous system, tears in his eyes, he could hear the tumultuous cheers of the crowd as he got slowly to his feet.

When play resumed, the Bruins, inspired by Adam's courage, came to life. The wings covered their checks,

allowing only seven long-range shots at the Boston goal and
playing most of the period between the blue lines.

With a minute and forty seconds left in the game, Philadelphia drew a minor penalty for having too many men on the ice.
Taking advantage of this break in the action, Ted McLennan
skated to the Bruins' bench and asked the coach to call a time
out. Redford complied, signaling Adam to stay in place while
the other players gathered around him.

"Ted has something to tell you," Redford said curtly and
gestured for him to speak. "Look," McLennan began, "you
don't need me to tell you we've been dead on our skates tonight
while McKinnon's been really busting his ass for us. Me, I'd
like to win the game for the old 'Magic Man.' So what say we
do it!"

Nodding vigorously, McLennan's teammates waited for
guidance. When he stayed silent, Brian Deaver spoke: "Okay,
Ted, how does this sound? The face-off is in their end. Just as
the puck is dropped, I'll break for the slot. Don't try to draw it
back, Ted. Just slap it to the right. I'll take it from there."

McLennan nodded, realizing, as did Deaver, that the
maneuver was risky and dependent on his winning the face-off.

The instant the referee dropped the disk, Brian Deaver
streaked from the point toward the slot and McLennan
pounced, beating Johnston to the puck and blindly knocking it
to his right, where normally there would be no player to
receive it. The puck hit Deaver on the skate, but he turned the
blade and nimbly deflected it to his stick. With a clear lane to
the Philadelphia goal, Deaver drove on it and blasted a slapshot
from fifteen feet out that the Flyer goalie blocked with his
shoulder pad. But, along with Deaver, McLennan, too, had
spurted for the net. The rebound came directly at him and he
slid it easily into the unprotected left side of the goal. The
crowd's cheering was almost seismic; the Bruins' jubilation so
great the whole team clapped their gloves and beat their sticks
on the ice.

But the Flyers were not finished yet. With thirty seconds left
to play, Al Johnston, determined to redeem himself for losing
the last face-off, carried the puck behind the Boston goal.
Swiveling his neck, Adam glanced right, then left, knowing
the Philadelphia style of play was to pass out from behind the
goal to wings, rather than trying to hit an open man in the slot.
But this time, they seemed inclined to do it differently.
Bullying through a Boston defenseman twenty feet from the

net, Don Scholl signalled his center for a pass. Johnston straightened and swept his stick in Scholl's direction, but the puck did not follow. It stayed on the ice in front of him as he drove to the net. Taken by surprise, Adam barely had time to shift in Johnston's direction before he backhanded the puck hard toward the open left-hand corner of the goal. Adam did the splits, blocking the shot with the edge of his skate and kicking it just wide of the net.

Two Boston defensemen descended on the puck as if it were a gold nugget and swept it toward the boards. Johnston muttered an obscenity and, knowing time was just about out, skated over to help Adam to his feet. "Very nice save!" he admitted.

The game ended, 2–1 in Boston's favor. Adam had stopped thirty-seven shots, while the Bruins had managed only seventeen at the Philadelphia goal. Wobbly, Adam skated to the bench, elated but exhausted. Shedding his mask and gloves, he accepted the congratulations of his teammates, careful not to let any of them thump him on the back or left shoulder. As he was about to leave the ice, Robin Redford held up his hand for him to stay. The Garden announcer's voice crackled over the public address system: "The number-three star of the hockey game is Al Johnston!"

Johnston skated a small circle near the visitor's bench, waving his hand at the cheering crowd.

"The number-two star of the hockey game is Ted McLennan!"

McLennan also skated in a circle to acknowledge the accolade before turning to watch Adam's face as the announcer boomed: "And the number-one star is . . . 'Magic' McKinnon!"

Adam flushed as he saw the crowd rise *en masse* to give him an ovation. Amid the clapping and stamping, he skated to midice and waved his goalie stick at each section. It was a crowning moment, marred only by his dread that it might well be his last in a sports arena. Each searing breath told him as much; told him his ride on the enchanted wave had probably crested and all too soon he would be plunged into a swirling backlash.

27

To the Garden spectators, even those at rinkside, it looked as if Adam had completed his turn around the ice and happily hugged teammate Ted McLennan—a comradely gesture they applauded lustily. Actually, Adam hadn't so much embraced McLennan as collapsed in his arms. "Hurt bad, Ted," he gasped. "Legs like rubber. Help me to the locker room."

"Right, Doc," said McLennan and, holding Adam under his armpits, called Danny Smith to assist him.

In the first-aid room, Adam almost fainted when Smith tried to pull his Bruins jersey over his head. He simply could not raise his left arm above his shoulder without excruciating pain. "Cut it off!" he cried. "I'll pay for it."

Worriedly, Smith said, "I better get the team doctor, Tom Johnson."

"No! I've got my own doctor here. Dan Lassiter. Get him."

Smith nodded, vaguely knowing who Lassiter was and what he looked like but having no idea where to find him. He took a pair of bandage scissors from his trainer's kit and handed them to McLennan. "Here. Cut Doc's jersey. I'll go get Lassiter."

He did not have to look far. Twenty feet down the corridor, Tom Johnson was talking to a man who also held a doctor bag in his hand. "Are you Dr. Lassiter?" Smith asked and, at his nod, said, "Adam McKinnon wants to see you." He gave Tom Johnson an embarrassed glance and added, "Alone."

"Alone?" Dan started to protest that Johnson, an orthopedic surgeon, was more familiar than he with sports injuries, but decided to find out what Adam's problem was first. "Stick around, will you, Tom?" he asked Johnson. "I may need your help."

"Sure, Dan," Johnson replied. "I'll be in the locker room with the boys. Tell McKinnon I don't know how he did it—and I'm not sure I want to know—but he put on an incredible show tonight. Best goaltending I ever saw. Hope he's not hurt too badly."

"It'd be a mixed blessing," said Dan over his shoulder and followed Smith to the first-aid room.

With his jersey cut off and his protective pads gone, Adam sat on the examining table in a sweat-soaked T-shirt. He took a last sip from the cup of water McLennan had brought him and muttered thanks as both the Bruin's center and Smith left the room.

Wordlessly, Lassiter observed Adam's grunting respirations a few moments before taking his right hand to check the color of his nail beds and time his pulse rate. "Where do you hurt?" he finally asked.

Adam pointed to the lower left side of his breastbone. "Lucas's head hit me there like a battering ram. Must've torn or cracked something, since I keep getting sharp stabs every time I breathe. . . . Think I'm cyanotic?"

"Not grossly—though it's hard to be sure in this artificial light."

"Better check me out for a pneumothorax, anyway."

"Exactly what I had in mind," said Lassiter. "I also plan to draw blood gases, stick a needle into your pericardial sac, and drill bilateral burr holes in your skull. Any other suggestions?"

"Okay, okay," Adam said. "I know doctors make lousy patients. But I'm really worried, Dan. I barely made it back to the bench after that last swing around the ice. Lakeman'll have a fit when he finds out."

Lassiter shrugged dismissingly. "Then, I'll treat him, too. But first, you." Opening his bag, he took out a stethoscope and blood pressure cuff and laid them on the table. Then, gripping the top of Adam's windpipe between his thumb and forefinger, he told him to take a deep breath.

"Well, at least your trachea's in the midline," he said before fitting his stethoscope to his ears. "Let's take a listen to your lungs."

Finishing his examination without further comment, Lassiter put the instruments back in his bag and met Adam's anxious stare. "Yes?" he taunted.

"What'd you find? I know damned well something's wrong."

"Something is," Lassiter agreed, "though based on my physical alone, I can't be sure what. Your skin's cold and clammy, but your blood pressure's okay, so you're not in shock. Any chance LBC produces hypoglycemia?"

"Not that I'm aware of."

"Then it's probably just a sympathetic nervous system response to the pain. Your breath sounds are faint but equal, making it unlikely you've suffered a pneumothorax of any size. No cardiac rubs or crunches, either. So, except for exquisite point tenderness along your left sternal border—which could represent either a rib fracture or avulsed cartilage—I don't find much else."

"Glad to hear that," Adam sighed. "What next?"

"A trip to the hospital for your weekly X-ray. Maybe an electrocardiogram to rule out cardiac contusion. And for the grand finale, a psychiatric evaluation to find out why you persist in behaving so idiotically. Any objections?"

"Not to the first few items. But I really don't need a shrink, Dan. Believe it or not, Lucas's hard head knocked some sense into mine. To prove it, I'm canceling my other exhibitions. Providing my chest X-ray doesn't show anything too bad, I'm going ahead with the Jackson fight and maybe a Ping-Pong match against the North Koreans in September, then hanging up my jock for good. That's a promise, not only to you but to Megan and Al Lakeman—both of whom are probably waiting to issue ultimatums of their own." He sighed deeply. "Maybe I ought to beg you to put me in the hospital. Otherwise, I've got a long night ahead of me."

"I wouldn't be a bit surprised. . . . Pro hockey, for Chrissake!" Lassiter said disgustedly. "What in the world possessed you?"

Adam shook his head. "As Napoleon might've said after the battle of Waterloo: it seemed like a good idea at the time. But even though my goaltending days are over, I've got a problem: I can't get off this table."

"What do you mean?"

"Just that if I'm going to make it to the hospital without the help of a stretcher, and explain myself to Megan and Lakeman later on, I need something strong for pain."

"Morphine?" said Lassiter, frowning.

"No. Morphine's out—for reasons I won't go into now. What I'd prefer is an intercostal nerve block. You can do that for me, can't you?"

Lassiter hesitated. "I suppose. There must be a bottle of Xylocaine around here someplace. But I'm an internist, don't forget. Haven't done one in years. Why not let Tom Johnson do it?"

"Uh uh. I don't know Johnson, but I do know he's quoted in the newspapers a lot. And it's essential to keep this quiet."

"Why?"

"Because, unless I miss my guess, Al Lakeman's going to descend on me shortly and tell me to either quit all my goddamned showing off or find myself another fight manager. And I'm going to look properly abashed and agree, providing he does something for me: get the date of the Jackson fight moved up. I don't know if Al can swing it, but I do know he'll have a much better chance if my injury's kept out of the papers. So, get the Xylocaine, will you, please, and if necessary, I'll show you how to do the block."

Lassiter's exhaled breath sounded like steam blowing from a safety valve. "You know," he said exasperatedly, "even if what you say makes sense, you're still a royal pain in the ass. And I'm getting damned tired of being manipulated. In fact, if you really—"

A knock on the door interrupted him. He unlocked it, spoke briefly to whomever was out there, and announced, "It's Todd Tanner."

"Let him in," Adam replied. "Just him."

"C'mon in and baby-sit, Todd," Lassiter said. "I'm going to get the keys to the medicine cabinet. Be right back."

"How you feelin', Doc?" Tanner asked.

"Like I've been kicked in the chest by a mule."

"You look it, too. Hate to add to your troubles, but Lakeman wants to talk to you bad."

"How mad is he?"

"Oh, Lord!" Tanner rolled his eyes heavenward. "Mad as I've ever seen him. He won't speak to Aaron. He had a run-in with the cop outside the locker room that almost got him arrested, and he is chewin' Tums a package at a time."

"Did you talk to Megan?"

"Yeah, and she don't sound too happy, either. I'm supposed to let her know if you're okay. Are you?"

"Doesn't she want to see me?"

"If you're dying, maybe. Otherwise, she wants to wait 'till she cools off. Far as I'm concerned, though, you played a hell of a game out there."

"Thanks," said Adam, "even if yours is the minority opinion. Tell Megan I'm a little banged up and Lassiter is taking me to the hospital for X-rays. Depending on how they turn out, I'll either call or come home right after."

"And Lakeman—what do you want me to tell him?"

Adam grimaced. "Tell Lakeman to have more respect for the fuzz. They're only doing their job. Then, after ducking, tell him to meet me at Commonwealth General in about an hour. We'll talk there."

Two hours later, after having had multiple X-rays, an electrocardiogram, an elasticized cloth-binder strapped to his chest, and his sanity questioned, not by a psychiatrist but by Al Lakeman, Adam was ready to leave the hospital.

"How does the rib feel?" asked Lassiter, after helping Adam into the front seat of his six-year-old Datsun and climbing behind the wheel.

"About as well as a cracked rib surrounded by a hematoma is supposed to feel. Not that I'm complaining. At least, the fractured ends aren't displaced."

"Is the intercostal block still holding?"

"Fairly well. The binder helps, too. I'll put some heat on it soon as I get home."

"And your talk with Al Lakeman—" said Lassiter as he started the engine, "how'd that go?"

Adam tried to laugh and immediately grunted with pain. "He didn't beat around the bush, I'll say that. He asked how I was, I told him, and then he just blasted away: either I quit all outside activities and go into serious training for the Jackson fight at some isolated camp in the Berkshires or I find myself another manager."

"Where in the Berkshires?"

"Some former horse farm outside of Lenox. Know the area?"

"Damned right. I was born and raised twenty miles away in Williamstown. It's pretty country. You'll like it."

"Maybe so. But Megan won't—since she's not invited. I had to argue like hell to get Lakeman's permission to see her once a week—conjugal visits I believe the prisons call them. On the bright side, though, Al promised to talk to Bucky Miller, Jackson's manager, and try to get the fight date moved up."

"How'd you persuade him to do that?"

"Told him the truth: that I'd developed a pinched nerve in my left wrist and needed it operated on as soon as possible. He'll probably want you to confirm what I told him—maybe in writing—and then do his best to re-schedule the bout for mid-June."

"Mid-June!" Lassiter exclaimed. "That's only a month from now. Your rib will barely be healed by then."

"Doesn't matter. Jackson punches so hard he can break any bone he hits. Especially forty-five-year-old bones. So I don't dare let him hit me anywhere. A regulation-sized ring's about four hundred feet square and I plan to use every one to keep out of his range."

"But a month!" Lassiter persisted. "Jesus, Adam, that rib you cracked sits right over the lingular segment of your left lung. A jagged edge from another rib fracture could not only puncture it but tear into your pericardium."

"I know, Dan. Better have an ambulance with a chest tube and suction waiting outside the arena for me. . . . Truth is, though, I don't have much choice. . . ."

"Mind explaining that?"

"You already know my biggest problem. You even predicted that, at the rate my peripheral nerves are growing, I'll need wrist and ankle and maybe even vertebral surgery by mid-summer."

"Is that what prompted you to take up hockey?"

"For one night—yes. Obviously, not my brightest idea."

"Better than bullfighting," Lassiter said generously. "But is that all there was to it?"

"No," Adam admitted. "About a week and a half ago, the pain in my wrist got so bad I shot up with morphine. Ever try it, yourself?"

Lassiter glanced at him sharply and shook his head.

"Well, I'll say this for it," Adam continued, "it certainly lives up to its billing. It opens all the doors in your mind at once, causing quite a traffic jam. But before you report me to the Medical Society, let me hasten to add that I ended up in nightmare alley and swore never to touch it again. Good thing that cortisone injection you gave me worked or else I would've quit sports right then. Now, I'm just hoping it'll hold me until the Jackson fight."

"And then?"

"The left wrist gets operated. I don't need my left hand to play Ping-Pong."

"And if the cortisone doesn't hold you?"

"Then I'm in big trouble. Maybe I can get my hands on some betaendorphin from the researchers around town. Or maybe I can learn to give myself anesthetic nerve blocks. Whatever it takes, I intend to go through with the Jackson fight."

"Why?" asked Lassiter with a mixture of exasperation and concern. "What are you trying to prove . . . ? Sure, you stand to make millions from it, but is any amount of money worth what you'll be risking? Wouldn't it be a lot smarter to grab all you've gained, including Megan, and drop out of the fight game now?"

"Don't think I haven't thought long and hard about it. But . . . I can't. Maybe if you'd known me and what I was like before taking LBC— what a loser I was—you'd understand."

"Understand what?" demanded Lassiter, braking for a traffic light. "Your death wish? I'm a devout death-hater myself. And, as you already know from a previous conversation, it nearly drove me off the deep end once, so I recognize the road signs."

"Is that where you think I'm headed—the deep end?"

"Based on your half-assed, macho reasoning for going ahead with the Jackson fight, I'd say you're right on the edge, or maybe even the downslope. Do you think anybody outside your camp and Jackson's camp really gives a damn whether you two fight or not? For the world at large, it's nothing more than a distraction. Which is not to say your exploits aren't making waves. I got hit by one of the bigger ones tonight. . . ."

The horn blast of the car behind them alerted Lassiter that the light had changed.

"What do you mean?" asked Adam.

"I suppose I should've mentioned this earlier, but there were a few things to be discussed first and I didn't want us to get sidetracked. Anyway, while you and Lakeman were talking in the X-ray lounge, I got a call from an old friend in Washington. You've heard of Nelson Freiborg, haven't you?"

"That economist who was recently appointed to some high-level government post?"

"That's him. Chief domestic advisor to the president. Nels and I have known each other a long time. It was mainly his recommendation that got me appointed to the National Commission on Health Care Costs. But that's not why he called. He called to talk about you."

"Me! Why?"

"Seems Nels and a few of his cabinet-level friends were watching the hockey game on closed-circuit TV tonight and afterwards, one of them, the secretary of defense no less, decided he had to meet you. So, knowing I was your doctor from somebody, probably one of the reporters at your press conference, Nels asked me to sound you out."

"About what? Meeting the secretary of defense. What for?"

"That's exactly what I asked him. But either he didn't know or wouldn't say. Instead, he gave me Andrew Mellinger's home phone number and asked me to call him."

"Well, let me know what he says when you do."

"I already did. Even though it was past one A.M., Nels insisted I phone him right away. Mellinger wants to meet with you urgently. In fact, tomorrow. He backed off from that idea when I told him how banged up you were, but asked me to talk to you and get you to Washington by Monday morning, if at all possible."

Getting no reply, Lassiter glanced at him, saw the perplexed look on his face, and added, "Look, Adam, I know the president's as big a sports nut as Nixon or Ford, and leaving on his ten-nation European tour on Tuesday, but Mellinger swore this had nothing to do with the president *or* sports. He wouldn't go so far as to say national security is involved, but he is the defense secretary, for Chrissake, so I suppose you have to take him seriously."

Adam nodded. "Anything else I ought to know?"

"Yes," said Lassiter and paused to clear his throat. "A real shocker. He thought you needed protection—by me on the way to Washington and by some federal agency from then on."

"Protection!" Adam cried. "Against whom? The Flyers? Coleman Jackson? The mob?"

Lassiter shook his head. "Beats me. But I must admit I'm intrigued. Things have been rather dull around the hospital lately, so I'm willing to go if you are. What do you think? I'm supposed to call Mellinger in the morning with your answer."

Adam pondered. "Tell him okay—with two provisos. One, Megan goes along, at least on the trip if not to the meeting. And two, I want Henry Kalisher in on it."

"The assistant secretary of health. Why him?"

"'Cause we both know what they're after, even if we don't know why: they want to know how I do what I do. And if it's really all that urgent I meet with them, then the possibility exists they not only want but *need* to know it for reasons I may not be able to refuse. That being the case, I might want to propose a little trade. And the guy with the goods is Kalisher. After all, he controls the myopic bastards at the N.I.N.M.D. who turned down my research grant."

Lassiter chuckled. "Neat. Just remember, though, Henry spent almost half his life in the military and shows it. He doesn't like to be pushed into anything."

"Neither do I. But if any pushing's to be done, I want the same pair of hands pushing him as me."

Lassiter parked his car in front of Adam's North Shore duplex and helped him out of the seat.

"Need any help up the stairs?"

"No," said Adam, "but maybe a little at the door. Megan's not much of a hockey fan."

Lassiter sighed and reached into his car to shut off the headlights.

Megan met them at the door in a long, silk lounging robe with Chinese dragons embroidered on its back. The robe clung to her flesh, outlining her svelte figure and making Adam feel a possessive pride in her.

"No hugs," he warned.

"I wouldn't dream of it," she said haughtily and, turning to Lassiter, asked, "How's my boy—and I do mean, *boy?*"

"A little cracked—in a rib, that is—but a dab of Krazy Glue took care of it."

"I see," she said coolly. "Well, thanks for bringing him home, Dan. Can I offer you a drink? Something to eat?"

"No, thanks. All I really want right now is a good night's sleep with a gorgeous woman beside me, and Kris has that franchise. Don't be too hard on him, though, Megan. If you listen to him long enough, he makes a certain amount of sense."

"He'd better!" she snapped.

"Would you please stop talking about me in the third person," Adam said, "and let me in the house!"

"Why not? You pay the rent. I suspect you're also responsible for the patrol car that's been passing by the house every ten minutes."

"Patrol car?" Adam exchanged glances with Lassiter. "Tell her about Washington, Dan."

"We've been invited there on Monday. You're welcome to come."

"To meet the president?"

"No, the secretary of defense."

"Oh, really? Is he having trouble with his tennis game?"

"We're not sure what his trouble is," Lassiter said with a shrug. "Why not come along and find out . . . for Kris's sake."

"Why Kris's?"

"If you go, she goes."

"She say that?"

"Uh, no. She doesn't know about the trip yet."

"You men!" Megan fumed. "You don't need wives, just puppy dogs."

Lassiter flushed in the heat of her stare. He smiled weakly, muttered good night, and left.

"Before you say anything—" Adam began after following Megan into the living room.

"Yes . . ." she hissed.

"Give me a kiss. You're irresistible when you're angry."

"Am I? Well, in that case, steel yourself, 'cause I'm going to be that way for some time. Not that you're likely to do anything about it. How badly are you hurt?"

Adam unbuttoned his shirt to show her the chest-binder underneath.

"You look like you've had open-heart surgery."

"I feel like it, too. Actually, though, I got away with one slightly cracked rib. . . . Anyway, it's over, I'm sorry for any anxious moments I caused you, and I do want that kiss."

"And I want an explanation, not just for what happened tonight but what's been happening lately. A good place to start is why you shot up with morphine a week ago last Wednesday."

He stared. "You knew about that?"

Megan's eyes flashed angrily. "Of course, I knew. I found you asleep on the couch the next morning with the empty morphine vial on the floor. I suppose I've had worse moments in my life, but that one ranks right up there. Made me realize you aren't the only one around here who lives in a dream world. But I decided to keep quiet about it."

"You have been pretty quiet lately."

"How observant! You've been so busy or exhausted the last few weeks I'm surprised you noticed anything I did. . . . Oh, sit down and I'll fix you a drink. Anything else you want—codeine? Morphine?"

"Easy on the sarcasm. The nerve block Dan gave me earlier is wearing off and I really do hurt."

"Well, damn it, so do I!" she exploded. "It hurts to realize that the man I love thinks so little of our future together that he risks his life in a silly hockey game. And for what? To get your name in the record books or your picture on a bubblegum card? Too bad you can't set any world records with me." His sudden wince made her pause, almost apologize. "Look, Adam," she resumed in a less strident voice, "I know you're exhausted and in pain, so I'll skip the bitchy remarks and get right to the point. When I get back with the drinks, I want to know exactly what you expect of me and I'll tell you the same. If our expectations aren't mutually incompatible, maybe we can negotiate a deal. Otherwise, let's break clean and *not* come out fighting—okay?"

"Okay," he said, sinking down on the couch and wearily closing his eyes.

When he opened them again, Megan stood before him, holding drinks. She handed him one and sat beside him, sipping her Scotch and water while he gulped his, and waiting for him to speak.

"What I want—need—is a month. A month to train for the Jackson fight." Purposely, he avoided telling her about Lakeman's planned change of scene until some more opportune time. "Win or lose," he went on, "I quit boxing, and all other contact sports, immediately afterward. We get married, take off on a Far Eastern honeymoon, and I go back to practicing medicine. That's it. Now, what do you want?"

"I'm tempted to say that I want you to stop all sports, especially boxing, right now, but I know that wouldn't be fair. So, in poor exchange, I want some answers—straight ones—

and if they're not too hard to take, I'll give you the month. Then, I, too, want to get married and have a baby. . . . Yes," she said, thrusting out her chin defiantly in response to his startled look, "a baby! And don't you dare pretend that's not important to you. The few times you've talked about Diana's abortion you've made it sound as if you're in debt to humanity; you owe the world a life. Well, so be it. I want a child, too. Your child. And soon."

Adam reached for her hand. "I really do want to kiss you now."

"Good, only don't pucker up just yet. There's more. I have a confidante—another man. But before you have a jealous fit, you'd better hear who. He's the man responsible for my meeting you. He gave me your address because he saw the same lonely look in your eyes as in mine. He's also noticed the change in you lately and is bothered by it for more than proprietary reasons. No, I won't keep you in suspense. It's Harry Patashnick."

"Harry!" Adam drew back in astonishment. "The same Harry who nicknamed me 'Magic'? He's even more of a promoter than I thought."

"And more of a friend. But wise as he is, Harry couldn't understand why you were on morphine. He suggested I talk to Dan Lassiter, but I was reluctant to do that before talking to you first. Does Dan know?"

Adam nodded. "He knows I took morphine *once*—the night you accidently kicked me out of bed and the pain in my left wrist, which had been building up for days, grew unbearable. I told him tonight. He also knows the experience scared the hell out of me and I swore never to do it again. I've kept that promise, Megan. I'm hooked on codeine and amphetamines until I get through the Jackson fight and some simple wrist surgery, then the drugs end. I'd like to keep my promise to Charlie Nash to help the American team beat the North Koreans in Ping-Pong which is why I wanted to honeymoon in the Far East—but that's optional, or as you put it earlier, negotiable. . . . Why the hell didn't you tell me before you wanted a baby?"

"I almost did, that lovely day we spent at Narragansett, but we'd sort of agreed to keep the talk uncomplicated. Then, the very next night, you took the morphine and that put a damper on that. It drove home to me how little I really know or understand about you. I don't know the fanatic who played goalie for the Bruins tonight at all. Who is he, Adam? Where does he come from?"

He gestured helplessly. "From the past, I suppose. From some distorted self-image. But I can't afford to indulge his whims any longer. Tonight's grandstanding cost me a cracked rib. The Jackson fight might cost even more, if I go through with it."

"If—?"

"I can take a lot of pain, Megan. I always could. But some things I can't—or won't—take. Losing you is one of them."

Megan blinked the sudden moisture from her eyes. "I don't want to lose you, either. I just hate to see you so driven and—" Abruptly, she broke off and pointed to the front window. "Oh, look—there are the flashing lights of that patrol car again. What's it doing around here?"

"Protecting me, I suppose. Only don't ask me from what. It'll probably take a trip to Washington to find that out."

"Washington?" she puzzled. "Explain."

Adam told her what little he had learned from Dan Lassiter.

When he finished, she smiled slyly and said. "Well, that certainly stirs my reporter's instincts. Think I will go with you, after all. Will we get a police escort to the airport?"

"Don't know," he said, yawning uncontrollably. "The only escort I need right now is to bed. I don't think I can make it without you."

"I don't think so, either," she said with tender conviction, "and not just to bed."

28

Adam had to admit he was impressed by the Department of Defense's travel arrangements. Anybody below the rank of cabinet member was bound to be. A siren-silent police car drove Megan and him to Logan Airport, a flight-line station wagon transported them, and the Lassiters, across the tarmac to an Air Force T-39 passenger jet, and when they landed at Dulles International, two long limousines were waiting to whisk them away. But Adam couldn't relax and enjoy the luxurious accommodations with the same enthusiasm as the others. Like the host of a lavish banquet, he kept wondering what all this was going to cost him.

There were four smiling security agents in civilian clothes— Secret Service, most likely, Lassiter speculated—assigned to their party. Two escorted Adam and Dan to the Pentagon in Arlington County, Virginia, and the other two drove Megan and Kris Lassiter to the National Gallery of Art in downtown Washington. Riding in the spacious back seat of the limousine beside Lassiter, Adam fidgeted as his chest-binder prevented him from sitting comfortably. Although the two of them had talked and joked throughout the flight from Boston, neither man spoke now. Adam had learned that Lassiter's face took on a deceptively stern, brooding expression in repose and it no longer bothered him. Both he and Megan had come to enjoy Dan and Kris's company enormously. They were two highly competent physicians with strong personalities who genuinely cared about and complemented each other. He would have envied Lassiter's apparent stability had he not sensed his inner tension and turmoil: the unappeasable restlessness of a man with a consuming mission. Under other circumstances, he could visualize Lassiter as a commando leader or a homicide detective—a man whose outlook was even more fatalistic than his own had become. Though it would be unthinkable to ask, he wondered what vital element was missing from Dan's life.

At the Pentagon, Adam waved off Lassiter's help and pulled himself out of the car. An army major, waiting at the reception desk, straightened up as they entered. "I'm Dawes, your escort officer. I understand you've been injured, Dr. McKinnon. Would you like a motorized cart?"

"How far do we have to hike?" asked Adam, looking down the long corridor.

"Maybe a hundred yards north and fifty west. We'll be using General Ricksey's office."

"And who, may I ask, is he?"

"Brigadier General Ricksey? He's a branch chief, sir. The Defense Intelligence Agency."

"I see. Well, lead on, Major. I'll try to keep up."

They followed the corridor to the second of the five concentric rings that comprised the Pentagon structure and turned left. Adam found himself thinking of the rats he had watched trying to find their way out of mazes during his memory-boosting drug research and sympathizing with them. Finally, Major Dawes stopped, slipped a punchkey card into a slot, and a door opened. Inside, a sturdy, fortyish-looking man with a silver star on his khaki shirt collar rose from behind a desk and extended his hand. "Greetings, Doctors. I'm Ricksey. Welcome to Paranoia Palace West."

"Where's East?" asked Adam.

"The Kremlin. They take vodka instead of Valium there and have Afghan rugs on the floor. Pleasure to meet you, Dr. McKinnon. I used to do a little boxing myself and would love to talk to you about it, but the others are waiting for us in the conference room."

The others were Defense Secretary Andrew Mellinger,

former Caltech engineering professor and founder of his own electronics manufacturing company, and Dr. Henry Kalisher, another native Californian, who had gone from chief of medicine at Letterman Army Hospital to president of the board of MEDCAL to his present post as the nation's leading medical expert. His immediate superior, Myles Mason, the secretary of health and human services, was a lay administrator who made no secret of his ambition to run for the U.S. Senate from his home state of Oregon at the end of his present term and left most medical policy decisions to Henry.

Mellinger was a handsome, thick-set man in his early sixties who impressed with his keen intellect and striking blue eyes. Elegantly attired in an Italian silk suit, he sat at the end of a small conference table, smoking a thin cigar. Kalisher sat to his right, a lank, lean, balding man about Mellinger's age whom Adam had corresponded with but never met and Lassiter knew slightly from medical meetings. He had a vague recollection of one such occasion, a late-night gathering in a hotel suite, when, after several drinks, Henry had unbent from his military posture and proved surprisingly witty. Shaking Dan's hand, he didn't seem so disposed now. If anything, he looked pained, imposed upon.

"Well," said Mellinger, waving everybody down, "now that we're through the introductions, let's get on with the intrigue. My apology, Dr. McKinnon, for failing to make clear the purpose of this meeting from the start, but there were a few field reports that needed verification. Obviously, my department is far removed from the world of sports and, except for a distasteful interest in biological warfare, from medicine. International sports competitions don't interest us, either. You, on the other hand, definitely do."

"Mind telling me why?" asked Adam as Mellinger paused to relight his cigar.

"I'd rather let General Ricksey do that, since he's the one who brought you to my attention. . . . Chet?"

"I'm embarrassed to admit this, Dr. McKinnon," began Ricksey, "but our agency was a little slow in realizing the full scope of your accomplishments. The moment we learned of the Russians' interest in you, however, we wised up."

Adam squinted in surprise. "The Russians, you say?"

"The Russian military, to be exact. We take them very seriously around here."

"I'm sure. And how did you come to learn of their interest in me?"

"A dozen of their top local agents have recently been ordered to find out everything they possibly can about you. That's a sizable contingent and they seem to be under some sort of deadline. Any idea why?"

"No, not unless one of their leaders has developed Alzheimer's Disease."

"Alzheimer's?"

"A progressive, memory-losing dementia," Adam explained.

"That's a happy thought! But since it's the Russian military, not their medical establishment, who've ordered the investigation, it's logical to infer that they think your discovery has military applicability. Does it, Dr. McKinnon?"

"I really haven't thought about it in that way."

"Nor did I, when I first read about you in the sports pages," Ricksey admitted. "But the Russians have a flair for the esoteric. They've still got an entire research division working on such arcane phenomena as mental telepathy and psychokinesis. In your case, however, they see a more practical use for your remarkable training method. To state it concisely: both we and the Soviets continue to design and build ever-more-sophisticated aircraft. But no matter what their performance capabilities or how many gadgets we pack into them, they're still flown by men. And in aerial combat, it's the skill of the pilot that counts the most. What worries the Russians is that their fighter pilots would be no match for ours if all of ours had your incredibly quick reflexes. Furthermore, and I suppose this is confidential until the details appear in *Aviation News*—both the Russians and ourselves are working hard to adapt laser weaponry for our aircraft. Computers, of course, can aim such lasers at slow-moving or stationary targets. But for air-to-air strikes they need human button-pressers, and that takes terrific hand-eye coordination. . . . Now do you see the potential problem you pose for our Russian counterparts?"

Soberly, Adam nodded.

"I was confident you would," Mellinger interjected. "It follows that we're every bit as anxious as they are to learn the details of your training method. In particular, the composition of your secret nutrient."

Adam rubbed the heel of his hand across his brow. He was not totally surprised by what had just been told him. He wouldn't have been *totally* surprised if, instead of the Soviet military, it had been their Academy of Music who was worried about how his discovery might affect the performance of the American entries in the next International Chopin Competition. "I understand your position, Mr. Secretary," he said. "Now, perhaps you'll help me to understand mine by telling what happens if I refuse to divulge that information?"

Mellinger smiled. "We've no intention of torturing it out of you, if that's what you mean? On the other hand, we are prepared to pay you a substantial sum of money for it. Just name your price. Everybody has one, I'm told."

"And I'm no exception. But just for argument's sake, let's say what I want doesn't translate easily into money. For example, some sports writers have accused me of trying to revolutionize and control professional sports. What if they're right?"

The defense secretary shrugged. "Some people regard sports as a metaphor for war, Dr. McKinnon, but I consider that naive. Animals compete for sexual domination and engage in what could loosely be called sporting activities. But only humans and ants go to war. So, whatever your ambitions in that field may be, they're of little concern to us. Our priority goal is to maintain military parity with the Russians and gain an edge on them whenever possible. Your discovery represents just such an opportunity. We simply need to learn, evaluate, and, if worthwhile, keep it for ourselves. If we can't, we have to make damned sure the Russians can't, either. We would have no choice but to guard you closely, even put you in protective custody if absolutely necessary. Does that help define your, ah, theoretical position?"

"It certainly does," Adam replied.

"Does it shock you?"

"Not at all. I accept your predicament and your contingencies. They're a matter of conviction and necessity. So was my decision to enter professional sports. As I've admitted publicly, my main reason was to make enough money to fund my research. Though not impossible, it would be difficult to carry on that research in 'protective custody.' Moreover, I'm as patriotic as the next man and want my country to be as strong militarily as possible. So, having made a few position points which may seem obscure but will become clearer shortly, I'm ready to start the bargaining."

Mellinger and Ricksey exchanged smiles. Kalisher, sensing

that he would likely be asked to contribute the lion's share to the pot, looked wary.

"Just to be sure we understand each other, Dr. McKinnon," Mellinger said, "am I correct in stating that you are prepared to confide every detail of your training method and give us exclusive and unrestricted rights to it in return for some form of payment on our part?"

"You are, providing the payoff is adequate to allow me to pursue my research goals—to find the cause and possibly the cure of presenile dementia."

"Very well. How much do you want for openers?"

"Not a cent," Adam said. "This isn't a Manhattan or Apollo project, it's basic research. So, instead of any specific sum of money, I'm asking for something better suited to my needs: control. I want to be appointed associate director of the National Institute for Nervous and Mental Diseases, with absolute authority over all government-funded research on dementia. Since no such position exists at the moment, it would have to be created by the secretary of health. And I'm hopeful Mr. Mason will do just that, on the strong recommendation of Dr. Kalisher here."

Mellinger swung around to face the assistant secretary. "What do you say to that, Henry?"

Kalisher squirmed in his chair. "Well, I don't know. To state the obvious, it's highly irregular. I'd certainly want to talk it over with the directors of the N.I.H. and N.I.N.M.D. first, get their input, then give it a lot of thought."

"Is that acceptable to you, Dr. McKinnon?" asked Mellinger.

"I'm in no hurry. But the longer it takes for the administrative wheels to grind, the longer you'll have to wait to find out what you want to know."

"Now, wait just a damned minute," Kalisher sputtered. "Do you mean to say you expect a decision from us right now?"

"It would certainly speed up our negotiations, wouldn't you agree, Mr. Secretary?"

"I would, indeed, Dr. McKinnon," said Mellinger. "We'd have our answer and you'd be free to resume your various activities, encumbered by a small security detail. So, what do you say, Henry?"

Kalisher compressed his lips. "Hell, I can't speak for Mason. You know that."

"No, but you can speak to him," Mellinger replied calmly. "I happen to know he's in his office now."

"What if he won't buy it on my say-so alone?"

"Then the president will talk to him."

"The president!" Kalisher exclaimed. "What's his involvement in this?"

"Look at it this way, Henry. The defense budget was over two hundred billion this year. How much was the N.I.N.M.D.'s budget? Half a billion?"

"Something like that."

"Five new fighter bombers cost more. Does that suggest to you which investment the president will want to protect?"

Kalisher scowled. "I'm beginning to feel like nothing more than a rubber stamp here. Has the president already authorized you to give McKinnon anything he wants?"

"Anything within reason. And his request sounds reasonable enough to me. . . . Dr. Lassiter, you've been conspicuously silent. What's your opinion?"

"I think the project review committee of the N.I.N.M.D. made a hell of a blunder when they terminated Dr. McKinnon's research grant a few months back and ought to be given a chance to make amends. Knowing something of the basic nature of Adam's discovery, I consider it enormously promising—in fact, a potential breakthrough in the treatment of a whole host of neurological diseases. In short, he has my vote."

"Mine, too," said Mellinger and looked at his watch. "Henry, why don't you call Mason? I promised the president that, if we couldn't get this matter resolved by three P.M., I'd let him know."

"Now, just hold on, Andy," Kalisher said with rising indignation, "I don't mind being strong-armed, but I do mind giving my boss the impression I'm a dunce. Don't you think I'd have a better chance of convincing Mason to give McKinnon the directorship he wants if I knew what we were getting in return? He's sure going to want to know what his training method consists of, and if it really works."

"It works," Lassiter assured him. "Ask a pro boxer named 'Mean Joe' Metcalf or the Philadelphia Flyers' team."

"Wait a second," interrupted Mellinger. "Henry has a point. Are you willing to brief us on the bare details of your method, Dr. McKinnon, just on trust?"

Adam hesitated. "On trust and on the condition that my appointment is announced to the press by the end of this afternoon. Of course, it could always be withdrawn later, but I'm willing to gamble that it won't."

"Sounds fair to me," said Mellinger. "Does it to you, Henry?"

"I'm not sure how fair it is, but it's bound to spare me a lot of hemming and hawing when I talk to Mason."

"All right, Dr. McKinnon," Mellinger said with a brisk nod, "the floor is yours. But you look mighty uncomfortable under that bulletproof binder you're wearing. Can I offer you a soft drink first?"

"That'd be appreciated," said Adam. "A blackboard would help, too."

After quenching his thirst with a bottle of Fresca, Adam rose stiffly to stand by the portable blackboard Ricksey wheeled out of a closet. He spent the first few minutes summarizing his previous efforts to find a cure for dementia and the many false leads followed. Then, picking up a piece of chalk, he sketched a synaptic nerve junction on the board to illustrate the key role played by acetylcholine in the transmission of nerve impulses. Glancing at Mellinger periodically to make sure he was neither bewildered nor bored, Adam explained the electrochemical process, step by step. Finally, he launched into his discovery of LBC and some of the professional setbacks that culminated in his taking the chemical himself. Kalisher and Ricksey stopped taking notes at this point and listened raptly. Leaning forward in his chair, Mellinger appeared equally enthralled.

When Adam finished, the defense secretary shook his head in wonder and exclaimed, "Extraordinary! That certainly entitles you to membership in the Walter Reed Club for medical self-experimenters. What about the special diet and exercises you mentioned in your press conference—where do they fit in?"

"The exercises are real enough. Al Lakeman, my fight trainer, prescribes those. And I do take calcium and glutamic acid supplements. Otherwise, my diet isn't anything special. I made mention of it mainly as a smoke screen."

"A smoke screen?" Kalisher questioned. "To conceal the fact you're taking this LBC?"

"More or less," Adam admitted.

"Well, is it a nutrient or isn't it?"

Adam glanced at Lassiter, saw him shrug, and said tersely, "It is for birds."

"Any idea how the stuff works?" Kalisher asked.

"It could work through any of five major rate-limiting mechanisms. They range from an increased affinity for the receptors on the postsynaptic membrane to the time it takes to activate the channel that causes the top of the neuron to leak sodium and generate an electrical charge. I'm fairly confident I can pinpoint its exact mechanism through a series of animal experiments, but, until then, I'd just be guessing."

"Any effect of LBC on brain function? You haven't mentioned anything about that yet."

"Far as I can tell, LBC doesn't affect normal brain function—which is not too surprising for several reasons. Whereas acetylcholine always exerts an excitatory effect at neuromuscular junctions, its action in the brain is mixed—firing some synapses and inhibiting others. And while acetylcholine serves as the predominant neurotransmitter for peripheral nerves, brain synapses are responsive to a large variety of chemicals, such as the endorphins and enkephalins. Whatever the reason, except for quickened eye movements, I haven't noticed any central nervous system changes. I'm hopeful, however, that Alzheimer patients, with their impaired ability to synthesize acetylcholine in their memory centers, will respond differently."

"That good enough for you, Henry?" Mellinger asked.

At the edge in the defense secretary's voice, Kalisher muttered, "I suppose."

"Then, go make your call to Mason while I arrange for some lunch."

As Kalisher rose, Adam and Dan exchanged searching looks.

Suddenly, Adam said, "Wait! There're a few more things you all ought to know. LBC seems to have one more remarkable—and troublesome—property." He paused until Kalisher retook his seat. "Somehow it stimulates *'nerve growth factor'*—not the substance described in the medical literature as essential for the development of sympathetic nerve ganglia, but something similar that stimulates the growth of peripheral nerves."

"Peripheral nerves!" Kalisher's eyes widened. "Jesus, that has implications! We treat a hell of a lot of nerve injuries in the military. How sure are you it can do that?"

"Painfully sure. Since starting on LBC, I've developed nerve-entrapment syndromes in both wrists, especially my left one, and incipient indications of the same process in both ankles."

"What's a nerve-entrapment syndrome?" asked Mellinger.

As Adam explained, the defense secretary's frown deepened. "So there's a glitch in the works after all?"

"Isn't there always?" Adam answered ruefully. "This particular side effect may be preventable, however."

"How?"

"Well, for one thing, I've taken LBC continuously for three months now. Perhaps if I'd taken it intermittently instead, or in smaller doses, I might've avoided the complication. Second, since we can synthesize LBC rather easily in the laboratory, we may be able to modify its molecular structure and come up with a derivative whose action is more selective; namely—one that will increase nerve conduction velocity without stimulating 'nerve growth factor.'"

"So, what you're saying is that the complication is serious but not necessarily insurmountable—right?" At Adam's nod, Mellinger pressed on. "But I must ask again—are you quite sure LBC doesn't produce any mental derangements?"

Adam smiled wanly. "Although Dr. Lassiter may wish to disagree, I'm not aware of any. I'm no more deranged now than I was before starting on it."

"Do you disagree?" the defense secretary asked Lassiter.

"That depends on whether Adam actually goes through with the Coleman Jackson fight—as he insists he is."

"I've seen Jackson in action," said Ricksey, "and I wouldn't challenge him in a closed space armed with a Colt .45."

"All right," said Mellinger, cutting the digression short. "Any other side effects we ought to know about?"

Slowly, Lassiter nodded. "A *potential* one that worries me plenty, since I'm going to have to deal with it if it occurs. Adam feels LBC might be useful in treating certain myasthenia gravis cases—particularly those patients whose disease proves resistant to conventional therapy. I've inherited just such a patient from him recently and he's been after me to try it out. But before I do, I've insisted Adam go off LBC first to see if he suffers any withdrawal symptoms. My fear—and his—is that he might well develop a form of myasthenia himself—hopefully mild and transient but possibly permanent and intractable. In other words, it could doom him to a life of in-hospital respirator support or even prove fatal. That's a possibility, however remote, that I feel compelled to rule out before I'm willing to give LBC to a patient."

"Sounds ominous," said Mellinger, "and, until you can exclude that hazard, it would be equally unconscionable to give LBC to one of our pilots." He smiled fleetingly. "It may turn out to be for the birds, after all. . . . When do you plan to withdraw from the drug, Dr. McKinnon?"

"In another month or two."

"Well, then, you wouldn't object to Henry making the starting date of your directorship a few months after that?"

"Under the circumstances—no. I could hardly carry out my duties confined to a respirator."

Mellinger murmured assent. "These last disclosures certainly put a damper on the situation. . . . Still, since you raised the possibility that the nerve damage you've suffered might've been avoided if you'd taken less LBC for a shorter time, let me ask this: might a brief course, even a single dose of the drug, eliminate the dangers of withdrawal?"

"It's highly unlikely a single dose would cause symptoms of withdrawal. Nor would it do your pilots any good. It took me several days to accommodate to my quickened muscular movements. A week-long course of LBC may well work, however, and deserves investigating. Given a large enough monkey colony to test out different dosages and treatment schedules, I could probably come up with the answer to that possibility fairly fast."

"Well, that's mildly encouraging," Mellinger said. "I think we could live with that, don't you, Henry?"

Making a pyramid with his hands, Kalisher pondered until Mellinger gave him a sharp glance. "Seems to me that what we've just heard changes things considerably. I'd like to convene a panel of top neurologists and get their consensus before making an official recommendation to Myles Mason or anybody else."

Seeing Adam grimace and drop his head, Lassiter spoke up sharply, "And if I were Dr. McKinnon, Henry, I'd tell you to take your consensus and shove it! As a fellow administrator, I think consensus-gathering is fine when it comes to matters of simple judgment—like whether to expand the parking lot or hire more nurses. But I wouldn't dare depend on it to decide the merits of original thinking! Remember the great job a panel of experts did when they advised the Ford administration to launch a crash mass-innoculation program against the Swine

Flu epidemic that somehow never materialized? Your department is still paying damages for that fiasco.''

Taken aback, Kalisher asked, "What would you have me do, Dan?''

"Quit your waffling and stick to your original intention. Or, if you're no longer willing to do that, at least don't add insult to injury by subjecting Dr. McKinnon's research findings to another panel of nitpickers. You know damned well that no major drug discovery from sulfanilamide on has ever been free of serious, sometimes life-threatening side effects. Besides, Adam didn't request this meeting, you people did. He didn't demand an exorbitant sum of money before divulging the nature of his discovery, he more or less gave it away free. And he didn't deliberately withhold any adverse information, Henry, he volunteered it—after you'd neglected to ask. So, how can you possibly justify holding back now?''

In the ensuing silence, Mellinger pensively puffed his cigar. Finally, he said, "You've built an impressive argument for pushing ahead, Dr. Lassiter, and I for one find it persuasive. But before I recommend we bypass Henry's office and bring the matter directly to the president for action, I'd like to give both sides a chance to make any closing arguments if they wish. . . . Dr. McKinnon?''

"Well," Adam began, his face reflecting his mounting fatigue, "between us, Dr. Lassiter and I have presented all the known facts. And since I trust you gentlemen to destroy your notes and keep confidential everything you've learned about LBC in the event we fail to reach agreement, I'm left to choose between two courses of action. I have a signed contract that guarantees me two million dollars for fighting Coleman Jackson. That's a minimum figure. My actual take may well be closer to ten. That sum would be sufficient to start my own research institute and operate it for a few years. The major attraction of that course is the complete independence it offers; its major drawback—the time it would take to plan, build, equip, and staff such a facility. Were I put in charge of the dementia research program of the N.I.N.M.D., I could embark much sooner on some of the crucial experiments that need to be done before LBC could be recommended for human use. Its military applicability, if any, would also be determined earlier as well. So, unless Dr. Kalisher insists on any restrictions which I find unacceptable, my preference would be to stay with my original proposal.''

Mellinger smiled appreciatively. "Henry—what's your answer to that?"

"Under no circumstances will I condone an arrangement which would allow Dr. McKinnon to create his own private empire in the midst of the N.I.H.'s structure. Nor could I allow him to become anything even approaching a law-unto-himself. Such a radical departure from the established order would be too disruptive to morale. However, if Dr. McKinnon is willing to work within the system, with its periodic audits and peer reviews and hierarchy of command, I could promise him a certain grace period in which he could carry out his animal experiments with considerable autonomy, as well as an initial operating budget of ten million dollars. That arrangement may not be totally to his liking, but, with a show of mutual trust and good faith on both our parts, I think it would stand a reasonable chance of working out."

"So do I," Adam said almost at once. "In fact, if it will make your selling job any easier, I'll withdraw my demand that my appointment be announced this afternoon."

Before Kalisher could respond, Mellinger said, "I'd rather you didn't do that, Dr. McKinnon. We *want* the Russians to know you're on our payroll, so to speak."

"Even if LBC turns out to be a complete bust?"

"Even then—providing we know that long before they do. You see, since cold war tactics are primarily geared toward preventing hot wars, it's important the enemy knows what you've got in your arsenal. It's even better if he thinks you've got more than you actually have. Right now, the Russians are very intrigued by you; should you beat Coleman Jackson, they'll be obsessed. Ustinov, their defense minister, will have worse nightmares than he did when the Israelis shot down a squadron of his latest MiG fighters over Syria without any losses of their own. In short, it buys us time."

"And don't worry about me, Adam," Kalisher said. "I'm no amateur when it comes to putting the best face on things. I'll tell Mason exactly what I feel he needs to know, not a word more."

"Good, Henry. Good!" Mellinger beamed. "And on that note of mutual accord, may I urge you to make that call so we can break for lunch?"

Watching Adam slump back in his chair, Lassiter wondered if he realized how tenuous his victory over Kalisher, his revenge on the N.I.N.M.D., his chance of ever assuming the directorship he had won, really was! Ostensibly, he had been dealing with a trio of powerful government officials; in truth, they were merely front men for a vast bureaucracy that fed on personal sacrifices. In an interplay vaguely reminiscent of a police interrogation Mutt-and-Jeff routine, Mellinger had taken the high road, invoking national security; Kalisher had fussed and fumed, while conceding very little. Dan had hoped the promise of the N.I.N.M.D. directorship would persuade Adam to forego the Jackson fight. But Mellinger's subversion of the event into a psychological ploy had doomed that chance. What worried him the most, though, was what might happen when Adam went off LBC. The worst Jackson could do was knock him out; the LBC withdrawal could kill him. Glumly, Lassiter reminded himself to warn Kris not to plan any out-of-town vacations for them this summer.

At the end of a last-minute private briefing before Adam left the Pentagon, General Ricksey told him: "Just remember, Doctor, our job is not only to protect you but your secret as well. And to do that we've got to stay ahead of those who are breaking their asses to find it out. Not only the Russians but the ferrets among the press. Suppose you were a hot-shot reporter trying to piece together the sports story of the century. Where would you start?"

After reflecting on the question, Adam told Ricksey how close Estebrook, the science editor of the *Baltimore Sun*, had come to making the connection between his expert knowledge of choline metabolism and his physical prowess.

"Hmm," Ricksey murmured appreciatively. "If you were Estebrook, how would you follow up on that?"

"I'd probably drop by the New England Medical Center Hospital and talk to the other neurologists there. Ask them what I'd been working on lately."

"And what could they tell him?"

"Very little. I haven't given a seminar on my research in almost a year. And the only other people who know about LBC—my two lab associates, Walt Carson and Jill Jamieson— are out of the country."

"Where?"

"Edinburgh. Spending six months in the laboratory of a Scottish neurologist named Christie."

"Do they know you've tested LBC on yourself?"

"No."

"Might they suspect it, in view of your rather remarkable transformation?"

"They might, especially knowing the state of mind I was in a few months ago."

"I see." Ricksey paused pensively. "Do you know they have a lovely old castle in Edinburgh? Sits on top of a hill overlooking the city and shines spectacularly in the moonlight."

"I've never been there."

"Neither have I. But I plan to be tomorrow—talking to your research associates."

"That soon?"

"My job is a lot like boxing, Doctor. Requires sharp instincts and reflexes. And my instincts tell me tomorrow won't be any too soon."

"What are you going to tell Carson and Jamieson when you see them?"

Ricksey grinned. "The simple truth should do nicely; that you're working on a top-secret government project and anything they know about LBC must be kept confidential under penalty of a fine, imprisonment, or both. Sounds a bit drastic, doesn't it? But that's the wording of the Official Secrets Act."

At the time, Adam doubted if Ricksey's rush trip to Edinburgh was really necessary. But, as it turned out, he beat Estebrook and his Scottish-born traveling companion, Harry McPherson, there by only a day.

29

Two hundred yards out, Adam settled into his morning run. His stride evened, he began breathing air instead of gulping it, his entire body moved more fluidly. Ahead of him on the dirt road that wound through the foothills of the Berkshires loped Todd Tanner. Far in front of Tanner was a car driven by a Secret Service agent named Kirk, who had lived in the Far East for several years and was expert in the Oriental martial arts of judo, karate, and tae-kwon-do. He and Adam had already held several discussions on the so-called "death points" of the human body—few of which actually existed. His partner, an older agent named Eglund, trailed Adam in a second car.

At first, Al Lakeman had objected to having Secret Servicemen in his training camp. But he quickly changed his mind—less from Adam's confusing explanation of why they were necessary than from a practical consideration: they saved him the expense of hiring extra bodyguards to keep out the press and other busybodies. Persuading Bucky Miller to move the date of the McKinnon-Jackson bout a month ahead had not only been difficult but expensive—costing Al five percentage points of their share of the proceeds and the potentially harmful admission that his fighter had an injured wrist. But Adam, backed by Dan Lassiter, had given him no choice.

The combination of Adam's spectacular goaltending for the Bruins and his appointment as associate director of the N.I.N.M.D. had caused as big a media sensation as a Martian landing in the White House rose garden. In fact, some reporters wrote about him as if he actually were from outer space. With cover stories in *Newsweek, Sports Illustrated* and *People Magazine* all in the same week, Al was thankful that he'd had the foresight to move Adam out of Boston to this rural, well-guarded training camp. Let Aaron Robards handle the press; they deserved each other. His job was training Adam for the Jackson fight—no easy trick, since he hadn't boxed a lick in over three weeks. About all that he could do comfortably was run, so Al had him running ten or more miles twice a day.

Adam did not mind the strenuous runs. The mornings, in particular, were usually tranquil—the only sounds for long stretches being his and Tanner's breathing and pounding feet. Although he never got a jogger's "high," running did seem to ease his pain, supporting the theory that vigorous exercise released endorphin, "the brain's own morphine," and could even be addicting. Best of all, the runs helped him think.

Between random reflections and idle musings, his thoughts kept returning to Jon Acheson and promises made during his recent conversation with him. . . .

The previous Saturday, after a passionate night with Megan in Boston, Adam had driven to Commonwealth General Hospital to see Dan Lassiter and have his wrists injected with cortisone again. Afterward, Lassiter had suggested that he visit Jon. "Frankly, Adam, he's got me worried. The pneumatic vest my bioengineers designed for him didn't work. His intercostal muscles are so wasted they couldn't pressurize it enough to help him breathe without risking rib fractures. And since Jack Morris has had some success in cases like Jon's by combining plasmapheresis with immunosuppressive therapy with Imuran, we decided to give it a try."

"What happened?"

Lassiter looked glum. "Nothing good. The plasma exchanges lowered his antimyoneural antibody titer as expected, but all the Imuran did was wipe out his white blood cells. Right now, he's running a white cell count of around fifteen hundred and a low-grade fever. He also shows clinical and X-ray evidence of a patchy bronchopneumonia. We've placed him in protective isolation and on antibiotics, and have multiple blood and sputum cultures cooking, but haven't identified the organism so far." He sighed deeply. "I don't need to tell you the problems we'll face if his pneumonia spreads. . . . Anyway, why don't you visit him for a while and then come back up here so we can discuss the situation?"

In an anteroom to the neuro-vigil unit, Adam donned a sterile mask and gown and entered Jon Acheson's room. The swoosh of the iron lung drowned out his footsteps and, before speaking, he stood for a minute observing his former patient with a professional eye. The change in Jon's complexion, from its usual sallowness to a healthy-looking pink, surprised Adam until he remembered that Jon was febrile. More disturbing was the evidence of recent weight loss. Because of it, he was beginning to develop the sunken-cheeked, beaked-nosed *Hippocratic facies:* the telltale sign of the terminally ill.

At his greeting, Jon's eyelids opened as wide as their feeble muscles permitted and he rasped, "Adam! Is that really you?" Holding his lids apart with his fingers, he managed a grin at Adam's masked face. "Jesus, am I glad to see you! I'm uh—" his voice cracked, "really glad. . . . Lassiter tell you what happened?"

Adam nodded.

"Well, it was worth a try, don't you think?" Jon smiled wanly. "My God, though, you've sure been making news! Playing goalie for the Bruins. Beating 'Mean Joe' Metcalf. It's simply incredible! I won't ask how you do it—that's obviously the biggest secret since Neanderthal man figured out sperm made babies—but mind if I ask why?"

"To make money," Adam said.

"Money?" Jon looked puzzled. "You need it that badly?"

"I do—or, at least, did—if I wanted to continue my research. The government grant-givers—of which I will soon be one—didn't give me any choice. It was either raise the money myself or let twenty years of hard work go down the drain. So I was desperate—desperate to make all those years count for something. Maybe even find a cure for odd-ball cases like you."

"Well, don't take too long. I'd rather you presented my case at grand rounds as a therapeutic triumph than at death conference. But we'll get into that later. Right now, I've a surprise for you. Diana was in town last Sunday and Monday to see me. She tried like hell to get in touch with you, but couldn't. I told her to try through Dan Lassiter, but he wasn't around, either. Just out of curiosity, where were you guys?"

Adam thought a moment. "In Washington. Both of us."

"Well, needless to say, Diana was plenty pissed. Wanted to talk to you about me, she said, but I'm sure she had other things on her mind."

"How is she?" Adam said it casually, though the thought of confronting Diana in his new persona stirred surprising emotions in him.

"Looks great—tanned, trim, dressed for a cocktail party at Hyannis Port with the Kennedys, if there were such a party. Her practice seems to be flourishing, too. Otherwise—" Jon grimaced.

"Otherwise, what?"

"She cried a lot. Cold sober, she cried—which is something new for her. Claimed it was because she was worried about me and I didn't dispute her. . . . Why don't you give her a call at her office? She'd really like to hear from you."

"Maybe I will."

Jon gave him a skeptical look. Removing his fingers from his eyelids, he rested his eyes a while. Then, prying them open again, he said in a low, compelling voice: "Level with me, Adam. How bad am I?"

Adam exhaled sharply to keep the paper mask from sticking to his lips. "That depends. If the antibiotics you're on keep your pneumonitis in check, you'll make it."

"And if they don't?" At his silence, Jon said forcefully, "I'm warning you right now—I won't let them do a trach!"

Taken aback by the mixture of anger and despair in his eyes, Adam asked, "Why not?"

Jon gave him a withering look. "Oh, c'mon! Don't forget who you're talking to! I may not have my boards in neurology, but there's damned little about myasthenia gravis I don't know. If I get a tracheotomy, I go on a volume-cycled respirator—right? And once on, the odds are I'll never get off. Aristotle Onassis, with all his megabucks, never did. Which means that one of the last things I can still do for myself—talk—I won't any more. How the hell do you expect me to make a dramatic departure from this vale of tears if I can't even mutter an exit line? Don't want to disappoint the nurses—one in particular, name of Karen, whom I'm rather smitten with." He smiled self-consciously. "We even kiss. Which is another small pleasure I'd hate to give up. So, forgive me for being uncooperative, but no way will I consent to a trach. Tell Lassiter, will you?"

Adam sighed, "If you wish . . ."

"Don't look so gloomy, for Chrissake! You did your best for me. All my doctors did. Sooner or later, though, every doctor runs out of ideas. Otherwise, no patient would ever die. Besides, this is just a friendly visit you're making, not a consultation. And I'm grateful. I know how booked up you must be these days. . . ." He stopped talking when it became apparent from the distracted look in Adam's eyes that he wasn't listening. Suddenly, Jon felt a flicker of hope. "You are out of ideas, aren't you?"

"Not quite. Only don't ask me to explain now. And don't depend on it. No decrepit forty-five-year-old crazy enough to climb into the ring with Coleman Jackson is that dependable. So stay loose while I try to convince Lassiter to give my idea a try."

"You mean it?"

"I do."

"And you won't tell me for fear of raising false hope? You figure I'm in Kubler-Ross's stage five of the dying process and you want me to stay here—right?"

"You've got it."

"Okay. You know, Adam, sometimes a visit from you can be as refreshing as Karen's kisses. One last request: will you please call Diana or give me a number where she can reach you?"

"No."

Jon grinned. "The blunt answer of a proud and pitiless man. Enough said." Shakily, he extended his hand and Adam squeezed it.

"How does he look to you?" Lassiter asked when Adam returned to his office.

"Sick, scared, determined to go out with grace and dignity if he can't be saved. Says that under no circumstances will he permit a trach, and means it. I suppose I'd feel the same way after being in an iron lung almost a year."

"You'd feel that way even if you hadn't."

"Perhaps. . . . Anyway, I hope the antibiotics work."

"And if they don't?" From across his desk, Lassiter stared hard at him. "I don't have to be a mind reader to know what you're thinking, so go ahead and say it."

"All right. If, despite antibiotic therapy, the pneumonia spreads—which is a good possibility, since he can't cough—I wish you'd let me treat him with LBC before you switch him from the iron lung to a respirator."

Lassiter nodded unenthusiastically. "Quite aside from the medical dangers, do you realize all the procedural problems that would present? First of all, I'd have to obtain permission from the F.D.A. to use it; fill out reams of investigational new drug forms. They'd also demand to know the chemical composition of LBC—which lets your secret out of the bag. Are you sure you're willing to risk that?"

"To save Jon Acheson's life—yes! Did you ever doubt it?"

"But what if it doesn't save his life? What if it has a strychninelike effect—so overstimulating his damaged nerve junctions that he develops tetanic muscular contractions, cardiac exhaustion, and death? I once saw a case of strychnine poisoning. It wasn't pleasant. What then?"

"Then, I'd just have to live with it. That's unlikely to happen, though."

"How can you be so sure?"

"Because I doubt he has enough receptor sites at his nerve junctions to over-respond that way. Most of them have been destroyed by his basic disease process."

"I'm not sure I follow your reasoning?"

"Then, bear with me while I take you through it, step by step. As you know, myasthenia victims somehow become allergic to some protein component of their myoneural junction and make antibodies against it. These antibodies then attack the acetylcholine receptors on the synaptic membrane—impairing nerve conduction. Early in the disease, drugs such as cortisone, which suppress antibody production, or plasma exchange, which washes out the antibodies from the blood stream, can control the process. But in its later stages, after most of the receptor sites have been destroyed, they're ineffective. Follow me so far?"

"Of course," Lassiter said impatiently. "Go on."

"Well, in addition to acetylcholine receptors on the membrane, there are L-butyrylcholine receptors, too. How do I know? Because they *have* to be there—in latent form, at least—otherwise, I never would've responded to LBC the way I did."

"Hmmm. That's an interesting thesis," Lassiter conceded. "Certainly fits the membrane physiologists' dictum of 'no receptors, no response.' Any ideas where these LBC receptors came from?''

"Well, if you believe Darwin, we must've picked them up from our avian ancestors somewhere along the line. We might even make and secrete a few squirts of LBC ourselves when we go into some sort of muscular overdrive. One of the first projects I want to launch when I get back to the laboratory is to develop an immunoassay for LBC. Might be interesting to try to detect it in the blood of sprinters or speed swimmers or any athlete engaging in strenuous locomotor activity."

"You're digressing," Lassiter reminded him.

"Sorry. . . . Anyway, since I have LBC receptors, so does everybody; including Jon Acheson. And assuming a couple more things; namely—that these receptors are structurally separate from those for acetylcholine and still intact—he should respond to LBC. Ergo, he will breathe on his own, cough up his secretions, and recover from his pneumonia."

"All right, say the fates are kind and all that comes to pass. What then?"

"Then, he's hooked on LBC just as I probably am. At least we don't have to worry about his developing myasthenia, if he has to withdraw from the drug, since he's already got it."

"And what happens when he starts to suffer the same nerve-entrapment syndromes you do?"

"Maybe he won't. It's just possible that, by keeping him on the lowest possible maintenance dose, he'll avoid that complication."

"Sounds like a big *if* to me."

"It is. But at least he'll be alive—really alive—instead of existing in a capsule. All things considered, I think it's worth trying, Dan."

"Perhaps you're right. But I'm still leery. I suppose I ought to discuss it with Henry Kalisher first. At least let him know that we're considering the possibility. If nothing else, he might help keep the lid on things at the F.D.A. . . . Are you quite sure there are no alternative treatments we could try first?"

"None I know of," replied Adam. "Kurt Eliasson at the Karolinska Institute has developed a compound which he calls 'activated choline.' I'm not sure what it is, only that it doesn't need the enzyme that's evidently missing in the brains of Alzheimer patients in order to be acetylated to acetylcholine. But I don't see how such a compound would benefit myasthenia patients. Apart from that, I can't think of anything that hasn't already been tried."

"Neither can Jack Morris. Which brings up another sticky point. Jack will have to be brought into this discussion, not merely as a matter of courtesy but because he's got legal responsibility for the patient. Though I doubt that he'll present much of a problem. Jack's very fond of Jon Acheson, too, and feeling pretty low over what the Imuran did to him . . ." Lassiter paused and then said with an air of finality, "All right, let's see how things go over the next few days. If his pneumonia resolves on antibiotic therapy, we wait."

"For what?"

"For you to stop LBC and see what happens."

"And if his pneumonia worsens?"

"Then Jack Morris and I have a tough decision to make." Lassiter held up his hand to stop Adam from speaking. "Enough discussion for now. I'm already an hour and a half behind in my appointments. Go back to Lenox and train for what the papers insist on calling 'The Fight of the Century.' In my day, it was Joe Louis versus Billy Conn. But the way the media's carrying on, I wouldn't be surprised if they end up comparing you and Jackson to David and Goliath!"

At his office door, Lassiter shook hands, patted him on the back, and was tempted to give Adam a slight shove when he seemed reluctant to leave.

"Promise you'll let me know the minute anything changes with Jon?"

"Oh, Jesus!" Lassiter groaned. "Give me credit for caring about what happens to Jon Acheson, too. You're obsessed with giving him LBC, aren't you?"

Reluctantly, Adam admitted it.

"I thought so. But you'll have to tell me why some other time. Right now, I've got more pressing problems. Like a chief surgical resident who's seven months pregnant and won't take maternity leave, even though she can barely get close enough to the table to operate. And a hospital trustee who's bugging me to start a division of holistic medicine—whatever the hell that's supposed to be. Would you believe there are doctors in this town, making two, three times the money I do, who fritter away Saturday afternoons on a boat or a golf course? The injustice of it all!"

·   ·   ·

A blast from Kirk's car horn jarred Adam from his reverie. They had reached the five-mile mark. With his calf muscles cramping, he was glad to rest. A few minutes later, as they approached a wooded area, he shouted, "Hey, Todd! Let's break."

Tanner trotted off the road into a shady grove and Adam followed.

"How's your chest feel?" said Tanner.

"Better. Only an occasional sharp twinge if I lift my left arm too high."

"Lakeman wants us to start sparring again tomorrow. You up to it?"

Adam shrugged. "Long as you don't hit me above the belt."

"Megan wouldn't like me hittin' you below it."

"Then I'll wear a wide belt."

Adam sat down on the grass, leaned against a tree, and began massaging his calf muscles.

Squatting in front of him, Tanner asked, "How come you been readin' all those medical books lately?"

"They're neuroanatomy texts. My secret weapon against Coleman Jackson."

"Oh, yeah?" exclaimed Tanner. "How so?"

"Sometimes, it's more important where you hit an opponent than how hard. And I'm going to hit Jackson in places he's never been hit before."

"Like where?"

"I'm not telling, since I plan to practice on you first. Three good punches and you'll not only be seeing double but unable to lift your arms."

Tanner blinked. "I hope you're just kiddin', Doc. I don't want to be no guinea pig. Why don't you practice on Phil Kirk? He's the karate man."

"Don't worry. Sixteen-ounce gloves are too big for what I want to do. I'm not even sure it can be done with regulation-size eight-ounces. But if it can, I'm going to do it—to Jackson."

Minutes later, Adam resumed his running and thinking. Lassiter was right, of course: treating Jon Acheson with LBC did obsess him. The reason was clear and meritorious on the surface, complicated and self-serving underneath. For some-one with Adam's medical training and dedication to the healing art, it was far more gratifying to save a life than beat up a ring opponent or block a puck from the nets. But even closer to bedrock was the haunting fear that his self-experimentation with LBC would end in ignominious failure unless he could successfully treat Jon Acheson and countless other myasthenia victims.

Once his secret was out—and the more people who knew about it, the sooner that was likely to happen—the sports world would be thrown into an uproar. He would be aswirl in controversy—vilified by the media and the fans. Never mind the gamblers and drug pushers, he would be branded the main malefactor of professional athletes, the Dr. Frankenstein of sports. Which was why Jon Acheson's fate, should Lassiter let Adam treat him with LBC, took on such crucial importance. By the definition of one group of fans, saving lives was a sport, too. If, as aficionados claimed, bullfighting, a contest to the death, was the one true sport, and all the rest mere games, then medicine, another contest to the death, was as much sport as profession—a line of reasoning, Adam conceded, that was as fanciful and fruitless as wondering whether he was caught up in the Promethean or the Faustian legend. The plain fact was that he wanted to save Jon Acheson's life because he was a doctor and because Jon deserved to live. Furthermore, the decision to treat Jon with LBC rested with Dan Lassiter; Adam could only hope he would make it while the drug still stood a ghost of a chance to succeed.

30

Shortly before nine the next morning, while sitting in an X-ray reading room with Jack Morris and staring at the chest film mounted on the illuminated view box in front of them, Dan Lassiter finally made his decision. The events leading up to it had begun in this same room fifteen hours earlier when a staff radiologist, unable to contact Morris, who was miles away giving a lecture, had phoned Lassiter to report that Jon Acheson's latest chest X-ray revealed complete collapse of his right-middle lobe—an ominous development in a patient already stricken with pneumonia. Lassiter had rushed to the X-ray department, reviewed the film, and agreed with the radiologist that the most likely cause of the collapse was a large mucus plug, lodged like a chunk of meat, in the bronchus. Because of Jon's inability to cough up his secretions, a mixture of mucus and pus had gradually filled the right-middle lobe bronchus and thickened by evaporation until it completely blocked the air passage connecting the lobe to the trachea. Thus, deprived of the air pressure needed to remain open, the hundreds of branching bronchioles and millions of tiny air sacs attached to their bases had collapsed, producing a dense white shadow on the X-ray and a dangerous decline in the oxygen supply to Jon's brain. Moreover, if the obstruction were not removed immediately, Lassiter knew, the airless lung tissue would rapidly become infected, abscessed, and destroyed. Seizing a nearby phone, he radiopaged Rick Raport, the thoracic surgeon on duty, and ordered an emergency broncho- scopy.

Minutes later, the two converged on Jon Acheson's room. While the surgeon set up his equipment, Lassiter tried to explain to Jon what they needed to do and why. But he was barely conscious, and Dan doubted that he understood a word of it. The iron lung Jon was in presented extraordinary problems, requiring Raport to be almost as flexible as his instrument. It took all his skill and dexterity to slip the tip of the bronchoscope past Jon's anesthetized vocal cords and down his trachea until its fiberoptic lens showed him the site of the obstruction. Powerful as the suction device was at the end of the yard-long scope, the plug proved too adherent to the bronchial wall to be removed in one piece. With a sigh, Raport resigned himself to a time-consuming cleanout.

It took him a harrowing half-hour to suck a cupful of thick, greenish-gray secretions from the right lung, but Jon's color improved noticeably in the process. Raport then spent several minutes lavaging the bronchus with a salt solution to loosen up and remove more mucus. At last, with his bent spine aching intolerably, he removed the scope, hoping the repeat X-ray would show that the lobe had re-expanded and greatly relieved when it did. But Lassiter remained uneasy—knowing the bronchus would likely plug up again. By this time, Jack Morris had returned to the hospital and the two discussed this disturbing development at length before going home to late suppers.

At eleven P.M., Lassiter phoned the neurology resident on the neuro-vigil unit, learned that Jon Acheson's condition was stable, and went to bed. But deep, dreamful sleep eluded him. He dozed intermittently, expecting the phone on his bedstand to ring momentarily, unnerved that it didn't. Finally, at five A.M., after Kris had threatened to banish him to the guest room, he gave up trying to sleep, dressed, and drove to the hospital.

To his surprise, he discovered that Jack Morris had preceded him there by a full hour. They met as Morris was emerging from Jon Acheson's room with a syringeful of blood in his hand.

"What are you doing here?" Lassiter asked.

"Drawing my own blood gases. The last set didn't turn out too good. No use kidding ourselves, Dan. We can't handle his secretions without a trach and we can't adequately oxygenate him without a volume-cycled respirator."

"Did you think over what I told you about LBC last night?"

Morris handed the blood specimen to a nurse and nodded. "Even though I watched the Red Sox go eleven innings before losing to the Yankees on the tube, I thought about little else."

"And—?"

"Sounds like a hell of a drug . . . and a hell of a risk. I've quit envying 'Magic' McKinnon ever since you told me what makes him magical."

"Never mind him. Do we use LBC on Jon Acheson or don't we?"

"Forgive the football metaphor, Dan, but that depends on whether you want to go for the short-gainer and first down or the long bomb and the touchdown. Nobody would criticize us for playing it safe, but let's not forget that we're playing catch-up ball here."

"I think I get your drift, Jack, but would you mind translating it into medicalese?"

Morris grinned. "Okay. I've treated well over a hundred myasthenia patients with pneumonia by conventional means: trachs and respirators. A fair percentage of the short-termers— those who are postoperative or early in their disease—have made it, and some of the chronic cases like Jon Acheson have improved. But I can count on my fingers the ones who've recovered enough to leave the hospital. So, if McKinnon really believes his LBC will work on Jon, and you're willing to handle the paper work, let's give it a shot."

Lassiter's scowl betrayed his uncertainty. "I don't know, Jack. I wish I wasn't so involved with Adam McKinnon in other ways and could be more objective about the decision. Maybe it's irrational, but I get bad vibes about LBC and everything about it."

"Well, if it's objectivity you're after, why not wait for the results of his latest blood gases, repeat his chest X-ray, and then decide on the basis of what they show? Does Jon have any family in the area?"

"No. Father deceased, mother somewhere on a tour of Europe and sister, Diana—an M.D. herself—in San Diego. I called her last night and she wants Jon transferred to the Scripps Clinic, but I told her he was too sick for that."

"You mention anything to her about LBC?"

"Not a word. I hope you like soap operas, because this could well turn into one. You see, Diana and Adam McKinnon lived together until a few months ago and apparently did not part on the friendliest of terms. There's an even more bizarre twist to the story, which I'll save for the next episode."

"I can hardly wait. You want me to order the X-ray or will you?"

"I'll take care of it."

"Good. Soon as I finish making rounds with the neuro-residents, I'll meet you in the X-ray department."

A nagging pain in his lower right calf, which could either represent a ligament sprain or the beginnings of another nerve-entrapment, had kept Adam from sleeping well the previous night. Even after his morning run, shortened to five miles because he was scheduled to spar with Todd Tanner that afternoon, Adam still felt logy.

Lassiter's phone call while he was finishing breakfast immediately swept the torpor from his brain. Summoning Phil Kirk, he briefed him on the situation and headed for the shower. He left it to Lassiter to explain his absence from camp to Al Lakeman. Telling Lakeman himself risked another hassle and, after all, he rationalized, Lassiter was Lakeman's chosen go-between.

"How fast do you want me to drive, Doc?" asked Kirk when they turned onto the Massachusetts Turnpike.

"As fast as your government-issue Chevy can go."

"It's only G.I. on the outside. Under the hood, it's turbo-charged and can cruise at a hundred and twenty."

"How about the highway patrol?"

"I've already alerted them. They'll just wave us on."

Adam nodded. "You play chess, Phil?"

"I prefer a Japanese board game call *Gō*, but I do play."

"And damned well, I'd imagine. You think two steps ahead. . . . Okay. Open her up."

With the speedometer needle hovering at 100 m.p.h., they crossed the state from Lenox to Weston in an hour and a half. Reaching Commonwealth General Hospital, Adam had Kirk drop him off at the front entrance and went directly to Dan Lassiter's office.

Neither Dan's receptionist nor Hedley, his private secretary, were at their desk. Seeing the door to the inner office ajar,

Adam entered without knocking and was immediately dazzled by sunlight streaming through the bank of windows lining one wall of the top-floor office. Vaguely, he made out the figure of a woman on the couch to his left and felt his scalp start to tingle.

"Hello, Adam," Diana said in her all-too-familiar voice. She rose in a self-consciously graceful movement, smoothed the skirt of her stylish suit, and stepped toward him out of the blinding sunlight. Dark glasses hid her eyes, but her lips glistened with fresh lipstick. When he merely nodded in response, she said, "I've looked forward to seeing you again."

He started to ask what she was doing here, but caught himself in time. After all, Jon was her half-brother, and as steadfast in his love for her as she was fickle in her love for others. Why hadn't he guessed she would be here and steeled himself for the encounter? At another time, he might welcome the showdown—he had the edge, the weapons—but now he was preoccupied with more urgent matters.

"You seem surprised to see me," Diana said. "Didn't you think Dan Lassiter would keep me informed? Jon's on the *critical list,* in case you didn't know."

"Of course, I know. . . . Look, Diana, I'm sure we have a lot to talk about, but this simply isn't the time. I have a new treatment I want to try on Jon, and his legal consent to use it, so if you'll excuse me . . ."

"*What* new treatment?" she demanded. "I have a right to know."

Adam drew a deep, calming breath. Time was short, his nerves raw, and he must keep his simmering emotions under control. "It's a new neurotransmitter called LBC that I'm hoping will act similar to acetylcholine at Jon's myoneural junctions. If it does, it could spare him a trach."

"A neurotransmitter?" She paused to remember the meaning of the term. "The same neurotransmitter you were working on for dementia patients? Is it dangerous?"

"It could be," Adam admitted. "It's only been used once before in humans. But believe me, Diana, it's Jon's only chance."

Unfolding her arms from across her chest, Diana's entire body seemed to sag. "I don't know what to believe," she said despairingly. "Lassiter never mentioned anything about it when we spoke the other night. All I *do* know is that Jon's the dearest person in the world to me. If he dies, I might as well bag it myself." Raising her sunglasses, she rubbed away the start of tears from her eyes.

"I want Jon to live as much as you do, Diana. And because I do, I can't spend time talking about it. I just drove all the way from Lenox at a hundred miles an hour to—"

"Lenox!" she interrupted. "What were you doing there? Why weren't you here—with Jon?"

Oh God, he groaned inwardly. Don't let her get irrational now. "Because I'm no longer Jon's doctor, Diana. I turned his case over to Dan Lassiter and Jack Morris months ago."

"Months?" She looked confused. "Oh, yes, I almost forgot. You're a boxer now—the darling of the press. Every middle-aged man's hero."

"Whatever I am, Diana, I'm in a hurry to get to the neuro-vigil unit and treat your brother while there's still time. We can talk later, if you wish . . ."

"I'll go with you," she said.

Adam exhaled sharply. *That* was the last thing he wanted and clamped his jaws to keep from shouting at her. Calmly, he said, "I really wouldn't advise it. From what Dan Lassiter told me on the phone earlier, Jon's in pretty bad shape."

"Well, I'm a doctor, too—remember? I won't go to pieces on you. And I'm sure Dan Lassiter won't mind. We're old friends, you know?"

"So he hinted."

"Hinted?" She chuckled throatily. "How discreet! I wonder if that was to spare your feelings or mine. . . . No," she said in response to Adam's incredulous stare, "I didn't go to bed with him." She shrugged. "His choice, not mine. He's a very attractive man, you know."

"Save it for your memoirs, Diana," he said curtly and swung around to leave.

"Adam, wait!" she cried. Taking a quick step toward him, she wobbled on her high heels and almost stumbled. "I'm sorry. I don't know why I tried to hurt you with that. But you seem so remote, so disapproving of my even being here. Please, let me come with you. I'll go crazy staying here all by myself. . . . Oh, damn," she muttered as her tears welled again. "Please, Adam. Don't make me beg . . ."

It would be a mistake, he knew. Just being alone with her made him edgy. But he simply couldn't be so hard-hearted as to refuse. "Okay," he said reluctantly. "You've got a right to be there."

"Thank you, Adam." She gave him a wavering smile. "Give me a minute—no more—to freshen up and I'll be right back."

While she was in Lassiter's private bathroom, Adam removed his money belt and transferred the three vials of LBC in its pouch to his coat pocket. Each vial contained fifty grams of the crystalline white powder. His supply was already low; if he had to share what remained with Jon Acheson, he would barely have enough to carry him through the Jackson fight. But if it helped Jon, it would be worth all the tricky arrangements to make more.

Lassiter was talking on the phone at the nurses' station when Adam and Diana arrived on the floor. Seeing them, he hastily concluded his conversation and said, "Adam! Glad to see you. Things are rocky in there." He gestured toward Jon's room.

"So I gather. . . . You know Dr. Diana Acheson, I believe?"

"Yes. We're old A.M.A. confrères. My secretary told me you were in my office, Diana, but it's been too hectic here to break away."

"I understand, Dan," she said and pushed her sunglasses to the top of her head. "How's Jon? Is he conscious?"

"Yes," said Lassiter, "which is an improvement over last night. But that's all that's improved. His right-middle lobe has partially collapsed again and he has fluid at both lung bases. Worse yet, his blood gases are rapidly deteriorating. His oxygen tension has dropped ten milliliters in the last few hours and he's retaining CO_2 for the first time. Jack Morris is in there now, suctioning him out personally. His X-rays are in the conference room if you want to see them, Adam."

"Later. Right now, I'd better go in, let him know I'm here. Want to come, Diana?"

She hesitated, visibly shaken by the implications of Lassiter's report. Leaning against a wall, she clutched her stomach.

"No, you go ahead," she finally said. "I need a little time to pull myself together."

Adam nodded and left for the anteroom to slip on a sterile mask and gown.

"It wasn't Adam's idea to bring me down here," she told Lassiter. "I insisted."

"Understandable," he replied. "Can I have the nurse get you anything?"

"Like a new nervous system? This one's on its last legs."

Lassiter made a comforting sound and put his arm around her.

"Funny—meaning sad—but I'm thirty-three years old, Dan, and in all that time I've managed exactly one lasting relationship—with Jon. All the others I screwed up."

"Don't be so hard on yourself, Diana."

"Hard!" She laughed harshly. "Except for my medical practice, my life's like a porno movie—no redeeming social significance. Jon's the only good thing in it. If I lose him, I honestly don't know what I'll do. I won't need a hotel room for the night—I'll need one of your padded cells."

"Well, we haven't lost him yet. He's a fighter—he wants to live. And Adam's fairly optimistic his new drug will help."

"Adam!" She shook her head in wonder. "I lived with a doctor by that name and general appearance for almost a year, but I don't know the man in there at all. People can't change *that* much in so short a time, can they, Dan?"

"Usually not, but Adam's an exception. And exceptional. He's also a brilliant neurologist. Trust him."

Presently a grim-faced Adam returned from Jon Acheson's room, trailed by Jack Morris. Before Lassiter could question him, he said, "Since he can't swallow and I sure as hell don't want him aspirating, we'll have to administer the LBC by stomach tube. Jack and I have agreed—we'll give it two hours to work. If it doesn't, we'll tube him and put him on a respirator." He glanced at Diana, who shuddered and said nothing. "Move a portable electromyogram in there, will you, Dan?" he went on. "That'll give some objective measure of his response."

Lassiter nodded. "How much LBC are you going to give him?"

"Twenty-five grams. The same loading dose I took initially."

"You!" Diana gasped.

"I had to test it on somebody."

"But you—you're not . . . Wasn't it—?"

"We'll discuss it later," Adam said brusquely.

"I'll get the EMG," Lassiter said. "Anything else you need?"

Adam gestured uncertainly. "Jack suggests we have a curarelike agent—Anectine or Pavulon—handy, just in case the LBC over-stimulates him. But they're so damned dangerous in myasthenics, and I've no idea whether they're capable of blocking the action of LBC."

"I'll order them up anyway. Anything else?"

"Prayers? Talismans? A rabbit's foot?"

"That, too."

"Jon!" Adam shouted in his ear and watched his eyes slit open. "I'm back and Diana's with me." Gently, he took her arm and pulled her into Jon's field of vision.

"Hi, darling," she said huskily.

"Hi, Sis!" He jerked his thumb at Adam. "Does he really know what he's doing?"

Diana smiled. "More than I ever did."

"Well, stick around just in case he gives us grounds to sue."

Stepping forward again, Adam said, "First thing we've got to do is pass a stomach tube. In a moment, I'm going to put a small ice cube in your mouth and I want you to suck on it. Suck hard and swallow as best you can. While you're doing that, I'll slip the tube through one of your nostrils. Got it?"

Jon made a sour face. "Better than a bladder catheter, I suppose."

"Much."

As Jon grimaced, gagged, and drooled, Adam maneuvered the naso-gastric tube in place. He then dissolved half a vial of LBC in a weak sugar solution, drew it up into a fifty cc syringe, and attached its nozzle to the flared end of the rubber tube. From the opposite side of the iron lung, Lassiter, Morris, and the day nurse watched intently. He was about to turn to Diana, make sure she was holding up all right, when he felt her squeeze his arm. By conscious effort, he blocked out the memories her touch evoked and slowly emptied the contents of the syringe into Jon's stomach. He tried to recall how long before his first dose of LBC had affected him—several minutes, at least. He steeled himself to wait it out.

"Hey!" Jon cried, pointing to the tube protruding from his left nostril. "How 'bout taking this out now?"

"Out? I had enough trouble getting it in," Adam protested. "Why do you want it out?"

"Tickles my nose."

"A small price to pay for making medical history. How do you feel, otherwise?"

Jon scanned the faces watching him. "Like a goldfish—

which is nothing new—and . . . like I'm going to throw up."

"Sorry, Jon," said Adam with a shrug. "That was the wrong thing to say. The tube stays."

"Ouch!" exclaimed Jon a moment later as Jack Morris inserted the first of two EMG electrodes into his forearm. "You're losing your touch, Doc."

"Sorry, Jon. I'm a little nervous." Turning to Adam, Morris asked, "How long before you expect a response?"

"Another ten, fifteen minutes, I'd estimate. If we get one at all."

Adam's estimate proved wrong. Jon responded much sooner and more violently than expected. Ending a long, tense silence, he said, "Adam! I feel funny—It's—I don't know— it's like I'm fluttering."

"Where?"

"Right here." With his free hand, he pointed at his stomach.

"Can you be a little more specific?"

"Not much. It's the weirdest feeling," he said in a tight voice. "Oh, Jesus!" he suddenly gasped. "Can't breathe!"

Adam and Jack Morris exchanged tense looks. "Diaphragmatic spasm?" Adam wondered, and Morris nodded.

"Oh, God, do something!" Diana shrilled. "He's turning blue!"

"Bag him!" Adam shouted to Lassiter, "while we break open the iron lung and get him out. The lung's useless against spasm."

The nurse seized the black Ambu bag from the emergency tracheotomy tray in the corner and handed it to Lassiter. Quickly, he raised Jon's limp head to strap its triangular cone over his nose and mouth and began compressing its rubber bladder to force air into his lungs.

Expertly, Jack Morris shut off the air-flow valve to the iron lung, undid its latches, and wheeled its long, lower portion away from the padded platform supporting Jon's body. "Look at his leg muscles! They're twitching like crazy," he said to Adam. "His hands, too."

Adam longed desperately for a calm moment to think, to collect his thoughts and figure out what was happening, what might be done about it. But the emergency situation permitted no such luxury. Lassiter's fear that LBC might exert a strychninelike action had been realized. In his eagerness to bring about a miracle cure, Adam had foolishly disregarded that danger. It helped not at all to tell himself that Jon Acheson was doomed anyway. Nothing could alter the fact that he had probably hastened his death.

Finally freeing Jon's neck and upper chest from the rim of the iron lung, Adam frantically wondered what to do next. He had to do something, if only to keep from panicking. Unwittingly, Dan Lassiter came to his rescue. "Grab the stethoscope from my pocket," he told Adam while continuing to knead the bladder of the Ambu bag, "and listen to his heart."

Adam complied, barely able to hear Jon's heart sounds through the scratchy surface noises made by his violent twitching. As he tried to listen, Jack Morris crowded in behind him and put his hand under Jon's right rib cage to feel for his diaphragm.

Straightening and removing the stethoscope from his ears, Adam heard Diana's sniffling and sobbing. She was slumped against the windowsill, her eyes wide with horror, hands pressed to her stomach. He felt an impulse to go to her, take her in his arms, and tell her he was sorry—for Jon, for all that had begun so brightly and gone so wrong between them. At least they had one thing in common now: they had both been dealt decisive blows by life.

"Well, what do you hear?" Lassiter demanded.

Clearing his throat, Adam replied, "Rapid, regular tachycardia." Almost as an afterthought, he accidently brushed Morris's hand away, felt for the femoral pulse in Jon's groin, and added, "Pulse fairly strong."

"That's good." Looking at Jon's twitching left arm and the blood trickling from the sites where the EMG needles had become dislodged, Lassiter ordered, "Nurse, try to slip a cuff around the arm and get a blood pressure reading." He started to ask Diana to help, but seeing her distraught state dissuaded him. Instead, he peered at Jack Morris, who had returned his hand to Jon's rib cage and was again feeling his diaphragm, and asked, "Jack, what about Pavulon?"

"What, Dan?"

"Pavulon," Lassiter repeated. "Will it help?"

"I doubt it," Morris said absently.

Lassiter stared exasperatedly at him. "Well, what do *you* suggest?"

Morris ignored him. "Adam, feel this for a second."

Adam replaced Morris's hand with his own and ran it over Jon's liver area. He looked up, puzzled. "Feel what?"

"His diaphragm. It's no longer fluttering. At least, I can't feel it. Can you?"

Adam tried again. "No."

"What are you two mumbling about?" snapped Lassiter, his right hand cramping from compressing the bladder of the Ambu bag.

"Dan," Morris said, "stop bagging him for a minute. Let's see if he can breathe on his own."

Looking skeptical, Lassiter unstrapped the triangular cone from Jon Acheson's face and watched him intently.

Several seconds passed. Then, to his relief, Lassiter saw Jon's chest rise and fall slightly—so slightly he might have imagined it. But the next chest excursion was definite. "Did you all see that!" he exclaimed.

Adam nodded faintly; Morris vigorously.

"Blood pressure ninety-five over seventy," reported the nurse.

"Good," said Lassiter. "He seems to be twitching less, too. . . . All right, gentlemen, what now?"

"Bag him a few more minutes until his cyanosis clears," suggested Morris, "and I'll get a tidal volume measurement on him."

"Sounds reasonable," Lassiter said and refit the Ambu bag over Jon's face.

In the lull, Adam moved to Diana, grasped her shoulders gently, and raised her up from her slumped position. "Diana, listen to me," he said. "Jon's better. He's breathing on his own now. He may just make it."

"I know," she said awarely. "Don't worry about me. I'm okay."

A few minutes later, Jack Morris slipped the mouthpiece of the tidal volume measuring device between Jon's lips and took a reading. "Three hundred cc, per breath," he announced. "Not great, but considering his lung pathology, not bad, either."

"Shall I try to rouse him? Get him to breathe deeper?" Lassiter asked.

"Not just yet. Just out of curiosity, I'd like to run an EMG tracing on him first. Okay with you, Adam?"

"Go ahead."

Morris reinserted the electrodes in Jon Acheson's forearm

and pressed the button on the machine that sent a weak electrical current down his ulna nerve. "Hey!" he exclaimed a moment later. "This can't be right. His nerve conduction velocity is one hundred and eighty meters per second! Nobody's ever had a reading that high. Nobody, except maybe you, Adam."

"No, my top reading was just over one hundred and thirty-six meters per second. But my nerve junctions weren't as hungry for the stuff as Jon's evidently are. Keep going and let's see if he shows the typical myasthenic fall-off."

Morris pressed the firing button several more times while Adam, joined by Lassiter, watched the depiction of the tent-shaped *action potential* on the oscilloscope screen. By the tenth shock, neither his nerve conduction velocity nor the amplitude of the *action potential* had decreased significantly.

"Well, I'll be damned!" said Morris, elated. "What do you do with reflex times that quick?"

"You start by being pretty klutzy. Knocking over a lot of things," Adam replied.

"You ought to know. Better be careful, Adam; if we can get Jon over his pneumonia and on his feet, he may give you a lot of competition."

"Not me," Adam avowed. "After the Jackson fight, I retire from boxing and all other contact sports."

"What's his respiratory rate, Nurse?" asked Lassiter, moving back to the head of Jon's platform.

"Twenty-eight and shallow, Dr. Lassiter."

"Want to try and wake him up now?" Morris asked.

"We'll have to. Even though Diana could just as easily sign the permit, I'd like his okay, too."

"Permit for what?" asked Adam.

"A tracheotomy," Lassiter replied firmly. "Look, Adam—all of you—I hate to be the one to dispel the euphoria we're feeling, but we'd better not lose sight of what we're dealing with: a cachectic white male with a collapsed right-middle lobe, extensive pneumonia, and bilateral pleural effusions. Even if he weren't myasthenic, that's still a high mortality situation—agreed?"

Lassiter scanned the faces of the three doctors until each nodded. "All right," he continued, "what we've got to do now is what we would've done if the LBC hadn't worked—get the pus and fluid out of his lungs. And there's no better way than a trach."

Adam started to speak and faltered.

Sensing his thoughts, Lassiter said, "I know, Adam. Bit of a let-down after all the excitement. And I know how Jon feels about a trach, too. But now that he's parted—forever—from his iron lung, he might be more willing to part with a small piece of his trachea." Gazing down at their frail, stuporous patient, Lassiter suddenly realized he was naked. He started to tell the nurse to cover him, but out of some obscure masculine impulse avoided calling attention to his nakedness by doing it himself. After draping a sheet across Jon's middle, Lassiter bent and shouted in his ear, "Wake up! Come on, Jon, wake up or I'll slap hell out of you like in that after-shave lotion commercial."

"Wha—?" Jon moaned and started to turn his head toward Lassiter. Anticipating what might happen next, Adam's hand shot out to cushion Jon's cheek before it slammed against the thinly padded metal platform.

At the impact, Jon's eyes opened wide—wider than they had in months—and his eyeballs oscillated.

"Easy, Jon," Adam advised. "Don't move a muscle. Stare at the wall until your vision comes into focus and then slowly, very slowly, turn your eyes this way."

"W . . . what's going on?" Jon gasped.

"How do you feel?"

"Cold! Shivering cold! Who turned the heat off in the lung . . . ? Is Diana still here?"

"Right here, darling!"

"Had the craziest dream. Sort of flew the coop or something. . . ."

"It wasn't so crazy," Diana said. "You did fly out—out of the iron lung."

Slowly, disbelievingly, Jon looked down, seeing the lower part of his body for the first time in weeks. "Your stuff worked, huh, Adam?"

"It sure did. At least, temporarily. That's the good news . . ."

"I'll tell him the rest if you want, Adam," Lassiter volunteered.

"No, I'll do it. You're out of the iron lung and you'll probably stay out—dead or alive. The consensus here is that we'd prefer you alive—which means you've still got to get over your pneumonia."

"Which means a trach?" Jon said glumly.

"A trach—but not necessarily a respirator," Adam explained.

"Hmmm," said Jon, brightening. "That's not such a bad deal. Liz Taylor had a trach and won an Academy Award for it. Give me a minute to think it over, will you?"

"All right. *One* minute."

"What's your hurry?"

"Every minute that passes, your lung sloughs off another million cells."

"Aw, that's just doctor scare talk and you know it!" Suddenly, Jon gagged and erupted in a fit of harsh coughing.

"Spit it out!" Lassiter ordered and shoved an emesis basin next to his mouth.

With his face flushed and contorted from the effort, Jon expectorated a glob of bloody mucus into the basin and slumped back, exhausted.

"Jesus, that hurt!" he said after catching his breath. "All right, call Raport and let's get it over with. I don't want to be raped by his bronchoscope again."

31

At four o'clock, the earliest Raport could schedule it, Jon underwent elective tracheotomy. The procedure, performed under local anesthesia, went smoothly. Afterward, with Diana near collapse from nervous tension and lack of sleep, Lassiter suggested that Adam take her to his office to rest while he and Jack Morris looked after Jon's postoperative medical care.

"Coffee or booze?" asked Adam after Dan's private secretary had unlocked his liquor cabinet and showed him how to work the stainless-steel espresso coffeemaker that sat on the shelf behind the desk.

"I need both," Diana replied. "Just bring a whiskey bottle and let me experiment until I get the right mixture."

As Adam stood in front of the espresso machine waiting for the water to boil, Diana sat in the desk chair. "I simply can't believe all that's happened to you in so short a time," she said. "I saw a TV replay of your fight with 'Mean Joe' Metcalf and was floored. You were so . . . so vicious! I'm glad you never got violent with me. I'm just not into S & M—though I wouldn't mind being one of your groupies."

Adam let the innuendo pass without comment.

"Are you actually going to fight Coleman Jackson in a few weeks?"

"I'd better, or a lot of people will be very upset with me."

"But he's so mean-looking it's spooky. A real monster."

"So am I. Jekyll-and-Hyde type."

"You're certainly different, I'll say that. You practically exude machismo. But as I recall the story, Hyde was Jekyll's evil side. Is 'Magic' McKinnon your evil side, Adam?"

Refusing to be baited, Adam did not reply. The thermostat light on the espresso machine flashed on and he said, "I'll get your coffee."

"And I'll go back to the powder room to freshen up again—though God knows why I bother. Short of an eye transplant, there's not much I can do to repair the ravages of a dissipated life. That LBC you're taking wouldn't help me, would it?"

"Help you what?"

"Oh, I don't know," she said airily. "We'll talk about it when I get back."

Alone in the office, Adam tried to phone Megan at his apartment, but nobody answered. Before leaving Lenox, he had asked Moe Malone to call and tell her he was on his way to Boston and would contact her from the hospital. Now he was afraid he might miss seeing her before returning to camp, and he *needed* to see her. Diana's blatant overtures made him uncomfortable, even a little angry at her apparent insensitivity to all the hurt she had inflicted on him—proving he was not as indifferent to her, and her still formidable beauty, as he hoped.

When she reappeared, Adam had two steaming cups of espresso and a bottle of Canadian whiskey on the coffee table in the middle of the room. She settled into the easy chair next to his, crossed her legs so that her expensive shoes and a few inches of nylon-covered thigh were prominently displayed, and laced her coffee with whiskey.

She smiled with satisfaction as she saw his gaze drawn to her legs. Her breasts were nothing to brag about, but Adam claimed that he had never been particularly attracted to big-breasted women, that her trim hips and long legs were the parts of her anatomy he admired most—evidently still admired from his lingering look now. Was it worth pursuing? She was utterly exhausted and from the effect of her first few sips of whiskey would soon be drunk; she could think of nothing more pleasurable than sprawling on a crisp-sheeted hotel bed while Adam brought her to orgasm. Or was she merely indulging herself in an impossible sexual fantasy—a recurring one ever since the Metcalf fight? Wouldn't it be wiser to wait and see where their conversation led? Wiser—yes, but too chancy. She couldn't count on being alone with him in Lassiter's office much longer.

"Well," she began after waiting for another sip of spiked coffee to stop burning in her empty stomach, "let's at least make a pretense of starting over. How are you really, Adam?"

He shrugged. "Fine."

"Just fine?" she said mockingly. "Somehow that sounds inadequate for the world's most-talked-about athlete, high-level government appointee, and potential Nobel Prize-winning discoverer of a cure for myasthenia. What more could you possibly want?"

"Nothing," he replied, avoiding the obvious trap in that line of inquiry. "How've things been going for you?"

Diana chuckled softly. It was a self-deprecating mannerism that he knew usually preceded a wisecrack or complaint, sometimes a whole litany of complaints. "How?" she said after a moment's reflection. "Well, let me see. I've proved one thing to myself in recent months: I can live without sex—have lived without it for all but the first week of my not-so-joyous homecoming. Ted and I barely speak, let alone screw. . . . You did know I was back with Ted, didn't you?"

"Yes. Jon told me."

"Did it upset you?"

"No. Having never met your ex-husband, knowing nothing about him other than what you've told me, he's almost not a real person to me."

"Ted has trouble accepting your reality, too. Or did until recently. Now he can't open a newspaper or turn on the TV without being reminded of you. . . . Anyway, Ted and I are finished. As soon as he finishes paying me off for my half of the house, I'm moving out. I'd leave San Diego, too, if I didn't have so much money invested in my new practice."

"Where would you go?"

"Maybe Chicago. To work full-time for the A.M.A. You know how I love medical politics. Maybe back here to Boston if Jon decides to finish up at Harvard or if you offer the slightest encouragement. I know this sounds shameless, after all I put you through, but I've missed you terribly. Missed talking to you and being in bed with you. I don't mind admitting, Adam, you're the best man I ever slept with."

"Yes, Diana," he said with surprising assertiveness. "I probably was. But that's because I loved *you* even more than your body, and once you realized it sex stopped being a power game with us." Rising abruptly, he said, "Now, if you'll excuse me, I've a phone call to make."

"Adam, wait!" she pleaded. "It's obviously not an urgent call, so at least let me answer your last charge. Yes, it's true. It's what made sex so good with you. And yes, I really do regret screwing it up—but what did you expect? I warned you before I moved in with you I have a flawless record—I ruin everything that's the least bit good for me. After six years of analysis, I'm finally getting a glimmer of why, although I certainly haven't got to the self-help part yet."

"Diana, forgive me, but I really don't want to hear any more. You're dead tired. You've been through a hell of a lot today. You don't have to bare your soul for me. It's pointless."

"It can't bring our baby back to life, if that's what you mean?"

The impact of her words sat him back down. "That's exactly what I mean."

"Would it be so pointless if that's what I wanted to talk about—the abortion? Oh, don't look so accusing. I've no intention of trying to justify it. How could I? I don't give a damn what the women's movement or the Supreme Court says. For me it was murder because I felt like a murderer afterward. I still do. In my own warped little way, I figured losing Jon would be my punishment. Ironic, isn't it?"

"What is?"

"That you, the one person in the world who knew how heartlessly I behaved and deserved to be punished, would be the one to spare me that punishment. So I'm grateful, Adam. Grateful and confused and so in awe of you that the main reason I'd like us to go to bed is to make you seem more human."

Wordlessly, Adam stared at her. What better revenge could he possibly want? But he no longer lusted for it. Nor for her. "Diana—" he faltered.

"Oh, you don't have to say it. Your eyes speak for you. You want—what's those words you threw at me so often?—commitment and continuity. And a good screw has no staying power. In fact, the only thing I have that could possibly interest you is an explanation—a gut-honest one—of why I went through with the abortion. Surely, you must still be a little bit curious about that; you asked me enough times before I left."

"I know," he said softly, momentarily recapturing the utter desolation he had endured during her silences. "It was important then. More important than you could imagine. Made me do crazy things."

"Like take LBC?"

The ease with which she made the connection startled him. "Yes," he breathed.

"Don't worry, Adam. Your secret's safe with me. I couldn't possibly do anything to hurt you after what you did for Jon. You believe me, don't you?"

"Yes, I believe you."

"Oh, look away while I wipe more damn tears from my eyes." Digging into her purse for Kleenex, she dabbed her eyes, and then took a long sip from her cup. "Jesus, I must be a real alcoholic. It used to be that I couldn't screw sober. Now I can't even carry on a sober conversation."

"Diana, stop! I get no particular kick from seeing you so down on yourself. What hotel are you staying at?"

"The Ritz-Carlton."

"Then let me take you back there."

"I'll try like hell to seduce you."

"I've got a bodyguard. Secret Service. He'll protect me."

"I'll try to seduce both of you. I may be a bit out of practice, but I still know which end is up. Or down. Whatever—"

"He's an ex-sumo wrestler who weighs over four hundred pounds. Definitely not your type."

"You're lying!"

"So are you."

"Teasing, not lying. There's a difference. I never lied to you. I was never unfaithful either. I just threatened too much. It was one reason you wanted me to stay pregnant, wasn't it?"

"A minor one. And one reason you didn't."

She sighed, "Also a minor one. . . . Adam, for God's sake, listen to me. I don't pretend to understand all of it, even with a therapist, but the abortion has brought me to tears at least once a day for months. And I've had the most horrible dreams about it. That's why I've been drinking so much—to try to suppress those dreams. Anyway, confession is supposed to be good for the soul and mine's a basket case! I was on drugs. Oh, not hard drugs. The usual uppers and downers I took. I couldn't stop them. I was afraid of having an abnormal baby. But that's not the worst part." Again, she reached for her cup, but could not hold it steady. "Oh, God," she groaned, "maybe you're right. Maybe I do need rest. I can't stop shaking." Suddenly, the cup tipped and spilled its contents on the table.

Leaping up to avoid soiling her skirt, she swayed and might have fallen had he not seized her. "Oh, hold me, Adam. Please! Until I can stop shaking. I must be hypoglycemic or something . . ."

He embraced her, inhaling the familiar fragrance of her perfume, shivering slightly at the caress of her hand on the back of his neck. Fragments of certain surpassingly sensuous scenes between them flickered through his brain: their first night of lovemaking together; the sheer, shameless joy they took in dirty-funny, treacherous sex. Between crises, Diana had been more fun to be with than any woman he'd previously known. *Fun*, he reflected; such a simple, childish pleasure, yet an irresistible lure to someone who had lived with so little for so long. With her almost manic exuberance, and wit, and keen insights into other people, Diana had gifted him with fun. If only they hadn't lived a continent apart, or fallen in love, they might have enjoyed an extended, uncomplicated affair. A host of *if only's* crowded his thoughts, but he refused to consider them. Instead, feeling his desire burgeoning, breaking through the constraints of conscience and experience, he shut his eyes to immerse himself deeply in the dreamlike state that had overcome him. He could no longer deny he wanted her. Whatever the consequences, he had to possess and comfort and heal her.

He was about to press his mouth to hers, lave the velvety underside of her tongue with his in the way that always aroused her when, with stunning suddenness, the dream dissolved; the impossibility of its fulfillment became inescapably clear. Not only did his love for Megan intrude, he was overwhelmed by a brutal reminder of the penalty for unrealistic ambitions.

After breaking up with Diana, he had talked to a colleague who had recently gone through a messy divorce and child-custody fight. Hearing the lurid details of his alcoholic ex-wife's conduct, Adam had asked his friend: "Why do we get involved with such women?" His reply, spoken more in sorrow than in anger, was devastating: "Because we think we can cure them." The insight was as sobering now as when he'd first heard it, ruthlessly exposing his physician's conceit and deadening his desire.

Sensing his withdrawal, Diana whispered, "What is it, Adam? What's wrong?" Intuitively, she knew that it was another woman: younger, prettier, more suited to his new celebrity. She tried not to accuse him of it, spoil the bittersweet nostalgia of the moment; resisted as an alcoholic resists the first drink of the day before yielding with self-loathing and relief. "Who is she, Adam—the new woman in your life?"

He slackened his grip on her. "There is a woman, a very special one," he said, realizing that would be the less punishing explanation.

"Meaning that it's gone beyond the tryout stage . . . ? Well, congratulations," she said wryly. "I'm all right now. You can let go of me. And I can just as easily take a cab back to my hotel. . . . Oh, don't look so abashed. I'm not that competitive any more. Lost my killer instinct, I guess. I've still got Jon, thanks to you. And I'm glad you were honest with me. It's easier being rejected now than if we'd gone to bed. Harder to lose on your home ground, so to speak." She yawned deeply and steadied herself with the chair. "I plan to stay on in Boston until Jon's out of danger. Will I see you again?"

"Whenever I visit, which will be every few days. Oftener, if necessary."

"I'd like that. And now that I know how things stand between us, I'll be more circumspect." She smiled fleetingly and he smiled back.

Both tensed at the knock on the door.

"Come in!" Adam shouted and Dan Lassiter entered, looked searchingly at both of them, and said, "Hope I'm not interrupting anything?"

"Hardly," Diana replied. "How's Jon?"

"Chipper. Wants the name of the plastic surgeon who removed Elizabeth Taylor's tracheotomy scar. Also wants to see you before you leave."

"My pleasure."

"I have a message for you, too," Lassiter said to Adam. "Megan's waiting for you in the lobby. With your bodyguard."

"The ex-sumo wrestler?" Diana inquired.

"The *what?*" said Lassiter.

"Adam was trying to get me to believe he's an ex-wrestler who weighs four hundred pounds. A private joke."

"Would you like to meet them?" Adam asked.

"The bodyguard? Maybe. Megan—no. Not in the shape I'm in. Mind if I use your bathroom again, Dan? I'll replace the Kleenex I used. And wipe off your coffee table."

"Be my guest."

As the bathroom door closed behind her, Dan studied Adam in silence. "You look like you've gone ten tough rounds."

"I have. Ended in a draw."

"Sometimes a draw is the best decision—providing there's no rematch."

"There won't be."

"Don't tell me, tell Megan."

"How's your patient?" Megan asked as Adam joined her and Kirk in the lobby.

"Much better, thank God."

"And *how's* Diana?"

Adam hesitated. "Phil," he said, "would you mind bringing the car around?"

"Will do, Doc."

"I repeat," Megan said a moment later, "how's Diana?"

"Outclassed, and knows it."

"She'd better! And you'd better know something, too. If I didn't trust you—really trust you—I'd have barged into Dan's office and punched her out at the slightest provocation."

"No, you wouldn't. Not after what your father taught you about poker. You don't kick over the table when you're holding a winning hand."

Megan laughed. "You're glib, McKinnon. Maybe a little too glib. If it's not too nosy of me, I'd like to hear exactly how good a hand it was. Preferably, over dinner."

32

"That's enough!" shouted Al Lakeman as the bell ended the second round of sparring between Adam and Todd Tanner. Face flushed and fury mounting, he muttered, "Jesus, that's more than enough." Standing beside him on the ringside grass, Harry Patashnick asked, "What's wrong, Al? What's got you so worked up?"

Lakeman gave him an incredulous look. "You blind or something? I've seen fighters throw fights—plenty of 'em—but that's the first time I ever saw one throw a sparring session. What a pair! One guy can't punch and the other can't act."

Harry looked baffled. "I still don't know what you're getting at."

"You don't, huh? Well, I'll show you." Lakeman climbed through the ring ropes.

"How come you're stopping us after only two rounds?" asked Tanner. "I thought we were going three."

"How come?" Lakeman snarled. "'Cause what you two clowns are tryin' to pull is an insult to my intelligence. Now, step aside. I'll get back to you later."

Striding up to Adam, Lakeman thrust out his chin and ordered, "Jab me on the jaw. Go ahead, jab me!"

Adam stared. "What for?"

"First jab me, then I'll tell you what for."

"What's the point, Al? What are you trying to prove?"

"That you don't have a jab," Lakeman sputtered. "And, without a jab, you don't have a prayer against Jackson. Now, go ahead—prove me wrong."

Adam shook his head. "Forget it, Al. I don't want to hurt you."

Lakeman raised his right hand, palm out. "All right. Never mind the jaw. Jab my hand—hard as you can."

When Adam remained motionless, arms hanging loose at his sides, Lakeman taunted, "You're afraid, huh? Afraid to show me—"

The next instant, Adam's gloved fist smacked loudly against Lakeman's palm, making him grunt.

"That jab enough for you, Al?"

After a moment's confusion, Lakeman cried, "Right jab! That was a right. Show me the left jab, not the right. What you plan to do, fight Jackson southpaw?"

Adam shrugged. "If I have to. Now cool off, Al, and let's talk calmly."

"Yeah, c'mon, Al," urged Tanner.

"You!" barked Lakeman, pointing a finger at Tanner. "Take a walk. And while you're at it, give a little thought to loyalty. A fight manager's no priest, for Chrissake, but certain things you don't hide from him. . . . As for you," he said to Adam, "go shower and meet me in my cabin in a half-hour. We'll talk there."

Walking up to Lakeman's cabin, Adam hoped Harry Patashnick would be there. More than once recently, Harry had interceded during Al's more unreasonable outbursts. But when Adam entered, Lakeman was alone in the small living room, looking sour and dyspeptic. He gestured Adam to the easy chair beside him and said, "So, you're finally ready to talk, are you? Well, that suits me fine, long as you realize talkin' isn't the same as levelin'. And it's high time you leveled with me about a few things. Like you're in no shape to fight an adolescent amateur, let alone Coleman Jackson. And by fight, I mean box—not that karate shit you and Kirk been practicing. That stuff's illegal in a boxing ring, you know?"

"I know," Adam said patiently.

"You know it all, don't you?" snapped Lakeman. "Well,

one thing you don't know is what my reputation means to me. I don't give a damn if it's the biggest gate of all time or the biggest thing to hit Detroit since the horseless carriage, I'd rather call off the fuckin' match than be a party to a scam! A hell of a lot of fans are paying twenty-five bucks and up to see a good fight, not a foot race or the fastest knockout on record, and a *good fight* is what you owe them. . . . Then there's that drug business," he said with distaste. "The papers been full of that lately. You realize you're going to be drug-tested like no boxer in history? It's in the contract."

"I know, Al. I'm stopping all painkillers tonight."

"Tonight! The weigh-in is in two days! You're going to be tested twice—then and just before the fight."

"Don't worry, Al, I'll pass."

"What makes you so sure? 'Cause the big drug you're taking can't be detected?"

Adam eyed him intently. "You really want me to answer that?"

Al made a negative noise. "No. In a roundabout way, Lassiter already did. If a top medical man like him can't decide if you're on a drug or a nutrient, why should I worry?" Standing up, he said, "I'm gonna get a beer. Want one?"

"No, thanks," said Adam. "I'm still gurgling from all the water I drank in the shower."

Shortly, Lakeman returned from the kitchen with an open bottle of beer in his hand. He sat down, took a long swig, sighed, and gave Adam a conciliatory look. "You know the saying: no fool like an old fool. Well, there's a reason. When you still burn with ambition at my age, you're not only bucking the odds but the calendar. The day you showed up at my gym, I got one of the biggest surprises of my life. What you did to Tanner I couldn't believe! And I don't mind admittin' I got a little too greedy where you were concerned." He swigged more beer and wiped his lips. "I wanted a title fight for Tanner—for my swan song, you might say—and the only way to work it was through you. You fight Jackson, Tanner fights Savitt; it was a package from the start and still is. So I got a reason for wanting you to go through with the Jackson bout. What's yours?"

"I think I can beat Jackson," Adam said.

"And I think you're crazy! So do the bookies who've made you a two to one underdog. But that's besides the point. Why do you want to beat him? Despite those hockey shenanigans, you don't strike me as a glory hound. And with your government job, you don't need the dough any more. What's left?"

"I'm not sure I can explain it, Al; not so it would make sense. Let's just say I want to finish what I started."

"No matter what the risk to life and limb? Jackson's already put five of his opponents in the hospital, ending the boxing careers of all of them. The guy's strong as a bull. From what Bucky Miller tells me of his African ancestry, he was practically bred like a bull. One good opening and he can crack your skull, brain-damage you permanently."

"I'm well aware of that, Al."

"And you're still willing to fight him, gimpy wrist and all?"

"Jackson just doesn't scare me as much as one or two other things. Compared to them, he's almost a distraction."

Lakeman lowered the beer bottle from his lips and gaped at him. Until now the talk had gone well; an honest exchange of views. But Adam's last remark created chaos in his mind. He couldn't have been more astonished had Adam looked him square in the eye and announced that he was the embodiment of the Holy Spirit, the Paraclete of the Ascension. Al gave up and said no more. If Coleman Jackson represented nothing more than a distraction to Adam, Al wasn't sure he wanted to know what his real fear was.

33

Normally the weigh-in ceremony for a prize fight is held the day of the bout and is a routine affair, especially for heavyweights, who don't have to worry about shedding excess poundage. A physician appointed by the State Boxing Commission measures each boxer's height, weight, and blood pressure; examines his eyes; and, as an added flourish, checks for hernias. By prior contractual agreement, however, the weigh-in for the McKinnon-Jackson fight occurred a day early so Adam could be drug-tested and turned out about as routine as the eruption of Mount St. Helens.

Adam had expected to suffer withdrawal symptoms after stopping the heavy doses of codeine and dextroamphetamine he had been taking the past month, but nothing as severe as what he experienced. Yesterday, he had felt lethargic and stiff-wristed, though not enough to interfere with his training routine. This morning, he could barely muster the strength to get out of bed, and the simple act of shutting off the alarm clock triggered an excruciating pain in his left wrist. While Megan was fixing breakfast in his Boston flat, he locked himself in the upstairs bathroom with his medical bag and, gritting his teeth, injected the area around the transverse ligament in his left wrist with a mixture of lidocaine and cortisone. Unable to direct the needle with any precision, the injection was largely hit-and-miss, numbing his fingers more than his wrist.

Even more disturbing, his muscular movements seemed slower, making him worry that, without amphetamine to augment its neurotransmitter action, LBC had lost some of its effectiveness. Since an amphetaminelike substance, ephedrine, had long been used as an adjunct to the standard treatment of myasthenia gravis, such a drug interaction seemed a distinct possibility. He wished he could run an electromyogram on himself to find out if the slowness he felt was real or imaginary. But he lacked both the dexterity and the time. Did he dare take an extra ten or fifteen grams of LBC, he wondered; risk an overdose? Or should he wait and see how he felt later in the day? The memory of Jon Acheson, twitching convulsively and gasping for breath, made him choose the cautious course.

He confided none of this to Megan at breakfast, not wanting to worry her or dampen her excitement over her menstrual period being three days overdue. She had made an appointment with her family doctor for a pregnancy test that afternoon, missing the chance to fly with him to Detroit in a few hours but planning to travel there the next day with the Lassiters. Adam had urged the doctor appointment action, wanting her pregnant but not wanting to hear her talk about it. Her blissful anticipation was too reminiscent of Diana's at the same stage and, opposites though the two women were, Adam found the blighted memory of those days almost physically painful.

Arriving at Logan Airport with his Secret Service escort, Adam was the last to board the private jet Aaron Robards had chartered to fly their ten-man group to Detroit. Seeking solitude, he merely waved to the others in the party and sat by himself up front.

In the rear, Aaron Robards, who had just telephoned the box office manager of the Pontiac Silverdome for the latest ticket-sale tally, could barely contain his excitement. No sooner had he strapped himself in his seat than he began punching his pocket calculator and feeding figures for Mel Waldman to jot down in his notebook. Al Lakeman listened to them chatter about sell-out crowds and record gates until he saw Adam come aboard. One glimpse of him told Al something was seriously wrong. He knew Adam had spent the night with

Megan and might be short on sleep. But, besides being bleary-
eyed, he looked wan and jittery; in the worst shape he had been
in since his hockey game pounding. More than a few of
Lakeman's fighters had gone to pieces on him just before a big
bout: one, who beat his wife half to death in a trivial argument,
was hauled off to jail from the dressing room; another had
broken a heckler's jaw on his way to the ring—the only solid
punch he landed all night. But Adam was too self-controlled to
give him that kind of worry. Too damned self-controlled. He
wished that Dan Lassiter's hospital duties had not kept him
from catching this flight so he could get the lowdown on
Adam's health from him. Lakeman decided to move into the
empty seat next to Adam after takeoff and ask him, point-
blank, what was wrong. But by then, somebody had handed
him a beer and he and Harry started reminiscing and, to his
later regret, he never did.

Promptly at noon, Adam descended from his fortieth-floor
room in the Detroit Plaza Hotel to the second floor in a service
elevator. He was accompanied by Lakeman, Tanner, and his
two Secret Service protectors. An assistant hotel manager met
them at the landing and escorted them to a large office where
State Boxing Commissioner Jack Madden and the ring physician, Dr. Andrew Tally, waited. Following introductions, Tally,
a thickset, balding man in his mid-thirties who was an assistant
professor of family practice at Wayne State Medical School
and a former college wrestler, took Adam into a small,
makeshift examining room and asked him to strip to his
undershorts.

"You look tense," he remarked as Adam was about to step
on the platform scale.

"Do I?" Adam said. "Tired, mainly."

"Want me to shut off the air-conditioner in here? You've got
gooseflesh."

Adam smiled briefly. "I'm not going 'cold turkey' if that's
what you mean?"

"Of course not," said Tally, grasping the implication.
"Look, Dr. McKinnon, as a fellow physician, there are dozens
of questions I'd like to ask you, but I'm sure you're in no mood
to lecture. So I'll limit myself to just one: any serious health
problems I ought to know about?"

"No," Adam answered.

"Very well, then. Let's see what you weigh."

While Tally was examining Adam, Coleman Jackson entered the outer office. With him was Bucky Miller, his manager; Jake Knowles, his trainer; Cleotis Gann, his chief sparring mate; and an expensively tailored middle-aged man, clutching a leather attaché case, whom Al Lakeman correctly surmised to be Garrold Dawson, a Memphis lawyer and head of the syndicate that sponsored Jackson.

Tanner and Gann broke into simultaneous grins at sight of each other. They had both boxed on the 1976 U.S. Olympic team and kept up their friendship by spending time together at various boxing events ever since.

Drawing Gann aside, Tanner asked, "Hey, Clete, how you doin'?"

"Lots better, now that I don't have to be Coleman's punchin' bag no more. I sure wouldn't want to be in your man's shoes tomorrow night."

"My man wears flyin' shoes," Tanner taunted.

"Yeah? Well, they'd better be gassed up and ready to go, 'cause Coleman's out for blood."

"How come?" asked Tanner. "He's gettin' a big payday out of this, too."

"I dunno. But he's been sulkin' and steamin' for weeks. Evenings, after supper, he used to watch a tape of the McKinnon-Metcalf fight and go around mumblin', 'Ain't natural for a man to move that quick. Just ain't natural!' till Bucky made him quit watchin'. . . . Lucky for your man there ain't goin' to be no handshake for the press. The mood he's in, Coleman would break his bones."

Tanner frowned. "He really *that* mean?"

"Naw," said Gann. "Plenty tough, but not mad-dog vicious or nothin' like that. What I mean is, I never seen him go out of his way to hurt nobody more'n necessary. Couple of times sparrin', he had me out on my feet and just stopped swingin'. But your man's got him spooked. Coleman thinks he's taking some powerful new drug and his doctor friends in the know are coverin' up for him. Besides, Coleman hates doctors from way back—white, black, don't matter. Says doctors let his mama die of T.B. when nobody else was dyin' of it no more."

"Lord!" sighed Tanner. "That man's sure carryin' a lot in his head. Mine, too, from the looks of him. I just hope they can control it till fight time. No sense givin' away free what people are willin' to pay millions of dollars to see."

As soon as he finished examining Adam and collecting the necessary blood and urine specimens from him, Tally left to repeat the procedure on Jackson. Adam put on his boxing trunks and shoes and waited for Al Lakeman to summon him.

When he did, Lakeman said, "Okay, here's the story. Once the doctor gets through with Jackson, we go down the hall to where the press and TV cameramen are waiting, let them take a few shots of you and Jackson together, and then back here to change. Bucky and I have agreed—no questions, no fancy poses, no tough-guy remarks. You and Jackson don't even have to say hello to each other and I'd just as soon you didn't. . . . Got it?"

Adam nodded.

"Then, stick to it." Lakeman paused to study him. "What you so tense about?"

Sighing, Adam said, "You're the second person to ask me that in the last ten minutes."

"Well—?"

"I'm not tense, just tired."

"Then get some rest, for Chrissake!" Lakeman snapped. "One look at you on TV and the odds'll jump to 10 to 1."

Adam did not reply. He saw no purpose in telling Lakeman that the incessant throbbing in his left wrist had returned, that he could hardly wait to get back to his hotel room to inject it again, and that he might have to keep re-injecting it every few hours until Lassiter arrived.

As Adam followed Lakeman into the main office, Kirk and Eglund fell into step behind him. A moment later, Coleman Jackson emerged from the other examining room and stopped short on seeing Adam in his path. Immediately, his belly muscles tightened and his hands balled into fists.

Adam blinked at his hostility, his smoldering presence. But, heedful of Lakeman's admonition, he decided to ignore him. He started to turn away when, on sudden impulse, he stepped forward instead, returning Jackson's glower.

Jackson's eyes widened with surprise, then narrowed menacingly. As the staring match continued, Adam sized him up— same height, thirty or so pounds heavier, hugely muscled but no more so than "Mean Joe" Metcalf. In fact, from the bridge of the nose down, Metcalf was the more physically imposing. Only Jackson's eyes, burning into him with laserlike intensity, made him more daunting. With his chest and shoulder muscles tense and twitching, he resembled a man straining at invisible shackles to get at a mortal enemy. But even more than his posturing, it was the glint in his incandescent eyes that forcefully conveyed to Adam the intense hatred Jackson felt for him. Suddenly, he grew afraid of the man and what the physical expression of his hate could do to him in the ring.

Perhaps it was in counter-reaction to this fear, perhaps a release from his maddening pain, but when Jackson's lip curled contemptuously and he hissed, "Junkie!" Adam lost control. In a blur of motion, his right hand shot out and he slapped Jackson's face three times in rapid succession.

Emitting an animal-like snarl, Jackson lunged for him, fists pumping. Adam sidestepped the charge and stiff-armed him in the back, sending him stumbling into a desk. Pushing off of it, Jackson spun around—into Todd Tanner's arms. But before he could lock his hands together, Todd was seized by the shoulders and shoved aside. Assuming one of Jackson's men had done the shoving, Todd quickly realized it was Adam; no one else was close enough. He caught a fleeting glimpse of Adam's face before he and Jackson closed and was astounded by its ferocity: eyes unfocused and wild-looking, neck muscles taut, mouth twisted in a killing rage. Even Jackson recoiled into a defensive crouch. Then, shifting his weight to the balls of his feet, he started to spring forward but was stopped abruptly— not by Adam's fists but by the Colt .45 Phil Kirk was pointing at him over Adam's shoulder.

"Freeze!" Kirk barked. "Freeze, or I'll shoot."

Jackson cursed savagely but unclenched his fists.

For a moment, nobody moved, spoke, hardly breathed. Then Jake Knowles shouted, "Psycho! The guy's psycho!" Turning to Boxing Commissioner Madden, he sputtered, "You saw it. I want him disqualified!"

"Hush up, Jake!" Bucky Miller ordered harshly. "Everybody stay cool. . . . Al, get your man out of here and I'll do the same. Never mind the press. They already got enough out of this to sell their papers."

Bleakly, Lakeman nodded and, seizing Adam's arm, turned him toward the door.

Outside the office, they waited for Kirk and Eglund to clear the corridor of reporters drawn by the shouting and headed for the elevator. Though still too shaken to trust himself to speak, Lakeman's brain was working furiously. Adam had not merely overreacted to Jackson's insult; he had snapped like an overwound spring. The incident proved beyond doubt that Adam was a sick man—mentally, if not physically—but left Lakeman uncertain how to deal with him. He had to get hold of

Dan Lassiter in a hurry, he decided; find out if that stuff Adam was taking could affect his mind. If Lassiter's answer was yes, or even a strong maybe, Al's course was clear. He had borne the burden of a guilty conscience long enough. Without consulting anybody—not Adam nor Aaron Robards nor any of the eighty thousand thrill-happy ticketholders to the fight—he was going straight to the boxing commissioner with the story and the consequences be damned!

34

At 10:20 Saturday night at the Pontiac Silverdome, before the largest paid attendance ever to see an indoor prize fight, the passage of time as perceived by Adam's hypothalamus hit a bump, staggered along in spurts and lapses for another thirteen minutes, and then ground to a halt. Without this essential dimension, other oddities of perception occurred, leaving Adam and all around him in a state of suspended animation. In the distance he could see a massive, cross-strutted, polyester cushion of air, the dome of the Silverdome, and, out of the corner of his eye, row upon endless row of faces, mouths agape, lips pursed in oohs and aahs, staring at him with morbid curiosity.

Unhurriedly, as if he had time to spare, he tried to deduce the cause of his condition.

Was it cataplexy? Or catatonia?

As a neurologist, Adam ought to have known the difference between the two, but at the moment, he couldn't remember. Neither sounded right, anyway.

Possibly sleep paralysis?

Possibly. But back to that later. At the next break.

Break? From what?

I don't know, he admitted. But something is definitely wrong. The supposition reminded him of the Yale medical professor, famous in life but even more for the manner of his death, who suffered a cataclysmic rupture of a cerebral artery aneurysm in the midst of lecturing to a class of medical students. Pausing in midsentence, he gazed at his audience with a thoughtful, stricken look, gave the correct diagnosis of his seizure, adding, "Something has definitely gone wrong in my head," and died.

Something has definitely gone wrong in my head, too, concluded Adam. Otherwise, why am I awake, on my feet, but unable to move?

Moments before, bells had been reverberating in his ears as loudly as if he were in a belfry; Coleman Jackson had loomed before him, inescapably close, malevolent as Satan, implacable as the Angel of Death. Never before had Adam seen a human face so enraged or ghastly-looking. With eyes bulging between blood-matted lashes and blood from his nose mixing with the saliva on his mouthpiece, Jackson looked like a man who had just smashed his face into a car windshield.

As Adam stared in fear and fascination, Jackson cocked his right arm as far back as his shoulder joint allowed and then whipped it forward and down in a tight arc at his jaw. Halfway through the swing, the rust-red glove with the Everlast trademark lettered across the wrist suddenly stopped . . . started down again . . . stopped . . . inching ever closer to Adam's face in jerky, cogwheel-like, slow motion. Synchronous with the action, the ring lights blazed and dimmed, the crowd noises swelled and faded; everything seeming to flicker like a reel of motion picture film that had lost its loop.

Oddest of all, Adam could see both himself and Jackson as if from a distance, as if he were suspended somewhere above the ring, observer as well as participant.

Was he having an out-of-body experience—a phenomenon postulated by certain death counselors that he had never believed in? Was it dream or reality? A nightmare would explain his inability to move, the slow descent of Jackson's punch. But the throb in his temples, the sweat stinging his eyes, told him this was no nightmare; it was some sort of adrenaline-induced, hallucinatory reality. Yet if it was real, why had he suddenly wakened to it with no memory of what had gone before?

Desperately, he tried to orient himself, to start at the

beginning—a beginning that kept wavering between a mid-March scene in the old Beacon Street apartment shared with Diana, the low point of his adult life, and the recurrent nightmare of drowning Megan had roused him from that morning. . . .

"Adam! You okay?"

At Lakeman's strident voice Adam blinked away Jackson's menacing image and found himself staring down at the dun-colored canvas in front of his corner. "Yeah," he replied. "What round is it?"

"What round!" Al Lakeman took him by the chin and peered into his eyes. "What kind of crazy talk is that? The fight hasn't started yet. You puttin' me on or something?"

Adam shook his head as if to clear it.

"Then what the hell's the matter?"

"Nothing, nothing. I just want to start from the beginning, that's all."

Abruptly, Lakeman released him and shouted at Todd Tanner, "Get Lassiter! Get him, quick!"

But before Tanner could descend the ring steps to Dan Lassiter in his front-row seat, the stadium lights dimmed and a voice boomed, "Ladies and gentlemen, our national anthem."

Half lifted off his stool by Lakeman's hand in his armpit, Adam scanned the sea of faces staring up at him. Some looked awed, others suspicious. Dully, he wondered what would please them more—for his "magic" to bedazzle them or to see it debunked?

The band, its brass section now blaring loudly, could hardly be heard a little earlier. Predictably, it had struck up the theme song from the movie, *Rocky*, when Adam emerged from the tunnel and started down the aisle behind his phalanx of protectors. But the snowballing shouts of recognition from the crowd soon drowned out the music. The familiar chant of "Magic! . . . Magic! . . . Magic!" swelled to a frenzied peak as Adam neared the ring, bouncing off the polyester fabric of the dome with echoes as eerie as they were deafening.

The hypnotic cadence of chant and echo reminded Phil Kirk of the hysterical *"Seig, heil! Seig, heil!"* of Hitler's Nazi followers. "Jesus!" he shouted to Adam at the ring steps, "this crowd is really revved up. . . . Just remember what I told you to do in case things get out of control."

Adam did not remember; he had been too torpid from lack of

sleep to remember anything told him in the dressing room. But he didn't tell Kirk. The outpouring of adrenaline that jolted him awake had left his mouth so dry he could barely speak. Instead, he nodded, patted the Secret Service agent's shoulder, and climbed to the ring platform.

Backing into his ringside seat, Kirk sank down next to Eglund, who held a powerful walkie-talkie in his hands. "Noisy crowd," he said.

"Like feeding time at the zoo."

Kirk grimaced at the comparison, but did not dispute it. He watched Adam scuff his shoes in the resin box and pondered the enduring enigma of the man. In their weeks together, Adam had usually been frank and open with him. Kirk alone knew his strategy for the Jackson fight and was the first person he'd confided in after the face-slapping incident at the weigh-in. Interpreting Adam's words through his own preconceptions, Kirk had concluded that his overreaction to Jackson's slur had been more calculated than impulsive. As any policeman or big-game hunter knows, the most dangerous quarry is the one whose behavior is most unpredictable. Unpredictability bred uncertainty in the pursuer, and uncertainty bred mistakes. By Adam's own admission, Jackson's formidable presence had intimidated him, made him afraid to face the brutish boxer in the ring. What perturbed Kirk, however, was that Adam showed none of the exhilaration that usually follows when a man overcomes his fear and acts decisively. Evidently, there must be something Adam dreaded more than Jackson's fists that he was loathe to reveal.

Better than anyone, Dan Lassiter understood Adam's secret fear and the morbid mentality that had turned his consuming ambition so joyless; Lassiter himself had been death-obsessed all his adult life. But his insight into Adam's psyche helped hardly at all to lessen the awesome responsibility he had assumed. From the moment of Al Lakeman's frantic phone call after the weigh-in until his arrival at Adam's hotel room just before midnight, Lassiter's brain had been in turmoil. Lakeman had made it abundantly clear that whether the McKinnon-Jackson bout went on or would be canceled at the last minute depended on his professional opinion. To Dan, it was like being asked whether or not to proceed with high-risk open heart surgery on a patient already on the operating room table with his chest incised, ribs spread, and heart in full view.

Adam's calm was trancelike when Dan finally confronted

him in his hotel room. Under Kirk's tutelage, he had been meditating, he hastily explained at Lassiter's disapproving look; it helped ease his pain. Reluctantly, Dan anesthetized his left wrist to make Adam comfortable for a long, private talk. Until then, he had been unsure what he most wanted to hear—a rational or clearly irrational explanation for Adam's violent behavior at the weigh-in. But Adam quickly allayed any doubts Dan had over his sanity.

The LBC, Adam argued, had not affected his mind at all. If anything, he was thinking *too* clearly, shedding delusion after delusion until the mental bubble that had sheltered him from reality all these months was close to collapsing. The millions of dollars he had set out to earn to support his research now meant little; the promise of LBC in the treatment of myasthenia gravis even less, especially if saving Jon Acheson's life with it had condemned him to the same hellish torture he was experiencing. These haunting realizations, brought to a head by Jackson's personification of Death, had so overwhelmed him with a sense of futility and utter powerlessness that Adam had simply exploded at Jackson's insult. He would be the first to admit that his behavior was inexcusable, but he was only human and helpless against such uncontrollable rage.

And Lassiter understood. He knew all too well the blinding rage provoked by a sense of powerlessness. At twelve, he had raged at the senseless death of his parents in a car crash. As a combat officer in Korea, he had raged at the death of his comrades. As a doctor, he had raged at death, the malicious marauder who struck without warning, without care. So he had readily accepted Adam's explanation. After a word with Megan, who was anxiously waiting to see Adam in the adjoining bedroom, Dan had so informed Lakeman.

Now, however, standing with Kris and Megan among the multitudes at the Pontiac Silverdome, Lassiter regretted his hasty decision. Having failed to use his power to stop this fight, he felt a heavy responsibility for its consequences. He was particularly concerned about Megan, who had not tried to influence his decision in any way but whose wishes were clear. Having given more of herself, her future, to Adam than anybody else, she stood the most to lose. But the torrent of events released by Adam's obsession had swept her up, too.

Outwardly, she appeared calm and composed as she mouthed the words to "The Star-Spangled Banner" and stared up at Adam's forlorn-looking figure in the ring. Only the hollow crescents under her eyes and the twitch at their corners betrayed her anxiety.

Having heard about the weigh-in scuffle on her car radio while coming home from the doctor, her elation at her pregnancy had been cruelly brief, her reunion with Adam tender but cheerless. Despite their reaffirmation of love, she couldn't help being angry with him, and herself. She had conceived his child *too* late to deter him from senseless battle with an opponent who hungered for both victory and vengeance. Regardless of his fearsome looks, his posturing, Coleman Jackson was not a monster, Megan realized; merely a man who ate, slept, and longed for love like all men. The real enemy of her happiness was Adam, the obsessed and driven being he had become. It was scant comfort that he knew it too and despised himself for the change.

As enthusiastic as he acted at the confirmation of her pregnancy, Megan sensed that the news only deepened his gloom. Lassiter understood his fear of death, Kirk his fear of fear, but only Megan knew the dominant truth: *how much Adam wanted to live*. At the end of a long, rambling self-analysis, frustratingly cluttered with such psychiatric jargon as "annihilation anxiety" and "savior complex," he had finally blurted it out.

Her pregnancy represented the ultimate irony, he explained; the twist of fate that had closed the circle for him and heightened his belief that life was an unwinnable shell game.

"What do you mean?" Megan had demanded.

"It's simple," he said, his tone indicating just the opposite. "I know this will hurt you, but until this morning, I cared less whether I lived or died than whether my life had meaning. I was afraid that all my years of research would wind up empty, LBC a dangerous therapeutic dud, and so I tried to make myself a living example of its worth. But, you, the look in your eyes this morning—something—made me realize how insane that was. Now I no longer give a damn about medical immortality. I want to live, with you, our child, and I'm afraid—afraid I'm living a horror story and, as in all such stories, *the monster must die!*"

Neither slept much that night. They had clung tightly to each other, shed tears together, and stared into the bedroom darkness at a future filled with uncertainty and eternal change.

· · ·

At the conclusion of the anthem, a stocky, tuxedo-clad man strode to the center of the ring with a microphone, turned to Jackson and announced: "In this corner . . . weighing two hundred and twenty-one pounds . . . in white trunks . . . from Memphis, Tennessee . . . the number-one heavyweight contender in the world . . . *Coleman Jackson!*"

That produced a spatter of applause, mainly from those who had bet on Jackson, and a long drum roll when he shed his robe. The crowd grew silent as the ring lights limned his rippling muscles and he raised a gloved fist in Adam's direction. Seizing the opportunity to solo, a trumpeter in the band blared forth a short, rousing *paso doble,* the one usually played at a bullfight when a fresh bull bursts through the Gate of Frights into the ring. But if Jackson recognized any subtle implication, he did not show it.

The tumult that followed Adam's introduction clearly showed he was the crowd's favorite—at least, for the time being. He neither smiled nor waved, and the expression on his creased face suggested bafflement. Adam did not want to slight his fans; he was simply distracted, the playing of the *paso doble* having triggered an intense sense of *déjà vu.*

When the referee beckoned the boxers to the center of the ring for instructions, Adam nodded at Lakeman's stern admonition that he do and say nothing.

"You *sure* you're all right?" asked Lakeman, worried by Adam's air of dreamy passivity. "What round is it?"

"Round two!" Adam answered brightly. "I won the first one on points yesterday."

"Wise guy!" grumbled Lakeman, unamused but secretly relieved that he would try to joke.

Surprisingly, Jackson neither glared nor scowled at Adam as the referee placed a hand on each of their shoulders. Instead, he looked as cool and confident as a fearless neurosurgeon Adam knew: a man who operated on any case he could get his hands on, however hopeless or far gone, not because he was greedy but because he enjoyed nothing better than operating on human brains.

After the referee finished his instructions, the fighters touched gloves and Adam wandered back to his corner, unable to shake off the odd feeling that all this had happened just a short time before.

Squirming on the hard stool, he let Todd Tanner insert his rubber mouthpiece, watched abstractedly as Lakeman kneaded his gloves to break the leather away from his knuckles, and thought how nice it would be to get back to his laboratory and Megan once this final ordeal was over.

The clang of the bell resounded through the huge, three-tiered stadium. Instantly, the eighty-one thousand spectators and five hundred or so media reporters went silent. Many realized boxing history was being made, but mostly they thought about the striking contrasts between the combatants: young versus old, black versus white, a natural athlete versus an artificial one. After the weigh-in scuffle, the odds against Adam had dropped from 2:1 to 8:5, many gamblers being impressed by his quick hands and reckless courage. Now, seeing the tremendous physical disparity between the two men, some who had bet on Adam began to regret it. They regretted it even more when Adam bounced on the balls of his feet and moved forward with the right glove in front of his left. A murmur swept through the arena as the crowd realized rumors about Adam's injured left wrist must be true. He was going to fight Jackson southpaw, possibly one-handed!

Jackson waited until his opponent had reached mid-ring before moving out of his corner—remembering how McKinnon had surprised "Mean Joe" Metcalf by rushing him at the opening bell. He was also still rankling over his humiliation at the weigh-in. There would be no quick knockout if Jackson could possibly help it. He wanted McKinnon to pay in pain for that blow to his pride and the unfair way the newspaper stories had slanted it.

McKinnon's right-hand lead did not surprise him. Bucky Miller had prepared him for that. Besides, the main danger when fighting a southpaw was from body punches and he was confident McKinnon couldn't hit hard enough to hurt him there.

Adam had reached the same conclusion. In an unheard of boxing strategy, he neither sought openings to Jackson's head nor his body. Instead, using his expert knowledge to the fullest, he went nerve-hunting, his first target being Jackson's median nerve as it wound down his humerus to control certain muscles in his forearm and hand. But that would have to wait until his opponent threw enough punches to grow a little arm-weary. In the meanwhile, Adam had to play the ring angles like a billiards champion, make sure Jackson neither cornered nor clinched with him.

At mid-ring, Jackson stretched forward on his toes and threw his first punches of the bout—a left jab and right cross that fell short as Adam easily leaned out of range. Nonetheless, Adam hastily backpeddled, impressed by his opponent's fast hands. Jackson closed and feinted with a left hook, hoping to move McKinnon right, where he could rush him into the ropes. But Adam did not react to the feint, keeping a safe five feet of ring space between them.

After two futile rushes at his nimble opponent, Jackson's pace slowed. Flat-footed, he pursued Adam until, passing his own corner, he heard Bucky Miller shout, "Get up on your toes!"

As Jackson glanced down at Miller, Adam darted in and stung him with a jab to the nose. Angrily, Jackson spread his stance to charge Adam again, but stopped short on realizing he was unlikely to cach him. Instead, he resumed stalking Adam around the ring, throwing jabs and combinations periodically to keep his muscles loose.

The crowd, fascinated but fearful that this might be the pattern for the entire fight, shouted at Adam to stop running and start punching. He ignored them, ignored as best he could the gut spasms that kept squirting bitter bile into his throat, and concentrated exclusively on Jackson's moves, on where the two of them were in the ring.

Having inspected it earlier, Todd Tanner had warned him about a danger spot in the ring—erected in the center of what was normally a football field—where the beam from a distant bank of lights shone directly in one's eyes. Adam had already been blinded momentarily by the low-set beam a time or two. Now, after luring Jackson into the spot, he saw him blink and drop his gaze. Instantly, Adam jabbed him twice in the face and rocked him back with a hard left hook to the temple.

"Atta way, Doc!" shouted Tanner from behind the ropes in Adam's corner.

Beside him, Lakeman nodded approvingly, although Adam's wince suggested that the hook had hurt him as much as Jackson. Lakeman was right. The pain, blazing from his left wrist to his shoulder, made him totter. In contrast, Jackson shook off the blow and charged forward. Bending low, Adam ducked under his lead left and weaved away from his right cross, making Jackson stumble past him. Suddenly, Adam was down—not from a punch but from a knee to his ribs. Lakeman and Tanner waved and shouted, "Foul!" at the referee, but

were unheard in the uproar. Almost the entire crowd had leaped
to its feet in a frenzy of excitement and protest.

The referee helped Adam up, wiped off his gloves, and, at
the barely audible bell, sent him to his corner while he
conferred with the two judges on whether Jackson had
committed a foul.

"That son of a bitch!" Lakeman fumed as he removed
Adam's mouthpiece. "You all right?"

"I'm not kicking," Adam said breathlessly. "He is."

Across the ring, Lakeman saw Jake Knowles in an animated
discussion with the referee. "Look at that weasel Knowles,"
he said scornfully. "Trying to convice the ref Jackson kneed
you by accident. *Accident,* my ass! It was a foul. A clear foul,
you hear?"

"I know, Al," Adam said laconically. "I was there."

"Can you punch with your left?"

"Not any more. But don't worry. Neither will Jackson,
soon."

"Oh, yeah?" Lakeman said skeptically. "How you gonna
manage that?"

"Just watch," replied Adam, and, rinsing his mouth with a
swig of water, spit it into a bucket. Rising from his stool, he
rubbed the bruise Jackson's knee had raised on his right hip,
stretched his arms, and awaited the bell.

For the opening minute of the second round, the ring action
was largely a repetition of the first. Quickening his pace,
Jackson pursued Adam relentlessly, but failed to force a
misstep or get within punching range. Then, with Jackson on
the brink of the blinding spot again, Adam made his move.

The time was 10:19.

Bouncing forward, Adam drew a left jab from Jackson,
which he deflected upwards; then, with his opponent's arm
extended, he slid to his right and brought up his right glove to
strike Jackson on the inner aspect of his upper arm just below
the armpit. It was risky, leaving Adam momentarily defense-
less against a right cross, and one of the strangest punches ever
thrown in a boxing match. But it accomplished its purpose—
crushing Jackson's median nerve against the shaft of his
humerus and disrupting the flow of nerve impulses to certain
muscles in his forearm and hand.

Directly below at ringside, Phil Kirk saw the blow and
smiled knowingly. He was the only spectator in the stadium
who was looking for the punch, appreciated its purpose, and

knew how it felt. The bruised nerve in his left arm still ached from Adam's practice punch the previous night. Kirk also knew that the paralysis it produced would last less than a minute. He tensed as he saw Adam position himself to deliver the crucial follow-up blow. His target now was the most vulnerable major nerve network in the human body, the brachial plexus, accessible to attack in the groove between the collarbone and the cervical vertebrae at the base of the neck. The brachial plexus comprised four spinal cord roots and controlled all the muscles of the shoulder and arm on its side of the body. Kirk knew from experience that a well-aimed karate chop could damage the plexus, but he had no idea whether or not a gloved fist could do the same. Neither did Adam, though he was about to find out. With his opponent's left arm hanging limp, Adam put all his weight behind a looping right hook to the side of Jackson's neck, feeling the impact transmit to his shoulder.

The time was exactly 10:20.

The next instant, Adam went reeling across the canvas into the ropes as Jackson caught him flush on the temple with a right cross. The crowd gasped, shrieked, and waited for Jackson to hurl himself at Adam, fists flying. Instead, he stood at mid-ring, trying helplessly to lift his left arm.

"Go after him!" Bucky Miller shouted. "Go!"

Jackson turned toward him, perplexed, but remained rooted in place.

The referee glanced at Adam, still on his feet and trying to shake the scintillating haze from his vision, and then at Jackson, puzzled by his immobility. "You all right?" he asked, and, at Jackson's nod, said, "Keep fighting."

The crowd grew unnaturally still as they watched Jackson strain to raise his left glove to chest-level. Once above his waist, however, it trembled so violently that he let it flop down in disgust and, charging Adam, unleashed a roundhouse right. Though still rubbery-legged, Adam evaded the punch, sending Jackson into the ropes, and moved out to the center of the ring.

With the television sportscaster describing the action in near-hysterical shrieks, Andrew Mellinger tapped Chester Ricksey on the shoulder and said, "Turn the audio down a little, will you, Chet?" Along with a contingent of high-level government officials they were watching the bout from a V.I.P. lounge in the Silverdome.

Ricksey lowered the volume on the TV set. "I hope the Russkies are getting a clear satellite picture of the fight," he remarked.

"So do I!" said Mellinger. "Especially their Air Force generals. McKinnon's amazing. Simply amazing! Can you imagine our pilots beating the Russian pilots to the punch like that?"

"My favorite bedtime fantasy," Ricksey admitted. "What we in the 'spook' business would consider 'a perfect ten.'"

The rest of the round was more spectacle than action: two boxers, one obviously dazed, the other bewildered, trying to fight each other one-handed. From their expressions, the bell came as a welcome relief to both.

"What'd you do to him? *What the hell did you do?*" Lakeman asked excitedly when Adam returned to his corner.

"Wha—?" Adam grunted and slumped back in the stool, his eyes rolling up.

"Jesus, he's out! . . . Smelling salts!" Lakeman cried.

Adam regained consciousness rapidly as the ammonia fumes scorched his nasal membranes. He jerked his head away. "Enough! . . . That's enough!"

"You okay? Tell me the truth now," Lakeman demanded.

"Okay," muttered Adam, tears streaming from his chemically irritated eyes. "How's Jackson?"

Lakeman looked across the ring at Miller and Knowles frantically rubbing and working on Jackson's left arm. Al's hopes for victory suddenly soared as he saw the referee and ring doctor move solemnly toward them. He still had no idea what Adam had done to Jackson's arm, but fervently hoped it would be enough to make Tally call the fight. After the referee instructed the time-keeper to hold the bell for the the next round, Tally examined Jackson's collarbone for breaks, tested the strength in his left shoulder, arm, and hand, and then, to Lakeman's disapointment, shrugged at the referee and walked away.

At Megan's urging, Dan Lassiter left his seat and came to Adam's corner during the delay. "Adam! How're you feeling?" he shouted, and was dismayed at the glassy look in Adam's eyes when he swung around.

"Okay," Adam said thickly. "Helluva headache, though."

"You took a helluva punch. . . . Can you keep fighting?"

Adam shrugged. "Maybe another round or two . . ."

"What do you think, Dan?" Lakeman interrupted.

"I think he's about had it. If it were up to me, I'd throw in the towel now."

"There'd be a riot," Lakeman said. "The crowd thinks Jackson's hurt, not Adam."

"The hell with the crowd!" Lassiter snapped. "Stop it!"

"No," said Adam. "Not yet. I want to see what my nerve punch did to him. I'll go down if I get hit hard again."

"You'd better," Lassiter warned. "You've seen enough autopsies to know what battered brains look like."

"I promise. Tell Megan I'm okay, will you, Dan?"

Grimly, Lassiter nodded and returned to his seat.

After a full minute's delay, the bell for the third round rang and Jackson came out of his corner, leading with his left glove again. Adam shuffled forward a few steps, stopped, waited. As he expected, Jackson feinted with his left and threw a long, overhand right. Adam sidestepped it and snapped a jab off his nose. Jackson countered with a left hook that grazed the top of Adam's head but did not hurt—confirming that Jackson had lost most of the punching power in his left hand.

Adam connected with another jab to the nose, drawing blood for the first time, and danced away . . . away . . .

The next thing Adam knew, he was back in his corner and dripping wet from Tanner's sponging. Fast round, he thought. "How'm I doing?" he asked Lakeman.

"Not bad," Lakeman conceded. "You're scoring with the jab. Keep it up."

"Sure, Al. . . . Sure," Adam said almost jauntily.

"But watch out," Lakeman continued. "He's getting more snap in his left and starting to go for your body."

"My body," Adam repeated, neglecting to tell Lakeman that he was still so numb he barely felt any bodily sensations.

"Al, look!" Tanner shouted and pointed at Jackson. "He's gettin' ready to rush Doc at the bell."

Pivoting, Lakeman saw Jackson rocking back and forth against the ropes in his corner. "Adam!" he warned. "You hear?"

But before he could answer, the bell rang and Jackson flew across the ring, his eyes gleaming with opportunity and malice as he saw Adam rise slowly, wearily, to his feet.

It's all over! thought Lakeman, feeling his heartbeat in his throat. Having missed a step, Adam couldn't possibly get out of Jackson's way. He didn't. He did the impossible instead. As

Lakeman blinked with astonishment, he seemed to disappear.
All he saw was Coleman Jackson, both arms raised to protect
his head, crash into the ring post and drop to his knees.

"What happened?" Lakeman shouted at Tanner above the
bedlam of the crowd.

Tanner grinned and said, "He played possum."

"He did—what? Tell me in plain English, for Chrissake!"
Lakeman growled while the referee wiped off Jackson's
gloves.

"He ducked low, bobbed to the left, knowing Jackson was
goin' to throw his right, then real quick the other way."

"I didn't see it," admitted Lakeman.

"Neither did Jackson."

Limp with relief, Lakeman looked at Tanner and laughed.
"Possum!" he jeered. "And you ain't even from the South."

"Talk about raw nerve," Mellinger exclaimed to Ricksey. "I
can't believe what McKinnon's doing down there. I swear, he's
operating on instinct alone—on automatic pilot, so to speak."

"It's damned impressive," Ricksey agreed. "I just hope he
doesn't get carried away. He could kill Jackson, you know."

"Kill?" Mellinger questioned. "How?"

"With his quick hands, he could crush his larynx."

"I suppose he could. But would he, do you think?"

Ricksey hesitated, thinking back to the one time in his long
military career when he was in hand-to-hand combat. The ugly
incident had happened in Vietnam, during the Tet Offensive
years ago, but he still had nightmares about it; still woke
sweating with the memory of that wiry little Cong's throat
crunching in his hands. "Probably not," he finally said. "He's
a doctor. But I believe I would—under the circumstances."

Between lucid moments, Adam's moves were as responsive
to Jackson's as if the two were veteran dance partners. His hip
hurt and a glancing body blow had started his cracked rib
aching, but otherwise he breathed and moved easily, circling
counter-clockwise whenever possible to avoid the danger spot
in the ring. Four rounds to go, Lakeman had told him during
his last rest period, making this one the sixth. Flashbulbs kept
flaring out of the darkness like fireflies and the taunts and
catcalls of the crowd seemed about equally divided now—half
demanding that he go on the attack, half demanding that
Jackson catch him.

"Thirty seconds!" yelled Lakeman as Adam skirted his corner and suddenly, with a loud pop and blaze of light, something exploded before his eyes. At first, he thought Jackson had hit him, even though he felt no pain. Then, vaguely, he realized that a bank of lights in his direct line of vision had shorted out, momentarily blinding him and throwing him off stride.

Frantically, Adam tried to locate Jackson through the blurry afterglow, but before he could, Jackson jolted him. The punch, a solid body blow, might have incapacitated Adam were it not for two things: it was a left hook, and Jackson still lacked power in his left hand; and it landed just to the right of his breastbone, partially knocking the wind out of him but missing his barely mended left sixth rib.

Staggering back, Adam sensed more than saw the vicious overhand right that followed and stepped inside it to clinch, feeling Jackson's forearm slam against the side of his neck. Using all that remained of his depleted strength, he tried desperately to pin his opponent's sweat-slick arms against his body, but Jackson was too powerful. With a mighty heave, he lifted Adam off his feet and flung him against the ropes.

"Stay down! Down!" Lakeman shouted as Adam slid to the canvas, and he did for an eight count.

Fifteen seconds remained in the round when the referee ordered them to resume fighting and Jackson immediately charged him. Whether he willed it or whether his imperiled body acted on its own, Adam didn't know, but he somehow slipped a straight right between Jackson's guard, striking the bridge of his nose and stopping him in his tracks. Blinking and snorting blood, Jackson wobbled back. Disgustedly, he looked down at the blood dripping onto his chest and shoes, wiped the thumb of his glove across his nose, and started forward again. But before he could take a full step, the bell rang and Jackson reflexively lowered his guard—a move that would be replayed on television repeatedly in the hours and days ahead and would cost him the fight. A split-second later, Adam, too, lowered his gloves, feeling a sharp stab of pain from the fresh bruise under his right nipple.

Mistaking Adam's mouthpiece-distorted wince for a smirk, Jackson suddenly lunged and smashed a right uppercut under his heart. The breath, which Adam had barely regathered, promptly left his lungs and, with a gut-sickening sensation, he felt something snap inside him. A searing pain spread up his sternum into his left shoulder and a pressure buildup in his chest seemed to shove its contents to the right and bring it close to bursting. Distantly, he could hear the bell clanging like a fire engine, but it didn't much matter; no one-minute rest between rounds could help him now. Intuitively, he knew his left sixth rib was cracked again—an internal dagger. The fight was clearly over for him, his illusion of magical invincibility shattered. As blood from his brain pooled behind his retina, he saw red and sensed he was on the verge of collapse. But before he went down, he knew he had to get out of the way of the follow-up punch Jackson had already launched. Primal fear shuddered through him as he realized he could neither block nor deflect Jackson's glove; it was too close, his arms too weak. All he had time to do was jerk his head sharply to the left and let it slide past his cheek. But could he? Would his stunned nervous system respond?

At the last possible moment, it did. Like an automobile swerving to avoid a head-on collision, first Adam's chin, then his jawbone, slipped out of the path of the punch, leaving only his temple and ear in jeopardy. Then, with the loudest bang he had ever heard, his right eardrum ruptured, his brain slammed against his skull in a concussive blaze, and a voice he had never before heard, rising out of the depths of his being, sighed in hopeless despair.

35

When the stadium was plunged into sudden darkness, Dan Lassiter was crouched protectively over Adam's unconscious form. The incredible events set in motion by Jackson's sneak attack flashed through his mind. The murderous punch to Adam's temple had sent him toppling sideways against the ropes, where he had hung suspended and helpless before Jackson's onslaught. Simultaneously, Lassiter, Kirk, and Eglund had sprinted for the ring, but it was Todd Tanner who stopped Jackson from hitting Adam again. Somehow—Lassiter was uncertain if he went through the ropes or over them— Tanner barreled into Jackson and sent him sprawling. Racing up the ring steps first, Kirk had seen Lassiter behind and, with a sweep of his arm, propelled him ahead. By then, Adam had slid, face-down, to the canvas and Dan had to thrust the referee aside to reach him. There was just time to roll Adam on his back, to observe his unfocused stare and the blood oozing from his right ear and check his carotid pulse, when the ring floor began to shake from the crush of enraged spectators trying to get to Jackson. Alarmed, Dan looked about for Kirk, who was standing a few feet away, shouting into a walkie-talkie. Returning to his examination of Adam, Dan saw that his chest was heaving faster and his face growing dusky. He tried to palpate the position of his trachea, but the ring was shaking so violently he could hardly keep his balance. He dropped to his knees and braced himself for the platform's inevitable collapse. It was then that every light in the huge Silverdome went out. He heard the crowd suck in its collective breath and from some unknown source an amplified voice, assured of total attention and authoritative as God, boomed:

"NOBODY MOVE! I REPEAT, NOBODY MOVE. ADAM McKINNON IS BADLY HURT AND MUST BE RUSHED TO A HOSPITAL. HIS LIFE DEPENDS ON YOUR COOPERATION. IN A MOMENT, THE LIGHTS WILL COME BACK ON. THOSE OF YOU IN THE AISLE LEADING TO THE LOCKER ROOM TUNNEL, MOVE TO ONE SIDE. IT MUST BE CLEARED IMMEDIATELY. THE REST OF YOU, STAY WHERE YOU ARE!"

The blackout had not caught Lassiter by complete surprise. Kirk had warned him it might happen. In spite of the extra Secret Service agents assigned him, and the stadium and city police, Kirk knew how useless they would all be if a crowd of eighty-one thousand fight fans turned into a mob. Wisely, he had stationed an agent at the light-control panel in the Silverdome and told him to throw the master switch in case of a riot.

So Dan recovered quickly when the lights went out, snapped on the powerful penlight Kirk had supplied him, and shone it on the man squatting beside him. It was Moe Malone, his dented forehead distinctive in the bright beam. Dan gave him the flashlight and showed him where to point it. Then, re-checking Adam's trachea and finding it shifted even farther to the right, feeling for the thrust of heart against chest wall and finding it shifted rightward, too, Dan knew there was no time to confirm his presumptive diagnosis of tension pneumothorax with either stethoscope or X-ray. He had to act at once. From his pocket he took a bulb-shaped needle, tore away its plastic sheath, and held it poised in one hand two inches below the middle of Adam's left clavicle. With his other hand, he checked its position between second and third ribs and then plunged it deep into Adam's chest. The sudden rush of air through the one-way valve at the top of the needle clinched the diagnosis. But Dan's sense of relief was short-lived. When the lights came on and he saw Adam's purplish face, his eyeballs rolled so far up only white sclera showed between the swollen lids, he was sickened by the suspicion that his heroic treatment was too little, too late. The human brain simply could not tolerate such a beating. In response, it might swell massively, herniate through the membranous opening at the base of the skull until it choked off all vital bodily functions. Or it might somehow limit the swelling to those centers in its neocortex that were the most advanced and greedy for oxygen. If that happened, Adam would live, but, in the cruelest of medical slang, only as a vegetable.

In the tunnel leading to the outside, as he strode briskly beside the ambulance attendants wheeling Adam towards their vehicle, Dan heard the ring announcer's stentorian voice:

"By unanimous decision of the judges, Coleman Jackson has been disqualified. The winner . . . Adam McKinnon!"

Unmoved by the crowd's stadium-shaking ovation, Dan muttered an obscenity to himself. Even if he'd bet on Adam, as countless of his doctor colleagues had, he could think of nothing to cheer about.

Al Lakeman, seated nearest the doorway of the visitor's lounge opposite the intensive care unit of Henry Ford Hospital, was the first to see Dan Lassiter come out of the unit and jumped up to greet him. He was immediately crowded by Todd Tanner and Phil Kirk. Behind them, Mel Waldman, Aaron Robards, and Moe Malone sat forward in their chairs, while Megan, who had been resting her head against Harry Patashnick's shoulder on a couch, straightened and tried to shake off her lethargy.

"How is he?" blurted Lakeman.

When Lassiter hesitated, Lakeman's eyes widened and his chin began to tremble. "J . . . Jesus, he's alive, isn't he?"

Lassiter nodded. "Barely. . . . Look, Al, let me talk to Megan in private first. This is hardest on her. Then I'll fill you in—okay?"

Blinking uncertainly, Lakeman muttered, "Sure, Dan. Sure. . . . But—"

"Later," said Lassiter softly but firmly and patted Lakeman's arm. To Todd Tanner he asked. "How's the knee?" Tanner had banged his left knee on the canvas when he'd crashed into Jackson, but stubbornly refused to let a doctor examine it until he knew how Adam was.

"No problem, Doc," Tanner replied. "It can wait. Adam comes first."

Megan tensed as Lassiter approached her and stared searchingly. His weary eyes and tight, pale lips offered no encouragement. "Oh, my God . . . no . . . " she wailed.

"It's okay," Lassiter said hastily. "He's alive. I swear it."

"How alive?" she whispered and clutched herself to keep from shivering.

Harry Patashnick rose so Lassiter could sit beside her. "Megan," he said, taking her hand, "there's a consultation room next door. What say we go there to talk?"

At her nod, Lassiter helped her to her feet and, gripping her arm firmly, led her to a small room with a desk, a few chairs, an X-ray viewing box, and a hotplate holding a Pyrex pot of coffee. He poured a cup. It was black and smelled stale. "Coffee?" he asked.

"No, thanks," Megan replied. "Afraid I'd vomit."

"Kris has cigarettes, if you're out?"

"I've still got a few. Where is Kris?"

"With Adam. She knows her way around an I.C.U. better than I do. She runs one."

"Oh . . . that's right." Although outspoken at times, Kris Lassiter was so much more relaxed and easier to talk to than Dan that Megan sometimes forgot what an outstanding internist she was. "What's she doing?"

Seemingly busy adding just the right amount of creamer to his coffee, Lassiter did not reply. Megan waited for him to carry the steaming cup to the desk and sit opposite her. Then, locking eyes with him, she asked, "Tell me straight, Dan. How bad is he?"

"Bad." He compressed his lips. "I won't mince words or mislead you about that. He's still comatose; his sixth rib is not only fractured again but displaced, and, despite the chest tube we've inserted, his left lung hasn't fully re-expanded yet. But there are hopeful findings, too. The CAT scan, for one. Shows a sizable contusion, but no hematoma—no blood clot pressing on his brain. . . . You asked what Kris was doing. She's performing a lumbar puncture to see if there's blood in Adam's spinal fluid. If not, or if just a little, so much the better. . . ."

As he paused to sip coffee, Megan stared penetratingly at him. "What are you trying to tell me, Dan?"

"That he *could* die, though the odds are against it right now."

"What would change them?"

Rubbing the flat of his hand across his burning eyes, Dan said, "A lot of things: Massive brain swelling, or a massive bleed into his heart sac from his broken rib. Naturally, we're taking steps to guard against both those dangers and a dozen others, too. Kris knows Boyd Frame, the head of the I.C.U. here, and says he's top-notch. She's just holding the fort until Frame gets here. Believe me, Megan, Adam couldn't be in better hands."

She tried to smile. "Whatever happens, I'll never be able to thank you two enough."

Lassiter shrugged. "It's been a team effort all the way. For a while there, when Jackson clobbered Adam after the bell and was about to again, I thought . . ." His voice trailed off as Megan nodded; there was no point in rehashing what she already knew.

"What was that needle thing you stuck in his chest before they carried him out of the ring?"

"A Nehme needle. Specially designed for the emergency treatment of tension pneumothorax. I packed a whole assortment of syringes and needles in my pockets, and though I guessed right on that, I screwed up royally on something far more important. I never should've let Adam go through with the fight. I should've lied, told Lakeman he was delusional, spaced out, anything . . ."

"Don't blame yourself unfairly, Dan. I tried to stop it, too. But Adam simply wouldn't listen. Kept insisting it was too late to back out now, though one of the reasons he gave me didn't quite make sense: something to the effect that the only way he could prove LBC's worth was as a living example."

Lassiter reflected a moment and said, "Not the *only* way, Megan, the quickest."

"Then you do understand?"

"I think so. At least, I'm not surprised at Adam making a remark like that. It's consistent with his state of mind ever since he started taking LBC. . . . You see, Megan, all too often the medical establishment takes a hell of a long time to recognize and act on major new discoveries. Adam just didn't want to wait."

"Why not?"

"Well, I'm guessing, but his research grant had been canceled, he was desperate, and one of his mentors—and heroes—was the late George Cotzias, who pioneered the use of

L-Dopa therapy for Parkinsonism. Adam knew the years and years of frustration George had endured while the so-called experts virtually ignored his findings." Lassiter shrugged. "Such things happen and for a good reason: 'The test of time' it's called, and a lot of wondrous-sounding cures simply never pass it. But before your discovery even becomes eligible for that test, you've got to publish papers in major journals, give lectures, organize symposia, corner your colleagues at national meetings. In other words, get your medical peers' attention. It's a long, drawn-out, often disheartening process—especially if you, yourself, aren't all that sure of the importance or practical application of your discovery, which Adam wasn't. So he took a shortcut; he became 'Magic' McKinnon, and made it impossible for the scientific establishment, the Defense Department, or anybody else to ignore him."

"Somehow it sounds so vain."

Lassiter shook his head. "Grandiose, perhaps, but not vain. Adam's a dedicated researcher. Maybe in his mind he saw himself as a 'hopeful monster'—as neo-Darwinists call mutants who accelerate mankind's evolutionary development. You can't fault him for that, Megan."

"No, I suppose not." She paused thoughtfully. "So that's what obsessed him, drove him, was responsible for this . . . this potential tragedy."

"A cure for pre-senile dementia, senility even, is no small thing," Lassiter pointed out. "Long as the odds were against LBC being such a cure, it's the reason I played along."

Suddenly, the door to the consultation room opened and a young white-jacketed doctor started in, saw them, excused himself, and left.

"One thing you haven't told me," Megan said a moment later. "And I haven't quite had the courage to ask . . . Assuming Adam lives, and I pray to God he does, will he be normal?"

Inwardly—imperceptibly, he hoped—Lassiter flinched. "I can't answer that, Megan, except to say the sooner he regains consciousness, the better his chances. Beyond that, there's no predicting. . . . Furthermore, even if he recovers completely from his ring injuries, he's still not out of the woods. He still has to go through withdrawal from LBC, and God knows what that'll entail. I plan to take him back to Boston for that, since I want Jack Morris in on it. So settle in for a long seige. . . . In fact, if I were you," he said, hoping to lighten the grim moment, "I'd think about finding a new boyfriend. Lots of dashing young doctors at Commonwelth General I can introduce you to. Browse around next time you're there."

Megan arched an eyebrow. "Hmm," she murmured. "Interesting offer. If I decide to take you up on it, though, it'll have to be soon, while I'm still a size nine. I may not be barefoot, but I *am* pregnant."

"So you are," said Lassiter and rose. "I'd better go speak to Al and the others and get back to Adam."

"When can I see him?"

"Oh, soon as we make him a little more presentable. I'll send Kris out to get you."

"Dan . . ." she faltered. "Thanks for taking the time to talk to me. It was kind."

"Forget it." He took a step toward the door. "Coming?"

"In a minute. I'd like to be by myself for a little while. Maybe smoke a cigarette . . ."

"Say a prayer for me, too," he said knowingly. "Considering what's ahead for Adam, I'd welcome all the divine help I can get."

36

Adam regained consciousness during the seven A.M. nursing shift change on the unit. At the time, Dan and Kris Lassiter were having breakfast in the doctors' cafeteria with Boyd Frame, director of the I.C.U.; the nurse assigned to Adam's case was in report; Megan slept on the couch in the lounge. Only Phil Kirk, who had scarcely left Adam's side since his admission to the hospital eight hours before, was in the room with him. Maintaining his vigil as much out of friendship as duty, Kirk had watched worriedly as teams of doctors— thoracic surgeons, radiologists, neurologists—worked over Adam's limp, seemingly lifeless, body. He had helped wheel Adam to the X-ray department, where a huge, revolving machine constructed computerized cross-sectional images of his brain on a television screen. He had even helped position Adam on his side, neck down and knees drawn up, as Kris Lassiter unflinchingly thrust a long needle into his spinal canal. Now, slumping in the chair by Adam's bed, a walkie-talkie at his feet, Kirk dozed intermittently while, out in the lobby, Eglund kept a more comfortable surveillance of the people entering the hospital.

Prodded by an assortment of painful sensations, Adam came

awake by increments. Opening his eyes, he felt a sharp stab in his right temple, saw a dazzling sunburst of light above him, and promptly, photophobically, closed them. A confusion of sounds filled his ears—a roar like incoming surf in the right one and an odd, disturbingly familiar, *beep-beep-beep* in the left.

He struggled to make sense of the bright lights and bewildering sounds. But it was no use; his bruised brain simply could not bridge the amnestic gap of the lost hours to orient him. Rapidly tiring, his curiosity waned and he was about to drift back to sleep when he suddenly recognized the monotonously repetitive *beep*. It was the audio signal of a heart monitor. What was a heart monitor doing in his Detroit Plaza Hotel room? His eyelids parted; he started to turn toward the *beep*. But an excruciating pain under his heart halted him and made him moan.

The faint sound galvanized Kirk. Springing out of his chair, he leaned over Adam. "Doc, it's me, Kirk. You all right?"

Adam's eyes opened wide this time. Through a blurry film, he recognized a distorted double image of Phil Kirk.

"C'mon, Doc, say something?" pleaded Kirk. Adam obliged with the only word that seemed appropriate. "O . . . Ouch!"

Relieved but uncertain, Kirk wondered whether to stay and keep Adam talking, or fetch the nurse. "That's good, Doc. Real good. Now, uh, now . . ."

Sensing his indecision, Adam groped about with his right hand and grasped Kirk's arm. "What happened?"

"Jackson went sort of crazy and hit you after the bell. Cracked your rib again. Knocked you cold. Look, Doc, I better get the nurse."

Feebly, Adam nodded. Kirk's explanation made no sense anyway. Confusion, double vision, splitting headache—these were symptoms of a head injury, Adam's neurology training told him. How he was injured, he had no idea, but at least he was conscious, hurting like hell, and able to reason after a fashion. That much was encouraging. The details could wait until morning. All he really wanted, needed, now was a good night's sleep. He hoped he had remembered to hang the DO NOT DISTURB sign outside his hotel room door before retiring.

But the deep, uninterrupted sleep Adam longed for did not come until the following evening when they transferred him from the intensive care unit to a private room. In the interval, he suffered an annoying stream of visitors, none of whom were welcome except Phil Kirk, whom he trusted and depended on, Dan and Kris Lassiter, whom he tolerated, despite their painful, probing examinations, and Megan, who made him warm with desire and wet with her tears. She was glad, so glad . . . she kept repeating, and each time he managed to smile or nod, though what she was glad about remained distressingly vague. Yet, Adam was not unduly upset over the day-long amnesia that made him unable to understand much of what was going on. After a good night's sleep, his mind was bound to be clearer, he assured himself, and he could sort it all out then.

Finally, the longed for sleep came. He woke refreshed, his double vision almost gone, and was ready to have the gaps in his memory filled in by Kirk, Megan, and Dan Lassiter.

Of the three, only Lassiter seemed less than cheerful about the progress he was making. After hearing his reasons, Adam was less cheerful, too.

Public interest in Adam's recovery was intense, demanding, and worldwide. The media gave it the most detailed coverage of a hospitalized patient since Eisenhower's first heart attack. From anchormen to camera grips, an army of network personnel invaded Detroit's affiliate TV stations. News bulletins, composed by Henry Ford Hospital's efficient public relations staff, were beamed over the airways every hour from midnight Saturday to noon Monday. The front-page layout of Sunday newspapers throughout the United States and much of the world were hastily revamped to play up the potentially tragic outcome of the McKinnon-Jackson fight. Half-hour news specials, put together by the three major television networks to air at eleven-thirty Sunday night, were moved up into prime time when it became apparent that viewer interest was soaring. Once authorized for release, the CAT scan of Adam's contused brain was reproduced in newspapers and on the cover of *Newsweek* magazine with all the eye-catching impact of Voyager One's telephotos of Saturn. Both the "Today" program and "Good Morning, America" booked local neurosurgeons and boxing experts for their Monday shows after trying futilely to line up members of Adam's inner circle. Dan and Kris Lassiter, Boyd Frame, even Andrew Tally all turned down on-camera appearances.

As expected, Adam's brutal beating by Coleman Jackson

rekindled arguments about the senseless savagery of prizefighting and efforts to abolish the sport. But this theme did not occupy the editorial writers for long. It was superseded by what came to be called "The McKinnon Fascination." That a forty-five-year-old doctor could display such masterful boxing skill against a muscular giant half his age was indeed astounding; even more newsworthy, however, was the massive outpouring of public admiration and sympathy for Adam as he fought for his life. Prayers for his recovery were included in many church services that Sunday. Telegrams, cards, religious articles, and talismans of every description flooded the hospital mail room. As spokesman for the group that represented Adam, Aaron Robards was inundated with lucrative offers for book, magazine, movie rights to Adam's life story. Unsolicited network bids for an exclusive TV interview with Adam following his recovery climbed past two hundred thousand dollars. Wondering how high the offers might go if suspense was maintained, Aaron urged Al Lakeman to postpone announcing Adam's ring retirement. But Lakeman refused. As soon as Adam's doctors pronounced him out of danger, the announcement came.

It surprised nobody; Adam would have been insane to box again. But the news that he was giving up all professional sports made his legions of admirers feel a sharp sense of loss at all the thrills he might have provided them. Even so, his fascination for them did not dwindle. If anything, it intensified, making Adam a sociological as well as a sports phenomenon.

The prevailing opinion among the editorialists and TV commentators who undertook to explain Adam's elevation from freak to folk hero was that it came from the public's belief that he had "paid his dues." Adam could have quit after Jackson had stunned him with that second-round punch, sparing himself further punishment. Instead, he had kept fighting, let Jackson beat him senseless, gone past the point where any sane man, regardless of his fantasies, would have traded places with him. By standing up to Jackson, taking the worst he could mete out, Adam had paid a hero's heavy dues in full. Nobody begrudged him his multimillion-dollar purse or his double entry in *The Guinness Book of World Records;* the skeptics who questioned his intention to spend his winnings on medical research were silenced now.

A bizarre incident came to Phil Kirk's attention too late for him to keep it from the newspapers. An unidentified man with

a foreign accent had offered a laboratory technologist at Henry
Ford Hospital a hundred dollars for a tube of Adam's blood.
When the technologist refused, the man, further described as
shifty-eyed and menacing, had hung around the hematology
lab until a security guard chased him away. It was the guard
who reported the incident to Kirk, but not before the
technologist had telephoned a cousin who worked for the
Detroit News and earned a hundred dollars for the tip.

The story renewed speculation about Adam's mysterious
nutrient and why the U.S. government put a lock on his
services. But even among purists worried about the future of
sports, the consensus was that if Adam's nutrient could do for
others, especially Olympic-class athletes, what it did for him,
better we should benefit than the damn Russians.

Though kept aware of the press coverage he was getting by
Mel Waldman and Aaron Robards, Adam was largely indifferent to it. The Jackson fight was over; much as he might enjoy
basking in his victory, another fight had already begun.
Because of the Defense Department's decision to keep secret
his discovery of LBC, the public could not know about the
battle being waged at his myoneural junction.

37

For the first three days of his hospitalization, Adam improved steadily. His IVs were discontinued, his chest tube removed, the wired ends of his fractured rib held together, and his left lung remained expanded. On the fourth day, however, his recovery stalled and he began to relapse. His double vision returned and he grew progressively weaker toward evening. By the morning of the fifth day, it was painfully obvious to both Lassiters that the myasthenia they feared Adam might develop off LBC had begun.

The hour he spent observing and examining Adam left Dan in a quandary. Adam's eyelids were drooping and his chewing and swallowing muscles wearied so rapidly he could barely finish his breakfast. Dan realized that he could not conceal Adam's incipient myasthenia from Boyd Frame and the neurologists on his case for long. Nor could he explain it away. Myasthenia gravis simply wasn't a complication of brain concussion. There was no known link between the two conditions, no way to account for their temporal occurrence in the same patient except coincidence—a coincidence that an astute clinician like Frame would find as hard to swallow as Adam did the steak served him for lunch.

For the rest of that day and late into the night, Dan pondered how best to deal with this dilemma. Much as he hoped Adam's myasthenia would prove to be mild and transient, his instincts told him it would probably be otherwise. It was Murphy's Law in the world of medicine. Dan had seen it prevail too many times to ignore its perversity. Just when a critically ill patient finally seemed on the mend, some unforeseen calamity struck: a pulmonary embolus, a gastric hemorrhage, shock lung—the possibilities were endless and impossible to guard against completely. No doubt there were medical exceptions to Murphy's Law, but he couldn't think of any. If a patient lived long enough, whatever could possibly go wrong with his body would go wrong. Dan's old nemesis, death, relied on it.

"Will you please stop flopping around and settle down!" said Kris exasperatedly as she lay beside him in the hotel bed. "God, sleeping with you is like sleeping with a beached fish. What's keeping you awake now?"

"Murphy's Law."

"Oh," she said after a pause. "Well, it's not going to be repealed soon, so get some sleep. Besides," she added, surmising that worry over Adam was making him restless, "it's always darkest before the dawn."

"You sure?" he challenged. The opposite seemed true.

"No." She yawned. "But if it'll help you sleep, I'll get up and check."

In the morning, after talks with Kris and Jack Morris over the telephone, Dan decided to correct Adam's myasthenic symptoms with one more dose of LBC and, with Phil Kirk's help, move him to Commonwealth General Hospital as expeditiously as possible.

Megan found the jar containing Adam's last ten grams of LBC and brought it to him. He responded rapidly—buying himself another few days before the myasthenia returned. Until yesterday, Adam had permitted himself the faint hope of escaping this crippling complication. Now that he knew better, knew with chilling certainty what was in store for him, he couldn't help feeling depressed. Alerted to this by the Lassiters, Megan urged him to talk about it, and after much coaxing, he did. The picture he painted of his future—generalized muscular weakness progressing to the point where he would be unable to eat, ambulate, even breathe—startled and shocked her.

"But won't it just be temporary?" she asked.

"That's what I'm hoping—though 'temporary' could mean months, and no telling where I'll bottom out. I may end up in Jon Acheson's old iron lung, or I may not be so lucky . . ."

His morbid words made Megan shudder. She had never even seen an iron lung, had only a dim comprehension of myasthenia gravis, but now hardly seemed the time to question him; these were things she could look up for herself in the medical library. "Couldn't you just stay on LBC?" she ventured.

Adam's mouth wavered between a smile and a grimace. "I could for a while. If the withdrawal gets too rough, I may have to. The trouble is, Megan, *I don't want to!* Short of dying, I'm willing to endure any ordeal, pay any price, to get that monkey off my back!"

The anguish in his face as he made this confession so touched and saddened her that she feared she would weep unless she turned away. From the bedside chair, she started for the window when he said, "Oh, by the way, I talked to Aaron; got my affairs in order."

She swung round. "Affairs? What affairs? You're retired—remember?"

He gestured placatingly. "I know. I'm also a millionaire. Which means, in case I don't make it, that you'll be—"

"I'll be what—?" she snapped. "Provided for? Taken care of? A rich widow, assuming you get around to marrying me before you kick off? Well, just forget all the euphemisms and largesse! I'll tell you what I'll be if you die: I'll be lonely! Terribly, terribly lonely, and no amount of money will change that." She glared at him, daring him to argue, nodding smugly at his silence. ". . . And don't tell me to be sensible, realistic, or practical. If I were any of those things, I never would've gotten mixed up with you! So just leave your millions to a medical foundation where they will do somebody some good and don't mention them again—understand?"

Meekly, he nodded.

Her anger was partly feigned, Megan knew, to conceal her anxiety. But had she overdone it? Did he have to look so contrite? "God, look at us," she mocked. "What a pitiful pair! Me knocked up and you knocked out! Imagine us being millionaires. We'd be the funniest couple since Maggie and Jiggs!"

Reluctantly, he grinned. Then they were both laughing. And hugging. And feeling better, for the moment.

· · ·

Under Phil Kirk's supervision, Adam's transfer to Boston was executed with military precision. Leaving Henry Ford Hospital before dawn, the group drove to little-used Willow Run Airport where a medically equipped Tristar jet waited.

Though rubber-legged from six days in bed, Adam insisted on climbing the ramp under his own power, each upward step stabbing his left rib cage like a stilleto. Making it to the passenger compartment triumphantly, he slumped into the first seat.

Lassiter gave him a disapproving look as he passed up the aisle, but said nothing.

When Kirk came aboard, Adam asked, "Hey, Phil, any chance of getting a Bloody Mary?"

Kirk glanced at Dan, who shrugged, and said, "See what I can do, Doc."

Turning to Megan, Adam asked, "Join me?"

"No, thanks," she said. "It's morning and, like any good Irish mother-to-be, I'm a little sick."

Adam and Dan Lassiter exchanged stares. Finally, Lassiter, wryly amused by Adam's bravado, murmured, "Why not? I can't blame booze for the mess we're in."

An odd sensation came over Adam as he was assisted from the limousine that had brought him to Commonwealth General and stood gazing up at the magnificent twenty-story strucure. The hospital was internationally famed for medical excellence and he was proud of the way his friend, Dan, ran it, but he took no comfort from these considerations now. Instead, he felt a sense of foreboding doom like a condemned murderer entering the portals of a fortresslike prison on his way to death row.

Shortly after Adam had slipped on pajamas and settled into his room, Jack Morris came to visit him.

"How's Jon Acheson doing?" Adam asked.

"Fine. In fact, extraordinary. His trach tube is out, he's up and around, and itching to see you."

"What sort of maintenance dose is he on?"

"Five grams a day. I'm planning to drop it to three grams in a few days and see how he does."

"That's great," said Adam, obviously pleased. "How much LBC do you have left?"

"Around a hundred grams. Enough for another month or so—providing you don't need any for yourself?"

"I won't," said Adam flatly. At Morris's silence, he added, "Those aren't just brave words, Jack. I mean them. I know damned well what's ahead; I've already had a taste of it. But I'm determined to go the limit, even if it means a respirator, to get off the stuff."

"Okay," Morris sighed. "Long as you realize we'll be stumbling around in the dark, dealing with all sorts of neurochemical unknowns. Among your other claims to fame, you'll be the first case of acetylcholine deficiency on record."

"I know. That's one entry I'd just as soon skip. But I'm betting my enzyme system for making acetylcholine will eventually recover and so will I."

"You're betting your life, Adam," Morris reminded him. "I'm not sure Dan and I can let you do that. Especially since yours isn't the only one at risk. We simply need your knowledge and experience to figure out how to prevent Jon Acheson from suffering the same peripheral nerve hypertrophy you did."

"Does Jon know about that?"

"He does, and accepts it with admirable equanimity."

"Well, I don't," said Adam. "I've done my body enough damage already with that stuff and it's got to stop."

"I understand," said Morris sympathetically. "And if it's humanly possible to get you off it, we will. Jon Acheson, of course, is another story. Where do we get additional supplies of LBC for him?"

"From Walt Carson, my research associate at Tufts. He's due back in Boston next month, but you can reach him at Christie's lab in Edinburgh if you need any sooner."

Morris jotted down the information in his pocket notebook. "Anything else?"

"It can wait," Morris said as he saw Adam's face sag with fatigue. "You look like you could use some rest."

Adam nodded. "A short nap would help. Tell Jon I'll see him sometime this afternoon."

"I will," said Morris, rising. "Oh, by the way, congratulations on the Jackson victory! Thanks to you, middle-aged neurologists are very 'in' right now. Even my ex-wife is showing new interest in me."

Adam smiled, waved, and sank back until his head hit the pillow. He made a quick calculation: He had taken his last dose of LBC on Thursday and it was now Saturday—which meant he had two, possibly three, days' grace before myasthenia sapped his strength again.

38

On Monday, a day earlier than expected, Adam began a long, slow descent into hell where, at its lowest level, not fire but suffocating airless space waited to envelop him.

On examining him that morning, Dan Lassiter had detected the first telltale sign of relapse. Sitting in bed, Adam was unable to gaze upward for more than a few seconds without his eyelids drooping. Nor could he maintain his arms outstretched, palms up, without his hands twisting inward in what was called "pronator drift."

"Well, it's starting," Lassiter said. At Adam's doleful nod, he mused, "Think it's worth giving Tensilon a try?"

Tensilon, the brand name of a fast-acting drug, blocked the enzyme that inactivated acetylcholine at synaptic junctions, thereby making more of the chemical available for nerve transmission.

Adam looked dubious but told him to go ahead.

Minutes later, Lassiter drew up ten milligrams of Tensilon in a syringe and injected one milligram of it into Adam's arm vein. When he showed no adverse reaction to the test dose, Lassiter slowly injected the rest, hopeful of a favorable response. But at the end of fifteen minutes, Adam's eye and arm muscles were as weak as before.

"Well," sighed Lassiter, "that was a waste of time."

"Not entirely," Adam said. "It told me something I'm not too happy to know. The reason Tensilon didn't work is because there simply isn't enough acetylcholine around for it to work on. Which pretty well pinpoints the problem . . ."

"To what?"

"To the transferase enzyme regulating acetylcholine synthesis in the nerve axon. Evidently, all the LBC I've taken the last four months has suppressed it." He shrugged. "You know the saying: 'What you don't use, you lose.'"

"Well, how do we get it back to work?"

"I could try oral choline, I suppose. The stuff tastes awful, but I'm willing to swallow a ton if it'll do any good."

From her reading on myasthenia gravis, Megan learned that it was first described in the medical literature in 1672 by Thomas Willis in a treatise quaintly titled, "Two Discourses on the Soul of Brutes," that it was caused by a defect in neuromuscular transmission characterized by weakness and abnormal fatigability of voluntary muscles, and that it could be classified in five stages, ranging from mild, localized, and stable to severe, generalized, and life-threatening. It was information that both enlightened and haunted her as she watched Adam run the gamut from stage one to stage five in the coming days.

By Monday evening, he either had to tilt his head back or hold his eyelids up with his fingers to see straight ahead. Since ocular muscle weakness was usually the first manifestation of myasthenia, this did not surprise him. But it came at an inopportune time. Earlier that day, the hospital librarian had brought him a stack of neurology journals—containing the latest research on choline metabolism—that he now found impossible to read.

When Megan visited Adam Tuesday morning, she saw Phil Kirk cutting up the food, even the toast, on his breakfast tray. His myasthenia had spread to the bulbar portion of his lower brain, making chewing, swallowing, and any repetitive movements difficult. Because of weakness in his neck and shoulder muscles, he could no longer sit up in bed unassisted. Nor could he lift a fork or spoon to his mouth more than a few times before having to stop and rest. Nonetheless, he stubbornly refused to let either Megan or Kirk feed him.

After two sleepless nights, Megan overslept the next morning and did not get to the hospital until noon. Had Phil Kirk been there, he doubtless would have intercepted her outside Adam's room and warned her what to expect. But Kirk was meeting with his superiors in Washington, D.C., that day, and, being unwarned, Megan was severely shaken by Adam's appearance. He had changed drastically. His sagging facial muscles gave him a jowly appearance, and, when he spoke, the corners of his mouth curved down in the classic "myasthenia snarl."

"Good morning, darling!" She leaned over the bed rail to kiss his cheek.

"Good morning," he replied, giving her a second unpleasant surprise. His voice had a distinctly nasal quality as if coming through pinched nostrils.

Heartsick, Megan spent an hour chatting with him and helping him cope with his lunch before his invalidism and valiant efforts to conceal it became more than she could bear.

Urging Adam to nap, she sought out Dan Lassiter, who took time from a meeting he was chairing to speak to her.

"For God's sake, Dan," she said the moment they were alone in his secretary's office, "can't you do something?"

He sighed. "We're trying, Megan. Believe me, we're working on it round the clock. Jack Morris made another computer search of the literature last night and talked to half a dozen neurochemists, one in Israel, about Adam's problem."

"Forgive my ignorance, Dan, but what exactly is his problem?"

"Your ignorance is shared by a lot of us. Far as we know, Adam's condition is unique. The LBC he's been taking has shut off a crucial nerve enzyme, choline acetyltransferase. Without it, Adam just doesn't generate enough acetylcholine at his nerve junctions for any sustained muscular activity."

"But can't you just give him some of the stuff he needs—this acetylcholine?"

"Afraid not. It can't be taken by mouth—stomach acids destroy it. And it's too toxic to tissues to be given intramuscularly or by vein. The nervous system needs just a little of it, but in the right places—at nerve junctions. And to get what it needs, it extracts choline from the diet and attaches an acetyl group to it by means of the transferase enzyme I mentioned."

Tight-lipped, Megan said, "I see. But will this enzyme Adam lacks come back?"

"Most likely. As the LBC still in Adam's system is used up, his body is demanding more and more acetylcholine to replace it, and the body usually gets what is demanded. If only we knew how to speed up the enzyme's production. All that the massive doses of choline we've fed Adam have done so far is produce a fishy odor to his breath. But Jack Morris is planning to start him on a new drug—an acetylcholine precursor—today. Maybe it'll help."

At the doubt in Dan's voice, Megan sighed despairingly.

"At least, his spirits are good," Lassiter pointed out. "He's holding up mentally."

"Is he?" she questioned. "I'm not so sure. He seems awfully detached to me—almost indifferent to all the horrible things that are happening to him. Are you certain this enzyme deficiency isn't affecting his mind?"

Lassiter frowned. He had observed Adam's odd placidity, too, but attributed it—perhaps hastily—to his stoical nature. "I honestly don't know, Megan. Let me discuss it with Jack Morris, see what he thinks. He might want to run some psychometrics on Adam. . . . In the meanwhile, how about dinner with Kris and me tonight?"

Megan forced a smile. "Thanks, Dan, but I'm afraid I'd be lousy company. And you deserve a break from this, too. Now, you'd better get back to your meeting."

Lassiter nodded. "We'll talk more later—okay?"

"Okay." Impulsively, she gave him a brief hug and left.

Megan spent the rest of the day with Adam, reading the newspaper to him, watching television while he dozed, missing Phil Kirk's company at meals. A second conversation with Dan Lassiter before she departed for home that evening left her faintly hopeful. At least, she couldn't imagine Adam looking or sounding any worse.

But the next morning, he did.

The moment she entered the room, Phil Kirk sprang from his chair to block her view of him. Taking her arm, he led her out of earshot of Adam and said, "He's bad, Megan. Real bad."

"How do you mean?" she asked, barely able to articulate the words.

"I'm no doctor, but looks to me like he's having some kind of convulsion involving his mouth muscles. Keeps making licking and smacking noises and sticking his tongue in and out.

Started around twenty minutes ago. I told the nurse and she paged Dr. Morris. He should be here any minute now."

Numbly, Megan nodded. Skirting Kirk, she anxiously approached Adam and recoiled in horror. Seemingly oblivious of it and helpless to stop, Adam kept smacking his lips and making slurping sounds. Even more shocking and sickening, tears streamed from his eyes, saliva drooled from a corner of his mouth and his tongue protruded out and up every few seconds like a lizard feeding off an ant colony.

Seeing Megan start to sway, Phil Kerk seized her shoulders and eased her down into a chair. "Just take it easy," he urged. "The nurse says it's nothing serious. He's in no danger."

"Nothing serious!" Megan cried. "It's grotesque!"

At that instant, Jack Morris strode into the room and straight to Adam's bedside. Megan waited for him to finish his examination before asking, "What's happened to him, Jack? Why is he doing that?"

"He's having involuntary spasms of his tongue and masticatory muscles—like a nervous tic or, in its more extreme form, St. Vitus's Dance."

"Then it's not a convulsion?"

"No, not in the usual sense. The medical name for it is *tardive dyskinesia;* it's usually seen in patients on high doses of antipsychotic drugs like Thorazine or Haldol."

"Is it dangerous?"

"It's not life-threatening, if that's what you mean."

"But it's not good, is it?" Megan persisted.

"No," admitted Morris. "In fact, it's ominous. The generally accepted belief is that tardive dyskinesia results from an imbalance between two key brain chemicals—one of them, acetylcholine. Which means Adam's deficiency has progressed to the point where it's affecting both his central and peripheral nervous system. To my knowledge, nothing like this has ever been reported before in myasthenia patients. I'd like to document it, if I may, by drawing some spinal fluid from Adam and sending it over to a colleague at M.I.T. to have its choline content measured."

"Could it possibly be a side effect of the new drug you started Adam on?" asked Megan.

"Deanol? It's possible, but highly unlikely. In fact, Deanol has been used successfully in the treatment of tardive dyskinesia. I must admit, though, it doesn't seem to be doing Adam's other problems any good."

"Will anything, Jack? Will anything change him back to what he was, or is it hopeless?"

Morris hesitated as if to weigh his words. "One thing, Megan . . . LBC. But that has to be a last resort."

"Why?" Megan cried. "Why does it?"

"Because that's the way Adam wants it. It's essential we find out whether or not LBC is permanently addicting before we dare use it on any more patients. And since it's his baby, Adam wants us to find out on him. It was part of our agreement before we let him try LBC on Jon Acheson."

"But surely you won't hold him to it? You won't just let him go on suffering like this for the sake of a medical experiment?"

Wearily, Morris rubbed his brow. "No, of course not. But Adam pretty well predicted most of the things that might happen to him off LBC and made us promise not to re-start it unless he was at real risk of dying."

"And you intend to stick to that promise—no matter what?" Megan protested. "That's inhuman!"

Morris sighed. "Right now, I intend to do two things. Talk it over with Dan. And watch Adam like a hawk for the next twenty-four hours. I know how hard all this is on you, Megan, but you'll just have to trust our judgment . . . and humanity."

"I suppose so," she said stonily, excused herself, and went off to a corner of the visitor's lounge to compose herself.

It was a nightmare worse than her father's slow decline from emphysema and mercifully swift death from a heart attack, worse than the Jackson fight, worse than anything she had ever experienced before.

Barely able to muster courage enough to return to Adam's room, she could now understand why Thomas Willis had titled his original treatise on myasthenia gravis as he did. If by "Brute" he had meant a non-human creature of brutal quality, Adam was rapidly turning into one. The monster must die, he had told her before the Jackson fight, and from Jekyll's Hyde to Frankenstein's creation, the monster invariably did. But no matter how he perceived himself, Adam was no monster; he was the bravest, gentlest, most humane man she had ever known. He had to get better, she told herself, and eventually he would. At least, she couldn't believe that Dan Lassiter and Jack Morris would let him get any worse.

But, unaccountably, they did.

At six Thursday morning, Dan Lassiter phoned to tell her

that Adam had suffered sudden respiratory muscle paralysis an
hour earlier and had been placed on an iron lung.

Speechless at first, Megan rapidly recovered and, before he
could elaborate, ended the conversation by saying, "I'll be
right there."

Forty minutes later, as she burst from the elevator, hair
disheveled, eyes reddened, lipstick chewed, Megan saw Jon
Acheson, whom she had come to know well in the last few
days, emerging from the respiratory support room where Adam
was being kept. "Oh, Jon," she wailed. "How is he?"

"His color's a lot better now. And he's conscious, though I
can't make much sense out of what he says."

She closed her eyes briefly in silent prayer.

"For what it's worth," Jon went on, "the iron lung's not so
bad. I ought to know. I spent almost a year in it. It's really
ironic, though, for me to be out, thanks to Adam's brilliant
discovery, and for him to be in."

"Your mind was never affected, was it, Jon?"

Misinterpreting her question, Jon said, "The confinement
gets maddening at times, and an itch can drive you wild, but
it's futile to even think of suicide. There's simply no way—not
even by holding your breath. So I managed to stay pretty
sane."

Unknown to Jack Morris, who was busy adjusting the iron
lung controls, Adam had gradually regained consciousness.
Not only was he awake but fully aware of what had happened
to him. For some reason—perhaps because the Deanol Morris
was giving him had begun to work, or because the brain
swelling from his concussion had finally resolved—he seemed
to be thinking clearer than he had in days. He knew he had
made a major miscalculation: he never thought the myasthenia
following LBC withdrawal would progress this far, this fast. If
it got any worse, the iron lung would be unable to ventilate him
adequately and he'd end up on a respirator. Then there was the
tardive dyskinesia he had developed. Incapacitating as it was,
it carried exciting research implications. LBC had affected his
brain chemistry, after all; lack of it had upset the delicate
dopamine-acetylcholine balance. But how?

Adam longed for solitude in which to think the problem
through, work out the biochemical interrelations. It was more
than an intellectual exercise, he realized. His life depended on
it. But the room, the iron lung itself, was too noisy, the busy-

bee activities of nurses and neurology residents too distracting. He needed to go off to some quiet place with paper and pencil or a blackboard.

Closing his eyes, he concentrated on a spot of orangish afterglow on the back of his eyelids and teleported himself back to a place where he could conjecture comfortably . . .

The lecture hall, located in a converted mansion on the north edge of the Yale campus was overheated as usual. Undergraduates were as welcome as medical students at his neuroscience lectures, but few ever came. Today, however, the room was packed. Word had somehow spread that Dr. McKinnon was about to announce a major medical break-through.

Barely able to contain his excitement, Adam strides across the stage to the blackboard, seizes a piece of chalk, and without his usual notes in hand, begins:

"This morning, if I can get it straight, I'm going to formulate a cure for Alzheimer's Disease, better known as presenile dementia. Like Parkinson's Disease, Alzheimer's is both a structural and biochemical disorder—the specific biochemical defect being lack of the enzyme, choline acetyl-transferase. By impairing the function of millions, possibly billions, of cholinergic neurons, this deficiency produces severe memory loss. Follow me so far?"

The class nods.

"Without replenishing this enzyme, it has proved impossible to supply the brain with the acetylcholine it needs to restore memory . . . until now."

The class stirs.

"As you can all see, I have tardive dyskinesia." For demonstration purposes, Adam exaggerates his bizarre move-ments. "From the L-butyrylcholine I've been taking, of course. And I must confess I'm thrilled by this development. It proves LBC has penetrated my blood-brain barrier and supplanted acetylcholine as my main cholinergic neurotransmitter. In short, it has bypassed the transferase. And since it's done this in me, there's good reason to believe it can do the same in Alzheimer patients."

The audience applauds.

Adam smiles modestly. "Any questions?"

Hesitantly, a student raises his hand and Adam nods at him. "But, Dr. McKinnon, you're dying—?"

"True, but—"

"Adam? You awake?"

At Megan's voice, he inched his head around with a smile that looked more like a snarl.

She tried to smile back but couldn't. He no longer looked grotesque. He looked moribund. He was going to die, she thought. Some invisible boundary line had been crossed, some irreversible process set in motion. An indescribable sadness gripped her. Yet, she felt more like screaming than weeping. Furiously, she lashed out at him. "Oh, damn you! Why don't you let them give you LBC? Must you be the ultimate experiment! They can't help you, Adam. Nobody can. You're going to die. And I don't want you to die. Please, Adam, please put an end to this . . . this insanity and take the LBC."

Slowly, he shook his head.

"All right," she sputtered. "All right, you damned fanatic! Do what you want. You got yourself into this mess, you figure a way to get yourself out."

To her surprise, Adam nodded. Now that he was able to think clearly, to correlate certain facts and observations, he had deduced a possible remedy.

"What's that nod supposed to mean?"

Spreading his lips, he managed to make a *ka* sound.

Megan leaned closer. "What?"

"Ka . . . kar . . . karrt."

After an exhausting effort on both their parts, Megan finally understood three words: Kurt . . . Eliasson . . . Stockholm.

The name meant nothing to her. Nor to Dan Lassiter when she repeated it to him. But Jack Morris recognized it at once, and after learning who Eliasson was and what he was famous for, Adam's reasoning began to make sense to Dan. He even had a vague recollection of Adam mentioning the Swedish neurologist's research when they were discussing possible alternatives to LBC to treat Jon Acheson. "What do you know about this "activated choline" of Eliasson's?" he asked Morris.

"Not much, except that it's supposed to get into the synapse independent of choline acetyltransferase."

"In other words," mused Lassiter, "it may be just what Adam needs. Is it available in this country?"

"Not to my knowledge, Dan. Far as I know, nobody outside Eliasson's group has used it."

"Well, how do we get hold of some?"

"From Eliasson himself. If he's willing to part with any."

Lassiter reached for his phone. "Let's find out."

Due to the six-hour time difference, Dan's call reached the switchboard of the Karolinska Hospital in Stockholm at two P.M. and was re-routed to Eliasson's office. Although Eliasson was in, Dan encountered maddening resistance from a thick-accented secretary reluctant to disturb him. Yes, Dan acknowledged, he knew Dr. Eliasson was a busy man, and yes, he knew, because she had just told him, that he was late for an important meeting, but it was imperative they speak at once. The life of a friend and colleague of Dr. Eliasson depended on it. Who? Dr. Adam McKinnon, the famous—

Hearing a click, Dan prayed they had not been disconnected and was greatly relieved when Eliasson came on the line. They spoke at length—Dan describing Adam's critical condition and Eliasson, after agreeing at once to supply the "activated choline," outlining its pitfalls. Eliasson concluded the conversation by promising to phone back within the hour to inform Dan what arrangements he had made to fly the medicine to Boston.

Hanging up the phone, Eliasson leaned back in his chair, lit his pipe, and, ignoring the fact that he was due at the Health Ministry in twenty minutes, pondered the curious circumstances that now linked him to Adam McKinnon.

Kurt Eliasson was no phlegmatic, stereotypical Swede. At fifty, he was a gifted neurologist and tolerated eccentric whose appetites for food, wine, women, and exuberant living were near-legendary. Having guessed what had transformed his old friend, Adam McKinnon, into an extraordinary athlete, Eliasson had thrilled at his accomplishments. What a man! he proclaimed to his wife, his children, his mistress. With cleverness and courage, Adam had satisfied that secret wish, deep inside every man, to turn by magic into a stunning athlete. Productive as Eliasson's life was, it did not remotely approach that kind of satisfaction. In fact, he brooded, it grew ever more Kafkaesque and tedious as he metamorphosed from research scientist to that lowly life form, a departmental administrator. He was no longer a clinical neurologist—he was a politician, a pie-cutter, an appeaser. As the stacks of paper on his desk rose higher and higher, his spirits sank lower and lower. He hadn't ridden a horse or played tennis in a month; made love in a week. And why? Because of the diabolical double bind he was in. Before becoming chief of neurology at the Karolinska, he had neither the freedom nor funds to fully pursue his research interests. Now that he was chief, he no longer had the time for it or for much else.

He looked at his watch, marveled at the havoc a half-hour phone conversation had wreaked with his schedule, and buzzed his secretary. "Inga, send for Lungren. I need him to prepare a package and instructions for me. Then phone the health minister and tell him I've been unavoidably delayed. And then call my wife and tell her . . . No, wait!" he suddenly barked and grinned mischievously. His spirit of adventure was not totally dead yet. "Before you do anything else, call the SAS office and book me on the very next flight to the United States, preferably Boston or New York. . . . *Ja*, that's right, Inga. The next.I'm leaving at once. And you're taking the rest of today and tomorrow off and going to the beach. That's an order. Let the hospital, the Ministry, the telephone company, think I've dropped off the face of the earth for a few days."

On the jet, a huge 747 whose first-class section was nearly empty, Eliasson had two quick Scotches and flirted with one of the stewardesses, a willowy young blonde with enormous seductive eyes. "Ah, my dear," he sighed when she made a point of telling him that she would be staying over in Boston for two days, "pity you're not ten years older, because I don't want to be ten years younger."

"Oh, Dr. Eliasson," she cooed, "I don't think age is all that important, do you?"

"Ordinarily, no. But the sad fact is, I have a daughter your age."

She forced a smile. "You know, you are the *first* man who ever admitted that to me."

With that pleasant diversion at an end, Eliasson leaned back in his seat to fantasize a bit over the missed opportunity and promptly fell asleep.

Dan met Eliasson when he cleared customs. Bluff-faced, rumpled, unshaven, he looked more like a cop or retired wrestler than a scientist as he ambled, suitcases in hand, past the last check post.

"Dr. Eliasson?" said Dan, "I'm Lassiter."

They shook hands.

"I'm deeply grateful that you'd come all this way to—"

"How's Adam?" Eliasson interrupted.

"Bad. In fact, critical. The iron lung simply isn't working. I have a surgeon standing by to do a tracheotomy if his oxygen tension drops much lower. But I'm willing to try your preparation first, if time permits."

"I should hope so. I didn't travel thousands of miles for nothing. But since time is so precious, let's not waste any. How long will it take to drive to Commonwealth General?"

"Too long. I have a hospital helicopter waiting."

"Uplifting, I'm sure—if you'll forgive the feeble pun. So lead on, Dr. Lassiter. We can fill each other in on the way."

Like Adam, Eliasson had devoted years of his life to dementia research, learned much about brain chemistry, cured nobody. He had tested dozens of choline-containing compounds, some original, some supplied by the pharmaceutical companies, on suitable patients without measureable benefit. Then, almost by accident, he had synthesized a compound that replenished acetylcholine at nerve junctions by some new, and as yet unknown, mechanism not regulated by the transferase. It was a complex molecule that changed form at least three times before cleaving into two parts, one acetylcholine, at the nerve axon. At least, that's how Eliasson postulated it worked. That it did work had more or less been proven by animal experiments in which it consistently raised the cerebrospinal fluid choline content of brain-damaged monkeys, and in patients with tardive dyskinesia. But it was hardly innocuous; several monkeys and two Alzheimer patients had convulsed while recieving large intravenous infusions of the compound, he told Dan. So its administration was not exactly cookbook medicine. Conceivably, it could kill, not cure, Adam. Which was the main reason, among lesser ones, why he had flown over the North Pole to personally give it to him.

At the time Eliasson began the infusion, Adam was unaware of his presence or his own precarious condition. To his mind's eye, he was standing in a vast field far from his Newton, Massachusetts, home—too far—and quite alone, although from time to time he could hear excited shouts coming from the playground behind the hillock at the far end of the field. He had gone there to fly the alcohol-fueled model airplane his father had given him for his eleventh birthday. Impatiently, he had waited for the spring snows to melt so that he could test-fly the plane. At last, they had. And although he had promised not to fly the plane without his father's supervision, his father was away at a physics meeting for a week and Adam could contain his curiosity no longer. Now, standing in the midst of the empty field gazing up at the rapidly darkening sky, he had cause to regret his impetuousness.

A flash of lightning startled him; its companion thunderclap made him cringe. Frantically, he looked for shelter. The nearest tree, its trunk no thicker than a telephone pole, was twenty or so feet away. After a moment's hesitation, he darted for it. But before he got halfway, a bolt of zigzag lightning streaked down and, with a pistol-shot crack, splintered the tree top, setting its branches ablaze and showering the ground with sparks. Terrified, Adam turned and dashed for the broad oak at the top of the hillock fifty yards distant. As flashes of lightning dazzled his eyes and thunder deafened his ears, he dropped his precious airplane and ran as fast as his short legs would go.

At the base of the hill, a few yards below the sheltering oak, something—a strange stirring in the air—made him stop, spin around, and look up. Before his terror-filled eyes, the dark sky split and a tongue-like blaze of electricity lashed at him, knocking him down, setting him aglow and twitching.

"He's convulsing!" shouted Lassiter and turned to Eliasson for guidance.

"I'm not surprised," replied Eliasson with studied calm. "The infusion has probably fired every cholinergic neuron in his brain at once."

"What do you suggest we do?" asked Jack Morris. "The iron lung won't ventilate him now."

"Reduce the rate of the drip and bag him vigorously. If his seizure persists, give him a muscle-paralyzing drug, intubate him, and put him on a respirator."

As Morris fitted the Ambu bag to Adam's face, Dan stared at Eliasson accusingly. "I know you're an experienced neurologist, Doctor, but you seem pretty damned unperturbed by all this."

"Please, Dr. Lassiter," Eliasson corrected. "Pretty damned pleased. Frankly, I didn't think my preparation would work at all. Certainly not this quickly. His nerve axons must really be ravenous for it. Now that they have the ammunition, it's no exaggeration to say that they're firing packets of acetylcholine across the synaptic gap like machine gun bullets."

"But what if the seizure is merely a side effect of your medication and it hasn't helped his myasthenia at all?"

"That's certainly a possibility," conceded Eliasson. "But if you'll notice—as I did, just before Dr. Morris applied the Ambu bag—Adam's eyelids are no longer ptotic. They're wide open." He shrugged. "In any case, we can always resolve the question with an electromyogram when he stops convulsing."

"*If* he stops convulsing . . ."

"Dan," Morris interjected, "I think he just has." Dropping his hand to the side of Adam's neck, he added, "And with a carotid pulse this strong, he's definitely not dead."

Dan eyed Eliasson with reluctant respect. "Doctor, it's a rare privilege to work with you."

"It's Adam, Dr. Lassiter, who deserves our respect. After all, he risked his life to save his research. How many other scientists do you know who'd be willing to do that?"

"None, I hope," said Dan fervently. "Especially if they expect *me* to take care of them. . . . But now that you seem to have pulled off this medical miracle, how about sticking around awhile as my guest so we can get to know each other?"

"My pleasure." Eliasson beamed. "Besides, Adam and I have a lot to talk about. Between his choline and my choline, we may just have the recipe for a potent therapeutic cocktail."

39

Five weeks later, Adam had recovered sufficiently from his myasthenia to leave the hospital. A single infusion of Eliasson's "activated choline" had not cured him; it took eight days of such infusions before he could breathe on his own and another twelve days to wean him off the medication. Shortly thereafter, he underwent a ligament-cutting operation on his left wrist to relieve pressure on his hypertrophied median nerve. The sutures had been removed two days earlier, the wound looked well-healed, and, though Adam still suffered twinges of pain in his right wrist and both ankles, it was decided to wait and see if they would abate, now that he was off LBC. At the conference, convened by Dan Lassiter, of the many Commonwealth General doctors and physiotherapists who had treated Adam, it was agreed that their extensive repair work was completed and it would be safe to discharge him.

As his physician and friend, Dan was happy for Adam and happy to see him go. Much as his Board of Trustees delighted in the publicity given the hospital during Adam's stay, Dan was weary of reporters prowling the corridors and waylaying him at every opportunity. While Adam had the Secret Service to protect him from the press, Dan had only Hedley, his harassed secretary.

As his last day in the hospital dawned, Adam felt charged with excitement by all he had to look forward to—marriage to Megan, an extended honeymoon on the lush Caribbean island of St. Lucia, a series of planning meetings with the staff of the National Institute for Nervous and Mental Diseases, and especially a reunion with Kurt Eliasson in Stockholm in mid-October to launch an all-out, collaborative effort to cure dementia.

He was also looking forward to the gala dinner at Anthony's Pier Four that evening when "Magic" McKinnon would bid final farewell to his most intimate friends and advisors. Al Lakeman and Todd Tanner were driving in from the Berkshires for the occasion, and Adam was eager to hear their strategy for Todd's upcoming championship fight. For a man who had been largely friendless and unloved a scant six months ago, he considered himself fortunate, indeed.

Yet, between such musings, Adam felt restless and subdued. He kept gazing out the window of his hospital room—as if the cloud pattern could somehow foretell what was in store for him next. Having nimbly evaded the clutches of death twice in two months, Adam realized he must now substitute caution for his lost agility or he might not be so lucky a third time. But more than luck, it had been competent colleagues and a special Providence that had kept him alive. If God did play stud poker with mankind, His hole card was neither Immortality nor Oblivion, Adam now knew; it was redemption through action. He couldn't help feeling he had been spared for a purpose. Far harder to accept was the premise that his father's horrible dementia and dehumanization had been a necessary prelude to that purpose.

At Kris's insistence, Dan Lassiter spent the afternoon at the beach with her, leaving Adam's discharge to Jack Morris. When the final battery of neurological tests Morris had ordered ran past five o'clock, Adam and Megan decided to stay on at the hospital and leave for the restaurant from there.

Although he had been ambulatory for days, hospital policy dictated that Adam ride from his room to the outside in a wheelchair and he did not protest. At the dock door in the rear of the hospital, he shook hands with Jack Morris, who would be joining him shortly at Pier Four, and, flanked by Kirk and

Eglund, waited for Megan to pull up in his car. But the
Corvette that rounded the corner of the building and stopped in
front of them was not the black, battered one he had reluctantly
bought from Diana. It was a silvery, shiny new model.

"Did you know about this, Phil?" asked Adam.

Kirk tried to suppress a grin. "It's my business to know.
We'll follow you in the Chevy."

"Like it?" Megan said from the driver's seat.

Adam climbed out of the wheelchair and, ducking his head
through the open window, gave her a kiss. "Love it. How 'bout
letting me take her for a spin?"

Despite her qualms, Megan let him drive—first to the end of
the hospital road and then, helpless against his boyish delight,
to the restaurant.

It was dusk when they exited off the expressway at Copley
Square and headed for the waterfront. Stopping at a red light,
Adam turned to her and smiled. "Be nice to see Al and Todd
again."

"Will Todd beat Savitt, you think?"

"I'm betting on it."

"How much?"

Before Adam could answer, the traffic light changed and
he moved forward. Suddenly, the blood-chilling sounds of
screeching brakes and blaring horn assaulted his ears. A car
had run the red light at the side street and was about to
broadside him. Adam caught a fleeting glimpse of a woman
driver's panicked face and prayed she would swerve her car to
the left while he swerved his to the right. The temptation to
brake was nearly irresistible. Instead, he twisted the steering to
its limit and flung out his right arm to protect Megan. In a time-
suspended moment, he heard her gasp, heard Kirk's warning
horn, and braced himself for what seemed a certain collision.
A vivid image of Coleman Jackson's knockout punch flashed
through his mind, but that was all before time speeded up
again. There was the grating sound of metal against metal as
the cars' rear bumpers made brief contact, and the Corvette
shook violently under him. Instantly, Adam hit the brake pedal,
reversed direction, and, with the car tilting on two wheels,
fought to keep it from jumping the curb and smashing into a
looming lamppost. Finally, the car righted itself, its four tires
gripped the pavement, its engine stalled, and it came to a
screeching, shuddering halt.

From his side window, Adam saw the other car stopped up at

the street. Its front door opened and a middle-aged woman, her pudgy face quivering, twisted around in her seatbelt to look at him. Too relieved by the narrow escape to feel anger, Adam waved at her and signaled Phil Kirk that he was unhurt. Then, he turned to Megan for her reaction.

She gulped and said, "Not bad . . . not bad at all for a man with normal reflexes."

"You want to drive?"

"No—faint. You drive, Mario."

Adam nodded. With his gut still knotted and his scalp electric from adrenaline, he started the engine, determined to concentrate on his driving. But after turning onto the side street leading to the restaurant, his mind began to wander. He had always been fascinated by automobile racing and, if the government job didn't work out, if he needed more research money, if he and Eliasson could somehow iron out the bugs in LBC . . .

Bestsellers you've been hearing about—and want to read